SHADOW SISTERS BOOK THREE

QUINN NOLL

Printed in the United States of America.

ISBN: 978-1-7353814-6-6 (Paperback)
ISBN: 978-1-7353814-7-3 (E-Book)
IBSN: 978-1-7353814-8-0 (Hardcover)

Warning: You are about to enter the mind of a serial killer. It is a playground for the demented—not a tourist destination. Within this book, you'll find scenes of murder, mayhem, and abuses of every kind. Enter at your own risk and proceed with caution.

This is a work of fiction. The only thing factual within these pages is proof of an author's dangerous mind. Any resemblance to actual persons, living or deceased, is entirely coincidental.

Cover photo: Constance Keller/Picsart
Cover design and interior artwork by Brian J. Quinn

www.QuinnNoll.com

For Mark
Our steps may be slower and our hair dusted with gray, but we are still 'us.'
A lifetime of memories; a story with chapters yet to be written.
Longer than... to forever.
I love you.

Evil needs but a willing heart and barren soul to live forever.

"Do not damage the earth or the sea or the trees until we have marked the servants of God..."

Revelation 7:1

"It was Pride that changed angels into devils;
it is humility that makes men angels."

St. Augustine

IN THE BEGINNING

"Therefore, stay awake, for you do not know on what day your Lord is coming."

Matthew 24:42

The end will come on a Tuesday.

Judgment Day, Armageddon, the day of reckoning. Whatever one chooses to call it, the facts remain unchanged.

The world is destined to die. And it will happen on a Tuesday.

Satan will descend upon the earth, wreaking havoc and destroying all in his path. Civilizations will collapse, the seas will boil, and all living things will perish from the planet.

And that destruction will occur on the second workday of the week.

The Apostle didn't know how he knew this; he just knew that it *was*. He knew it as he knew his own name, his mission, his destiny: everything familiar in this world, all that is known, will come crashing down.

And just as the end of the world is preordained, so too is the timing of that end.

At exactly 8:46 a.m., the precise time a hijacked commercial airliner hit the North Tower of New York's World Trade Center more than two decades ago, Earth's final Tuesday will see fire rain from the sky. The sun will become black as ash, and the moon will become as blood.

All a cruel mockery, commissioned by the devil himself, meant to capitalize upon the pain of one of the greatest wounds in human history.

On the anniversary of the moment that hellfire rained down from the skies, evil will once again seize control, weaponizing the power inherent in that horrific sliver of time.

Because there is nothing more telling, more symbolic, than the hidden meanings found on the face of a clock.

For instance...if one were to compile a list of the precise times relating to the terrorist attacks on September 11th, 2001, the results would be chilling. Most notably, the digits pertaining to each individual event, from the hijackings and subsequent crashing of all four planes to the inevitable collapse of both towers, when added together, total 9,110: nine, eleven, zero.

But the coincidences don't stop there. The number eleven in particular plays a pivotal role, numerologically speaking, in what happened on that fateful day.

September 11th is the 254th day of the year. The digits in that number, two, five, and four, add up to eleven. There are 365 days in a year, and 365 minus 254 is 111.

Additionally, before the attack, the twin towers themselves resembled the number eleven as they stretched up into the skies over New York.

And the first airliner to hit the World Trade Center was American Airlines Flight 11.

Yes, as a wise man once said, there is no such thing as coincidence, only design.

But none of this surprised Gabriel Devine. Ever since he was a child, he'd been fascinated by numbers. Early on, he would play a game where he would focus on a significant event and add or subtract the numbers involved, trying to glean a deeper meaning.

Like the uncanny similarities between the assassinations of Abraham Lincoln and John F. Kennedy—for example, the hypnotic interplay of each event's dates and facts. Or the timeline of the bombing of the Alfred P. Murrah Federal Building in Oklahoma City in 1995. When added together, the numbers on that particular timeline—from the detonation of the bomb to the execution of perpetrator Timothy McVeigh—totaled 168.

Not so coincidentally, the dead from that event also numbered 168.

Gabriel soon came to realize that numerology was more than just a silly pastime; it was a doorway to knowledge, perhaps the key to existence itself.

Before long, numbers dominated his life. He washed his hands for a length of time calculated by adding the current year, month, and date. He knocked on a door three times before entering, even if he was alone.

He was born in 1987; his father, Rowan, was killed in 1996. The sum of the digits in the two years was the same: 1+9+8−7 was 25. Similarly, 1+9+9+6 also equaled 25.

And 2+5 was 7, the most mystical, magical number of all. As foretold in the Book of Revelations, the end of days would begin with Christ himself opening of the seven seals on heaven's sacred scroll. This would herald the Tribulations, the seven-year period where catastrophic events would befall mankind in preparation for Judgment Day.

Yes, seven was possibly the most significant number in the universe.

And now, Gabriel knew, Earth was beginning her final rotation. She was taking her closing bow and would soon see her last sunrise. A fierce battle between good and evil, between morality and indecency, between the promise of life and a violent, agonizing death, was nigh.

And it would all occur on a Tuesday.

Father Gabriel sat on the dingy floor of the rectory bathroom, Bible in his lap, and openly wept. His were tears of joy, his heart light and bursting with pride and humility.

Although not an ordained priest, Gabriel considered himself holy, devout. Every bit a man of the cloth.

Surely more deserving of the title of 'Father' than some of the cleric impostors he'd become acquainted with.

Losers and drunks, the lot of them. Men who spoke of a 'calling' but wouldn't know piety if it bit them in their collective asses. Men who, in the pitch black of night, saw only darkness and gloom, where Gabriel saw light, possibilities, sun.

Because he was the Chosen One.

He sniffed and rubbed his eyes with the back of a hand. There was no shame in crying, he reasoned. Many a great man wept in both unbridled joy and heart-wrenching defeat. Tears could be uplifting and cathartic.

In this case, tears were a sign, proof that he was on the path to greatness, to immortality.

He tipped his head back and studied the pocked ceiling tiles above the shower. In one corner, two intersecting lines depicted an all-too-familiar symbol.

The number seven.

He sighed, reveling in a knowledge gifted to but a few of heaven's soldiers. Seven represented wholeness and perfection and appeared in countless biblical passages and proverbs.

It appeared in life itself.

God created the world in seven days. There are seven days a week and seven colors in the rainbow. We celebrate seven seas, seven continents, and seven wonders of the world.

Revelation, Gabriel's favorite book of the Bible, speaks of seven churches and seven seals upon the heavenly scroll. Within that scroll lie the seven plagues, seven trumpets, and seven bowls that represent God's wrath and judgment. There are seven deadly sins, seven virtues, and seven sacraments.

Even Snow White knew the power of the number seven.

But the biggest validation of his belief, his faith that his destiny was bound to the number seven, lay in his past. On the seventh day of the seventh month in his seventh year, Gabriel attended a birthday party where, in the throes of a temper tantrum, little Bradley Maxwell threw a rock at the back of Gabriel's head.

The stone hit the base of his skull, splitting the skin open and requiring seven sutures to close.

Gabriel wiped his face with his sleeve and stood to wash his hands. A jagged break in the mirror above the sink split his image in half, creating the illusion that he was not one man but two. His lids fluttered, and he sighed.

'Two are better than one, for if either of them falls, one can help the other up.' Ecclesiastes 4:9–10.

Although the image reflected was merely a trick of the glass, he fantasized about how much work he could do if there were, indeed, two of him. Deep in thought, he left the rectory and walked to St. Michael's church. His was a small parish in Sheridan, Wyoming, ministering to fewer than three hundred Catholic worshippers. Entering the church, he made his way down a side aisle and ascended the altar's steps. Genuflecting, he headed toward the right, to the sacristy.

He had a phone call to make.

It had been four weeks. Four weeks of bliss, silence, and hope that, perhaps, the priest who'd cornered him in that back alley, threatening him with unspeakable violence, had forgotten all about him.

Forgotten about the pathetic man who had been shaking with fear in that alley and now cowered at home, biting his nails to nubs, afraid of his own shadow.

Four weeks. Twenty-eight days of praying that the Apostle, with his piercing eyes and ragged scars along his face, had changed his mind and moved on.

Six-hundred and seventy-two hours of worry, daring to believe that the psychopath outside Benny's Bar and Grill was gone.

Or, better yet, dead.

And forty thousand, three hundred and twenty minutes trusting that he would never get the call to join the Apostle in his quest for vengeance.

As his newly named, albeit unwilling assistant, Simon of Cyrene.

Anticipating that call to action was wreaking havoc on the man's body. Crippled with fear, the man had missed more days of work than he cared to remember. He'd rarely taken a sick day in the past, but now, the emotional anguish had begun to manifest as physical ailments: stomach issues, unexplained fevers, crushing chest pains. He'd even developed an angry-looking rash on his face and torso.

Sitting at his kitchen table, chewing the side of his thumb and bouncing a knee, he did what he'd done for the last month—stare at his phone. Lately, his pattern had been the same: wake up, make coffee, glare at the phone.

Today, he was particularly anxious, though he couldn't say why. He'd been in the same chair for hours, worrying, debating his next move. Logic dictated he tell his friends, make a report; fear told him if he did, he was as good as dead.

So, he continued to fret, sob, and gnaw at his fingernails until they bled.

Eventually, he talked himself into getting off his chair. Famished, he microwaved two slices of yesterday's pizza, grabbed a can of Dr Pepper, and headed to the living room. He would watch some mindless sitcom, preferably one starring a pretty woman with huge tits, and try to relax.

Halfway to the couch, the peal of his cell phone caused him to yelp with fright. His arms flew into the air, sending his plate and soda hurling across the room.

Knees shaking, he stepped over his ruined meal and crept back to the kitchen, where the phone lay vibrating on the counter. Hesitating, hyperventilating, he finally picked it up.

"He—hello?"

"Did you miss me?"

The man gulped and closed his eyes.

"Are you there, Simon of Cyrene?" the Apostle asked.

"Yes, yes, I'm here."

"Excellent! We have much to do! We must prove ourselves worthy! We must demonstrate we are deserving of His trust."

The man swallowed. "His trust?"

"Yes, my son."

"Wh—what do I have to do?"

"Oh, you have the easy part. All you need do is find me my sinners."

"Your sinners?"

"What are you, a fucking parrot?" the Apostle shouted. "Yes, *sinners!* The masses who commit the deadliest of sins. Keep up, man!"

Aware that any answer would be met with anger, the man said nothing.

"I need you," Gabriel said, "to help me find those guilty of the most grievous of sins. Do you have a problem with that?" His voice was tight, as if he were speaking through gritted teeth.

The man crumpled to the cool kitchen tile, defeated. He was trapped, and the only way out was to do what he was told.

"No, no problem," the man said quietly. "What would you have me do?"

There was a long pause; the man could almost feel the air humming with tension. And then the Apostle whispered, "Find me a pig."

CHAPTER ONE

"GLUTTONY"

"And put a knife to thy throat if thou be a man given to appetite."

Proverbs 23:2

It was a stupid way to die.

Rebecca Sue Caraway kneeled on the dusty floor of her prison, arms shackled in irons above her, and watched as droplets of blood splashed to the ground below.

Seven cuts over seven minutes in the seventh hour of the day. Her punishment for committing one of the most grievous of offenses, one of the most cardinal of sins.

At least, that's what her captor had told her.

She tipped her head back and examined the slashes marching in formation down her forearms. As a nurse, she understood she was in no danger of bleeding to death. Although painful, the cuts were superficial and too shallow to hit an artery. No, her immediate concern was dehydration, shock, or hypothermia.

And, of course, her captor. The man who held her prisoner was the biggest threat of all.

Becky Sue had no idea how long she'd been trapped in the old barn.

The hours and days seemed to fuse, melting into a succession of horrors her mind could not process. She closed her eyes and took a calming breath, willing her racing heart to slow down. It was a relaxation technique she'd demonstrated for many of her patients before they faced a painful procedure.

She was learning firsthand that the method was useless.

Fear was fear, and pain was pain. No amount of measured breathing could ease the agony of skin debridement in a burn victim or alleviate the anxiety a patient felt before undergoing cardiac bypass.

And no number of cleansing breaths could erase the spine-chilling terror that came with knowing a psychopath wanted to end you.

She tugged once again at the chains that bound her and winced. Every movement sent blinding pain through her body. The delicate skin under the iron cuffs was raw. Her knees throbbed from kneeling, while the intense heat spreading across her shoulder blades threatened to become an inferno.

Besides the shackles biting into the flesh of her wrists, the angle of her body was contributing to her misery. She was strapped by the waist to a column behind her; a pair of iron chains looped menacingly over a beam above, ensuring her arms hung at least a foot in front of her. With her upper torso suspended, her shoulders were forced to take the brunt of her body weight.

Admittedly, it was a considerable load to carry.

Becky Sue wondered if her being fat—obese, truth be told—would be a deciding factor in her survivability. Could she have escaped if she were thinner? Model thin, like Kate Moss or Angelina Jolie? A petite girl with slender, graceful hands that could easily slip out of the restraints? She studied the cold steel around her wrists and shook off the idea that skinny would equate to survival.

Becky's wrists were the only thing one could consider slim on her two-hundred-seventy-pound frame.

Which helped her to realize that, under similar conditions, even Kate

Moss would be screwed.

Rebecca's inability to slim down was not for lack of trying. She'd lost track of how many diets she'd tried, how many gym memberships and pills and 'quick-loss' programs she'd paid for in her quest to drop the pounds.

Nothing worked.

In the end, the only thing lighter was her wallet. Like a needy friend or an unrelenting virus, her weight was always there, lurking in the background, an unwanted guest that wouldn't leave. Her doctor attributed it to hormones, while her friends blamed the high-stress career she had chosen. Phil, her personal trainer, accused her of binge eating and 'not wanting it badly enough.'

Soon after Phil had given her his 'professional' opinion, she'd fired him and gone out for fries and a milkshake.

Because Becky Sue understood it was a combination of problems—issues that would take years of therapy, calorie counting, and strenuous workouts to resolve. At this point in her life, it all seemed too overwhelming. So, for now, she accepted her weight, had even learned to live with it. After all, she still believed herself to be an attractive woman.

What was it they said? There was just more of her to love.

But 'they' had obviously never considered a madman seeking to punish people who, in his eyes, had committed one of the seven deadly sins.

Apparently, Rebecca Sue Caraway's sin was gluttony.

The Apostle stood before the mirror in his bedroom, naked and slick with sweat, gazing at his reflection.

He'd just completed a ten-mile run—a hobble, truth be told—and the muscles of his right leg burned as though on fire.

He rubbed his aching right quadricep, the still-tender flesh a reminder of where FBI Agent Jake Devereaux's bullet had pierced his thigh. The round had gone clean through, taking a large chunk of muscle with it and tearing a gaping hole in the flesh, front to back.

It was a hole that had required twenty-five precisely placed, painful sutures—administered by Gabriel himself—to close.

The puckered skin was a memento of all he had suffered, and it reminded him, each time his fingers stroked it, why he loathed those who opposed his work. Devereaux's bullet had nearly taken his ability to walk. Now, here he was, not only walking but running.

Glory be to the Father!

He smiled at his image, liking what he saw. Chiseled jaw, ripped abs, arms the size of tanks. During his time at St. Michael the Archangel Church, he'd worked diligently to increase his size, stamina, and strength.

All in all, aside from his hideous left eye, milky-white and sightless, he thought himself a magnificent creature.

So many trials, and yet still, I stand! A rusty nail—not unlike the spikes pounded into Jesus's palms—blinded me, yet still, I see!

To Gabriel, the parallel was further proof that he was the Chosen One.

It was his sister, Callie, hiding the metal spike within her fist, who had dealt him the life-changing blow. Her aim had been true, and the ten-penny nail that had poked out between two fingers of her hand had torn through the sclera and cornea of his left eye. The severe bleeding and subsequent infection had resulted in complete vision loss on that side.

But it was his ability to adapt to his partial blindness that had cemented his belief he was destined for greatness. Every challenge was a gauntlet designed to test his faith, just as surely as the bullet that had punched through his right thigh continued to test his fortitude.

The road before him would not be easy. His task? To prepare for his place on earth, to become qualified to wear the crown offered to him. And the only way to do that, to prove himself, was to unmask the evil ones who walked among the righteous. He must expose the beasts who had committed the most egregious trespasses and eliminate them one by one.

Seven sinners. Seven sins. Seven lives.

He would begin with the swine in the barn. To achieve greatness and power, to be gifted with the vision to see what lay inside the pages of the Heavenly Scrolls, he must offer a sacrifice.

And once the seven sinners had died seven deaths, he would see what no mortal had ever seen.

The Four Horsemen. The arrival of the Antichrist. The Apocalypse.

His was an honor afforded no other. Because not everyone was chosen; not everyone was given the key to eternal life.

Not everyone was worthy of becoming the Messiah.

Rebecca Sue sniffed snot back into her nasal passages and, once again, scrutinized her prison. As a healthcare worker and patient advocate, she'd seen more than her fair share of hopeless situations, of dire circumstances. Each time, she would forge ahead, implement a plan for her charges, refuse to give up.

But her current predicament was proving more challenging than any other.

Who was the man who had taken her?

She remembered little outside of leaving the hospital at the crack of dawn. She'd just pulled a double shift and could think of nothing except a big plate of sesame chicken and an egg roll, leftovers that awaited her at home. But somehow, she'd ended up here, hanging from the rafters, trussed up like a Christmas turkey.

The sound of the barn doors sliding open snapped her focus from the past to the present. A glistening shadow, huge and looming and full of ill intent, emerged from the entryway. Becky shook, her breaths coming in ragged, quick gasps.

He was back. And he was naked.

Gabriel tilted his head and studied the woman in the barn. Her eyes were wide, the pupils dilated and blacker than night. To anyone else who might have chanced upon her, her pale skin, tear-stained face, and panting breaths would have telegraphed her terror.

But in Gabriel's warped mind, these became something entirely different.

To him, her fear was a living, breathing thing; an animated, weak, bloated monstrosity that mirrored her physical appearance.

An abomination that needed to die.

He felt his groin stir and tried to temper his excitement, but the look of horror on her face as she fixated on his growing erection demonstrated his failure.

Don't worry, Slim. Fat chicks ain't my thing.

Rebecca Sue waited, and when he didn't say anything, she spoke. "I...I don't know what you want, what you need. I'm just a nurse, mister. I have no enemies. I've done nothing wrong." She bit her upper lip, already raw from chewing on it for hours. "I have money, stocks, and bonds, jewelry. It's yours—just don't hurt me!"

Gabriel steepled his hands under his chin as if considering her offer. His chest was slick with sweat, while his erection throbbed in the waning sunlight. "But what of *your* worth? Are you aware of your value?"

Becky Sue frowned in confusion.

"I suppose not," he breathed, disappointed. "You are the first to pave the way. Because of you, many will be saved. Your sacrifice will not go unnoticed."

At the word 'sacrifice,' Becky Sue began to howl.

Unaffected, Gabriel looked on, eyes hard and face neutral. He sighed and studied the woman before him without pity, without empathy.

Understanding her fate, Rebecca's demeanor changed from unbridled terror to outrage.

Who the fuck does he think he is?

"You scum-sucking son of a whore!" she screamed. "What gives you the right to judge me? You're a limp-dicked scumbag who probably has mommy issues and never got laid! Fuck you and your sacrifice!" Then, more quietly, she said, "You chose the wrong girl, shit-for-brains. I may not be nimble, but I'm strong. When I get my hands on you, I will break you in half."

The Apostle smiled, moved to what had once been a horse stall, and picked up a long baton from a dusty table in the corner. Barefooted, he made his way back to her and squatted, almost nose to nose with her. Using his fingers, he pushed back a strand of damp hair from her eyes.

"You will never get the chance," he said softly.

Seconds later, Rebecca's mind registered that the item he held in his hand was, in fact, not a baton.

It was an electric cattle prod.

The first shock, delivered to the delicate skin of Becky Sue's throat, sent a jolt so intense her jaw clenched, and her body jerked violently. Paralyzed by fear and pain, her vocal cords could only produce a soft grunt as her neck sizzled where the prongs connected to flesh.

Gabriel giggled and did it again.

Rebecca's head flew backward, and spittle leaped from her mouth. Tears of anger and pain streamed down her face as, convinced her neck was on fire, she struggled to raise her bowed head.

"Why are you doing this?" she rasped. "Why?"

He ignored her question, instead continuing to enjoy the show. He had made several alterations to the electrical output of the prod and was pleased with how well it was working.

"Please," Rebecca pleaded, her voice weak, "don't do this!"

Gabriel squinted, studying her form as she flopped forward, suspended by her chains. The string of drool seeping from the corner of her mouth lengthened as she struggled to straighten her spine.

The sight disgusted him. He shocked her again.

Rebecca yelped once more. "Stop!" she moaned. "Please—just stop it! What do you want from me?"

Snarling, Gabriel pointed the prod at her neck, then lowered the device until it was directly above her left breast. "What I want, you could never understand."

When the jolt went through her blouse and into her breast via her left nipple, Rebecca Sue Caraway, mercifully, lost consciousness.

When she opened her eyes a few moments later, the first thing Becky Sue noticed was Gabriel standing close by, his sinewed back and taut ass staring her in the face. His left arm dangled loosely at his side, his hand wrapped around the hilt of a gleaming Bowie knife.

She moaned, and he turned to face her.

"Welcome back," Gabriel said. "I wasn't sure if you'd make it. A pig your size, well, much of the time it's the ticker that gets 'em."

Becky used every ounce of strength she possessed, willing herself to lift her head. Despite her ragged breathing and the pounding in her chest, she would show him no fear.

Even if she had to fake it.

"Go to hell, fucker," she said between gritted teeth.

Amused, Gabriel responded, "On the contrary, Miss..." He stopped, searching his memory for her name. "Oh, yes. It's Caraway, right? On the contrary, Miss Caraway, hell is the last place I am going. But don't worry. You aren't going there, either. I'll make sure of that."

He crept closer, the twinkle in his eye nearly as bright as his shimmering blade. He tugged at the back of her hair, exposing her throat.

"Did you know that, during biblical times, animal sacrifice was considered a way to atone for one's sins?" Whispering, he added, "You're welcome."

"Please!" she sobbed. "Don't!"

In one swift motion, the blade of the knife tore through the delicate skin of Rebecca's neck, slicing her from ear to ear.

Her eyes widened, and she wheezed, a gush of blood cascading to the floor from the gaping hole in her neck. Oddly, either because of the adrenaline rushing through her body or the stark terror of knowing she was about to die, she felt no pain.

Her last thoughts were of her mom, her cat named Chowder, and how easy it was to drain a body of its lifeblood.

∽

After releasing Rebecca Sue Caraway from the chains that bound her, Gabriel laid her body gently on the ground. Her death, the first in his quest to prove himself worthy of the title he sought, marked the beginning of the end.

He moved back to the table in the stall and picked up a cast-iron rod and a pair of welding gloves. Half-walking, half-limping—

Because this leg is hurting like a motherfucker!

—Gabriel stepped outside, the cool evening breeze drying the sweat from his body. A fire pit sat before the barn, kindling and fuel already stacked neatly inside it. After dousing the kindling with a hearty dose of lighter fluid, he struck a match, dropped it onto the woodpile, and stepped back. Bright orange flames danced in the center of the pit, smoke licking and curling its way to the heavens.

It was a breathtaking sight to behold.

Donning his gloves, he adjusted his grip on the rod and leaned forward. After jabbing the end of the rod into the blaze, he twirled the steel, ensuring an even heat distribution. A circular pattern emerged at the rod's tip.

Bold, beautiful, and white-hot within the flames.

Gabriel hobbled back to the barn and Rebecca Sue Caraway's lifeless body. Leaning forward, he brushed back her hair and pressed the still-glowing branding iron to her forehead. The sickly-sweet scent of burning flesh permeated the air as her skin sizzled.

When the metal cooled and the hissing stopped, he pulled the rod away, revealing an imprint centered above her brows. He stared in wonder, marveling at the mark that was left behind.

No, not quite a mark. A seal.

The seal of God.

For, in the end, Rebecca, too, had been selected. Only her destiny was fated not for glory but for sacrifice.

CHAPTER TWO

Fredericksburg, VA
June 10

Callie Callahan twirled in front of the closet mirror, checking and rechecking the length of the maxi-skirt she wore.

As if by staring at her reflection, the dress would magically become shorter. Or she would become taller.

Tossing a glance over her shoulder, she said, "Come on, Devereaux. You gotta admit I look pathetic. I'm too short for this skirt. It looks like I'm about to put a loaf of bread in the cast-iron stove before I head out to help plow the back forty."

Jake Devereaux lay on top of the mattress in Callie's room, a toothpick in his mouth and an arm behind his head. He wore jeans, a pale blue jersey, and an amused expression.

"I think you look adorable. In fact, I will see your loaf of bread and raise you a venison stew bubbling in a copper pot over an open flame."

"You're not helping. Seriously, I'm meeting my half-sister for the very first time ever, and I want to make a good impression."

Jake jumped to his feet and walked over to stand behind her. Wrapping an arm around her middle, he rested his chin on her shoulder and stared at her in the mirror. "Blaze, the only thing you need to make a good impression is you. Amara will be so thrilled to meet you I doubt she will even take notice of your skirt."

Today was the day. After recuperating for a month at her home in Fredericksburg, Callie Callahan was finally going to meet the sister she, up until recently, never knew existed.

Amara.

Amara Grace Davies, daughter of Rowan Callahan and Meredith Sterling. Half-sister to Katie, Callie, Finn, and Ryan Callahan.

And biological sister to a madman named Jeremy Sterling.

Jeremy, a sadistic serial killer, had murdered over a dozen people, including Callie's twin and Amara's half-sister, Katherine Callahan.

After convincing himself he was omnipotent, Jeremy Sterling had changed his legal name to Gabriel Devine in honor of the archangel Gabriel. He believed it better reflected his status as a messenger of God. But not everyone called him Gabriel.

To his victims, he was simply 'The Apostle.'

"I hope you're right, Jake. Anyway, doesn't much matter now, does it? By dinner this evening, we'll be in Denver." She extricated herself from his embrace and limped to the suitcases beside the bed. "Damn, I was going to ask you something, but I've totally forgotten it now. Must have gotten distracted by this pile of luggage. It boggles the mind—how do I have more stuff now than when we arrived from Montana?"

Jake smirked. "Because you're a woman, Callahan. Packing light is a guy thing, right up there with flexing in front of a pretty girl and burping the alphabet after a few beers."

Callie chuckled. "If that's a challenge, I accept. Give me a good porter, and I can belch the Declaration of Independence."

He laughed, then nodded toward her left leg. "You still have a pretty good gimp there. How's it feeling?"

Callie plopped down on the corner of the bed and flexed her knee. "Sore and stiffer than hell, but the pain isn't too bad. The donor who provided the ligaments believes my upgraded knee joint can now withstand bungee jumping and mogul skiing. At least, it did when he was alive."

Jake's eyes widened. "Wait, you actually talked to the cadaver who provided the graft?"

"No, I spoke to the *man* who provided the graft. His name was Joe, and, from the way he talks, he was a hell of a poker player and an all-around good guy."

Stunned, Jake took a seat on the opposite corner of the bed. "We've been hanging out for weeks, Callahan. I am over here every day after work, cooking your supper and adjusting your knee brace. Not once did you mention you've been communicating with ghosts. Not once."

Callie shrugged. "I'm sorry, bud. It literally just happened a few days ago." At Jake's dubious look, she added quickly, "Swear on my eyes, may I never eat a Happy Meal again. It started with a conversation in my head. I couldn't hear the words with my ears, but his sentences sort of, I don't know, assembled in my thoughts? I'm still in the dark about how it happened, but I knew exactly what he was trying to convey."

"Like telepathy?"

"That's as good a word as any. Anyway, it isn't just Joe making an appearance. There have been other visitors and a few strange events that have occurred in the last forty-eight hours. I swear, it's as if the other side knows I am leaving for Montana and is pressed for time or something."

Jake stood and moved to the window. He pulled back the curtain, absently watching the flow of the Rappahannock River out back. "How do you mean?"

"I mean, it wasn't just Joe communicating with me. Yesterday afternoon, I saw a woman in white standing right about where you are now."

Jake jumped a few feet to the left, and Callie smiled. "Don't worry, Barney. She isn't here now."

When Jake had first begun calling her Blaze, a nod to her auburn hair, she had quickly retaliated. Barney Fife was the name of a bumbling country cop in an old sixties sitcom. And although Jake Devereaux, FBI agent, was as far from bumbling as one could get, the nickname had its desired effect.

Jake hated it.

"So, did she speak at all? This lady in white?" he asked, pointedly ignoring the jab.

"Whispered mostly, so I couldn't grasp much of it. It wasn't like with Joe, where the words sort of formed in my mind. This spirit was weaker, less able to manifest or something. But I did hear *'You must find her.'*"

"Well, I won't say that ain't creepy. Who do you think she meant?"

Callie rubbed her face. "Take your pick. A missing girl we don't know about yet? Faith or Emily? Maybe even Amara."

Jake, the wheels of his mind churning, said nothing.

"Anyway, this morning, I had another spirit encounter. I heard what sounded like panting as I stood by the front window. I swear I could even feel a puff of warm breath on my legs."

"Oh, that? That was me," Jake said with a wink. "When I got here, you were wearing one of my shirts. Sexy as hell, and it dropped me to my knees."

"Oh, please," she said, trying to hide her pleasure at his words. Embarrassed, she picked at an imaginary piece of lint on the bedspread. "I think it was Chance, Jake. I think Chance came to visit me this morning."

Chance, a goofy and lovable golden retriever, had been Katie Callahan's pride and joy. She'd spent hours with him, training him to be the best cadaver dog Virginia had ever seen. Gabriel had killed him with unparalleled viciousness, and it had nearly broken her

And weeks later, when Gabriel had ended Katie's life, equally viciously, with a bullet to the chest, the loss had nearly broken Callie. Truthfully, in the beginning, there was no 'nearly' about it.

Callie had been smashed into a thousand pieces, her very soul shattered almost beyond mending.

That frigid day in December, as she'd cradled her sister's lifeless body, as she'd watched the brilliant light of Katie's soul ascend to the heavens, something had cracked. Some essential 'thing' that made Callie Callahan who she was, had fragmented, raining a thousand shards of glass over her inner core.

After Katie died, well-intentioned friends had rallied around Callie. They told her it was normal to feel like a part of her had died with her sister. They explained it was reasonable to assume Katie's death would leave a hole that would never be filled, but at the same time they promised that one day soon, the sharp pain Callie was feeling would fade to a dull ache.

Platitudes and cliches, all of them, that could never come close to Callie's torment, her 'living death.'

Her profound grief had been almost palpable. Loved ones patted her hands, kissed her cheeks, and brought her comfort food. Unsure how to soothe her, they went along with her pretense at living—all the while whispering behind her back about her pale skin and sunken eyes.

Nothing had been able to blunt her pain; no kind remarks, no encouraging statements, no well-intentioned anecdotes had come close to touching it. Most people got that, mercifully. Those who didn't continued to search for the magic words that would heal her.

Words that did not exist.

All she'd wanted was the freedom to grieve in her own time and her own way. She had no interest in sympathy cards or special-intention masses. And, unless the offers to 'say a prayer for the family' included a petition to raise the dead, she was uninterested in any of that either.

Callie had stumbled through the days and weeks following Katie's death in a zombie-like trance, a shell of the person she once had been. Her body yearned to concede to the darkness inside herself, to curl into a ball, to follow Katie into the abyss.

But, although her soul was splintered and her heart shattered, a part of her wanted to stay, to fight. She yearned to exact justice on the man who'd taken everything.

That inner turmoil, that sensation of drowning on dry land, never truly went away. Some days, she still had to force herself to get out of bed, to put one foot in front of the other, to take that next breath. Days where the pain was so raw, so overwhelming, she was sure she'd die from a broken heart.

The fact that the one responsible for her misery was still free to kill, to live, just added to her grief.

Lost in the past, she was shaken back to the present by Jake's voice.

"Hello? Earth to Blaze?"

Callie smiled softly but, not trusting her voice, said nothing.

"Look, sweetheart," Jake began, "you're stressed out. You've been through hell and back, physically and emotionally, for months. Give yourself a break. I don't pretend to understand this ghost business, but it doesn't seem like they want to hurt you. For now, let's just accept that they are here to help. And that's not a bad thing, right?"

Except for the dark entities I've seen; except for the sensation of dread dripping off their shadowed forms whenever they appear. Yeah, except for that.

She had yet to explain those sightings to Jake. After all, she'd barely understood them herself. All she knew was that whenever they appeared, it wasn't a little-bitty fan the shit was about to hit.

It was a big-ass wind turbine.

While Jake finished loading up their rented Bronco, Callie took one last pass around the house—checking door locks, closing drapes, bundling memories.

She loved this house—loved the location, loved having family nearby, and loved sitting on the deck and listening to the rhythm of the Rappahannock River. Mostly, she loved that it was here she felt most connected to Katie. She picked up a photo on the mantel that depicted a smiling Katherine Callahan crouched by the river, Chance and Blue at her side.

"Damn it all, but I miss you, Kates," Callie said, eyes glistening. "It's stupid nuts how badly I miss you. Sometimes, I find myself waiting for the front door to open, for you to sashay in with a dopey grin and a cheesy bow, shouting, 'Man, had you going, didn't I? You really fell for it!' in that high-pitched voice you used whenever you were joking. I know, I know—it's the fantasy of a crazy person. But there it is."

"No, not crazy," a voice whispered. "Just coping."

Callie whirled around, her eyes finding Katie's glimmering form standing by the French doors that led to the backyard. The late morning sun shining through the glass highlighted her brilliant glow.

"Kates," Callie said, breathless. Despite the number of ghostly visits she'd received, her physical reaction was always the same. Her heart pounded, her hands shook, and her lungs were suddenly devoid of air. When appearing in spirit form, the dead required mountains of energy to manifest. Some days, that energy seemed to suck the life out of whatever room they entered.

Suck the life out of Callie.

Would those physical effects eventually impact her health? Maybe even decrease her life expectancy? Perhaps. But Callie was willing to risk anything to keep Katie in her world, if only in brief doses.

Taking a gulp of air, refilling her lungs with precious oxygen, Callie said, "You always seem to know when I need you. Cute parlor trick. How are things on the other side? How's Michael?"

Michael Trent, a former Civil War soldier, was a spirit Katie had encountered and fallen in love with when she was still in high school. After a few months of enjoying each other's company, Michael had made the painful decision to stop his visits, hoping Katie would forget about him and live her own life. She had been devastated.

It was only after they'd reconnected in the afterlife that Katie understood his decision. It was a selfless and agonizing choice for him, demonstrating how much he adored her.

And proving to Katie that Michael was her true love and soulmate.

"He's great. I was hoping to bring him with me, but he got slammed in traffic on the way in."

Callie frowned. "Traffic? You're joking." Then, because she had no idea if heaven had highways, said, "You *are* kidding, right? 'Cause if not, I need to rethink the whole afterlife thing. Traffic sounds like the opposite of heaven."

Katie chuckled. "Of course, I'm joking. Come on, Cal-Pal. Traffic? You know, you're too easy anymore."

Callie laughed. "Yeah, whatever. Anyway, I hate to be the butt of your jokes and run, but Jake and I have a plane to catch."

"Amara Davies. Yes, I know. I'd tell you to give her my love, but let's wait and see how she handles the whole 'I see dead people' trick you have. Just be careful, Shadow. There's a shift in the universe, an unsettling in the air. Darkness surrounds both you and Jake."

"Thank you, Debbie Downer," Callie groaned. "But, yeah, I feel it, too. Hell, I even see it sometimes. The lurching shadows, the black mists that telegraph some kind of impending doom. But don't worry, we'll be careful." Smiling sadly, she joked, "Mind the traffic on the way home, Kates. Love you."

"And I love you, Cal-Pal. Remember, I'm never far away."

Callie and Jake drove in silence to Reagan National Airport. The flight from Arlington to Denver was about four hours; from there, the condo Amara Davies called home was a forty-five-minute drive.

Jake sat behind the wheel, checking Callie's profile every few minutes. Her head was turned slightly as she watched the landscape fly by. The reason for her silence and the thoughts that occupied her brain remained a mystery.

Eventually, the quiet unnerved Jake, and he spoke. "I'd say a penny for your thoughts, but I'm fresh out of change. You okay, darlin'? You're awfully quiet for a Callahan."

Callie turned to him and quirked a brow. "Really? I figured you'd be enjoying the silence." She angled in her seat to study his features: chiseled jaw, high cheekbones, hair as black as night.

He truly was a gorgeous man; the fact that he didn't know it made him even more attractive.

"I guess I'm a bit nervous," she said unnecessarily. A blind and deaf man need only be in the same hemisphere to sense her unease. "Amara knew nothing of us, as we knew nothing of her. If I hadn't run that ancestry test looking for Gabriel's extended family, we never would have found each other." She turned back to the window and wiped away the condensation blocking her view. "I can't help but wonder...."

"Wonder what?" Jake asked.

"What she's like. Is she like us?"

"You mean clever, witty, remarkably attractive?" he said with a grin.

Amused, Callie said, "Well, of course. It goes without saying she'll be a knockout."

"Sometimes I forget how humble you are, Callahan."

"Hah! You started it! Anyway, I'm talking about what she's like on the inside. Do you think she's a good person? Could she, God forbid, have gotten the ugly genes? Like Gabriel?"

Jake snorted. "No one is like that bastard. Relax, Blaze. I'd bet my left nut she's a peach."

Callie laughed. "Why is it always the left one? Why not the right? These are the things that keep me up at night."

Smirking, Jake reached for her hand and raised it to his lips. "You're really something, you know that? So, what's the plan? Are we meeting Amara directly at her house? Bringing dinner, maybe? How do you want to play this?"

Callie shook her head. "I have no clue. It's not like I've done this before.

I mean, what do you say to a sibling you never knew you had? 'Hello, I'm Callie, your sister. I like long walks on the beach, dancing in the rain, and, oh, by the way, I communicate with dead people. How about you?'" She sighed. "See what I mean? No way this isn't an awkward first meeting."

Jake blew out a breath. "Not necessarily. Look, there's no need to immediately jump into the 'I see dead people' stuff. Just feel each other out, start with the basics. What does she do for a living? Where did she go to school? Did she always live in Denver? Does she have a weird pinkie toe or a dimple on one cheek like you? Stuff like that."

"So, in other words, engage her in small talk? Pretty up the nasty and refrain from throwing her in the shit immediately? That I can do."

Jake pursed his lips. "Come on, Blaze. Compared to what you've been through, this is a picnic. You just need to adapt, something I've seen you do a thousand times."

Callie snapped her fingers. "That's what I started to ask you before! How are you dealing with the whole change of location for work? You're leaving the friends and co-workers you've worked with for years. You're leaving Sully."

Ian Sullivan was Jake's partner in the Quantico office and had become a trusted friend.

"Yeah, don't think that doesn't sting. Sully and I have been through the shit, all right. But it's time for a change. I think the Billings office will be a new challenge for me. I've not worked on that side of the country. The crimes seem... I don't know... tamer than what I've seen in downtown DC."

Callie scrunched her face. "Well, sure. I mean, all you see in the Wyoming and Montana area are serial killers running amok. Nothing to that kind of policing." She rolled her eyes, then reached over and gently elbowed him in the ribs.

Jake laughed. "Touché. Anyway, Quantico is giving me a kind of honeymoon period in Montana. They will leave my position unfilled for three months, which gives me plenty of time to decide if Billings and I are a good fit." He pointed out the windshield. "Look, there's the airport. And we're an hour early. See that, Blaze? Miracles really do happen."

Callie looked out the window, watching as jets with wingspans the size of football fields took off and landed. Her palms were damp, and her legs trembled.

The promise of new beginnings waged war with the threat of heartbreak.

Because either she was meeting a wonderful new sister, or she was inviting into her life a sinister replica of the man she despised.

CHAPTER THREE

"Every high priest is selected from among the people and is appointed to represent the people in matters related to God, to offer gifts and sacrifices for sins."

Hebrews 5:1

"Padre? You here?"

Bob Dietrich, groundskeeper of St. Michael the Archangel Church, pulled open the weathered barn door an inch or two and peered into the darkness. The outbuilding was part of the property St. Michael's had secured after fire destroyed their rectory many years ago. Needing a place to house visiting priests, Bob had found this parcel on a realtor site, and the church had snapped it up for a song.

Since that fire, however, the rectory had been rebuilt. Now, this old barn, along with the aging farmhouse and twenty acres of land that went with it, had ceased to be of value. Bob wanted to sell it, get money for a new roof the church was begging for, but Father Gabriel was hesitant. He believed the house could still be used for visiting priests, while the land could be rented for farming, creating a steady income for the church.

"Howdy ho—anyone in here?" Bob called out, again rapping his knuckles against the door. He adjusted his John Deere cap over his graying hair and slid his glasses up the bridge of his nose. At seventy-one years old, he was in decent shape physically but 'blind as a bat,' according to his wife, June. Indeed, without his impossibly thick glasses, he could barely make out an image three feet away. His eye doctor had diagnosed him as legally blind years ago, but Bob continued to insist he could still spot a snake or a pretty girl at fifty paces, and that was 'the best this old coot could ask for.'

He paused for a moment, listening. While his eyes were failing him, he had the hearing of a man half his age. He could've sworn he'd heard scuffling or scraping when he'd first cracked the door open. Now, the silence that greeted him convinced him that what he'd heard earlier was just a mouse scrounging for a meal.

Opening the door another few inches, he poked his head inside and waited for his 'blind as a bat' eyes to adjust to the darkness. The odor of hay and manure and something he couldn't identify assailed his nostrils.

It was an unpleasant, pungent smell, like a mixture of metal, sweat, and urine.

"Anyone home?" he tried again. Father Gabriel's car was in the drive, so Bob knew he couldn't have gone far. He'd tried the old farmhouse first and, when there was no answer, walked around the structure, peeked into windows, called out.

The house appeared empty.

By the time Bob made his way to the barn, he was more concerned than curious. The farmhouse was, literally, in the middle of nowhere. There was nothing for miles, certainly nothing one would walk to. The closest neighbor was more than three miles away, the nearest business, an all-night diner, six or seven miles down the road.

He knocked once more before pulling the barn door fully open. The hinges squeaked, and the bottom of the door scratched against the dirt, creating small puffs of dust that swirled upward, landing on his shoes. Head swiveling, he took a few steps forward, the sound of his boots as they crunched against a thin layer of hay echoing through the barn. The space was largely empty, with a few of the usual farming tools hanging on one wall to his left and a sawhorse that held some two-by-fours on his right.

Six open stalls, ghosts of a past when the property was a successful working farm, lined the right-hand wall. Against the back wall, a solitary ladder leaned against the bottom lip of the hay loft. The loft was empty now, with only the random scrap of hay or rodent droppings lining the wooden floor.

In the center of the barn, two rusty chains, about eight feet long, dangled from a rafter in the ceiling. Behind them, a leather strap of some kind was wrapped around a center support beam.

"What in tarnation...." Bob mumbled, walking closer. He picked up one of the chains and stared at the manacle at the end. Splotches of red nestled into the crevices near the locking mechanism, but it was another substance, chunks of it on the inner circle of the device, that turned his blood to ice.

Unwilling to accept what his eyes were seeing—because, after all, he *was* blind as a bat—he held the handcuff close to his nose and sniffed. The smell of copper assailed his nostrils, confirming that the red-colored spatter was blood.

Holding the device mere inches from his nose, he studied the flecks of material stuck to the metal.

It looked a lot like skin. Like flesh.

Stomach roiling, he dropped the cuff as if it had teeth and stepped back. In a panic, eyes scanning the barn floor, he caught sight of a dark stain he hadn't noticed before. It was round, large, and had seeped through the cracks between the floorboards.

More blood.

"What in the hell?" he whispered.

Gingerly, he stepped over the stain, pushing himself to examine the west side of the barn. It was dark, darker than night. He wished he had a flashlight, a lantern, a cell phone even. But old Bob didn't believe in cell phones. Instead, he contended that 'a man ain't much of a man' if he constantly needed a cell phone for company.

Now, he was cursing his pompous stand on cell phones.

Squinting toward a black mass in the corner of the barn, he licked his lips, craning his neck toward the inky shape. His throat was bone dry. "Hello? Who's there?" he croaked, feeling a droplet of sweat run between his shoulder blades. He was nervous—terrified, truth be told—though he couldn't put a finger on why he was so spooked.

He knew every inch of this property and had visited the barn all hours of the day or night. Still, he trembled.

"This ain't funny no more," he called out, his voice a mere rasp. "My name is Bob Dietrich, caretaker of this here property. Ya'll best come out of there now."

But the form didn't move.

"Gosh hang it and fuck yer granny! You gonna make me come over there, ain't ya?" he yelled.

The figure remained motionless.

His heart kicked wildly, threatening to burst through his chest. Muttering an oath, he tiptoed, taking baby steps, to the unidentified mass slumped on the floor. When he got close enough to see what it was, bile rose in his throat.

"Jesus, Mary, and Joseph," he whispered, blessing himself while moving backward.

A broken slat on the exterior wall provided just enough illumination to make out the body of a woman. She was lying on her right side, unmoving, the slit in her throat glistening in a sliver of light. In the center of her forehead, an impression had been burned into her flesh, still raw and red. It was an unusual symbol, one that Bob recognized.

The Sigillum Dei: the seal of God.

He'd seen a similar design before.

Years ago, during a Bible study class, a fellow congregant had passed around a photo they'd copied from the internet. It was a diagram of sorts, an image of what laypeople assumed was the mark of the Almighty. The design consisted of various geometric shapes said to be labeled with the name of God and his angels. The design's purpose? To protect the faithful, the chosen, from divine judgment.

According to the Book of Revelation, those who carry the seal of God will be spared from His wrath on Judgment Day.

But this woman was already dead, no longer in peril of the horrors of the Tribulations. Even if she weren't, even if the seal placement were genuinely divine, it should not have been visible to mortal men.

Sickened and confused, his mind stubbornly refusing to process what he was seeing, Bob took a quick, wheezing breath and moved backward.

He moved slowly at first, legs weak, bowels cramping. When comprehension of the horror here began to trickle in, he moved faster, twice tripping over his own feet and landing on the ground.

He got up, then fell a third time.

Staying on the ground, tears streaming down his face, Bob Dietrich crab-walked toward the door. He could think of nothing beyond leaving here, getting to his car, hugging his wife June.

As he continued backing up, wrists aching from holding his weight, he at last found a swift rhythm and was close to the barn door when his head struck something solid.

A bare leg.

Screaming, he flipped over onto all fours, tilted his head back, and gazed up at the naked, bloody man in front of him.

"Padre?" Bob asked, confused. "I...I don't understand." Then, because he could think of nothing else, he said, "Gabriel? Where are your clothes?"

Gabriel smiled, ignoring the question. "Do you realize how special you are, Bob? You fell three times! I witnessed it! Just as Jesus fell three times while carrying his cross on the way to Calvary!"

Bob swallowed hard, his mind swirling. *Father Gabriel is naked; Father*

Gabriel is bloodied; Father Gabriel is talking nonsense.

Too terrified to ask about the corpse in the corner, Bob tried to stand, but his legs shook violently, and he fell back to his knees.

"Here," Gabriel said, extending a hand, "let me help you."

Bob shrank back. He was a Vietnam veteran who had joined the army at seventeen with his momma's blessing. He'd seen battles, witnessed man's inhumanity to man. Hell, sometimes, he had been the cause of it. He'd fought in hand-to-hand combat, taken cover inside foxholes, and watched buddies blown up in minefields. But this? This was, perhaps, the most frightened he'd ever been.

And at seventy-one years old, that was saying something.

"Oh, come now, Bobby," Gabriel said, drawing closer. "How long have you known me? Give me your hand."

Torn, Bob glanced wildly around the barn as if he could find the answer within its notched beams and worn siding. Finally, his eyes met Gabriel's once more and, resigned, he stuck out his hand.

Once he'd pulled the older man to his feet, Gabriel searched Bob's face, then shook his head sadly. "I'm sure you have questions. For someone like you, it's a lot to process."

Someone like me? Bob thought. *What the blazes does that mean?*

Turning away, Gabriel walked toward the dusty table in the corner as, uneasy, Bob watched. Although wary about what was on that table, his mind seemed stuck on the priest's nakedness. Like a record skipping on an old Victrola, he kept coming back to the same thought.

He's naked, he's naked, why is he naked?

It was as if the dead woman, the one in the corner with the gash in her throat and the brand on her forehead, existed elsewhere. In his fright, Bob could handle only one thought at a time.

Otherwise, he feared he'd go mad.

Gabriel returned to the center of the barn, his pace smooth, leisurely, his hands tucked behind his back. Stopping in front of Bob, he cocked his head.

"You look troubled, Robert. Uncomfortable. Do I make you uncomfortable?"

Sweat gathered under Bob's armpits as he sized up his opponent. His eyes moved over the priest, assessing his body language, trying to catch a glimpse of what Gabriel held in his hands.

It was obvious he was hiding something—horrifically, chillingly obvious.

And, although it had been almost fifty years since Bob had served in the military, he recognized the signs; tense posture, wandering eyes, wide stance. He'd bet his last dime that Gabriel was contemplating a strike.

Planting his feet, muscle memory and past training kicking in, Bob prepared for an assault. He was not as tall as Gabriel, not as strong, but he still possessed the instincts and experience to fight well. He'd done it a thousand times.

Fought for a cause, fought for what was right. Fought for survival.

The change in Bob's posture, the steely determination in his eyes, did not go unnoticed. "I want you to know, Bob," Gabriel said, "I have nothing against you. But this is bigger than our friendship, more important than the fate of one man, one dot in the universe."

Bob raised his hands in readiness for combat, calculating the best place to land his first blow. As he moved forward, he never registered that his enemy was moving just as swiftly; never saw the electric prod his opponent held in his right hand.

And never saw the blade Gabriel held in his left.

Seconds later, electricity buckled Bob's knees just as the knife sliced through his heart muscle.

He wondered why there was so little pain.

Clutching the hilt of the knife, panicked, Bob yanked it from his chest. It was a novice mistake, one he would never have made under ordinary circumstances.

Of course, these circumstances were anything but ordinary.

He was dying.

Once he'd pulled the blade free, nothing was tamping the severed vessels. With each beat of his heart, a spray of blood jetted from his body. He'd witnessed the effects of arterial bleeding firsthand and knew he would be dead in minutes if he didn't act.

When his silent plea to his attacker went unanswered, Bob slapped both hands over the hemorrhaging wound in a feeble attempt to stop the bleeding. Blood gushed beneath his palms and between his fingers as pink foam bubbled from his mouth.

"Don't worry," Gabriel whispered. "You will be saved, honored with the mark of God's chosen. You will carry the seal."

Just as Bob's vision faded and his heart slowed, just before he prayed for his family and succumbed to the darkness, he heard Father Gabriel's voice for the last time.

"I really will miss you, Bob-O. Say hello to my bitch sister."

After showering and having a bite to eat, Gabriel laced up his boots and walked back to the barn. He felt lighter than he had in years, his mind so much clearer.

The old barn and the farmhouse were his now. He'd made sure of it. Once he'd found the deed for the property, it was just a matter of changing the title to his name. He'd created a forged document—uncannily good— and hacked into the town records. Now, if anyone asked, the farmhouse and its twenty acres belonged to J. Gabriel.

Because he was a cautious fellow.

Not that he expected anyone to question it. The only one who knew the land wasn't his was Bob Dietrich, and he wasn't talking.

Still, one could never be too careful.

Property tax records were public documents. Since the name 'Jeremy Sterling' was in the system, Gabriel couldn't use it. And, after the events of the last six months, 'Gabriel Devine' would also raise a flag to authorities.

But no one had heard of J. Gabriel.

He grabbed some tools from the shed—a few shovels and a rake—and tossed them into his pickup truck. He would bury Bob on the property, maybe give him a lovely cross to mark his grave.

It hadn't been bullshit when he'd apologized as Bob took his last breaths. Gabriel really did hate to kill him.

But remorse was something he would never experience, could never feel. Remorse was for cowards and fools and lesser men. Remorse was for mortals.

But he did have regrets in life.

He regretted missing the opportunity to watch Katie Callahan die. He regretted not killing her sister, Callie, when she sat chained in a basement— broken, bleeding, still defiant.

He regretted not ending his mother, Meredith, sooner; regretted not starting his mission to wipe out the filth and the unworthy earlier in his life.

And he regretted Bob.

He returned to the barn, intent on dragging his caretaker to the truck. Later, he would concoct a story for June Dietrich that told of her husband's deep secrets and wanton desires. It would explain his disappearance, and, with any luck, the woman would be too embarrassed and angry to notify the police of Bob's absence. It mattered little either way. Gabriel was a meticulous planner.

No one would know what had occurred here.

As for Rebecca Caraway, he had something special planned for her. Something that would show the world exactly how she had sinned in life.

He reached the body of Bob Dietrich, shook his head sadly, and began to drag him to the barn door by his ankles.

Sorry, Bob-O, but you gotta crack a few eggs to make an omelet, am I right?

Just as he got to the door, a soft moan from inside the barn caught his attention. Ignoring it, he pulled Bob the next twenty feet to the fire pit. Stacking kindling within the circle of rocks, he doused the wood with lighter fluid and tossed in a match.

His Sigillum branding iron was in the barn. So was his next pressing problem.

After watching the fire burn for a moment, he walked to his truck and reached for the toolbox in the truck bed. Grabbing his medical kit, whistling a happy but nonsensical tune, he re-entered the barn and moved immediately to the last stall on the right.

The woman on the floor, blindfolded and bound, tried to raise her head.

"Shh, hush now. You'll wake Rebecca," he giggled, pulling a pre-filled syringe of midazolam out of his bag. "You are a feisty one; I'll give you that. But since I can't very well have you leaving here..."

He rolled up her sleeve and injected the sedative. She moaned again.

"There, now. Rest," he whispered into her ear. "I'll be back before you can miss me."

Before she succumbed to the darkness, the woman on the ground felt a solitary tear slide down her cheek.

"Where are you?"

Gabriel sat in his idling truck, cell phone in hand, irked that Simon of Cyrene did not pick up on the first ring.

"I-I'm at work. I was in the back and didn't hear the phone ring." Simon of Cyrene dabbed his face, wiping sweat from his upper lip.

"Then I suggest you purchase pants with pockets. I'll not be trifled with, sir. This is important work, and you must be there when I need you."

The man gulped and took a seat at one of the desks in the room. It was early, and he was the first to arrive at the office. Sinking into the chair, he curled forward, a throwback to when he was a child and feeling uncomfortable.

If he could have rolled himself into a ball and disappeared entirely, he would have.

Whispering now, fearing the answer, he asked, "What is it you need me to do?"

"Meet me at the farmhouse. I have a disposal."

Simon of Cyrene held his breath, waiting. Surely more information about this 'disposal' would follow. When no explanation came, he said, "Um, I can't really leave now. It would look—suspicious. Can it wait?" As soon as the words left his mouth, he wanted to call them back.

Stupid, stupid, stupid!

Gabriel pulled out his pocketknife, opened it, and held its edge against his right palm. Angling the tip, he pushed down, using tiny jerks and small flicks of the blade, watching as pockets of blood pooled around the center of his hand.

Creating his own stigmata and never feeling a thing.

Clearing his throat, Gabriel said, "I'll forget you asked such a stupid question. See you here in an hour."

The click of the phone as it disconnected reverberated in the man's ears. As he rose, defeated, he began rehearsing the excuse he would give his supervisor for leaving work early. The man's greatest fears had come true.

The Apostle had summoned him. And it was a call he could not ignore.

CHAPTER FOUR

Callie stood in front of Amara Davies' home, taking in the exterior of the condo. The streets of the small community were lined with cobblestone sidewalks, the roads all named after flowers. On the way into the neighborhood, Jake and Callie passed Primrose Drive, Heather Way, and Jasmine Circle to arrive at their destination.

Twenty-one Magnolia Lane. Amara's home. The pale blue structure, highlighted with black shutters shaped like barn doors, was modest sized and well kept. There was a colorful garden, bright with early-blooming impatiens, marigolds, and begonias, to the left of the entry steps. In the center of the garden, a double shepherd hook held a 'Welcome' sign on one side and an old gas lantern on the other.

Beside her, Jake nudged her elbow. "Blaze? You good?"

Callie stared at Amara's front door. "I—I think so. I don't know. It's so odd, knowing that behind that door is a stranger who is my sister, my blood. My belly is in knots. You know, once that door is opened, it can never be closed again." She took a deep breath, both excited and terrified to meet the person on the other side of that door.

Trying to lighten the mood, eyes twinkling while holding back a smirk that was dying to get out, Jake shrugged, "Yep, you're right. Once you open that can of worms, there's no going back. Kinda like losing your virginity, huh? I mean, once that genie is outta the bottle...."

Callie turned to him and wrinkled her nose. "Always the comedian. Come on, Barney. Let's do this."

Amara Grace Davies peeked out from behind the living room curtain and watched the couple on the sidewalk. They seemed comfortable with each other, familiar, close.

She studied the woman's features, looking for a hint of resemblance, a flicker of familiarity. She searched her mind for a word that adequately described Callie physically, finally settling on the word 'stunning.'

Long, waving strands of auburn hair, shining in the waning light of day, were the first feature to draw Amara's attention. Amara's own hair was more a strawberry blond, shoulder length, thinner than Callie's.

Strike one—different hair color, she thought. *Still, we're both camped in the same 'red' family.*

She continued her covert inspection, taking in Callie's dusting of freckles and heart-shaped face. Her eyes were bright and warm. A single dimple creased her right cheek when she smiled at the man.

Amara's face was more oval than heart-shaped, and she had no dimples. She did, however, have an army of freckles.

Okay, she thought. *We're getting warmer here.*

She watched as the male leaned close and said something to Callie. When he smiled, Amara felt her heart flutter. At first glance, he was attractive, but when he grinned, he was breathtakingly gorgeous.

Yeah, you are a looker, aren't you? If I were into older guys, I might give Callie a run for her money.

Amara moved from the window to a hall mirror when the couple approached the steps. Checking her appearance for the thousandth time, she took a calming breath and stepped to the front door.

Callie pushed the doorbell just as Amara grasped the doorknob. The thunderous volume of the chimes was unexpected, and Callie jumped a bit.

Amara opened the door wide in greeting. Somewhere in the background, a lamp flickered on and off.

"Hel—hello," Amara said, breath caught in her throat. Standing two feet from the woman at her doorstep, it hit her.

I know you! I know the curve of your face, the warmth of your smile, the tilt of your head! How is this possible?

"Amara Grace Davies, I presume?" Callie asked, raising her brows. "Actually, scratch that. No presumptions are needed. You have our father's eyes."

Amara smiled, the initial shock of seeing Callie waning, and joked, "Hopefully, I don't have his ears." Her voice was clipped, the end of her words cut short. "The function, I mean, not the size."

Callie frowned, confused.

"I'm deaf, you see," Amara said. "Well, not entirely. I have about twenty percent hearing in my right ear. In my left? Let's just say it's a good ear to turn toward a person I no longer want to listen to." She chuckled and stepped back, inviting them in.

"Oh, I'm sorry. I had no idea," Callie said as she and Jake stepped into the foyer.

"No need to apologize. I've been hearing impaired my entire life. But I'm one of the lucky ones. Even a small degree of hearing can be the difference between being a participant in life or a spectator."

"I get that. Do you read lips?" Callie asked, sure to keep her eyes on Amara's face.

"Yes, I do. Occasionally, I miss a word or two, but I can generally get the gist of what's being said. I hear certain pitches, mostly male, and loud tones somewhere around seventy decibels. I have a hearing aid for my right ear, but it usually sits in my bedside drawer. While it does help some, most days, the small benefit doesn't offset the annoyance " She shrugged. "I

42

would rather sign or read lips, honestly. But I do have it in for your visit." She smiled and turned her head to showcase the device.

"Well, just so you know, I can sign a bit. I took a few elective classes in college. Funny, because I never understood why it felt so important to do so. Now I know."

The three stood awkwardly in a circle, unsure whether to nod, shake hands, or hug. Amara chose for them.

"Welcome to my humble abode," she said, extending a hand.

"Thank you for seeing us," Callie said. She shook Amara's outstretched hand, then turned to Jake, intending to introduce him. He beat her to the punch.

"Jake Devereaux," he said, grabbing Amara's hand warmly. "It's a pleasure to meet you."

"The pleasure is mine. Please, come in. I hope you'll stay for dinner?" Amara asked them. "I made a big pot of chili and some cornbread."

Callie nodded. "We would love that."

Amara beckoned them into the small living room, and Callie took in her surroundings. The room was modern looking and tastefully decorated in various shades of blue and gray. A mahogany coffee table took up a large portion of the space. An abundance of artwork hung on the walls, mostly ocean pieces depicting lighthouses nestled amidst stormy seas.

"You have a gorgeous home," Callie said. "Those paintings are beautiful. Local artist?"

Watching Callie's lips closely, Amara snorted. "You could say that. They're mine."

Callie's eyes widened. "Shut up! Seriously? And here I am, unable to draw a straight line. Why are you not famous?"

Amara blushed. "I-I guess I sort of am. At least here in Denver. I make a decent living with my portraits and watercolors. I have several more in my studio I would like to show you if you're interested."

"Yes, please! I would love that!"

Another wave of uncomfortable silence washed over them. It wasn't that they had nothing to discuss. It was more that they had so much catching up to do, no one knew where to start. Jake broke the silence.

"Amara, if you show me where the dishes are, I can set the table while you girls chat."

Callie felt a warmth spread from her cheeks to her toes. Some days, she took Jake's consideration for others, his ability to 'read the room,' for granted.

Not today.

After orienting Jake to the kitchen, Amara escorted Callie upstairs to her loft-like studio. Three free-standing easels stood in three corners of the room. One easel was empty; the other two were covered by drop cloths.

In the fourth corner of the room, an overstuffed chair and ottoman sat beside a floor-to-ceiling case filled with various hardcover books.

On the right side of the room, lining one wall, hundreds of brushes and artist tools, some unfamiliar to Callie, sat on top of a built-in thigh-high dresser. Above that dresser, an arched window looked out over the back of the building complex. It was a lovely view, with a common area that held flowering trees, a hand-built babbling brook, and several tables and chairs. The faint outline of a vast mountain expanse could be seen in the distance.

"Wow. This view is spectacular!" Callie said. "How on earth do you get any work done?"

Amara looked around the room. "I'll admit, sometimes it isn't easy. There are days when I park myself on that big ol' chair with a glass of red wine and a thick book." She twisted her hands in front of her, suddenly troubled. "But most days, I'm left with little choice but to work. The pull of the canvas is too...." Walking to the window, she sighed. "Too strong."

Callie followed Amara to the window, and the younger woman turned to her. Staring into her sister's pained eyes, Callie frowned. "I don't understand. I thought you enjoyed painting."

Amara studied the white porcelain floor, her frown foreshadowing her indecision. She was apprehensive about opening this door into what her life had become. "Oh, I do. I love it. Well, I love it if it's on my terms."

"Meaning?"

"Oh, boy. Okay, what I am about to tell you, to show you, may have you running away from this room, this house, even from me," Amara said nervously. "But, once I saw you up close and personal, I understood."

Impatient, stomach in knots, Callie waited for an explanation. Something told her that, whatever this secret was, it would alter the course of their lives.

When Amara said nothing, Callie probed. "What is it? Tell me, Amara." All at once, a horrible thought crept into Callie's mind, unexpected, unsolicited, and unwanted.

What if what she tells me is disturbing? What if she's done something terrible, something criminal?

And then, the most terrifying thought of all shoved its way into her psyche. *What if she is like Gabriel?*

"I think it's better if I show you," Amara said. "This way."

Callie followed Amara to the closest easel. A paint-speckled, cream-colored tarp covered half of what lay beneath; the edges of the canvas seemed to push and strain against the fabric. For reasons she couldn't understand at first, Callie felt her pulse quicken and her stomach clench.

The sight of Amara's work, smothered beneath that simple tarp, struggling to break free, conjured an image in Callie's mind of a dank space, a cold prison.

A moldy basement, a kidnap victim whose limbs were immobilized by chains.

My limbs, my childhood basement, my torment!

She squeezed her eyes tightly against the mental picture forming in her brain. It was a memory that threatened to transport her back to a time when, shackled to a Lally column, beaten and nearly broken, she waited for Gabriel to finish her.

Instead, he finished Kates with a bullet to the chest; a bullet that was meant for me.

Unsettled, Callie forced herself to snap back to the present. Worrying her bottom lip, she stood shoulder to shoulder with Amara, waiting for the unveiling.

"Fair warning," Amara said, hands steepled and resting against her lips. "You're in for a shock. Once you recognize the subject here, once it hits you how impossible it is..." She shrugged, unable to finish her thought.

"Don't worry," Callie signed while speaking the words. "I'm not going anywhere."

Amara smiled. "Impressive. Signing is usually a use-it-or-lose-it kind of thing for people. Not for you, apparently. Or do you have another deaf person in your life?"

"Nope, no one else. But knowing American Sign Language is a great tool for a psychologist. To keep it fresh, I take a quick workshop class several times a year."

"That's dedication!"

Callie winked. "Once you get to know me, you'll learn my tenacity is due more to my Irish genes than any dedication. I am stubborn, I walk to my own, very odd, beat, and sometimes, I don't play well with others."

Amara giggled. "You just signed 'I don't yellow with others.' You need both of those hands going with the word 'play.' Like this." She held up her hands, formed the letter 'y,' and moved her hands back and forth. Then, patting Callie's shoulder, she grinned. "But don't worry. You aren't *terrible* at signing."

"Okay, wise guy," Callie joked. "Let's see what's behind door number one."

Amara nodded, lifted both sides of the tarp, and pulled it free. The motion blew a puff of air, fragrant with the scents of oil paint and charcoal pencils, into their faces.

Callie digested the painting for a moment before her mouth went dry and her eyes widened with disbelief. It was a portrait of a woman lying on a damp cement floor, her right wrist tethered to a length of chain and her right leg in a shackle. Although the subject's head was low and the lighting dim, her features were clearly identifiable: auburn hair, high cheekbones, battered face.

This is me! Callie's mind screamed. *This is me!*

"I—I don't understand," she said, confused. "This cellar is... How could you have known?"

Amara shook her head. "I didn't. At least, not consciously." She walked to the ottoman, legs shaking, and took a seat. Tucking her hands between her knees, she said, "I suppose I should explain."

Spellbound, Callie remained still.

"Toward the end of December of last year, I woke up with an indescribable urge to get to the loft, to my art. Granted, I enjoy my work, but this was more than that. This was, I don't know, more like need? Desperation? I was compelled to get to a blank canvas, set it on my easel, and paint. But once I got up here, once I grabbed a brush, something happened." She pointed a finger to her temple. "Something happened in here."

"What?" Callie whispered, mesmerized.

Amara shrugged. "I went away. Mentally, I mean. The last thing I remember is picking up that brush. When I 'came back,' I saw I had painted this."

Callie shook her head. "But that's impossible! This is clearly me, in the basement of my house as a child. How could you know about this?"

"That's what I'm trying to say. There's no way I could have known about what happened in that cellar, let alone painted it. Hell, I just recently learned I even had a sister. We just met twenty minutes ago." Amara stood again. "That's not all, though. The same thing has happened to me two more times. I have no idea what these drawings mean, but I think you need to see them."

On heavy legs, Amara plodded to the next corner, the next easel. Hesitating a moment, she pulled off the tarp. The painting depicted, once again, the basement of the Callahan family's first home—the site to which Gabriel Devine had lured Callie and Kate, the place where Callie's worst fears had come true.

Callie studied the picture now, horrified at the content but impressed by the talent of its artist. Amara was very good at her craft. There was no mistaking the figure of Katie Callahan—on the cement floor with a hole in her chest, a pool of blood surrounding her body as Callie cradled her head. To the side was a man's hand, strong and soaked in blood, applying pressure to the wound.

Jake's hand.

Callie clamped a hand over her mouth. "This is...this is crazy. You're telling me that you have, what? A supernatural ability to paint the past? An uncannily accurate way to reveal what was?"

Amara frowned, pouting like a three-year-old. "It's not like I asked for this, Callie. Do you think I enjoy this? Do you think I want to see the only family I have left relive the worst pain imaginable?" She nodded toward the painting and whispered, "So, this is her then? Katie? I painted a picture of her death?"

Callie nodded, shaken by the impossibility of what she was seeing. "Sure looks like it. Tell me, when did you say this ability first appeared?"

"Oh, that's an easy one. It happened without warning, just after Christmas. I remember because I had a whole week of projects planned. I was going to try my hand at some abstracts, maybe do a few 'Holidays at the Ocean' themed paintings, capitalizing on the twelve days of Christmas. Instead, I found myself in a fugue-like state, painting things I could not possibly know."

"Like Katie's last moments," Callie said softly. "Timewise, I guess it makes sense. Your ability started around the time Katie died, and right when I…" She stopped, not sure if she wanted to reveal her 'gift' to Amara yet.

"When you what? Come on, spill. I just told you my deepest, darkest. It's only fair you do the same."

She's not wrong, Callie thought. *It's not fair that she spills her guts, and I leave her hanging.*

Callie nodded and signed, "Okay, but when you wake up screaming in the night, cringing as you hear my words over and over in your mind, don't say I didn't warn you."

Amara grinned. "Well, since I can't hear shit, that shouldn't be a problem." Growing serious again, she added, "But before you tell me your secret, I need to show you one more painting. I did it last week and still have no idea who I painted or why. Or even if it has anything to do with our family."

Stepping around a center table, Amara made her way to the empty easel in the back corner of the room. Behind it, a painting stood propped against the wall, the finished side hidden. Reaching past the easel, she pulled out the canvas, keeping its finished side turned away. "I moved it here and turned it to face the wall because I ran out of drop cloths. It's too creepy to look at for long, and I couldn't bear to have it just sitting there, uncovered."

"Well, that sounds encouraging," Callie deadpanned.

Amara shrugged, lifted the canvas, turned it, and set it on the easel. Horrified, Callie stared at the painting. It was an image of a young, heavy-set woman bound in chains, her head bowed. Beneath her slit throat, creating a macabre abstract of its own, a fan-like pattern of blood stained the ground.

Callie had never seen the woman before. "Good God," she said softly. "Who is she?"

Amara lifted a shoulder. "No idea. I'd hoped you would recognize her, or at least recognize the surroundings."

Callie scrutinized the painting again. The woman in the drawing was in some sort of outbuilding, with open rafters and old wooden floors. Several ragged hay bales were stacked in the distance. The space was unfamiliar to Callie.

"When did you say you painted this, Amara?" she asked.

"Four days ago. I remember because I wasn't feeling well and planned to take the day off. Apparently, this new ability, gift, or whatever you call it, decided it was more important to paint than to rest. Do you know her?"

"No, I've never seen her before. This all has to mean something, though, right? In at least two of your paintings, you've drawn an event from the past. This third one? Maybe it's another echo of a previous crime. Or perhaps it's a depiction of a future one." Callie wrapped an arm around Amara and led her to the staircase. "Let's get back to my gorgeous man in your kitchen and sit down to some of your delicious chili. Jake and I can fill you in on everything you want to know while we eat. But I warn you— what we disclose will be a lot to take in. You may kick us out before we take a bite of that heavenly-scented cornbread."

Amara chuckled and began to descend the steps, arm in arm with Callie. "Not a chance! After I lost my folks, I thought I would be alone forever. But now, I know I have family out there. Trust me when I say nothing you can say would make me turn away." Pausing on the steps, she turned to Callie and beamed. "And, since I just showed you what I can do, I doubt anything you tell me will scare me off."

Callie threw her head back and roared. "You think a couple of psychic-induced pictures are scary? Well, hang onto your shorts, sister! I'm about to blow your mind!"

CHAPTER FIVE

"LUST"

"If a man commits adultery with another man's wife, even with the wife of his neighbor, both the adulterer and adulteress must be put to death..."

Leviticus 20:10

Annie McCormack sat on a stool in Murphy's Irish Pub, sipping a Guinness draft while staring at her reflection in the bar mirror, counting all the reasons she should leave her husband.

She'd lost count of those reasons somewhere around twenty-seven.

To be fair, Trevor Oakley wasn't always a drunk and a cheat. In the first years of their marriage, he had been attentive, kind, generous. He and Annie had a magical future planned, filled with endless love, plenty of money, adorable children.

They'd met in their sophomore year of college. Annie, or 'Mac' as she was called back then, was a photography major while Trevor studied music. She used to joke to her friends that it was his voice, not his looks, that had swept her off her feet. She also joked that if they were ever to marry, the name 'Annie Oakley' would never work for her.

She would always remain Annie McCormack.

Back then, before it all fell apart, Trevor was a talented singer and songwriter, even writing a song for her on their wedding day that he'd titled "Forever, Annie Mac."

But, as with everything in life, reality eventually knocks on the door—first as the slightest tap, then as a resounding boom. Trevor, although gifted, would never tour the country with a kick-ass rock band; Annie would never get rich snapping pictures of snot-nosed children in birthday tiaras or sixteen-year-old girls wearing wrist corsages and prom dresses.

Four years after saying "I do," they were barely keeping their heads above water financially. Money worries, combined with Annie's inability to conceive and Trevor's drinking problem, had escalated their marital issues.

But it was the lipstick on the collar, the late-night jam sessions with an imaginary band, that had changed their union forever. Trevor hadn't done much to hide his steamy affairs—which, in some way, was more offensive to Annie than the affairs themselves.

Yes, Trevor Oakley wasn't always a drunk and a cheat. But now, he'd sell his mother's soul for a pint and a kiss and never look back.

Their marriage was now more or less a free-for-all. They each did what they wanted when they wanted.

And who they wanted.

Annie scanned the strangers in the pub, twisting her wedding ring around her finger, searching for a new hook-up. At the moment, she didn't give two shits about her marriage, her husband, or her career.

She just wanted to feel again.

"Can I get you another, milady?" the bartender asked with a cheesy grin.

Annie smiled. She'd been coming to Murphy's for a year now and knew the bartender, Terry, well.

"'T'would be grand, milord," she said with a slight bow.

While she waited for her next round, she twirled her glass on the cork coaster and continued to surveil the bar. Moments later, her eyes met the steely gaze of a man sitting at a corner table. Even seated, she could tell he was muscular and attractive, in a raw kind of way, even with the eye covering. She wondered what had happened to him, what lay beneath the patch over his left eye.

He looked dangerous, feral, confident; he looked like he knew his way around a woman's body.

He looked like her next fuck.

You Jezebels are so fucking predictable.

Gabriel watched the woman at the bar with disgust. The flip of her hair, the fake laugh while talking to the mustached bartender, the way she ran her fingers suggestively up and down the lager glass. There was no doubt in his mind that she was a wanton woman, a slut willing to spread her legs for anyone with a dick.

At once, it both sickened and excited him. He'd found what he came for—another sinner. This would be number two in his quest to find seven offenders, seven evildoers practicing one of the seven deadly sins.

Number three, if you counted the woman currently sedated in the barn. Although to be fair, he wasn't sure what he'd planned to do with that one. When he first saw her, he'd been taken back by her beauty, by the brilliant beam of light that played around her face and seemed to surround her. She was stunning and vibrant, and sacred. Almost immediately, deep within himself, he'd heard a voice command, 'Take her.'

So, he did.

He still hadn't decided if he wanted to worship her, fuck her, or kill her. Maybe he'd do all three.

As for the other immoral fiends, extinguishing their light was up to him. Those guilty of committing the vilest of sins—cardinal sins—needed to be punished.

His task was daunting. He would pave the way and cleanse the earth for the start of the Tribulations. That seven-year period, beginning with the opening of the seven seals, would herald the end of days.

And the first of those seals, once opened, would release the Four Horsemen of the Apocalypse.

Conquest, war, famine, death.

Once freed, the first horseman, known as the Antichrist and riding a white horse, would wreak havoc on man, filling humanity's heads with empty promises and false hubris. He—or she—would come cloaked, disguised as a force for good, the salt of the earth.

All lies from the beast whose number is 666.

Yes, Gabriel was confident he would have no problem recognizing the beast, despite its façade of purity. Soon, the Antichrist would descend, and Gabriel would pounce, proving beyond a shadow of a doubt that he was the true Messiah.

But first, the bitch at the bar—the Whore of Babylon who wore a wedding ring yet paraded her vulgar desires for all to see.

The woman who chose the capital sin of lust over the capital virtue of chastity. She sat there, tight skirt hugging her perfect ass, her slim calves sliding up and down the leg of the stool. She wore false innocence like a crown, demurely dipping her head while sneaking him furtive glances that spoke of a quiet naivete.

I got your number, girly. Tough to play hard to get when you're creamin' your panties, isn't it?

He licked his bottom lip and rolled his eyes over her body.

Yeah, I can play that game, too.

Gabriel, sans clerical collar, stood and moved next to her at the bar. "Good evening, pretty lady," he said, voice deep, a slight drawl to his vowels. "Can I buy you a drink? I have a quiet table in the corner." He displayed his most charming smile, bright white teeth gleaming under the bar lights. "Might be a tad more private. I'm Bob, by the way. Bob Dietrich."

He said the name loudly, hoping the bar patrons heard him. Later, if asked by the cops about the one-eyed stranger last seen with this woman, people would recall his name before any physical description. As a rule, humans were not very observant. Of course, a man wearing a patch over his eye wasn't all that common.

Fuck it. Let them know I was here!

As for Bob Dietrich, he hoped the dead caretaker didn't mind him using his name. But when the idea had come to him, it had been too perfect to ignore. Small-town gossip never failed. Eventually, word would reach June Dietrich that her husband had been hanging out at Murphy's, cementing the notion that Bob was a liar and a cheat.

Besides, it wasn't like Bob-O was going to be using his name anytime soon.

He stifled a chuckle and waited for the woman to respond.

Holding out a slim, well-manicured hand, she said, "Nice to meet you, Bob. I'm Annie McCormack, and, yes, I'd love to join you for a drink."

Gabriel ordered another round and escorted Annie back to the table. They sat in awkward silence, waiting for Terry to signal their drinks were ready.

As they waited, Gabriel played with the tiny package of powder in his jeans pocket. One of the perks of parading through life as a priest was the access it gave him to society's underbelly—halfway houses, hospital detox units, and court-mandated group therapy sessions. Places where some addicts had no true desire to get 'clean' and stop using their drug of choice but were forced to participate under threat of incarceration.

All easy targets for a man of the cloth.

Gabriel would choose the ones he knew were on edge, those who would likely pick up a needle as soon as they were sprung. He'd dangle money in front of those unfortunates like a carrot, promising a finder's fee for a lead to their dealers.

The rest, as they say, was history.

Once he obtained the names of their suppliers, he was able to buy any street drug he wanted—liquid X, roofies, ketamine. Of course, *he* didn't make the purchases himself.

Mingling with such people was beneath him.

Instead, he sent Simon of Cyrene, kicking and screaming, into the bowels of the dealers' dens. The man did surprisingly well, scoring enough junk to keep Gabriel's sinners quiet and malleable until judgment was passed.

And Annie McCormack?

Annie would soon be on the receiving end of a generous dose of Rohypnol, an odorless and tasteless amnesiac. After just one dose, 'roofie' users often felt drowsy and appeared to be drunk. Considering Annie was on her fourth drink, her stumbling gait and slurred speech would be chalked up to inebriation.

Gabriel had studied the drug, learning that symptoms usually began thirty minutes after ingestion.

Thirty minutes didn't give him a lot of time.

He planned to drop the powder in her beer, then buy one more round of drinks, bolstering the illusion that it was alcohol, not drugs, at the root of her behavior. He would need to work quickly once her symptoms appeared, getting her to his car before she collapsed entirely.

He had no desire to carry her skanky ass to his truck.

Twenty minutes later, Gabriel watched in fascination as the Rohypnol took effect. Annie's words became garbled; she swayed in her seat, and her eyes blinked rapidly. Her shaking hands fought to hold her glass of Guinness but failed, the dark liquid sloshing over the rim into her lap.

I thought I'd have more time! Maybe the alcohol hastened the drug's effect? No matter. I need to move...now!

"Hey, are you okay?" Gabriel asked, grabbing her elbow, his voice telegraphing mock concern tempered with urgency.

Annie giggled and waved a hand. "Oh, me? I'm juss fine! Never better!"

Gabriel glanced across the room at the bartender, who had stopped washing glasses and was staring intently. After twenty years of mixing drinks, Terry had seen the worst of humanity, witnessed the vilest of cretins as they preyed on the fairer sex.

As a result, he was extremely cautious regarding his female customers.

Nervous now, sensing he was being sized up, Gabriel found the bartender's eyes and mouthed, *'I think she's had too much.'*

Terry paused, waiting for his inner alarm to silence, then nodded discreetly. Satisfied that Annie wasn't in the hands of a rapist or worse, he went back to washing his dishes and tending his bar.

A day would come when Terrence Donnelly, bartender of Murphy's Irish Pub, protector of women, and creator of the best martini this side of the Mississippi, would kick himself in the ass for missing the signs.

Not today, though.

Less than five minutes later, Gabriel was escorting Annie McCormack to his pickup truck with the stolen, out-of-state plates and a removable decal that read 'All Bark, No Bite Tree Service' on the driver's side door.

Because Gabriel really had thought of everything.

Annie grabbed the passenger-side dashboard and moaned. Craning her neck, she peered out the window at the darkened landscape, lit only by the full moon. They were on a winding road that lacked streetlamps or lane markings. The rush of trees flying by made her queasy.

Eyes heavy, limbs like lead, all she wanted was to lay her head down and rest. Instinct, however, demanded she stay awake. She searched her muddled mind, trying to remember where she was going, who she was with. Nausea burned her belly and throat, threatening to morph into an unrestrained vomit-fest.

Gabriel reached over and patted her leg. "Welcome back, Annie. Quite an evening, am I right?" Chuckling, he gave her thigh a hard slap. "You should be more careful, woman. Imbibing too much—well, that can lead to trouble. I think we need to get to my place and make you a nice cup of coffee, no?"

Annie shook her head. "No. I-I just want to go home." The name of the man behind the wheel suddenly popped into her head. "I don't think I'm drunk, Bob. I think I'm sick or something." Her words sounded distant, foreign to her ears.

"You want to hear something funny, Annie?" he asked, ignoring her physical complaints. "When I first saw you sitting at the bar, I watched you for a moment. I thought maybe I had you all wrong. I thought maybe you were waiting for your man instead of looking to get laid. Which would mean maybe, just maybe, you weren't the chippy little slut I took you for."

Annie moaned, convinced she was dying. She pulled the seat belt away from her abdomen, releasing the pressure. It was too tight, and she had to pee.

She felt awful.

"But, alas, I was wrong," Gabriel continued. "What is it they say about putting lipstick on a pig?"

Annie groaned again, the first real tickle of fear shooting down her spine. "I-I want to go home, Bob," she said, more firmly this time. "Take me home now!"

Gabriel pulled abruptly to the shoulder of the road and twisted in his seat. Frowning, he said, "My name is Gabriel Devine, but do you know what they call me, Annie? They call me the Apostle, messenger of God. And the Apostle takes orders from no one."

Without hesitation, he pulled back his arm and slammed his fist into her jaw. Annie's brain ricocheted back and forth inside her skull, rendering her unconscious.

Gabriel pulled back onto the darkened street and whispered, "As far as taking you home, don't worry, Annie McCormack. I'll get you there. You'll be home soon."

The first thing Annie noticed when she regained consciousness was the impossible weight on her chest. Something was pushing against her ribcage, making it difficult to inflate her lungs fully. Lacking the strength to lift her head, she turned it to the left instead.

The scent of raw earth filled her nostrils, while the taste of mineral-rich dirt lingered on her tongue.

She was on the ground, partially buried beneath a mound of soil, a heavy rock compressing her upper torso. Her heartbeat quickened, vibrating like thousands of winged insects beneath her breastbone.

Where am I? Sweet Jesus, what's happening?

Sensing a presence, she turned her head the other way. Bob or Gabriel, or whatever he called himself, stood about five yards away, arms crossed, jaw clenched, completely naked.

And he was watching her.

At that moment, Annie McCormack had never been more terrified. She struggled under the crushing weight of the stone, attempting to wriggle to her side while working to buck free. But she was weak and uncoordinated, her body still processing the Rohypnol, and her limbs refused to obey the signals from her sluggish brain.

Her attempts to dislodge the stone, using a chaotic dance of twisting and jerking, only succeeded in sending more dirt tumbling into her face.

"Tsk, tsk, little Annie," Gabriel said, moving closer. "I don't believe you have the strength to release yourself." He picked up a small stone and tossed it high in the air, catching it as it dropped to his palm

He repeated the action several times—toss the rock into the air, catch it, move forward a step—until he was about five feet away.

Horrified, Annie tried to swallow the lump in her throat but found her mouth was bone dry. "Why are you doing this?" she croaked, gasping.

It was getting harder and harder to breathe.

Gabriel smiled and pitched the rock at her head. It hit its intended target, bouncing off her temple.

Stunned, Annie yelped in pain.

Picking up another stone, Gabriel said, "Do you know how they dealt with adulterers and whores in the Bible?"

Annie's heart raced even faster, and her pupils dilated.

"They would restrain them, sometimes bury them clear to their necks, and then pelt them with stones. To the death, usually." He clucked his tongue, then picked up another rock and flung it forward, once again connecting with her head. "Actually, 'stoning,' as it's called, is still practiced in certain countries. Yes, indeed, if a woman is caught cheating on her spouse or flirting with another man, she may be stoned to death. Brutal, really."

He picked up a third rock, this one twice the size of the others, and launched it at her. It made a grotesque popping sound as it ricocheted off her forehead, opening the skin and sending a river of blood over the bridge of her nose.

Panicked, Annie started to howl. "Help! Somebody, please! Help me!"

"There is no one for miles, Jezebel," Gabriel said coolly. "Save your breath." His dark eyes seemed to pierce through to her core, invading her body, exposing soul. After a moment, he spun and walked away, head down, as though looking for something.

Annie watched him go, daring to hope that he was leaving, at least for a little while. She needed some time, even just a few moments, to think, to move, to calm her panicked mind.

Oh, God, help me! I can't breathe!

Eyes tracking his every move, Annie watched as Gabriel bent forward, grunting with effort, and lifted a huge object with both hands. Comprehension dawned, and Annie shrieked in horror.

He was holding a flat, slate-like rock, about sixteen inches long and a foot in diameter. The stone was heavy, as evidenced by Gabriel's labored breathing. Struggling with the stone's weight, he lumbered back to where Annie lay and then hesitated.

Oh, please! Annie silently prayed, hoping his delay meant indecision. *Please, God, I'll be good! I swear I will never cheat on Trevor again! Just please, let me live!*

"I want you to know that your sacrifice will not be in vain, Annie McCormack. You are one of the chosen. You will wear God's seal and be protected from His wrath."

Annie recognized the change in Gabriel's stance, saw his fingers flex as he adjusted his grip on the rock, and knew what he was about to do. She screamed, awkwardly raising her weakened arms in a vain attempt to protect herself.

She was a second too late.

Thankfully, before the juicy thwack of the stone that crushed her brain could reach her ears, Annie McCormack was already dead.

After showering off the gray matter that clung to his body, Gabriel returned to the barn to await the arrival of Simon of Cyrene. There were now three bodies to attend to, three sacrifices to dispose of. Each corpse carried the Sigillum Dei—the seal of God. They were now protected, shielded from the horrors to come.

Marked safe from Judgment Day.

As he waited not-so-patiently for his assistant to arrive, he contemplated the three people he'd recently eliminated: Rebecca Sue Caraway, Bob Dietrich, and Annie McCormack. He had placed seven cuts on each of their forearms, representing the seven deadly sins.

Bob, although he hadn't committed a capital sin, had received the cuts as well.

Because one can never be too careful when it comes to the Rapture.

After Rebecca and Annie were dead, Gabriel tucked a rosary in each of their pockets and took a marker to their abdomens. Using a circle with a slash—the universal symbol meaning 'no'—he referenced the cardinal sin they'd committed on each woman's body. For Rebecca's sin of gluttony, her abdomen was marked with 'No Temperance'; for Annie's sin of lust, 'No Chastity.'

As an afterthought, he placed an additional 'clue,' one only a few would understand, within the palm of Annie's left hand.

Then, he took photos.

Once the pictures were delivered to Callie Callahan and Jake Devereaux, there would be no doubt who was responsible or the lesson he was trying to convey.

For what good is a lesson that never reaches an audience?

His only regret was that he'd yet to witness the Splendor. The Splendor was a term he'd coined, describing the moment the soul leaves the body. Gabriel had looked for it with each death by his hand but had yet to see it.

He knew it would be breathtakingly beautiful—a shimmering glow of essence rising from the corpse to the heavens. He needed to be a part of it, thirsted for it as a man on a desert island thirsted for fresh water to drink.

So far, he'd witnessed no such metaphysical transition. But he had faith that such a transcendental experience awaited him.

And he hoped to find it with his next sinner.

He hoped to find it with Greed.

CHAPTER SIX

After dinner, Callie and Amara sat in the living room, sipping coffee while trying to digest everything they'd learned about each other's lives. Jake stayed behind in the kitchen, finishing up the dishes.

"Hey, Jake," Amara called out. "I have a dishwasher, you know. Leave those and join us, won't you?" Turning to Callie, she added, "I feel terrible. He set the table, poured the wine, served the chili. Now, he's cleared the table and is cleaning up." Raising a brow, she joked, "What's wrong with him, anyway?"

Callie smiled. "Not much, I can tell you. But don't let him hear me say that."

"Too late!" Jake shouted from the kitchen.

Callie laughed and shouted back. "Don't flatter yourself, Devereaux. I was talking about the dog!"

"You're lucky," Amara said quietly. "Most women would kill to have a man so attentive. My mom..." She stopped, voice cracking.

"Tell me about them," Callie prodded. "Your adoptive parents."

A soft smile touched Amara's lips. "Finest folks I've ever known. They were hard-working, church-going people without a mean bone in their bodies. My mom, Vivian, was a schoolteacher, and Dominic, my dad, worked in the security field. Dad adored Mom. He was lost without her when she passed a few years ago."

"I'm sorry. I lost my mom, too, so I understand. How did she die, if you don't mind my asking?"

"No, I don't mind. It was a brain tumor—unexpected, quick, ugly. She was diagnosed on a sunny day in October three years ago. By Christmas of that year, she was gone. After she died, Dad was never the same."

"So, your dad is still alive then?" Callie asked.

"Unfortunately, no. Late last year, he suffered a heart attack. The doctors could never understand it, though. His autopsy showed a healthy heart and arteries as clean as a whistle, leading them to believe the malfunction was a cardiac electrical issue rather than a structural thing. His rhythm got out of whack, eventually stopping his heart and causing sudden death. Personally, I think it was the grief that got him. He couldn't fathom a life without Mom, so he made sure he didn't have one."

"Oh, that's so sad. I'm very sorry, Amara. That had to be unbearable for you."

"For a few months, it was," Amara said, nodding. "But I finally concluded that it was for the best. They really did belong together, whether here on earth or somewhere else." She took a sip from her cup. "Anyway, their deaths left me with no family. My grandparents are long gone, and both my parents were only children. I think that's why they never adopted any more kids. 'One and done' was all they knew growing up. So, when I found myself with no adoptive relatives, I decided to search for any blood relations using an ancestry test."

"And found me," Callie smiled.

"Yes—you and the rest of your family we spoke of in your emails."

"Oh, we're quite the crew. You'll meet everyone soon, I hope. Grams, Finn, Ryan. Oh, and you are going to love Darby! She was Katie's best friend, and now, it seems, she may be mine." She nudged Amara's elbow and wiggled her brows. "You know, it might be easier if you lived closer.

Like, I don't know, maybe somewhere in Montana or Wyoming?"

Amara laughed. "Subtle, aren't you? But sure, I could look around. I'm not married to Colorado. It just happened to be the last state we moved to as a family when Dad retired. Before that, we lived in Virginia, Nebraska, and even Florida for a year or two. My dad specialized in business security and had to go where the jobs were."

"Virginia, huh? Did your parents ever tell you..." Callie stopped speaking when Jake walked into the room.

"Sorry," he said sheepishly. "Didn't mean to interrupt." He took a seat across from Callie and Amara.

"Not interrupting at all," Callie said, turning to Jake. "I was just going to ask Amara if her parents ever told her anything about my dad. Or Meredith."

Amara leaned forward. "I didn't get much of that Callie. What did you say?"

Callie blushed and turned to face her. "Oh, I'm sorry! I asked what your parents told you about my dad and Meredith Sterling. You have great communication skills; it's easy to forget your hearing loss."

"Don't apologize. That's probably the nicest thing anyone has ever said to me. That you forgot about my disability is music to my ears." Amara smirked. "No pun intended."

Callie clapped her hands. "Spoken like a true Callahan! No doubt you've inherited the family's 'wit' gene."

"Hopefully, that's a good thing! So, you wanted to know what I've been told about my birth parents. Not a lot, I'm afraid. My mom was wonderful but overly protective of me. I think she was afraid that if she said too much, I would begin a search for my biological parents and, maybe, the outcome would not be what I'd dreamed."

Callie listened sympathetically, trying not to become distracted by the spirit that had entered the room. She was an older woman, plump, with short curly hair and kind eyes. The woman stood in the corner, hands clasped together, smiling warmly at Amara.

"But my dad," Amara continued, "did tell me some stuff. After Mom died, I think he was looking for a way to connect with me. Mom had always been the nucleus of the family, the glue that held us together. Once she died, we started to fall apart." Draining her coffee, she stood. "I need a refill. Anyone else?"

Callie shook her head. "No, thanks. I'm good."

"Me, too," Jake said. As Amara left for the kitchen, Jake got up and went to sit next to Callie on the couch. Bumping her shoulder with his, he said quietly, "Okay, Callahan, spill it. You've become distracted the last few minutes."

"Have I?" Callie asked absently.

"Big time. You have that 'I see dead people' look in your eyes, and it's giving me hives."

"Oh, no—am I that obvious?" Callie gasped, mortified. "I don't want Amara to think I'm not listening."

"Not obvious at all. At least, not to someone who doesn't know 'the look.' What gives?"

Callie tucked her hands between her thighs, one knee bouncing in place. "There *is* a spirit here...a middle-aged woman, focused solely on Amara." Whispering, she added, "I think it may be Vivian, her adoptive mom."

"Why are we whispering?" he joked. "Amara is deaf, remember?"

Callie rolled her eyes. "Whatever. Seemed appropriate somehow. So, sue me."

Jake smirked. "Getting back to the ghost lady. Can't you do your 'hocus pocus' thing and talk to her telepathically? Do you think she is the lady wearing white that you saw? The one who told you to 'find her'?"

Callie shook her head. "No, it isn't the lady in white. She was—oh, how do I say this without sounding mean? Let's say the lady in white is extraordinarily beautiful, while this woman is pleasant looking with kind eyes. As for communicating, I can't hear any of her thoughts. It's as if she doesn't even notice us, as if Amara is the only person in the room."

"Speaking of..." Jake said, nudging her again and jutting a chin toward Amara, who was walking into the room with a fresh cup of coffee. He moved back to the chair, giving Amara her seat back.

"Sorry. I had to send out a search party for another carton of creamer. Where were we?"

"You were telling us what you knew about your birth parents," Callie answered.

"Right," Amara said, taking a seat. "So, as I said, Mom gave me no history at all. On the other hand, Dad told me what he knew—that my birth mom lived in Texas, and my dad was killed before I was born." She blew on her steaming coffee and took a sip. "A social worker told my parents that my birth mother didn't feel like she could handle my medical issues at the time. She'd contracted rubella, better known as German measles, during her pregnancy with me, which led to many problems. I was born at a smidge under three pounds with congenital heart defects and severe deafness. Apparently, my birth mother was dealing with something complicated when I was born. It was an issue that occupied all her time, and she didn't feel she could give me the love and attention I needed."

Jake scowled. "Complicated?" he said under his breath. "How about impossible? Evil? Maniacal?"

Callie gave him a warning glance, then turned back to Amara. "Um, tell me something. Did your dad say anything else? Anything about, er, siblings?"

Amara blinked. "Siblings? As in you, or...."

"No, I'm talking about a full sibling."

Amara's eyes widened. "Now you have me curious. My dad didn't say anything about that, but I'm guessing he divulged all the info he had. Adoption agencies are quite selective about what they disclose to potential parents." She swallowed hard. "Are you telling me I have a full-blooded brother or sister out there?"

Callie grabbed Amara's hand. "You do. His name is Jeremy Sterling, and he's the biological son of our dad, Rowan, and your mom, Meredith Sterling." She shifted her weight, straightening out her injured leg. Her pain level amped up whenever she sat for too long with a flexed knee. "Jeremy was, to say the least, a troubled child. Meredith did her best, but, in the end, even she couldn't save him. I expect she was simply overwhelmed, knowing how much care you would have needed, how many doctor appointments and surgeries would be required. Especially on top of caring for Jeremy."

"That bad, huh?" Amara asked.

"Oh, Amara," Callie said, her heart breaking. She would rather suffer a thousand cuts from a dull blade than deliver such painful news to her sister. "Jeremy was—he *is*—a sociopath. Recently, he legally changed his name to Gabriel Devine and began calling himself 'the Apostle.' In his twisted mind, he believes he's a messenger of God and was put here deliberately to weed out the unworthy."

"Jesus," Amara whispered.

"Yeah, he's that kind of crazy. We have a long and horrendous history together, and he has taken so much from our family. I want to make sure he doesn't have the opportunity to take any more." Callie let go of Amara's hands and stared at her lap for a moment; she picked at a cuticle, steadying herself for all she was about to reveal. "He killed Katie, exactly as you have depicted in your painting, with a single gunshot to the chest. He also killed my best friend Stacy, my mom, and Kate's ex-boyfriend, Kyle. Even Katie's dog, Chance. Some suspect he is responsible for the death of your birth mom, Meredith, while she was lying in bed in a nursing home."

"Oh my God. That's horrible," Amara said, wide-eyed.

"He took out several others, as well," Jake added. "Many of his victims were connected to Kate, but some were just in the wrong place at the wrong time. This guy kills without conscience, indiscriminately, to further his nutso agenda."

Amara frowned. "What, exactly, is his agenda? Do we know what he wants?"

Callie stood, knee throbbing, and stretched her leg. The ghostly woman in the room continued to ignore everyone but Amara. "I'm guessing he wants recognition. Acknowledgment that he is an all-knowing, all-seeing being. I believe he is flexing his muscles, so to speak, tiptoeing into new territory. There is no doubt that he suffers from delusions, hallucinations, and paranoia. Early on, a behavioral specialist from the FBI created a profile for him. Unfortunately, his actions have escalated since that profile was developed. He is morphing into a whole new persona."

"Meaning?"

"Meaning he is close to being out of control and reckless. Up until now, he was cautious, methodical. I fear that is no longer the case." She took a few limping steps, stretching out her knee.

"Did he do that?" Amara asked quietly, nodding at Callie's leg. "Did he hurt your knee?"

"Not the knee, but he did take great glee in shattering my ankle. This," she looked at her knee, "is the work of yet another serial killer. What can I say? Some people collect coins; I collect crazy people."

Amara raised her brows. "Maybe pick up stamp collecting, huh? So, you were telling me how Gabriel is losing control or something?"

"Right," Callie said. "Truth is, I think he may have something to do with the woman in the barn. You've painted two other crimes he has committed. Could this be a third?"

Jake groaned. "If you're right, we are in trouble. That girl could be anyone; that barn, anywhere in the world." He caught Callie's eye. "Can you ask her? The lady in the room?"

As soon as the words left his mouth, he regretted them. Callie had yet to divulge her secret to her sister. He coughed into his closed fist, embarrassed. "Uh, never mind. I—I..." He stopped, flustered.

Callie walked to him and kissed the top of his head. "It's fine, G-man.

You just opened the door for me, is all." She walked back to where Amara sat and squatted in front of her. "Remember when I told you I had a secret that would blow your mind?"

Amara nodded slowly.

"Um, okay, well, it's similar to what you can do, only instead of painting the past, I see it."

Amara looked confused. "You see it? How do you see the past? Are you a time traveler? Do you have a DeLorean parked outside?"

Callie laughed lightly. "Nope, nothing like that. I can see, um, well, dead people. Ghosts, spirits, whatever you want to call them." She cleared her throat. "In fact, I am seeing someone right now. I think it might be your mom."

Amara's gaze flicked around the room. "Momma?" she whispered. "My momma is here?"

Callie sat next to her on the couch. "Maybe. She's a middle-aged woman with dark hair and a warm smile focused solely on you. I can usually communicate telepathically, at least a little. But with this spirit, it's like there is no one in the room but you."

"Oh, that's my mom, all right! She doted on me." Amara's eyes filled with tears. "Can you tell her something for me? Tell her I miss her madly. Tell her I love her."

"I don't have to," Callie said gently. "You just did."

～

A few hours later, after photographing Amara's paintings, Jake and Callie rose to leave.

"Thank you so much for having us," Callie said. "And thank you for showing me your pictures. We'll take the photos we took of them back to Jed's house to refer to later."

"Not a problem. I could ship the paintings to Montana, but it would take too long, I think." She linked arms with Callie, and they headed to the front door. "I wish you guys hadn't booked a hotel. I have a spare room you could have stayed in,"

"It's fine," Jake said. "Besides, both of us sharing a room? What would the neighbors say?"

Callie pushed her shoulder into his. "You know, I would feel better if you came to stay with us in Montana, Amara. As far as I know, Gabriel doesn't know you exist, but I fear what he will do when, or if, he ever finds out he has another sister."

"But this is my home, Callie. I have all my stuff here: paints and easels, canvases, and brushes. Heck, I even have the lights synched to the doorbell. You know, they flash when it rings."

"We can get you whatever you need. And it is only for a little while, just until we catch him. Please say you'll come."

"Think of it as a mini-vacation," Jake added with a wink. "My brother has plenty of room and a beautiful view to inspire you. Plus, you and Callie have a lot of time to make up for. What do you say?"

"Your brother will be okay with taking on an orphan?" Amara joked.

"Are you kidding? He lives for it. Night and day, he scours the streets, beating his chest, hoping to find a waif to shelter from the storm."

Callie smirked. "Listen up. Jed Devereaux is one of the kindest men I have ever known. He will love the idea of you staying with us."

Amara chewed her bottom lip, a gesture famous among all the Callahan women. "Um, okay. I can't believe I'm agreeing to this, but yes, okay. Give me a few days to work out the logistics. If I book a flight, could you pick me up at the airport?"

Callie clapped her hands together. "Yippee! Yes, you bet we will pick you up! Can I see your phone?" Amara slipped it out of her pocket and handed it over. Callie worked the keys, tapping the number pad. "Okay," she said, handing it back. "I've programmed my cell phone number into your phone. Just give me a text or call when you've made the arrangements.

I am so thrilled!"

"Really? A deaf sister walking around with a bum ticker and a talent for singing out of tune thrills you?" Amara said. "Not to mention, I seem to be painting dead people, maybe even before they are dead. Maybe being 'thrilled' is overrated. You think?"

Callie grinned. "And just like that, a Callahan was born!"

~

June 11

At ten a.m., the jet carrying Callie and Jake landed at Billings-Logan International Airport. After collecting their luggage, they rented a car and started the thirty-minute drive to Jed's home in Billings.

Callie said little on the drive; her thoughts were centered around Amara and her paintings. Jake, noting her silence, spoke first.

"Hey, where'd you go, Blaze?"

"Sorry. I've been thinking about things. Worrying is probably a better term. What if we can't connect Amara's last painting to a victim? What if we're too late? What if Gabriel somehow discovers that he has a sister?"

Jake gave her a side-eyed look. "And what if the hokey pokey really is what it's all about? Come on, sweetheart. Don't go borrowing trouble to bake a pie no one wants to eat."

Callie chuckled. "That's the silliest saying I've ever heard. Yours?"

"Grandma Devereaux's, thank you very much." He tipped his head back, pretending to talk to the heavens. "I'm sorry, Mimi." He looked back at the road, and then glanced at Callie again. "She's Irish and not much of a baker."

"Funny. Seriously, Gabriel will be a real problem if he finds out about Amara." She turned in her seat. "Have you spoken to Jed yet? Did you fill him in about Amara and what she can do?"

"I called him last night after you fell asleep on the couch."

"Yeah, my neck is killing me, by the way." Callie groaned.

"Hey, I offered you the bed, Blaze," Jake said. "And just so we're clear," he said with a wink, "it was delightful. Best sleep I've had in a long time."

"Oh my God, could you—" She stopped, the ring of her phone interrupting her. She didn't recognize the number. "Hello?"

Silence greeted her.

Jake glanced over. "Secret admirer? Bill collector? Telemarketer?"

Callie shook her head. "Hello? Is anyone there?" she said again.

A glow from the back seat reflected off the outside mirror, and Callie turned, coming face to face with Katie.

Jake noticed the change in the atmosphere, noticed Callie's anxiety kick up a notch when she turned to look behind her. He looked up at the rearview mirror but saw nothing.

Katie scooted to the edge of the seat and put her hands on Callie's headrest. "Hang up, Shadow," she pleaded. "Listen to me! Just hang up!"

But before Callie could end the call, her ear caught a deep, familiar voice through the phone, causing the hairs on her neck to jump to attention.

"Hello, little sister," Gabriel whispered. "Miss me?"

CHAPTER SEVEN

C allie's lungs grew tight, and she took a great gulp of air.
"Gabriel," she said, her voice shaking. "How did you get this number?"

Jake tapped the brakes and pulled to the side of the road. Releasing his seatbelt, he unholstered his Glock and looked around. They were still fifteen miles from Billings, on a back road, exposed.

And sitting ducks for a maniac with a hard-on for Callie.

"There are many things I can do, little one, countless ways of getting my information. Do not delude yourself that you are beyond my grasp."

Callie's mind whirled. *Is it a coincidence that just yesterday, I was with Amara? Is that why he's calling? Oh, please, don't let him know!*

Livid, Jake tried to grab the phone. "Let me talk to the fucker, Blaze. Seriously, I need to talk to him!"

Holding up her palm, Callie pulled back. "What do you want, Gabe? You understand I'm not afraid of you, right?" she said, sounding braver than she felt. In truth, she was terrified of him. She'd witnessed firsthand what he was capable of.

Gabriel clucked his tongue. "*'Do not be afraid of those who kill the body but cannot kill the soul. Rather, be afraid of the One who can destroy both soul and body in hell.'* Matthew 10:28. I don't suppose you've heard of it, have you, Callista? Pity. I fear you will only see the light after it begins to dim."

"Are you going to get to the point while I'm still young, asshole? I have places to go and psychos to catch."

There was a long pause before he spoke again. "Your words only serve to confirm what I've suspected all along. You have been unleashed on the world, tasked with wreaking havoc on earth, and I have been tasked with making things right. I know my mission now, understand that I must prove myself worthy by shedding the blood of those who've trespassed against Him. And then, once the cardinal sinners have been punished, I will be bathed in the light of God, free to take my place beside Him."

Callie shook her head. It was sad how Gabriel's mind was so fractured, so detached from reality.

She almost felt sorry for him. Almost.

Then, like a blast of frigid water to the face, she was shocked back to reality. That bastard had taken everything from her; the only thing she felt toward him was rage.

"You are a sick fuck, aren't you?" she said, slightly annoyed at herself for her choice of words. She was a psychologist, a supposed professional. The last thing she should do when handling her brother was to get down into the mud with him.

But she couldn't help herself—anger was overriding her mastery at dealing with the human mind.

"The next thing you will tell me is that you actually believe you *are* God."

Gabriel's voice boomed through the phone. "You haven't been listening, Callista! I am not the ruler of the universe!" He cleared his throat, and when he spoke again his voice was calmer. "I am not the supreme being, the creator of all things. I am his son. I am the Messiah!"

The line went dead.

Jake palmed the cell phone from Callie's shaking hands and dropped it into the console.

"How the fuck did he get your number?" he growled.

"I don't know, Jake. How has he gotten his hands on any of this? He discovered my cell number, knew my email, and somehow ended up in the same part of the country as us. It's like he really does have help or a connection to a higher power."

"Bullshit, Blaze. He has a devious mind and, I hate to say it, good instincts. Maybe it's his military training. But if he has an 'in' with a special power, I'm Miss Marple."

Callie twisted her mouth. "I'd probably find that funnier if I weren't so terrified. What if he knows about Amara?" Groaning, she held her stomach. "God, I feel like I'm going to be sick."

"Just breathe, sweetheart. Let me think a minute."

"Okay, but think fast. Something tells me we are miles behind this asshole."

Jake buckled his seat belt and pulled back onto the road. "That's because we haven't pushed hard enough. We've been using zone defense rather than playing man-to-man coverage. Gabriel has too many moves to leave holes in the field."

"Super," she joked. "We're all about to get dead, and you're *tossing* out football analogies...no *punt* intended."

"Funny. But seriously, we need to be extremely cautious now. No matter what he professes to be after, I still believe his end goal is you." He turned left, got back on Interstate 90, and felt his shoulders relax. "You know what we used to say in my academy days about bad guys?"

She shook her head.

"We'd say, 'A guilty fox will always hunt his own hole.' He is hunting on comfortable ground, Blaze. Eventually, with someone this fucked up, we always see them return to the familiar. The only thing we have to figure out is where."

Callie nodded glumly. "And who."

Father Gabriel entered St. Michael the Archangel Church, a spring in his step despite the load on his mind. He needed to make an appearance to avoid suspicion, if only for mass and the confessional. Yet, he knew he had grander plans to make, bigger fish to fry than tossing out a few Hail Marys for some inferior congregant's perceived transgression.

As he walked toward the front of the church, he spotted an elderly woman in the first row of pews. She was perched on the kneeler, one ass cheek on the seat, forearms resting on the bench in front of her. She held a rosary and, head down, appeared to be crying.

Well, shit, I don't have time for this!

He tried to go around, cutting through the row of pews several feet behind her. Just as he made it to the side aisle, just when he thought he was safe, her head snapped up, and they locked eyes.

Fuck, it's Bob's wife! Now what?

"June," Gabriel said, approaching her. "Are you ill?"

Sniffing, June Dietrich dabbed a tissue at her eyes and sat back in the pew.

Great, here it comes...

"Oh, Father Gabriel, I'm so upset," June began, twisting the Kleenex in her hands. "Bob hasn't been home, you see. Not since Thursday morning. It's so unlike him. What if he's missing? What if he's met with..."? Her eyes widened, and she gasped in horror. "What if he's met with foul play? I must call the police!"

Gabriel's belly clenched at the mention of cops.

"Are you sure you want to involve the authorities, June? The result could prove, um, embarrassing. After all, Bob is, well, he enjoys the company of other women on occasion."

June made a squeaking sound, like a mouse caught in a trap, and clutched her pearl necklace. "Whaaaat? He does no such thing, Father! I would know if he—if he had a lady friend."

Gabriel clucked his tongue and patted her shoulder. "June, it pains me to say this, but while I would never betray the sanctity of the confessional, you have a right to know the truth. Without violating my vows, I can tell you that Bob has, um, urges. He has been associating with shady people, hopping from bar to bar while on the hunt for companionship. I know for a fact he's been telling tall tales, exaggerating his wealth, and drinking too much of the devil's juice, trying to gather the courage to...."

"To what?" June asked, lips trembling.

Gabriel was enjoying the look of agony and horror on June's face. "To sweet-talk his way into another woman's bed. I'm terribly sorry to be the one to tell you this, but, as I said, I feel you have a right to know. In fact, I believe he met someone recently. Annie something, I think her name was—a harlot with questionable morals. But perhaps I'm being too judgmental? After all, it is only the Lord who has a right to judge us. Wouldn't you agree, June?"

In the short time it took Gabriel to plant the seeds of doubt in her brain, June Dietrich's expression went from worry and confusion to sadness and pain before finally setting on anger. "I cannot believe it! How could he betray me like this, Father? What shall I do?"

"Let him go, little lamb," Gabriel said softly. "Let him go and pray that, someday soon, he will realize the error of his ways and come back to you."

Of course, his appearance would be as a ghost, Gabriel thought, holding back a smile.

June wiped her nose. "If you think that's best, Father. But please, if you see him, if he comes to you, tell him I'm not mad. Tell him he can call me, and we will figure it out. After all, fifty years of marriage must count for something, right?"

Gabriel nearly rolled his eyes. *This is so fucking boring. Go away, little June bug, before I stomp your ass into the ground.*

"Of course, of course. Now, dry your eyes and run along home. The best thing you can do is hand your burdens to the Lord, for only He can right this wrong."

He guided her to the front door of the church, struggling against the overwhelming urge to grab her by the hair and smash her face into the baptismal font. In his mind's eye, he did just that, 'hearing' the wet thwack of her skull against the porcelain font and 'seeing' the blood splatter leap to the ceiling.

Of course, he didn't fulfill that vision. He was far too smart and disciplined to make such a hasty decision.

But later, as he lay in bed, the sucking splat of June Dietrich's head cracking in half, the gray matter oozing down the side of the basin, played on a loop in his brain, lulling him to sleep.

$\sim$

The first thing Jake and Callie noted as they pulled into Jed's driveway was the black Labrador retriever, ears flying comically in the wind, bounding toward their car.

"Blue!" Callie cried from the passenger seat. "Do you think he knows it's us?"

"If I had to guess? Nope. Don't forget—we're driving a rental car he doesn't recognize. I think he just loves company and isn't too particular about who it is."

When they stopped, Callie hopped out and got down on one knee. Blue practically knocked her over, slobbering her with kisses and nudging her neck.

"Doesn't care about who it is, huh?" Callie said over her shoulder. "I'd wager he not only knew it was us but couldn't get to us fast enough."

Jake laughed. "You might be right about that. He certainly is glad to see you."

After a few seconds, a golden retriever came bounding toward them, her gangly legs seemingly too long for her frame, giving away her youth.

"Lucky, my friend!" Callie squealed, taking the dog in a bear hug. "How's my baby girl?"

Jake popped the trunk and took their suitcases from the car. "Wonder where everyone is? I expected to see a welcoming committee once Jed knew we were on the way here." Pouting, he added, "We've been gone for weeks. I'm starting to feel unloved."

Callie straightened and grabbed one of the lighter bags from him. "Or maybe they're just busy. Come on, let's go find them."

"You shouldn't be carrying anything, Blaze," Jake admonished. "How's the knee after that ride, anyway?"

"I'm okay," she said. "It's a bit stiff, but I have the brace on." At his dubious look, she added quickly, "Seriously, Dad. I'm fine."

Jake mumbled something she couldn't hear and closed the trunk lid. They heard the front door creak open, and a split second later the sound of little feet racing across the pavement reached their ears.

"Callie!" Tyler screamed, arms wide. "You're back! I'm so glad to see you!"

Callie's heart squeezed with pride at all Tyler had overcome. Early on, she'd learned that, following an undetermined trauma, the child formerly known as 'Caleb' had lost the ability to speak. It was while trapped in an abandoned well with Callie, waiting to die, that he'd uttered his first words to her.

"She's not my mother...."

His words, plus the fact that he had spoken at all, had shocked her to the core. Fiona Clark, the woman parading around as Faith McTavish—Caleb's mother—was, in fact, not his mother but his nanny. After taking the boy from his parents, she had changed their names and left the family's home in Philadelphia, heading west to Montana and Jed Devereaux's ranch. Once there, she had wormed her way into Jed's heart, and his business, by living in the guest cottage and working as his assistant.

Callie still had no idea why Fiona had run away with Tyler, how she'd decided on Montana, or who she had been running from. But none of that mattered right now.

"Ty!" she yelled, dropping her bag and wrapping him in a hug. "My gosh, you've grown two feet since I saw you last! What are Jed and Darby feeding you?" She ruffled his hair.

He grinned, then grabbed Callie's bag and started to lug it into the house. It was heavy, and he struggled but never gave up. Callie smiled and shook her head. The boy had been through hell and back, yet somehow remained upbeat and sweet.

And that pretty much summed up Tyler. He possessed courage and strength beyond his years. Several weeks earlier, after Medical Examiner TJ Palmer had kidnapped Callie and Tyler and thrown them into a deep, dry well in the mountains, Tyler had displayed a bravery that Callie had never witnessed before, even among grown men.

Most people, when faced with the madness of a killer, would roll into a ball, too terrified to think.

Tyler didn't. He remained helpful and calm, comforting Callie as much as she comforted him.

But he was still just a boy, only six years old. He deserved the chance to be carefree, to play ball and catch butterflies and stare in wonder at the Milky Way while camping under the stars.

He deserved to be a child. And, come hell or high water, Callie would see to it that he had that opportunity.

"Tyler, you're making me look bad," Jake called after him jokingly. "That suitcase weighs more than you do, and yet, there you are, carrying it like a badass."

"Language," Callie warned.

"Oh, right. How about 'carrying it like a bad *butt*'? Tush? Hiney?"

Tyler turned back to them, still clutching the bag, and giggled.

"Oh, brother!" Callie groaned, heading for the front door.

"It's about time you two got home!" Darby yelled from the small porch. "I was about to send out a search party!"

Callie's heart soared at the sight of her friend. "I missed you too, Darbs," she called back. "And Jed and the Scooby Gang. I missed it all."

Darby Harrison, Katie's best friend and the owner of a specialty shop in Virginia, had decided months ago to open a second store in the Billings area. 'Time and Time Once More' would carry most of the same merchandise as its sister store, 'Time and Time Again,' but would include a selection of old-time western wear and boots.

Darby missed Katie desperately and believed the smartest way to keep her best friend alive was to get closer to the person Katie adored most.

Her twin sister, Callie.

"Well, don't dawdle, then," Darby said, opening the door wide as the little group mounted the steps. "Come on in and cop a squat. I am dying to hear about your adventures in Virginia and all about your visit with Amara."

∾

Twenty minutes later, Jake, Callie, and Darby sat with Jed Devereaux at his dining room table. Tyler was outside, playing with Blue and Lucky.

Turning her coffee cup in her hands, Callie said, "Jed, I want to thank you, once again, for letting us all invade your home. You've been a wonderful friend to Darby and me and now to Tyler, and I am so very grateful."

"Most welcome," Jed said with a smile. "Tyler is a great kid, and I've enjoyed getting to know him. And honestly, with all that has happened with Faith, Darby has been a lifesaver. She really stepped up, helping me with the business and the upkeep of this place." He reached across the table, took Darby's hand, and squeezed. "I have no clue what I would have done this last month without her."

Darby blushed and smiled shyly.

Eyes wide after witnessing the display of affection between Jed and Darby, Callie kicked Jake under the table. His head snapped up, and he nodded at her knowingly, a slight grin on his face.

"Um," Callie started, "I had no idea you two had gotten so involved. In the business, I mean."

Darby drew in a breath, then kicked Callie under the table.

"Ow," Callie grunted, rubbing her shin.

"Lotta feet flying around here," Jake joked. "Contagious spasms, maybe?"

He felt the swift breeze of a foot moving under the table just before Jed's size eleven boots kicked him in the left leg.

"Jesus. Okay, let's change the subject," Jake said. "What do we hear about Gabriel's whereabouts?"

Jed cleared his throat. "Nothing so far. Curtis and Sawyer have been following some leads relating to Gabriel's relationship with TJ Palmer, but we still have no idea how those two jokers found each other."

Curtis Valdez, a special agent with the Wyoming Division of Criminal Investigation, and Sawyer Mills, an FBI agent out of Casper, Wyoming, were part of Jed's part-time investigative team. Another member of the group included a crackerjack computer whiz named Abby Moore.

They were all assisting in the search for Gabriel.

Jed's business, "Private Investigative and Personal Protective Services," or PIPPS, was a PI firm he had built from the ground up. His team would help him with his investigations, and, in return, Jed would assist them in uncovering background information on suspects, sometimes using means that were frowned upon in the criminal justice arena.

"TJ Palmer," Callie shivered. "Every time I hear the man's name, I want to scream. I'm hoping you'll tell me the bastard is still in a coma. Or, better yet, dead."

Jed shook his head. "Afraid not. He's still comatose."

"Have you seen him, Jed?" Jake asked. "It's been over a month since he was given that insulin overdose." Turning to Callie, he added, "Seems like a long time to be in la-la land, doesn't it?"

Callie nodded. "For this type of injury? It is, unless he suffered severe and irreversible brain damage." Her eye caught a tall shadow flickering in her periphery, and she chased its path to the corner of the room before it disappeared. "A megadose of insulin to a non-diabetic can be deadly. In most cases, though, if treated early with glucose, an individual can be roused from their comatose state. In this case, it took a bit of time for doctors to diagnose the cause of TJ's coma. At first, they weren't looking for an insulin-type injury because he isn't diabetic."

"And during that time frame, brain damage occurred?" Darby asked.

"Maybe. Or maybe not. We don't know how long it took to get him from that bar where he was poisoned to medical help." Callie rested her chin on her hands. "There is one other avenue to consider."

"What's that?" Jed asked.

Callie frowned. "Thomas Palmer is a smart man with a strong background in medicine. He's exactly the type of person who could successfully prolong his illness for his own benefit."

Jake slapped the table. "Son of a bitch! I never thought of that! This prick is slicker than snot on a doorknob! He knows the minute he regains consciousness, he's getting locked up."

"He sure does."

"But could someone fake a coma for weeks?" Jake asked.

Another fast-moving flicker of darkness crossed Callie's vision. A chill ran down her spine, and goose flesh crawled across her arms.

Something was there, lurking.

"Um," she said, trying to ignore the sudden chill in the room, "it'd be very difficult but not impossible. You'd have to remain in the same position, avoid flinching when an examiner inflicts pain to elicit a response. Certainly, it would take a disciplined individual. Or a sociopath. I've heard of cases where people have done it for years." She shrugged. "Maybe you and I should take a ride to that hospital, Jake."

"Only if I get to punch him in the face," Jake said. "You know, to check that whole 'response to pain' thing."

Jed laughed. "Stand in line, brother. There are a lot of folks waiting to take a swing at that bastard."

Callie stood on shaking legs. The air had become not only colder but heavier. It felt as though the entire room had suddenly been covered in a shroud, sucking out the oxygen and blocking the sun. None of the others in the room seemed to detect the change. "If you'll excuse me, I need to unpack and reach out to Amara regarding her travel plans."

"The cottage house is empty now, Cal," Jed offered. "Why don't you set up there? Amara can move in with you, and Darby can take the apartment. Jake has his room here in the house, and Tyler has a nice bedroom on the west wing. That way, everyone has their own space."

"That would be perfect. Thanks a million, Jed."

Jake stood and walked with her to the door, tucking his hand gently beneath her elbow. "You okay, Blaze? You seem distracted."

"We'll talk later. Meet me in the cottage in an hour?"

He kissed her cheek. "Count on it, sweetheart."

CHAPTER EIGHT

"GREED"

"No one can serve two masters. Either you will hate one and love the other or you will be devoted to one and despise the other. You cannot serve both God and money."

Matthew 6:24

"Uh, Gabriel? I'm finished with the old man, but what about the... what of the women?"

Simon of Cyrene stood holding a shovel in the blazing sun and wiped his brow with one wrist. They were somewhere south of the farmhouse, in the back acreage and away from prying eyes. Several yards behind him sat an old backhoe and what appeared to be a rusted woodchipper. A fresh mound of dirt lay at his feet as though vomited from beneath the earth.

And five feet under that mound, the decomposing corpse of caretaker Bob Dietrich.

Gabriel, who was sitting on a tree stump, ignored him and continued reading the Bible. His truck, still advertising "All Bark, No Bite Tree Service," was on his right and contained more digging equipment, along with the bodies of Rebecca Sue Caraway and Annie McCormack.

"Um, excuse me? Father?"

Gabriel held up a hand to silence him.

Simon of Cyrene blinked rapidly, a retort caught in his throat. The clipped wave of Gabriel's hand, as if hushing a precocious child, made him angrier than any words could have. He was itching to snap back, to tell Gabriel to find someone else to do his dirty work.

To tell the piece of shit priest to fuck off.

But, of course, he said nothing. Instead, he tried to steady his pounding heart, tried to will away the ominous rumbling in his bowels, and waited. In his 'real' life, Simon of Cyrene would never be considered a virtuous man. He could be snide and obnoxious and a bit of a bore.

But he wasn't a criminal—just an asshole.

Five minutes later, Gabriel yawned and stretched. Squinting up at his assistant, he said, "I do enjoy a good Bible story, don't you?"

"Yeah, uh, sure I do," the frightened man said. "But I-I do have to get back to work soon. Can we take care of...?" He inclined his chin toward the truck bed. "Where do you want me to bury them?"

Gabriel stood. "Oh, we aren't burying them, my good man. I mean, all of this is meant to be a lesson. We are at the end time, son. The Almighty will soon pass judgment, and His son will walk among us."

Simon of Cyrene swallowed hard. "You're talking about Armageddon? Things in the Book of Revelation?"

"See that?" Gabriel said. "You aren't as stupid as you look." He rubbed his hands together, seeing dirt where there was none. He hadn't lifted a finger to carry Bob or lay him in the ground. "We will be—how should I say?—displaying them. Seven bodies, seven sinners, seven sins. Did you know that the First Seal is about to be opened? That the Antichrist who rides the white horse will soon be unleashed? They will come with false promises of unity and peace, all the while planning the destruction of what God has created!"

Simon of Cyrene's heart galloped, and he shifted uncomfortably.

Gabriel's demeanor had changed from laid back, almost bored, to wild, intense. His eyes had grown wide, and spittle gathered in the corners of his mouth.

He appeared manic, feral, dangerous.

A moment later, as though a switch had been flicked off, Gabriel became calm once again. "Come now, my friend. We have much more to do. I know exactly where to take these women, how to get the whole world's attention." He clapped his assistant on the back. "And think about it, man! You get to be a part of my holy journey! But first, I need to take the truck back to my farmhouse. I have a few more preparations to make before we begin. Put a marker on poor ol' Bob's grave and then meet me at the barn."

Gabriel hopped into the driver's seat of his truck and leaned over, cranking open the passenger window to shout out his parting words. "Don't dawdle, my son. You know I hate to be kept waiting!"

The man watched as the pickup truck advertising the nonexistent tree service drove over the grass and onto a dirt path leading to the house. Hanging his head, mind swimming, he half-heartedly searched for stones or tree limbs to serve as a makeshift headstone. As he looked around, he felt his eyes well with tears. How long would he have to do this? Should he go to the police, try to explain? Would they understand, even sympathize with his plight?

No, he decided. He was in too deep and had blood on his hands, albeit from a distance. It was he who had come across Rebecca Caraway working in the hospital, he who had given her daily schedule to the Apostle.

I handed that fat girl over and gave her to a bat-shit crazy psycho. Of course, no one will sympathize with me!

He found a few large, flat rocks and piled them on Bob's grave, along with a handful of wildflowers growing in the field. He felt obligated to do something, say something, out of respect for the dead.

Not due to some sense of human decency or an urge to do right by Bob, mind you, but merely to gain favor with a higher power. He felt he needed someone celestial in his corner and was not above bullshit and bribery to win them over.

Never one for organized religion, Simon of Cyrene nonetheless stood in front of the small hill that hid the body of Robert Dietrich and whispered seven simple words.

"I am sorry for who he is."

Twenty minutes later, Gabriel and his assistant stood on either side of the truck, scrutinizing a map spread out on its hood.

"This is where we position Rebecca." Gabriel tapped a spot on the map. "There is an abandoned pig farm out in the Buffalo area. And this," his finger slid up Highway 90, "is where they will find Annie."

"Ranchester? What's there?" Simon of Cyrene asked.

"A strip club. It's called Bushes and Boobie Traps, a place that hosts all sorts of debauchery. It is precisely the location one would expect to find a harlot like Annie McCormack."

Simon of Cyrene tucked his hands into the pockets of his jeans. "So, we just, like...drop them off? No burial or hiding them or anything?"

"Focus, man! I've told you before that our purpose is to teach. How can people learn if they have no access to the lesson? We will wave the bodies of these sinners like flags, flapping in the morning sun." He raised his brows comically. "We will leave clues for the authorities, breadcrumbs for the imbeciles to follow. Most importantly, we will leave a message for my sister."

The pair reached their destination in Buffalo, Wyoming, in under forty minutes. Exiting their vehicles, they surveyed the property.

"See?" Gabriel said, pointing. "Over there, in front of the barn."

Simon of Cyrene followed Gabriel's finger. "It just looks like an old trough in a broken-down pig pen."

Gabriel slapped his back. "One would think that, wouldn't one? But it is so much more than that! Come, I will explain as we work. Fast feet, my boy! Once we finish here, we will take Annie on her last ride to Ranchester before I take my leave. I have an appointment to find the sin of 'greed,' you see! Busy, busy, busy!"

Gabriel walked to the back of the truck, stepping lightly and whistling an unfamiliar tune. He tossed off the tarp that covered the corpses in the truck bed, grabbed Rebecca beneath the armpits, and pulled.

"Are you coming," he grunted, "or shall I heave this hefty bitch all by my lonesome?"

His accomplice shuffled to the truck bed, head down and mouth dry. Now and then, bile crept into his throat, threatening to erupt. He was trapped in a nightmare, caught in an endless maze with no beginning and no end. He wished he were stronger, smarter, more cunning.

Most of all, he wished he had the balls to stand up to the Apostle, tell him to find someone else, tell him he was no longer a pawn in his games. Instead, he grabbed Rebecca Sue Caraway by the ankles and helped Gabriel carry her to the trough.

While they worked, he prayed for the day he would no longer be known as Simon of Cyrene and could return to who he really was—a ladies' man, a former FBI intern, and Wyoming DCI's top forensic investigator.

Tucker Simon.

~

Harry Tinning was pissed.

Not your run-of-the-mill, kick the dog and smack your momma kind of anger, either. He was livid. For weeks, he'd been grooming Elaine Wilheim, a woman he referred to as a "dried-up rich bitch," hoping to take over her finances.

Her husband, "old fart" Morton Wilheim, was dead. At the time of his massive heart attack, brought on by Mort's love of booze, steaks, and gourmet cheeses, he was worth somewhere in the neighborhood of forty million dollars.

It was a neighborhood that Harry Tinning would love to live in.

So, as he'd done in the past—with great success, mind you—Harry flattered and wooed and courted Elaine Wilheim. He hoped that, during her devastated state, she'd jump at the chance to hand the family's financial planning over to him. Morton had been a whiz at investing and had a portfolio rivaling those of even the wealthiest men. With his death, Elaine would need to find someone to handle the estate.

And all that beautiful, green money.

Several other investment firms were angling to get a piece of Morton Wilheim's fortune. As of this morning, though, Elaine had yet to decide who would wear that crown. The old biddy refused to be rushed into anything despite Harry's magnetic personality and smooth-talking charm.

It was his crappy mood, and Catholic upbringing, that had brought him to church today. Afraid he would say something to Elaine he would regret, effectively killing the deal before it was even made, he'd decided a trip to the confessional would clear his mind. In the sanctity of confession, he was free to think and say anything he wanted without consequence.

All it required was an air of remorse and an act of contrition.

The sun was setting when Harry Tinning entered St. Michael the Archangel Church. An older building created from stone and wood, with a beautiful spire and ornate stained-glass windows, its quiet sanctuary brought unparalleled peace to the soul.

But it wasn't just the church itself that inspired. The grounds, beautifully landscaped and maintained, were a sight to behold. Harry was no green thumb, and his yard could use sprucing up. On more than one occasion, he had complimented the caretaker, Bob Dietrich, and even asked if he did work on the side.

He entered the sanctuary and walked up the side aisle toward the confessional. The church was empty except for Lucia, the woman who cleaned the building. His shoulders relaxed, and he sighed, grateful he would not have to stand in line to unburden his soul.

He had no time for such nonsense. Time was money, and money was everything.

Taking a seat on the penitent's side, he waited for the small screen to open, a signal the priest was ready to hear his confession. Eventually, the tiny window made of polished wood slid to the left.

"I'm here," the voice behind the partition murmured.

"Oh, um, hello," Harry said, his mind suddenly blank. It really had been a long time since he'd sat in a confessional booth. "Bless me, Father, for I have sinned. I won't lie—it's been a while since I've done this."

"God doesn't keep a scoreboard, son," Gabriel said, bored. His mind was on more important things than listening to some sad sack's confession. "All He asks is for your honesty and genuine remorse."

Harry cleared his throat. "Well, see, you hit the nail on the head right there. Remorse is, well, it's something I don't seem to have, Father. See, I believe that God wants us to be happy, right? So, it seems that whatever it takes to make that happen is fair game. And a life spent in remorse rather than happiness is not worth living, is it?" He ran a hand over his balding head. At just forty-two years old, he had the thinning hair and hefty paunch of a much older man.

"I see," Gabriel said, intrigued.

"Anyway, there is this lady, right? Filthy rich since her husband kicked the bucket a few weeks ago. Don't get me wrong; I feel for the old bat. I do. But her loss can be my gain, am I right?"

Gabriel's stomach fluttered in anticipation. "What exactly are you saying, son? What do you seek from her?"

Harry chuckled. "It must be odd to be a priest, always trying to find good where none exists. I sometimes wish I had your faith, Father. But no, there's nothing pure or selfless about my intentions. I want her PINs, her credit cards, her property. I want all of it."

"So, you—what? Want to become her accountant?" Gabriel asked, suddenly feeling deflated. This was not going at all as he'd hoped.

"Accountant?" Harry frowned. "Oh, no, Father, you misunderstand me. Sure, getting a gig as her financial adviser is the first step to my plans, but I don't want to manage her wealth. I want to *take* it. If that makes me a greedy bastard, so be it."

Gabriel relaxed. "Greed can manifest in many forms, my son, and not all of it is bad. A dying person can be greedy for more life; a lonely person, for love. And who's to say what good you may spread, even if it's unintended, with vast wealth."

"Uh, sure. Of course. So, what now, Padre? What do I do?"

Gabriel smacked his lips. "For your act of contrition, say three Hail Marys and repeat the Lord's Prayer twice. Afterward, meet me in the sacristy. I think I may have an idea that will sit well with us both."

Gabriel waited for Harry to leave the confessional, then tipped his head back and whispered, "Thank you, Father."

$\approx$

Harry Tinning groaned, blinking rapidly to clear his vision. The last thing he remembered was sitting in the passenger's seat of Father Gabriel's truck, heading toward Morton Wilheim's palatial home on the outskirts of Billings.

Now, as he lay on the floor of what appeared to be, judging by the lingering stench of manure, a barn, he tried to piece together the last few hours.

Gabriel had suggested Harry visit Elaine Wilheim in person once again, this time with a priest at his side. All the priest wanted in return was Harry's pledge to donate a good portion of the money to the charity of his choosing.

Harry had no intention of donating to anything but his own bank account.

Gabriel knew this. He had no illusions that Harry would ever go through with such a generous gesture, just as he had no illusions that Harry would survive beyond this day. His only goal was to bring the man back to his farm, to get Greed to the barn and prepare him for his chosen path.

"Hello, Harry. Welcome back."

Harry struggled to stand but succeeded only in sitting up. Dust and dirt swirled around him as his leaden feet scrambled for purchase. His brain felt like it was drowning in mud. "What the hell is going on? What did you give to me?"

Gabriel patted Harry on the cheek. "Oh, just a mild sedative in the water I offered you. But judging by the speed of its effectiveness, perhaps I was a bit too generous in the dosage? Oh, well. No harm, no foul, right?"

Warily, Harry watched as Gabriel moved past him to the rear of the barn and the last horse stall. Once there, the priest crouched down, leaned into the booth, and began to whisper.

Harry couldn't hear the specific words Gabriel used, but his tone was gentle, as if speaking to a frightened child. The bizarre scene lasted for several minutes—Gabriel leaning into the stall opening, whispering, then moving back to sit on his haunches.

Always keeping one ear to the stall as if expecting an answer.

And, although Harry could not see anything from where he sat, he could swear he heard the soft moans of a female.

"Hey, uh, Father? I'm not sure what this is, but I'm done here. I don't think you can help me."

Gabriel stilled but never turned from the stall. After a pause, he resumed whispering for another minute or two before standing and slowly turning toward Harry.

The dark stare, the raised corner of Gabriel's lip, sent an icy chill down Harry's back.

But it was the condescending smile—and the cattle prod in his hand—that sent a stream of urine down Harry Tinning's leg.

"Do you know of the seven deadly sins, Harry?"

Harry, tied to a beam, hands above him, raised his bowed head. His brain was a scrambled mess, the stun of several hits from the cattle prod rattling his mind. One of those shocks had been delivered near his left eye, leaving his vision blurred.

With his good eye, he followed a trail of blood that dripped from seven gashes in his forearm, snaked around his arm, and eventually wrapped across his bare chest. A sticky film coated his throat, and he struggled to collect enough saliva to moisten it.

"What?" he croaked, momentarily stunned to realize he was not alone.

"The sins? Cardinal sins that lead us all down the path to eternal damnation?"

Harry shook his head, trying to break the cobwebs blanketing his brain. "I-I dunno what you mean." He turned his head, staring at the cuts on his arm again. Slowly, clarity came as the fog cleared, and he began to remember. Childlike, tears in his eyes, he said, "I'd like—I want to go home now, please. Please, take me home."

Gabriel crouched beside him. "Oh, I plan to take you home, good sir. Not the home you seek, but the place we all call home." He stood and folded his hands as if in prayer. "You have trespassed against the Almighty, Harry Tinning, and conspired to steal from the weak to line your pockets. Your sin is greed—the punishment, death. But fear not, my son! I shall place the seal of God upon your forehead, which will protect you from the plagues and fires of Judgment Day."

Harry yelped—a strange sound, he thought with a sense of detachment, coming from a grown man—before he began to bellow. Gabriel ignored him, walking to the table at the far wall and picking up a silk satchel from the table's edge. He carried the pouch back to his prisoner, the jingle of coins inside the bag filling the air.

"Do you see this silk purse, my son?" Gabriel said, shaking the bag until the room reverberated with the clatter of loose change. "What do you feel when I shake it? Excitement? Joy? Maybe even arousal? You have spent your life in the service of riches rather than in the service of God. You have forsaken His word for the words on a dollar bill."

Tears streamed down Harry's face as he pulled against his restraints. "No, no, that's not true! You've seen me in church! I've just said my confession! I swear I will do anything, follow the church, change my ways forever! Please!"

Gabriel smoothed a comforting hand over the top of Harry's head before suddenly placing a palm on his forehead and shoving his head backwards. "It's too late for that, my son. Take these coins, for you may need them to pay the devil as you work your way out of hell."

"Wait, wait!"

Gabriel forced Harry's mouth open and poured out the pouch's contents, stuffing hundreds of coins into the gaping void. "As you've lived, so shall you die!"

Harry felt the cold metal pouring into his mouth, the taste of copper bathing his throat. He gagged as the coins slid beyond his tongue and into his windpipe.

Attempting to cough them up, eyes tearing as he struggled to breathe, Harry Tinning didn't take long to choke to death on the only thing he had ever truly loved.

Money.

CHAPTER NINE

"Knock, knock." Jake tapped at the cottage door. "Blaze? You decent?"

"Yes, come on in," Callie called out. "I'm in the kitchen."

Jake walked through the front door and made his way to where Callie was working at the counter, a devilish grin on his handsome face. "While I love the pretty skirt and green blouse you got going on today, just once, could you tell me that you are *not* decent? That you are, in fact, so far from decent, you'd make a stripper blush. Or you could give me a rush by telling me how you've just gotten out of the shower and are dripping wet, wearing only a towel and a smile."

"What, and destroy the mystery?" Callie teased, turning to face him. "Anticipation beats expectation any day of the week. You want something to drink? Looks like Faith—I mean Fiona—left the place stocked."

"Well, at least there's that. Dammit, if that woman didn't do some damage, though. Between you and me, I think she broke Jed's heart."

"Yes, but I think Darby is mending it. Did you see the looks between them? Something is brewing there." She grabbed a couple of bottles of water from the fridge and handed Jake one.

"Thanks," he said, cracking open the bottle. "So, what happened back there? Did you see something?"

Callie took a swallow from her bottle. "You could say that. You may want to sit down for this."

Jake raised a brow, then took a seat at the table. "Okay, fire when ready."

She took the chair opposite him. "You know, someday we will have a normal conversation that doesn't include ghosts or serial killers. I don't even know where to start."

"Start wherever, Blaze. We can fill in the chronological order later."

"Right. Okay, so, for some time now, in addition to seeing the dead, I have seen other things. Darker things."

Jake sat up straighter. "Darker? Like evil dark?"

Callie bit her lip. "I'm not quite sure what it is or even what it represents. I only know how it feels. Strong, overpowering, mysterious. The energy emanating from it is so intense it saps my strength. And it seems whenever it appears, negative things happen."

"So, it's like an omen? A harbinger of bad?"

"Maybe. Katie has seen it, too. She said there was a darkness surrounding the both of us."

Jake sighed and slumped back. "Perfect. Just what we need, Blaze. More darkness."

"I know it. Anyway, I've seen it several times. Once was right before we left Virginia, when Gabriel called me." She reached for his hand. "Another was before we found Jim."

Months ago, James Ford, fellow agent and Jake's long-time friend, had become a casualty of a serial killer with a penchant for fairy tales. Dubbed the 'Grimm Reaper' by the media, suspected killer Thomas John Palmer was a medical examiner who had worked with the FBI and local agencies on many criminal cases.

During the Reaper investigation, when Jim Ford was close to uncovering the truth, Palmer had attempted to frame him by planting evidence to suggest that Jim was, in fact, the Grimm Reaper.

Then, Palmer had killed the FBI agent by slashing his wrists, making it look like suicide.

In the end, TJ Palmer had been taken out not by the authorities but by his mentor. Once Gabriel had discovered a teenager was among the Reaper's victims, he'd decided Palmer was not worthy of being his Disciple.

Because the Apostle, although a morally depraved sociopath, apparently had a soft spot for children.

"So, it's a warning then," Jake said. "A foreshadowing of the shitstorm that has been, or the one that is coming. Which begs the question: what's next?'"

"A stellar question, and one I have no answer for. Right now, I think we need to concentrate on TJ Palmer. I'd like to know how he came to work with Gabriel. Most importantly, though, I'd like to see for myself that he isn't a threat, especially with Amara coming."

"Speaking of Amara, do you know when—" Jake was interrupted by his cell ringing. The caller ID was from Portland, Oregon. "Sorry," he said, getting to his feet. "I'd better take this. I don't think I know anyone in Oregon."

As he walked out to the front porch, Callie tilted her head in thought. She remembered someone connected to them, someone they'd recently contacted who lived in Portland.

Someone they would, hopefully, stay in contact with for years to come.

"That was Patrice, wasn't it?" Callie said to Jake when he returned to the kitchen.

Jake stopped in his tracks. "That psychic stuff is creepy, Blaze. How do you do it?"

Callie laughed. "No psychic skills this time, just a good memory. I recall Ford's alleged suicide note mentioning his sister lived in Oregon."

Middle-aged, confirmed bachelor Jim Ford had discovered he'd fathered a child just months before he was killed. Eleven-month-old Cassidy Vaughn, the beautiful but unexpected result of a one-night stand, had also lost her mother, Naomi, to the Grimm Reaper. When Naomi died, Jim had updated his will, leaving his estate and the care of Cassidy to the only family he had—his sister, Patrice.

"Suicide note, my ass. Palmer screwed the pooch on that one. He never counted on us knowing Jimbo wasn't the author of that note."

"He never counted on *you* knowing Jim didn't write it," Callie corrected him. "Decades of friendship and loyalty beat Palmer at his own game."

"Yeah, well, I wish I could have helped him more." He rubbed a hand over the back of his neck. "Anyway, you're right about the phone call. It was Patrice checking in with me. She wanted to let me know—let *us* know—that Cassidy is doing great and thriving under the care of Patrice, her husband, and their teenage daughter. She promised to send us pictures."

Callie chewed her thumb. "So, what's wrong, then? I know you well enough to know when you're troubled, G-man. Is everything okay there?"

Jake shrugged. "It is, and I should be grateful. Patrice was all the family Ford had, and despite the falling out they went through years ago, she was kind enough to take his kid in as her own."

"So, what's the problem?"

Jake sighed. "I guess the problem is that I feel guilty. I was the closest thing Jim had to a brother. Should I have stepped up, taken custody of his daughter?"

Callie hugged his neck. "You know the answer to that. It sounds as if that baby has found a loving home with an aunt who truly cares for her. And the fact that Patrice thinks enough of you to check in and give updates on Cassidy's well-being? Man, that's gold, Barney. Treasure it."

Jake smiled and brought his lips to her mouth. "Lady," he murmured before kissing her, "do you ever tire of being right?"

∾

Thirty minutes later, after Jake had returned to the main house to check on dinner, Callie sat at her table, brainstorming a list of baby items to purchase for Cassidy. She felt it was the least they could do, helping Patrice with expenses while doing their best to support Jim Ford's daughter.

"Don't forget anesthetic gel for her gums," a voice behind her said. "I hear eleven months is prime time for teething."

"Hello, Kates," Callie said, smiling. "Good call. I know nothing about babies. I mean, they eat, sleep, and poop, right? So aside from that, what else does a baby need?" She chewed on a nail. "Thank God Patrice stepped up. I would suck as a foster parent."

Katie laughed. "You would not suck at it, Cal-Pal. How could you? You're essentially fostering Tyler right now. And don't forget, you mothered me most of my life."

Callie snorted. "Yeah, and look where that got us!" She squinted at her sister. "Don't get me wrong, Sis. You know I love seeing you, but why do I feel this is more than just a 'Hey, I'm dead but never too busy to chat' kind of visit? What's up?"

"You tell me, Shadow. I don't just pop in and out of your life willy-nilly. I come when I'm summoned."

"Summoned? You've got your wires crossed, Kates. I wouldn't know how to command your presence even if I wanted to."

Katie smiled. "Easy, peasy, lemon squeezy, Cal. I am there when you're lost or frightened or at a crossroads. I feel the pull of your need and I come." She raised a brow. "Which means something is seriously bothering you right now."

Callie smiled sadly. "I'd almost forgotten how often you used to use the 'easy, peasy' line on me, Kates."

"Always worked like a charm to get you out of your own head."

"Maybe," Callie said.

"So, what gives?"

"Gosh, I don't know. What could possibly be bothering me?" Callie said, more sharply than she intended. "I mean, aside from being hunted by a lunatic who wants me dead or fearing a face-off tomorrow with another killer who almost took me out? Not to mention wondering how the bloody hell I can search for Gabriel and still care for Tyler."

Katie nodded. "Okay, fair enough. But I think there is more. And I think it has to do with the darkness you see."

Callie chewed her lip. "It's everywhere, Kate. I see it in the light of day and the darkest of nights. I see it in the beauty of a rainbow or the stillness before a storm. I see it in my sleep and smell it in the mountain breeze. It's nowhere and everywhere all at once." Whispering, she added, "It's like I can't escape it."

"Close your eyes," Katie said softly.

Callie quirked a brow. "You know, sometimes when I close my eyes, I can't see."

Katie laughed. "Wiseass. Okay, don't close your eyes. Just listen. The darkness is telling you something is brewing, something evil. But maybe you're thinking about it all wrong. Instead of believing it's a curse or an albatross, why not think of it as an asset? Listen to it, Shadow."

As Katie began to fade, Callie mumbled, "Listen to it? I'd rather bathe in honey and sit naked on an anthill. But for you? I'll do it."

∾

Sheridan Memorial Hospital, West Wing
Rehabilitation and Infusion Center
June 12

"What room is it again?" Jake asked Callie as they got off the elevator.

"West 306. The fact that he is still here, in this hospital, boggles the mind. Did you call the locals yet, let them know we were coming?"

The Sheridan police department, along with the county sheriff's office, was coordinating an effort to keep Thomas Palmer under guard during his stay in the long-term care wing of Sheridan Memorial. It had been an ongoing operation, lasting nearly six weeks now, and Callie wondered how long the county could afford the overtime.

"I did. Guess who pulled the OT card today? None other than John Paul Burke!"

"Burke?" Callie said, surprised. "The Tongue River Canyon Burke? I thought he was in the Forest Service."

While investigating the murders attributed to the Grimm Reaper, the team had met the young law enforcement officer in Tongue River Canyon, part of the expansive Bighorn Mountains. JP was a bright, eager-to-please young man who had stumbled upon the charred remains of one of TJ Palmer's victims.

This would have put most people off, but not JP. Once he'd become immersed in the thick of a grisly murder case, he'd decided criminal investigation was where he wanted to be.

"He was, but from what I hear, he caught the 'investigative bug' after finding that body. He applied for a position in the sheriff's department and was hired a month ago. Jed is recruiting him for PIPPS as well. The kid has excellent instincts. Besides, we can always use fresh, young eyes."

Callie smirked. "For real. Yours are getting stale and downright ancient."

Jake winked. "Luckily for you, I can still spot a pretty girl with no problem. Especially a redheaded one."

Callie laughed. "Smooth."

They walked down the hall, nodding in greeting to hospital workers while checking room numbers, before spotting John Paul. He was seated in a metal chair, forearms resting on his thighs, in front of what Jake assumed was TJ Palmer's room.

As they approached, JP stood and extended a hand. "Agent Devereaux, sir. My supervisor told me you were coming. It's great to see you again."

Jake shook his hand. "Please, call me Jake. I understand we will be working together at PIPPS, and we don't stand on formalities there." Smiling, he gestured to Callie. "You remember Callie Callahan?"

Burke smiled and shook her hand warmly. "I do, indeed. Pleasure to see you again, ma'am."

Callie snorted. "Ma'am? Oh, hell no! Callie is just fine, JP." Growing serious, she nodded at the door and asked, "Have you been notified of any changes in his condition?"

JP shook his head. "No, nothing. I will say the hustle and bustle I saw in the staff just a week ago is gone. Now, they only pop in a few times a shift to check his vital signs. I sometimes wonder if anyone would even know it if he woke up."

"That's exactly why we are here," Callie said. "I'd like to get a peek at his level of responsiveness. Something isn't sitting right with me."

"You know, despite your 'special' radar going haywire," Jake said, choosing his words carefully in front of JP, "are you sure you want to do this, Blaze? Speak now or forever hold your peace. This scumbag nearly killed both you and Tyler. There's no shame in deciding it's too heavy to deal with now."

"Are you kidding? I've dreamed of the moment I could face the bastard, whole and on my terms. There's not a snowball's chance in hell I would chicken out of seeing him now." Throwing her shoulders back, she grabbed the doorknob and raised a brow. "You ready? Let's do this, G-man."

Jake smiled. "Yes, ma'am."

Thomas John Palmer, tucked up to his neck in crisp, white sheets, looked almost...dead.

Callie studied the subtle up and down motion of his chest muscles, watched his eyelids for any sign of movement, and glanced at the full catheter bag secured to the bed frame. By all appearances, the man known as 'the Grimm Reaper' was, indeed, unconscious.

And she didn't buy it for a second.

She moved to the bed and bent close to TJ's ear. "Hello, asshole. Comfy?"

The man didn't stir.

"I know you can hear me," she said softly. "The last time we met, you threw me into a well, expecting me to die. But guess what? You're so pathetic that you couldn't even do that right. I beat you. *We* beat you." Standing taller, she glanced at the IV bag of antibiotics hanging next to the bed.

"Looks like you picked up a nasty infection while you've been here. Pity." She patted his shoulder. "Oh, and to be clear...I don't believe for a second you're still comatose."

Jake began drumming softly on the footboard, the steady beat of his fingers against the wood somehow ominous in the sterile environment.

Tip tap, tip tap.

He stilled his hand for a moment. "Hey, Blaze? How about I try and elicit a painful response? You said that was one method to determine level of consciousness, right? I could break a few fingers or yank that catheter right outta his tiny little dick. See if he cries like the bitch that he is."

The gentle thumping on the footboard resumed, soon growing into a series of sharp knocks that shook the end of the bed.

Thud, crack, thud, crack.

"I think that could work," Callie smirked, enjoying the routine. "Go ahead. Give it a try."

Callie watched TJ closely for any hint of a response to their words, but his face was a mask, emotionless and still. And then... Just when she'd convinced herself she was wrong, that he was, indeed, comatose, she saw it.

A tiny bead of sweat running down his temple. Currently, the room was a cool sixty-eight degrees.

Jake spotted it at the same time and smiled. *Gotcha, fucker!*

Giving Jake a knowing look, Callie turned her attention back to the man on the bed. "So, here's the deal, Palmer. We know you're awake. But we also understand that we are giving you a lot to think about. And what I mean by that is, if you continue this charade, we tell not only the doctors but the prosecutor as well. I don't think that will garner you much mercy when it comes to the charges against you. Will it, Jake?"

"Nope, you're right," Jake said, playing along. "The county prosecutor demands honesty above all else. You fuck with that, you lie to him? Man, he will jam it up your ass every time."

"Right," Callie said, adjusting TJ's gown over his shoulder. "On the other hand, if Thomas were to, I don't know, suddenly wake up tomorrow and cooperate with investigators, he might have an actual shot at getting out of jail while he still has a pulse."

"I'd say that's a fair assessment," Jake said with a wink.

Callie snapped a photo of the now-excessive sweat running down TJ's face, then cocked her head toward the door. "Then let's leave Thomas to his decision, Jake. If we don't hear of his miraculous return to the living by tomorrow, we will take our story and this evidence to the authorities."

Exhilarated at having cornered an animal, they stepped lightly to the door. "We hope to hear of your recovery tomorrow, Thomas," Callie threw over her shoulder. "Sleep well."

Under her breath, she added, "Or die. Either works for me."

≈

The drive back to Jed's was quiet, each lost in their own thoughts. Eventually, Jake broke the silence.

"You did excellent back there, Blaze. Had that bastard on the ropes and literally sweating."

Callie smiled. "Actually, he didn't start to sweat until you mentioned ripping the tube out of his—" She stopped, heat rushing to her face.

Jake chuckled. "You're blushing. Having trouble with the word?"

She turned to him. "Of course not. I just...I was trying to be diplomatic."

He gave her a sideways glance. "Diplomatic, huh? Blaze, I've heard you swear like a sailor. Why the hesitation now?"

Because when that part of the male anatomy is mentioned, I think of the only man I'd like to explore that appendage with!

The truth was, despite their declarations of love, Jake and Callie had yet to consummate their relationship. Physical injuries and the emotional scars of loss doused passion's flames whenever they ignited. As a result, it just never seemed to be the right time, the 'golden' moment, to seal the deal.

Callie wasn't sure if it was her problem or his.

Ever the gentleman, Jake moved the conversation forward. "So, I spoke to Patrice at length again. It sounds like they've settled in well with Cassidy. It's a relief, to be honest. I'm in no position to care for a baby now."

"Of course you aren't! Being caught in the middle of a serial killer investigation, not to mention the seemingly endless search for Tyler's mom and Fiona Clark leaves little time for diapers and formula. But," she reached over and squeezed his hand, "if there ever comes a need for someone else to take over Cassidy's guardianship, a time when Patrice can no longer care for her, we could do it. Together. After all, we are already practicing with Tyler!"

When they'd discovered Tyler was, in fact, not the son of the woman they knew as Faith McTavish but a kidnap victim, they had some decisions to make. Little was known about Tyler's family other than he was the only child of attorney Graeme Duncan and his wife, Emily, daughter of billionaire Randall Weston. Several months ago, Graeme had been found face down in the family's kitchen, shot to death by an unknown assailant.

That same day, Emily Weston Duncan had vanished without a trace.

Fiona Clark, the Duncans' nanny, had left soon after with Tyler. She had changed her name to Faith McTavish, introduced Tyler as her son,

'Caleb,' and headed to Montana.

Like parts of an onion, the mysteries of the Duncan and Weston families were revealing themselves one layer at a time. Jake and Callie still had no idea about the relationship dynamics between family members, what had happened to Tyler's mother, or who had killed Graeme Duncan.

Emily's father, Randall Weston, was a powerful man who also happened to be caught in the middle of several ongoing investigations, including the kidnapping of Tyler by Fiona Clark, Emily's disappearance, and the murder of her husband, Graeme.

So, until they knew for sure whether he or any of the Weston/Duncan family could be trusted, Tyler wasn't going anywhere.

∽

Gabriel tucked the phone under his chin, anger growing with each unanswered ring. What good was having an assistant if he never answered the blasted phone?

"Pick up, Simon!" Gabriel hissed into the receiver, wondering where the devil his charge could be. The last he'd seen him was in Ranchester, near the back dumpster at Bushes and Boobie Traps. There, the two had positioned Annie McCormack, arms slashed, legs splayed, skirt hiked up over her hips. The left side of her face was warped, her skull pulverized into a dozen pieces.

Placing the Sigillum on Annie's crushed forehead had proved challenging.

The concave shape of her head reminded him of a doll he'd found while going through a trunk belonging to his mother. At the time, he was about eleven years old and knew better than to go through his mother's personal items. She would not be pleased to learn he'd invaded her privacy.

He didn't give a shit.

The doll was lying on its side, wedged against the wall of the chest, her face smashed against the wood of the trunk. At the back of her head, a heavy crate of silverware pressed down, compressing half of her skull. When Gabriel pulled her free, he found her face sunken, her eyes protruding grotesquely beneath painted eyebrows. He turned the doll over and over in his hands before pushing on one side of her face.

He smiled as the doll's head filled with air, reverting to its intended shape.

Intrigued, he used his palms to squash the head flat again, clapping his hands together and giggling at the farting noise the toy made whenever he squeezed it. He did this again and again, finding it hilarious.

It had been a long time since he'd thought of that doll, a long time since he wondered why the hell his mother had it in her possession in the first place. It was a newer model, certainly nothing she would have used in her youth, and he was an only child.

Curious.

Dragging his thoughts back to the present and now outraged at his assistant, he ended the unanswered call and studied Harry Tinning's corpse on the barn floor. He'd have to handle this one himself. And once he did, he'd handle Tucker Simon.

For good.

CHAPTER TEN

"Welcome back," Jed said, opening the front door of his expansive home. "I've got two fingers of my finest whiskey for each of you in the dining room. Figured you'd need a stiff drink after visiting that comatose bastard."

Callie, greeted by the wagging tails of Blue and Lucky, moved into the foyer ahead of Jake. "You've no idea. Just being in the same room with that sleazeball—I think we need a shower in addition to that drink."

Jed shook his head. "That bad, huh? I'm sorry, Callie. Maybe I should have gone with Jake instead. It had to be incredibly difficult to face him again."

Jake wrapped an arm around Callie's waist. "It was, but you should have seen her! It was like she hit him with a sledgehammer, helped him up, then clocked him again. He was sweating it out. Honest to God, it was poetry in motion."

Callie nodded, smiling. "It was cathartic, Jed. I'm glad I went; glad I confronted him. It was freeing. I was no longer his victim, no longer fearful for Tyler's well-being or my own. I took control back, and it was amazing." She tightened the ponytail holding back her long, auburn locks. "Where are Darby and Tyler?"

Jed extended an arm, motioning them into the dining room, and followed them in. "Hiking. Darby thought Tyler could use the exercise and the distraction. He's been...." Jed struggled to find the right words. "He's been a bit sullen lately. Both Darby and I sense the change in him. It's like everything that's happened was buried under a layer of—something. Denial? Shock? Or, perhaps, pushing it away was a way to survive the horrors inflicted on him. Between the horrors he witnessed at home, being kidnapped by Faith, and not knowing whether his mother is dead or alive, it's no wonder he's confused. It's a lot for a kid."

"On top of that, he was taken by a madman, thrown into a well, and left to die," Jake added sourly. "Frankly, I'm surprised he's communicating at all."

"He'll be okay. The kid is tough. And that stuffed animal you sent really lifted his mood. He takes it everywhere. Mother of pearl eyes, silk stitching. It must have cost you a bundle. Not the kind of toys we got as kids, that's for sure."

"Stuffed animal?" Callie said, looking at Jake. "Did you send it?"

"Not me. I'm more of a toy truck and Play-Doh kind of guy. Maybe Randall Weston?"

"Yeah, sounds like the type of gift a grandfather would get," Callie said. "No note or card?"

"Just a generic 'For you' card that introduced the teddy bear as 'Porter.'"

Callie felt an icy chill snake down her spine. "Got to be a coincidence, no?" she asked Jake almost pleadingly.

"I'm sure. It's just a bear, Blaze. Don't read into it."

Jed raised a brow. "Gonna tell me what you're hinting at, Callie?"

Jake jumped in. "Gabriel, when he was a teenager known as Jeremy Sterling, was in foster care for a while. The people caring for him were Billy Ray and Jolene Porter."

Jed whistled. "Well, that is quite the coincidence."

"And we don't believe in coincidences, only design." Callie said.

"Right, G-man?"

Jake smiled. "We also don't believe in borrowing trouble. The worst-case scenario is the psycho got the kid a stuffed animal as a message to us. Kind of like a 'Yeah, I can get to you whenever I want' type of threat. Typical Gabriel bullshit."

"Or," Jed chimed in, "it could be from Faith. Porter is her favorite kind of beer."

"I hope you're right, Jed," Callie said. "Otherwise, it means that Gabriel knows where we are."

"We'll cross that bridge when we know for sure," Jake said. "My money is on Faith sending it. Nothing says 'guilty conscience' like a child bribe. What do you say we forget about the bear for now and focus on the kid, okay?"

Callie felt her eyes well up with tears. "Yeah, you're right. Poor Tyler. Of course, everything is weighing on him now. He's had time to process it all and is left with more questions than answers." She sat heavily in one of the dining room chairs. "I'll reach out to a colleague of mine, a woman who specializes in childhood trauma. She might have a recommendation for a therapist out this way. He needs to speak with a professional, but it can't be me. I'm too close to it."

Jake sat next to her. "Whatever he needs, Blaze. Say the word, and we make it happen. He's become important to us all." He squeezed her hand before addressing Jed. "So, brother—where are we with the search for Gabriel?"

Jed slid a white folder across the table to Jake. "I just spoke to Curtis Valdez and Sawyer Mills. They're on the way here to fill us in on their end of the investigation. They've been looking into the connection between Gabriel and TJ Palmer—where they met, how they found each other. If we can find a common thread between them, it may lead us to wherever the hell Gabriel is."

Callie cupped her chin in her hands. "I don't get how he's living.

Where does he get his money from? He has to have food and shelter, right? So, does he work? Is he just a run-of-the-mill thief?"

Jake frowned. "Nah, I can't believe he's stealing money. Weird, but as I've gotten to know how this asshole thinks, I believe he would feel common thievery was below him." He scrubbed his face. "I think... Oh, hell, I don't know. Maybe picking pockets and getting away with it gets him off."

Blue put his head on Callie's lap, and she rubbed his ear. "No, your gut instinct is right, Jake. Overt stealing is 'beneath' him. That's not to say he won't take what isn't his; it just means he will find a way to do it with finesse."

"May I?" Jed asked, pointing to the folder in front of Jake. Jake slid it back. "Okay, as far as the team goes, Abby has been working a specific angle. You remember the video Gabriel sent to your email, Callie?"

How can I forget? It was a video documenting the last day of Katie's life.

But Callie didn't voice those thoughts. Instead, she said, "Yes, I remember. And if I ever forget, I have her absence and the scars on my body to remind me." She rubbed her leg, trying to erase the crude tattoo seared into her thigh.

The tattoo that said "Gabriel."

Jake cleared his throat, uncomfortable. "We're gonna get that asshole's name off your body, sweetheart. If it's the last thing I ever do in this life, I'll make sure you never have to see or hear his name again."

Too late, Jed realized his words had taken Callie to a darker place. "Oh, shit, I'm sorry, Cal," he said, seeing her stricken face. "If it's any consolation, Abby is working on triangulating Gabriel's location to discover where he was when he sent the email. Piece by piece, we'll nail down a perimeter showing where he could be hiding out."

"Or not hiding," Callie said.

"How do you mean?" Jake asked.

Callie bit her lower lip. "What if he's hiding in plain sight? Like working as a rent-a-cop or a bouncer or something? He has military experience, after all. He could very well be doing a security gig somewhere."

"Damn," Jake said thoughtfully. "That would be a brilliant cover. As you say, hiding in plain sight."

The doorbell jolted them all from their thoughts.

"That will be Curt and Sawyer. Be right back," said Jed, getting to his feet.

Jake stood and stretched out his hand. "Hey, I'm going to grab a bite from the kitchen. I've been told my ability to slice a tomato is downright sensual." He waggled his brows. "Want to come with, get a firsthand look at a master in action?"

Callie grabbed his hand and smirked. "You know, I will follow you anywhere, Devereaux. But if food is involved, you don't even have to ask."

~

Curtis Valdez was at the table when Jake and Callie returned to the dining room, arms filled with assorted snacks, sandwiches, and bottled water.

"Hey, Curt," Jake said with a nod. "Good to see you again. Water?"

"Thanks," Curt said, taking one. Smiling at Callie, he asked, "How was your trip back home? Feeling back to normal yet?"

Callie snorted, a gleam in her eye. "Normal? What's that? No, it was good, thank you. I think we," she nodded toward Jake, "both needed a reset."

"And I'm glad you got it," Jed said. "But, since you are back, let's dig in, shall we?" He grabbed a handful of pretzels, a salami on rye, and a water bottle. "You have anything new, Curt?"

Jake held up a hand. "Before we start, I know the kid, JP, pulled babysitting duty for Palmer at the hospital. But shouldn't we wait for Sawyer and Abby?"

Jed shook his head. "Sawyer was unexpectedly called into a court proceeding but will stop by later this afternoon. Abby is out of town at some tech conference in Vegas. She's still working the case, but any developments will have to be done virtually."

"Maybe we should start recording these brainstorming sessions," Callie suggested. "That way, we can pass on the information to anyone missing and we won't have to get hand cramps writing everything down."

"Great minds think alike." Jed dipped a hand in his front pocket, extracted a digital recorder, and placed it in the center of the table. Pushing the record button, he began the meeting.

"Let's start with the latest news, or rather, concern," Jed said. "Callie has discovered she has a sister, which means Gabriel has a sister. Her name is Amara Grace Davies, and I'd be lying if I said we're not worried about her safety."

Callie nodded and spoke directly to Curtis. "Terrified is a more appropriate word for me. As far as we know, Gabriel doesn't know of Amara's existence yet, but once he learns he has a full-blooded sibling, I'm afraid he'll...."

She swallowed hard, finding it difficult to complete the thought.

"He'll what?" Curtis asked. "Do you think he would harm her?"

Jake grunted. "Why the hell not? He hurts everything he touches. Truthfully, there is no telling what the son of a bitch will do."

Callie shivered and rubbed her arms. She was suddenly chilled from the crown of her head to the nape of her neck but unsure why. An automated temperature system controlled the room's environment. It simply could not vary from the pre-determined settings on the smart thermostat, currently set at seventy-two degrees.

Groovy. I wonder which ghost is dropping by this time?

She scanned the room but saw nothing. "Jed was kind enough to open his home to Amara," she said. "I will feel much better when she is here, under our protection. She's only twenty-two, hearing impaired, and unschooled in just how awful some people can be."

"I get that," Curt said. "When will she arrive? I can pass an 'unofficial' word to our friends in the sheriff's department to beef up patrols around the house. Not sure how often they can do a drive-by, but even an extra pass or two can add a layer of protection."

"We'd appreciate that, Curt," Jake said. "Amara called while we were in the kitchen. She has a flight tomorrow morning from Denver. Callie and I will pick her up at the airport and be back by lunchtime."

Curt rolled his water bottle between his hands. "On my end, I'm afraid I've hit a wall. Witnesses in Benny's Bar and Grill, where Palmer was given that nearly lethal dose of insulin, recall his companion only as a tall, good-looking man with whiskey-brown hair, scars on his face, and a patch on his left eye. Nothing we didn't already know." He took a gulp of water. "I suppose I had hoped that Gabriel spoke to other patrons while he was there, maybe let some personal details slip—occupation, where he lived, maybe a favorite hangout? But according to Bobby, the 'I don't give a fuck about your investigation' bartender at Benny's, the man he dubbed 'cyclops' spoke only to Palmer."

"Cyclops. Cute. I don't suppose the bar has cameras, right?" Jake said skeptically.

"Nope. Just a ton of mirrors and a barkeep with a stick up his ass."

"Okay." Jed sighed. "What else? We know they were working together in some capacity. We also know that when Palmer killed teenager Maddie Gibbs and kidnapped young Tyler, Gabriel went ballistic."

"Right," Jake said. "And we know Palmer killed those he believed echoed certain characters in a storybook. Hence, the tag 'the Grimm Reaper.' So, is the connection the Grimm's Fairytales book? Maybe they met in an online chatroom that discussed or reviewed the stories. We know how much TJ loved those anonymous chatrooms."

"I don't know, but somehow Gabriel in a chatroom doesn't jibe for me," Callie said. "Too impersonal. But I can see him in a bookstore or library." She scrubbed her face, frustrated. "Honestly, though, does it matter how they connected?"

116

"It does," Curtis answered, somber. "It gives us something, a starting point. Wherever they met, Gabriel may be repeating that behavior."

His phone rang, and he stepped out to take the call.

"Okay, so what else do we have?" Jake asked. "Anything from the others?"

"Yes," Jed said. "Abby reached out to let us know she's set up a program that will flag any credit card applications, car loans, or real estate transactions made by either Jeremy Sterling or Gabriel Devine. If anything pops up, it can tell us where he's been, maybe even where he is now."

"Good idea," Jake said.

"As for Sawyer," Jed continued, "he's been monitoring the waves for any suspicious person complaints that fit Gabriel's physical characteristics. He's also keeping an eye on any warrants created or arrests made of a one-eyed suspect. But so far, nada."

Callie frowned. "You know what this comes down to, right? We need help pinpointing where Gabriel is and what he's doing. We need inside intel. We need..." She paused, loath to say the name.

Jake swore softly before finishing her thought. "We need that prick, Palmer."

Ten minutes later, Curt rushed back into the room.

"Christmas came early this year, my friends," he said, holding up his phone. "I just got off the phone with the prosecutor's office. It seems—"

The click of the front door closing caused them all to look up.

"Hey, folks," Sawyer said as he walked into the dining room. "Hope you don't mind my letting myself in. The doorbell doesn't seem to work." He handed Jed a sealed manila envelope. "I found this leaning against the door."

"Thanks, Sawyer. I have a new mail carrier, so I'm finding mail all over the place. As for the doorbell, it's been acting wonky all week. Have a seat. Curtis was just about to share some news."

"Wish I could," Sawyer said. "On my way here, I got called out to help process a homicide scene in Buffalo. A woman's body has been discovered on an abandoned farm, leaning against a pig trough, her throat slit. I don't have many particulars except that it sounds exceedingly gruesome."

"Damn. Poor lady," Jed said.

"No kidding. I'm heading there now. Sorry to miss the meeting."

Jake stood and clapped Sawyer's shoulder. "You go do what you gotta do. We recorded the session and will send it to you later."

"Thanks. I'll be in touch."

After Sawyer left, Jed said, "Where were we? Oh, yeah, Curt. You have something?"

"I do. News from JP Burke at Sheridan Hospital."

Callie clutched her throat. "Palmer? Oh shit, is he dead?"

Curtis smiled. "Better than that. He's awake."

Thirty minutes later, Curtis finally reached the hospital specialist in charge of Palmer's care and learned more about the former medical examiner's miraculous recovery.

"Well, that was interesting," Curtis mumbled when he ended the call.

Jake raised his hand. "Let me guess," he said dryly. "Shortly after we left today, the bastard started to stir."

"Something like that. The doctor claims TJ became restless about an hour after his last visitors left, which, I assume, would have been the two of you. Apparently, he became combative and tried to pull out his catheter. They gave him a mild sedative to calm him down." Curtis laughed lightly. "Imagine that. Giving a sleepy-time drug to a man just emerging from a coma."

"Aw, bullshit," Jake spat. "That fucker has been faking his illness for some time. I'd bet my left..." He looked sheepishly at Callie. "On second thought, I'd bet my right nut on it."

Callie raised her eyes in feigned shock. "My gosh, you must be sure, then! But, kidding aside, I agree with you. Let's give him today to stew. We can go at him hard tomorrow afternoon after we grab Amara from the airport and get her settled here."

Jed cleared his throat. "Sounds like a plan. Um, on another note, I was thinking about the living arrangements. Darby has been staying in the west wing of the house to be closer to Tyler. As I said, he's been having a tough time, experiencing some pretty vivid nightmares. I think maybe moving him, moving them, out of the house now would be detrimental to his mental health." He lifted a shoulder at Callie. "But you're the expert. What do you think?"

"I think it's a valid argument. Tyler's life has been upended lately. He could use a little stability about now."

"So, what did you have in mind, Jed?" Jake asked.

"I think we should keep Darby and Tyler where they are for now."

Callie gave Jake a subtle wink.

Jake peeked under the table, ensuring her feet were not aiming for his shins.

"What?" Jed asked. "I miss something?"

Callie sensed Jed was trying desperately to convince himself his concern for Darby was strictly professional.

He wasn't doing a very good job of it.

"Uh, nope. You didn't miss a thing," Callie said, amused.

"Okay," Jed continued, "so I thought maybe you two could take the carriage house, and we'll give Amara the garage apartment. Darby and Tyler can stay put."

"I can work with that," Jake smirked.

Callie squinted at Jake. "Of course you can. Truthfully, it's the best solution. Amara can work on her art in the second bedroom. It has the best lighting, I think."

Curt's cell rang, and he once again excused himself to answer it.

"Busy guy," Callie said.

"Indeed, he is," Jed responded. "Wyoming DCI agents are invaluable assets to our local law enforcement community. As remote as we are, our departments count heavily on each other for assistance, information, and backup on dicey calls. Sometimes, Curt works with two or three agencies at a time." He reached for a bag of chips on the table. "So, tell me more about your sister, Callie. She's an artist, right? Paint or pencil? What type of subject matter?"

Callie looked at Jake, eyes pleading for direction, but he just shrugged.

"I think we need to tell him, Blaze," he said after a beat.

"Well, I know that, Captain Obvious! I was looking for advice on how we tell him."

"Tell me?" Jed said. "Tell me what, exactly?"

"Better to show you, maybe," Callie took her cell phone out of her pocket and scrolled through the photos of Amara's art. She reached across the table and laid the phone down in front of Jed. "I've snapped images of three pieces my sister has painted since December. Somewhere around the holidays, she began to experience a strange, almost dreamlike urge to paint. Several times, she was drawn to her studio by some unseen force and compelled to pick up a brush."

"Uh, okay. So, what am I looking at here?" Jed asked, nodding to the first picture.

"This is the basement of my childhood home in Virginia. The same basement Gabriel took me to when he kidnapped me."

Silently, Jed scanned the picture. The artist's attention to detail was impressive, from the smudges under the subject's eyes to the lacy pattern of corrosion etched into each chain link that bound her. "Holy crap!" he said finally. "This is you, isn't it?"

Solemn, Callie nodded.

"But how? How could she draw not only you, a person she'd never met, but your circumstances all those months ago?"

"Another of the famous Callahan gifts, I'm assuming," Jake answered for her. "Somewhere around the time of Kate's death, Amara was given her supernatural ability." He glanced at Callie. "Or am I reading too much into this paranormal stuff?"

Callie smiled. "No, that's my assumption as well. My sister had two unique skills—the ability to see the dead and the ability, as an empath, to feel what others feel. When she...when Kates died, it created a sort of tear in the universe, like a sucking void or something."

"Or a vacuum," Jed said.

"Exactly. And, if I had to guess, those gifts needed to go somewhere to close that void. Amara was given an artistic 'second sight' instead of an empath ability, and I received my sister's gift of seeing the dead.

"So, essentially, things are in balance again?"

"Well, that's my theory," Callie said. "I could be all wet, but it makes the most sense to me."

She felt another chill and looked to her right, long enough to see the lady in white gliding across the room. The woman stopped, turned, and looked Callie directly in the eye.

You must find her.

"So," Jed said, startling Callie back to the present. "Let's look at the other paintings you mentioned. Maybe between us all, we can figure out what—"

Jed stopped speaking as Curtis re-entered the room.

"Sorry to interrupt, Jed. That was Sawyer on the phone. He wants me to meet him in Buffalo at that homicide he's out on. It seems this victim may be the work of our guy."

Oh, please! Callie thought. *No more deaths at his hands!*

Jake listened to Callie's quick intake of breath and saw her spine go rigid. He gently took her hand and whispered in her ear. "Breathe, Blaze. Just breathe."

"Can you tell us anything else, Curt?" Jed asked. "What makes this look like Gabriel's work?"

"The signature left behind, mostly. Sawyer said they found a set of rosary beads draped over a fence post at this abandoned farm. Rosary beads were his calling card, no?"

"They were," Callie said.

Curtis nodded. "And there's this." He placed his phone at the head of the table, and Callie, Jake, and Jed gathered around it. "Sawyer sent me two shots. One is of the position they found the body in; the other was taken after the woman was laid out on the ground. There is a peculiar inscription on her abdomen. It looks to read 'No Temperance.' Temperance is, what? Moderation? So, is this killer saying their victim lacked self-control?" Curtis shrugged. "And take a gander at her forehead. Call me crazy, but that looks like a religious symbol."

Callie craned her neck over Jake's shoulder and looked down at the picture on Curtis's phone. The quality of the snapshot was not great, the sun's brilliance casting glimmering waves of light and shadows on the figure in the forefront, but Callie could see enough. Clutching Jake's forearm, throat dry, she said thinly, "Jake? Do you see it? That woman looks familiar."

Grunting, mind swimming with questions, Jake said, "Yeah, I see it, Blaze." Turning back to Curtis, he asked, "That mark on her forehead does look religious. What is it?"

"Not sure. I'm going to head over to the scene. I'll take a few more pictures and send them on."

"Thanks, Curt," Jed said. "Keep us in the loop, huh? If this is Gabriel's doing, we need to know about it."

"Okay," Jed said after Curtis had gone, "what aren't you telling me? I could tell by your reaction to the photo that you guys know something."

Wordlessly, Callie reached for her phone and pulled up the third picture from Amara's collection. "I don't know her name," she said dully, handing Jed the phone, "and I'm not sure what killed her. But Amara knew she would die long before we did."

Jed chewed the inside of his lip, his stomach doing a small flip as he stared at the image in front of him. The woman was on her knees, the angle of her bent head obscuring her face. But there was no mistaking the gaping wound at her neck or the massive amount of bright, red liquid surrounding her body.

"Dear God," Jed whispered, sure he could almost smell the coppery scent of the victim's blood. "How could a man do this to a woman?"

"He's not a man, Jedidiah," Jake said through gritted teeth. "He's a fucking monster."

CHAPTER ELEVEN

"Behold, I am coming soon, bringing my recompense with me, to repay each one for what he has done."

Revelation 22:6–12

The Apostle lay on his back in a field, a long piece of dried grass resting between his lips, and studied the sky. Lazy circles of swirling white clouds drifted above, their patterns changing with the wind. In the distance, a mere dot on the horizon, sat the home of Jedidiah Devereaux.

Gabriel had been coming to this very spot for nearly a month. Whenever he felt troubled or doubted his mission, he came here. High on this hilltop, he would monitor the comings and goings of the Devereaux family, planning their demise, secure in the knowledge they hadn't a clue they were being watched.

Studied like lab rats. Studied and dissected.

It wasn't kismet, fate, or coincidence that had compelled Gabriel to leave Virginia and come to Sheridan, Wyoming, after he killed Katherine Callahan.

It was research.

While Gabriel recovered from the injuries sustained in the Callahan basement many months ago, he had begun a rigorous campaign of studying

Jacob Devereaux, looking at his friends, family, and work connections.

Trying to stay one step ahead; trying to anticipate a location for the inevitable showdown with his sister.

Who was important to that FBI asshole? Where would he and Callista go if they left Virginia? Where would they feel safest?

He knew enough about Callie to know she would go to the ends of the earth to find him. She wanted payback for Katie's death.

But she also wanted to protect her remaining family members and would put as much distance as possible between herself and her loved ones until Gabriel was caught.

Which left her with one option—leave Virginia. Probably with Jake Devereaux.

Once Gabriel understood that concept, he began uncovering Jake's family and background. His search gave him a few close contacts to investigate, but only two seemed likely—Jed Devereaux, Jake's brother in Billings, and Asa and Jane Devereaux, their parents who owned a farm nearby.

When Gabriel was well enough to travel, he feigned a background in theology, claimed to be ordained, and took over as parish priest for St. Michael's church.

Then, he waited.

Weeks later, he discovered Callie and Jake had come to Montana after all, just as he knew they would. That confirmation came from his disciple, TJ Palmer, in the form of a photograph taken during a murder investigation in the Big Horn Mountains. In it, Callie and Jake could be seen in the distance, observing the crime scene, heads together in thought.

Once Gabriel discovered Callie and Jake were in the area and part of the 'Grimm Reaper' investigation, he began to plan. Instinct sent him to Jed's house first, and he monitored the home from the same hill he now occupied. A few days later, just when he had been about to give up, Darby Harrison had come running outside, followed by a couple of dogs, and he knew he was at the right place.

He could finally get his revenge.

Because, as Khan would say, 'Revenge is a dish best served cold.'

Gabriel always did love Star Trek.

Pulling out a small notebook, he began to jot down his thoughts. A meticulous note-taker since grammar school, he understood that while the brain is a powerful computer capable of receiving data and processing information, it contains only a finite amount of storage space.

The most successful men knew this and adjusted accordingly. The most successful men took notes.

Given the import of his work, given the timelessness of his mission, Gabriel believed his journey should be documented. After all, did God not document His word in the Bible? Did He not use parables and proverbs and prophecy in his teachings?

He flipped to his belly and lifted his binoculars to his eyes. Days ago, his bitch sister and the FBI douchebag had returned, tails between their legs, from whatever hiding place they'd crawled out of. Despite a considerable limp, Callie Callahan looked well rested, healthy.

Enjoy it now, little one. Your time is coming soon.

He lowered the binoculars, picked up his pencil again, and began to list the players vital to his mission. Each was an integral part of the plan; each had a role to play.

And each would, at some point, fall to him.

Callie and that FBI puke, sweet Darby with the gentle smile and big tits, and the puke's younger brother, Jed.

But not the little boy. No, the one with the sad eyes and innocent face would live.

The crunch of gravel beneath tires drew his attention once again to the house. A black SUV pulled to the top of the driveway and idled for a moment. Gabriel could make out the silhouettes of the driver and passenger, even without the binoculars, because he was gifted with almost hawk-like vision. He could clearly identify Callie and Devereaux. Even if he'd not known it was them, the tilt of their heads, the way they carried themselves, gave away everything.

They wore crowns of arrogance and conceit—especially that FBI puke.

Gabriel understood that, in God's teachings, the deadliest of the seven capital sins was the sin of pride.

Agent Jake Devereaux had it in spades.

An abundance of faith in oneself eventually led to vanity and an inflated sense of self-importance. In contrast to the cardinal virtue of humility, pride led a sinner down a thorny path rife with narcissism, directed by Lucifer himself.

In ancient times, the punishment for excessive pride was the 'Wheel,' an archaic torture device with the ability to break bones and rip limbs. It was a harsh, brutal, and fitting end to the most grievous of sinners.

Of course, Gabriel had no wheel.

But he could design one, just as he'd designed the Sigillum he'd burned into the trespassers' foreheads.

He began to draw a rough outline, a crude sketch of what, in his mind, the 'wheel of hell' would look like. Along with the wheel, and using only his flawless memory, he sketched the branding iron with the Sigillum at the tip that sat waiting outside his barn.

Because accuracy and precision mattered when documenting the works of a supreme being. The masses would be eager to hear his thoughts and witness his brilliance. Of this, he had no doubt.

And soon, with a dash of luck, his version of the Wheel would send Jake Devereaux straight to the burning fires of hell.

Callie, on the other hand, was another sort of beast. She was not one to trifle with the sins of the ordinary; rather, his sister's interests lay in the more grandiose of transgressions—evils committed solely to further her reasons for being.

Yes, Gabriel knew exactly where she fit into his plan. And it wasn't among the piddly sins of the few. She would soon become the catalyst for the end of days.

So, yes, Callie Callahan was a bigger fish to fry. She was courageous, intelligent, and strong. Stronger, even, than her sister, Katherine.

But that mattered little to him. Because in the end, she, too, would fall. They always did.

∿

The Apostolic Word.

Gabriel smiled, instantly in love with the title he'd decided upon for his works. It was fitting, powerful, perfect.

Because he was the Apostle and, quite literally, a genius.

Besides, the name for the most revered book in the world, the Holy Bible, was already taken. He needed his own text, his own lesson plan, to preach the word of the world to come.

He envisioned a universe of students studying just two books—the Bible of God, the Father of all things great and small, and the Apostolic Word of Gabriel Devine.

It was times like this when, humbled, Gabriel wondered how it was he was the Chosen One. Sure, he was extraordinary. He was brilliant and talented and deserving of glory. Still, with almost eight billion people in the world, could he truly be the One?

Of course he could. He was.

He closed his eyes, dreaming of the day he would sit at the right hand of the King and join the table prepared for the true Christ.

Jesus of Nazareth, the purported child of God, was an illusion. He was an idea, a figment of the imagination, created by mortal men until the undeniable son of God was revealed.

Until Gabriel, the Chosen One, had risen.

He licked the end of his pencil because he had seen it done in a movie once and, even though he thought it was bullshit—*because who licks a fucking lead pencil?*—it looked cool. He began to write the opening mantra for what he anticipated would be billions of faithful readers.

The Apostolic Word of Gabriel
Canons and Catechisms
Doctrine 1:1

Peace unto you, my Gabrielites! I share with you the word of the one true Christ, Gabriel Jesus Devine!

Be it known that during the twenty-first century, in the third millennium Anno Domini, a savior will be chosen.

This man, this anointed one, shall be the bringer of all great things. He shall be wise and strong and deserving of the people's worship. He shall pepper the heavens with his wisdom and cast down those who rail against him.

This son of God, this miracle sent from heaven, shall be called Gabriel.

Those who follow his teachings and abide by his word shall be saved from eternal damnation. But those who forsake him, those who cast aside his counsel and lie down with the devil, shall burn for all eternity.

Gabriel looked over the passage, content with his beginning. Later, when time allowed, he would review it again, perhaps make a subtle change or two. But, for the most part, he'd said all he wanted to say in a few short words.

He had demonstrated his power. His worshippers must know that he could take them all on, squash every one of them into dust, and still have time for breakfast.

He got to his feet, tucked his drawings and notes beneath an arm, and started back down the hill toward his car. He was suddenly anxious, a tinge of fear bubbling in his gut, though he didn't know why.

Heart pounding, he started to run.

His hair flew in the wind as he rushed toward his car, tossing glances over his shoulder as he picked up speed. Once or twice he tripped, his feet moving ahead of his legs, but caught himself before he fell.

In his haste, he'd forgotten all about Callie and Jake, his calling, or his church.

Instead, his thoughts centered around a deep, undeniable dread and the overwhelming urge to flee, hide, get back home.

Home to safety, control, and the woman in the barn.

~

The glowing figure atop the bluff smiled as she watched Gabriel stumble down the hill. She'd been watching him for a while, wondering what he was doing here. At first, he seemed oblivious to her presence. Now, as she watched his eyes widening with each step he took, she sensed his fear.

So, you can feel me, huh, brother? Feel me judging you, mocking you, watching you? Good! Hope you piss your pants on your leather car seats, asshole.

Kate smirked again as Gabriel jumped into the car, speeding off with the car door still partly ajar. It gave her immense satisfaction knowing that the man who seemingly feared nothing was scared shitless. Despite the glorious weather, the air around her was suffocating and thick with ill intent.

Evil, it seemed, lived among the clouds and waltzed within the breeze whenever Gabriel was nearby.

What the hell are you up to, Gabe? What were you drawing?

She moved to where her brother had sat with his notebook, searched the ground, and saw nothing. Except for a slight bend in the blades of grass, he'd left no trace.

As if he were never here. As if he, too, were a ghost.

CHAPTER TWELVE

"Cal? You here, girlfriend?"

Darby tapped on the door to the guest cottage and waited a beat. "You realize you can't hide from me, right? Because I know things, ma'am. I know all the things!"

"Yeah, yeah, whatever!" Callie yelled from the bedroom. "I know things, too, missy! Come on in. I'll be out in a sec."

Darby walked inside and made herself at home. After making a vodka tonic, she sat on a stool in the kitchen, checking the weather forecast on her phone. The air outside felt heavy, while storm clouds darkened the sky.

A few minutes later, she heard Callie's stocking feet pad into the kitchen and looked up from her phone.

"No, really, don't be shy," Callie joked. "Help yourself!"

"Oh, I did! I never figured you for a top-shelf vodka gal, but man! This here is proof positive that the right alcohol makes the drink!"

Callie chuckled. "I can't take credit. I think it's Fiona's stash."

Darby grinned wider. "I hope so. I hope I'm drinking her most expensive shit. Bitch."

Callie shook her head and took a stool. "Yeah, she is not in the best standing right now. But she did take care of Tyler. Although, we still have no clue why she kidnapped him."

"About Tyler," Darby said. "We had a nice hike today, but I gotta say, that boy is seven shades of hurting. I think it's all finally hitting home— Fiona taking him on the run, him coming close to dying at the hands of the Reaper, his mom going missing, and, by all accounts, probably being dead." She took another sip of her drink. "Funny how just a few bad weeds can choke out a garden, right? Speaking of weeds...where are we in this mess?"

Callie reached across the breakfast counter for the vodka and tonic. "Well, there are some developments," she answered, pouring herself a drink. "Let's see. Gabriel and Fiona are still missing, and we have no clue where they are. TJ Palmer miraculously 'woke up' from his coma, so Jake and I are going to speak with him tomorrow after we fetch Amara from the airport. Palmer is the only one who may know where Gabriel is hiding out. We hope, anyway."

"Ya'll been busier than a one-armed fisherman in a rowboat! What else you got for me?" Eyes lighting up, she said, "Oh, I know! Tell me all about Amara!"

Callie rose and went to a small cabinet. She grabbed a bag of pretzels and sat at the counter again. "Oh, Darbs, you will freaking love her! I do already, and we just met! She is drop-dead gorgeous. And so young! She's sweet and caring, and I loved spending time with her." She sighed and cupped her chin in her hands. "I don't know. I just felt an immediate connection with her. It was like I'd known her forever, even though we just met."

Darby smiled. "Your whole face lit up like a Christmas tree just now. She must be pretty darn special."

"She really is. She's smart and amazingly talented and, oh, about eighty percent deaf. So, if you have any tricks up your sleeve as far as communication goes, pull 'em out now!"

"Deaf?" Darby frowned. "For reals? How sad."

"Doesn't seem to bother her as much as you'd think," Callie explained.

"She handles it like nobody's business. It seems her hearing issues were discovered at an early age, a result of her mother contracting German measles. Her mother being none other than Meredith Sterling."

"Gabriel's mother?" Darby gasped. "I thought Amara was a product of a random affair by your dad."

Callie shook her head. "Nope. Meredith and Rowan had a long relationship that produced Amara. But early in the pregnancy, my dad died in that plane crash. Meredith, alone and in charge of a psychotic ten-year-old boy, contracted rubella and was advised to terminate the pregnancy because of possible neonatal abnormalities. Instead, she had the child, then gave up her parental rights."

Darby gasped. "Back up! So, Amara is actually a full sister to psycho-boy?"

"Unfortunately, yes."

"And, through no fault of her own, she's deaf?"

"Well, to be precise, she has a bit of hearing, but essentially, yes. Although, there is a bright side to her story. She was adopted by amazing parents and had a wonderful life. Truthfully, a better life than if she'd stayed with Meredith."

"Wow." Darby paused a moment. "So, does she look like a Callahan?"

Callie grinned widely. "She does! Well, somewhat. She has our freckles and chin, for sure. Actually, I see a lot of Kate in her." Waggling her eyebrows, she added, "In more ways than one."

It took a minute for Darby to grasp the double meaning in Callie's words. "Holy macatolli, Batman! Are you telling me she sees spooks?"

Callie stretched her spine like a cat. She'd been tense for days and was starting to feel the strain on her back muscles. "She doesn't exactly see them, but she definitely has an ability. You know she is an artist, right?"

Darby nodded.

"You have to see her stuff, girl. Beautiful ocean scenes, pencil sketches of lighthouses, gorgeous beach sunsets in watercolors. But the coolest drawings are the ones she paints while in a trancelike state. She recreates the past for sure, and maybe the present. Or some sort of play-by-play as the events unfold. We aren't sure of the timeline yet." She shrugged and popped a pretzel in her mouth. "Some pieces she paints could even be depicting the future."

Darby frowned, not comprehending.

"She drew me in the basement, Darbs! Chained and bleeding after being taken by Gabriel. And Kates. She drew the last moments of Katie's life."

"You're joking," Darby said in disbelief.

Callie pulled her phone from her pocket and showed Darby the pictures of Amara's work. "This last one might be Gabriel's latest victim. Sawyer Mills of the Casper FBI office is on the scene now. He sent us a picture of a dead girl identical to the one in this painting."

"Holy shitbags," Darby breathed.

"Yeah, and that's not all. Guess what they found at the scene?"

Darby, eyes wide, slowly shook her head.

"Rosary beads. And a biblical message on her abdomen. Who does that sound like?"

"Gabriel. It sounds like your douchebag brother Gabriel."

"Bingo. I mean, we knew he was in the area. His attempt on Palmer's life, his call to Jed to tell him where Tyler and I were being held in that well. In fact, it wouldn't surprise me if that email he sent me months ago, the one with the video of Kates dying, turns out to have come from around here."

"And how in the blazes would we know any of that?"

"Abby Moore is how. Once she breaks through whatever program the asshole is using to cloak his location, that is. I thought once he thought the Reaper was dead, he would disappear until things cooled off. He's normally quite cautious."

Darby remained silent.

"What?" Callie asked. "What are you thinking?"

Clearing her throat, Darby said sadly, "I'm thinking Gabriel Devine is uglier than sin on Sunday. And God don't like ugly. He's not gonna quit you, Cal. Not until one of you is dead. He's a crazy person whose cornbread ain't done in the middle. Besides, his ego is too big to let it go."

Callie stood and carried her glass to the sink. "True story." She rinsed it out and set it to drain, then turned and leaned on the counter. "Kates has been visiting a lot lately. We both have sensed a darkness. Hell, I've seen it. Shadows so ominous, so black, they defy explanation. Kates thinks it portends a lingering evil bent on destruction."

"Well, sugar honey iced tea! What in the Sam Hill are we supposed to do about that? How do we fight a shadow? An evil we can't even see?"

Callie walked behind Darby and wrapped her arms around her shoulders. "Hell if I know, Sis. All of this comes back to my brother. All of it."

Darby groaned. "This whole thing stinks like a barrel of chicken shit in July."

Callie laughed and sat back down. "Look at you with the creative expressions today! You'd better be careful, though. Men go nuts over a truly southern girl!"

Darby rolled her eyes. "What can I say? When I get scared or pissed, Mamaw Harrison comes shining through. Gosh, but I wish she was here! She'd know how to skin this cat!" She chugged the last of her drink before sitting up straighter and snapping her fingers. "I got it! We woo him!"

"We what? We woo him? Woo who?" Chuckling, Callie added, "This is starting to sound like an Abbott and Costello sketch."

"Hear me out!" Darby said. "If we can make him think we like him and understand his brand of crazy, he might drop his guard long enough for us to get a bead on his location. It's like my Mamaw used to say. She'd say, 'You know, Darby darling, sometimes you gotta hug people you don't like just so's you know how big to dig the hole.'"

Callie giggled. "I think I love Mamaw Harrison! But Gabriel is too far gone to play nice. He would never believe it, and I don't think I could ever hide my disdain and disgust for him. I see him, and I see an oozing, festering malignancy that needs to be cut out."

Darby waggled her brows. "For real. Burned out, cut to the bone, incinerated. I'm with ya there!" She hopped off the stool. "Say, I spotted some margarita mix in the cabinet. All it needs is tequila, a lime, and some triple sec. How about I pop over to Jed's and steal some booze? We can make adult beverages, and you can tell me all the dirty deets about you and Jake!"

Callie narrowed her eyes. "Only if you tell me the skinny on you and Jed! But yeah, that sounds amazing. I'll dig out the blender, and we can drink and talk."

"Sounds groovy! Be right back!"

Callie had her head bent down under a cabinet when she felt the temperature in the room drop.

"Gosh, how I miss that girl," Katie said from behind her. "Darby was such a great friend."

Callie turned and smiled. "I know. I am so glad she and I have become closer. You know, not too long ago, it was you and Darby against Stacy and me. We challenged each other in tug of war, kickball, even hangman. Now, it's you and Stacy over there versus Darbs and me on this side. How weird is that?"

Katie smiled sadly. "Pretty weird. But I told you, Shadow...Stacy is fine here. Did you know her grandpa passed last month? The two of them have been hooting up a storm over here, catching up on family gossip. So please, don't worry."

Callie smirked. "You do know who you are talking to, right? My picture is in the dictionary next to 'worry' and 'anxiety.' Sometimes, I chew my lip damned near to the bone—if lips had a bone—and wring my hands until they cramp. I make our old neighbor's paranoid Chihuahua look positively

Zen."

Katie laughed. "Oh, Mr. Beans! I'd forgotten about that neurotic pup! You know, you're pretty funny, Shadow!"

"But I'm dead serious." She smirked, feigning embarrassment. "Oh, my, did I say that aloud? *Dead* serious? Sorry, that was in poor taste." She clucked her tongue, indicating to Katie that she was more amused than sorry. "Anyway, although I could have my own floor in a hospital wing dedicated to anxiety, I am improving on some other hiccups of my personality. I still won't go anywhere near a pool, but my fear of enclosed spaces is letting up. Sort of."

Katie lifted a glimmering brow. "Uh, yeah. Sure, it is. You forget I was with you while you were stuck in that well, Shadow. I'm surprised you didn't soil your pants."

"Oh, goodie. Happy to see that being dead hasn't blunted your wicked sense of humor."

Katie grinned. "Hey, I can't help it if I'm a riot. You should see me during meet and greets at the pearly gates. The people love me! Serious as a heart attack, though—or a bullet to the chest..." She laughed, then teasingly stuck out her tongue. "See? I can joke about being dead with the rest of them. Anyway, for real, Cal, you are doing amazing. I admit I was concerned at first, but you are stronger than either of us anticipated. Good on you."

Callie blinked, the familiar sting of tears burning her eyes. "I'm trying so hard to stay level, focused. To just keep swimmin', as they say. Some days are harder than others." She pulled out the blender she'd almost forgotten about, set it on the counter, and turned back to face her sister. Frowning, deep in thought, she asked, "Is there really such a thing as 'meet and greet' there, though?"

"Yep. Officially, it's called 'Intake and Inventory,' but basically, it's a time when newcomers meet their ethereal guides. Remind me to tell you about it sometime. For now, though, we're running out of time, and you need to know something important. I spotted Gabriel a little bit ago, hiding on top of a hill in the distance."

Callie gasped. "Here? At Jed's? Shit, how does he know where I am?" She chewed the corner of her thumb. "What was he doing?"

"Watching the house, I assume. He had binoculars and was writing in some kind of journal or diary. I'm pretty sure he was drawing something, too, though I couldn't see what."

"Dammit! How the hell am I supposed to bring Amara here if he knows where I live?"

Katie shrugged. "I don't think you can, Shadow. At least, not until we figure out where he is and what he's up to."

"Fan-fucking-tabulous! I swear on my eyes, Kates, if it's the last thing I do, I will take that asshole down!"

"I have no doubt. Just be careful, Shadow. I fear he is more disturbed than any of us realize." Energy draining, Katie started to fade. "And one more thing, Cal. I think he knew I was there."

"He saw you?"

"At the very least, he felt my presence. Tread carefully, Shadow. He may have a family trait or gift we aren't aware of."

"Perfect," Callie muttered. "This just keeps getting better and better."

～

"Ice up the blender, baby! I'm back!"

Darby tore into the kitchen, two bottles tucked under her arms. "Jed has the good stuff, too!" She noted Callie's posture, the draw to her brows. "Oh, for criminy sake! I swear, girl! I can't leave you alone for a second! What in grandma's Christmas cookies could have happened while I was gone?"

Callie took a seat and rubbed her forehead. "Katie happened. She came for a visit while you were gone. Guess who she saw watching this place?"

Darby set the bottles down with a thud. "Oh, shit. Gabriel?" When Callie nodded, Darby continued. "But how? Do you think Palmer told him?" Then, horror-stricken, she gasped, "Oh my gosh! Could he have followed me? Did I lead him straight to you?"

Callie, puzzled at first, finally comprehended. "Oh, Darbs, no. Just no. That prick has been here for a while. I would bet my left—" She stopped, the corners of her mouth curving when she thought of Jake. "Look, I'm sure you didn't cause any of this. Gabriel was here weeks before you arrived." She started pouring the ingredients into the blender. "In fact, I wouldn't be surprised if he was in this area even before Jake and I arrived."

"Well, what does Kate think?" Darby asked. "Does she have a sense of what he's doing?"

"Same as us, really. She figures he's watching me, watching Jake, and making notes of what we do. If nothing else, my brother is anal about planning his evil deeds. Kates said—" Callie stopped, suddenly remembering something. "Oh crud! I wanted to ask her if she knew the lady in white that I keep seeing."

"Um, who is that now?"

"Right—I haven't told you yet. So, a beautiful woman dressed in white has come to me a few times. I have no idea what she wants, though. Her presence is weak and hard to see, as if she hasn't the energy to manifest fully. I don't know, Darbs. This is all new to me, but I can say I've not seen this yet. Her inability to communicate makes this whole thing even weirder."

"As if." Darby smirked.

"Right? When she appeared to me, all I got was the same phrase over and over."

"Which was?"

"'*You must find her.*'"

"Find her? Find who? Why are these spirits so obscure? Who makes up these cockamamie rules, anyway?"

Callie laughed. "Beats me on all counts. That's why I wanted to ask

Kates, but whenever she comes, something more pressing takes center stage. Today, it was the information about Gabriel spying on us."

"Hey, I wonder," Darby shouted over the roar of the blender, "if the lady in white is talking about Jake and Jed's missing sister, Lacy Jane? Or even Emily Duncan?"

"Yeah, that was where my brain, and Jake's, went as well."

Darby pulled two margarita glasses from the cabinet and salted the rims. "Speaking of that hunky man of yours...how are things?" She waggled her brows. "Getting spicy? Heating up?"

"Things are, for lack of a better word, steady. We love each other and enjoy each other's company. He is my biggest cheerleader and my best friend. We just haven't...you know...yet."

Darby gasped. "Oh, come on! Seriously?"

Callie shrugged sheepishly.

"Well, what in tarnation are you waiting for, girl? You need to seize the moment; grab the bull by the horns." Darby plopped a lime wedge into each glass. "You need to get on the stick!"

There was a pregnant pause before they giggled, finally getting the double entendre.

"You know," Callie wheezed, still laughing, "I could say the same for you and Jed. You seem to have gotten much closer since we were in Virginia. So, I ask you—how close *did* you get?"

Darby poured the contents of the blender into the glasses. "Let's just say I haven't climbed aboard the stick either!"

Callie grinned. "So, you like him, then?"

"Good Lord, woman! What's not to like? The man is drop-dead gorgeous. And tall? Geesh, he could fall to the ground and be halfway home!"

"Of course, at five-two, anyone over the age of ten is Gulliver to you," Callie joked.

"Oh, short jokes," Darby said, smiling. "Nice. I figured they were beneath you."

Callie snorted at the pun, then clinked her glass with Darby's. "Here's to us. To friendship, new beginnings, and catching Gabriel."

As Darby touched Callie's glass, she added, "And to us both getting on the stick!"

They folded over in laughter again.

CHAPTER THIRTEEN

Philadelphia, Pennsylvania
Eight months earlier

Thinking back, Emily Duncan couldn't pinpoint how long the abuse had been going on. The days soon melted into weeks, weeks into months, and months into years. All she could be sure of was that she'd married a monster who had twisted her perception of time and space, of right and wrong. Of normalcy.

Emily hadn't had any sense of normalcy in years.

'Normal' left the station the moment she laid eyes on Graeme Duncan.

As a young student in her final year at Montserrat College of Art in Beverly, Massachusetts, Emily Weston had prided herself on her study ethic. Eager to learn photography and even more eager to excel in it, she had often wandered the area, exploring countless libraries and soaking up the information she'd found at her fingertips.

She'd met Graeme in a library close to Harvard. He was a law student at the university and happened to be in the same library, cramming for an exam.

They were sitting at the same long table, both with piles of books before them, when their eyes met. Emily smiled; Graeme waved shyly.

It was electric.

Eventually, he got up and moved closer to her. They started a conversation, and he asked her out. She readily accepted, and they began dating.

She was twenty-three years old, and he, twenty-eight.

A year later, after passing the Bar Exam, Graeme took a job in a law firm near the Weston family home in Philadelphia. Their year-long courtship was magical. Emily had never felt so loved, so alive. On her twenty-fourth birthday, smitten, she accepted his marriage proposal.

It would prove to be the worst decision of her young life.

The Duncan Home
Two days before the murder

Graeme Duncan stood quickly from the kitchen table, his face crimson, hands curled into fists.

"Please," he said through gritted teeth, eyes locked on his wife. "please tell me you didn't just fucking second-guess me, Emily."

Emily recoiled, pressing her back painfully against the wooden spindles of her chair, desperate to make herself a smaller target. For years, nearly the entirety of her marriage, Graeme had abused her physically.

Emotionally? That abuse began on their honeymoon.

Stomach cramping, she tilted her head back and peeked at him through long lashes. His eyes had changed from their usual gray-blue color to a smoldering black.

She was in trouble. Deep trouble.

Her only blessing was that Tyler's nanny had taken him to the park. He didn't need to see more beatings; he'd already seen plenty in his short life.

"Of course not, sweetheart," Emily said placatingly, feeling trapped. "I-I just wonder if Tyler is too young to spend an entire summer at your parents' summer home in Scotland. It's so far away, and I couldn't get to him for days if he needed me."

Graeme moved closer. "I will be going back and forth, remember? I have a few clients in Scotland."

"Yes, yes, of course. It's just with the baby coming...."

His eyes narrowed. "You don't think my parents can handle an emergency? Is that what you're saying?"

"Graeme, please."

"Do you think you're the only fucking woman who has ever carried a kid?"

"No, no, of course not. I just think...."

Graeme howled, his vibrato ringing in her ears. He kicked the legs supporting Emily's chair, and it toppled over, sending her sprawling to the floor.

She landed on the Italian marble tile with a thud, her lungs heaving for air.

He reached down, enraged, and snagged a fistful of her hair. Instinctively, she brought her hands to her scalp, grabbing at his fingers to loosen his grip, shrieking as he pulled her body toward the far wall.

"Did you just say 'I think'?" he yelled. "Well, there's your first mistake, Em. You don't get to think. Your opinion means shit in this house."

He jerked her head back and punched her in the mouth with his free hand. Her bottom lip burst open, spraying blood all over the intricate molding.

"Quiet, dear," he said when she yelped. "You'll wake the neighbors."

She screamed again, twisting to escape his grasp and raking her nails across the back of his hand. Swearing, furious, he pulled his hand away and sucked at the scratch before reaching for her again. He grabbed hold of her collar and dragged her across the kitchen floor. Her scalp burned, her tongue tasted like blood, and her skull throbbed where it had smashed into the floor.

Incomplete, scrambled thoughts assaulted her from all angles. Should she plead with him? Try to get to the steak knives? What time would Tyler and Fiona be back? Did she turn the stove off after breakfast?

Attempting to rise from her crab-like position, she bent her knees and dug her heels into the smooth tile. Her legs worked furiously, pushing as he pulled, *sliding for purchase in a lousy imitation of a Slavic squat dance.*

She'd never seen Graeme so furious, so out of control. She feared he really might kill her this time.

She fought for air as the vee of her neckline dug into her throat. When he reached the door that led to the cellar, he halted abruptly, jerking her closer to the wall.

Emily heard the doorknob twist and felt the cold whoosh of air traveling up the basement steps as he threw open the door. Hauling her to her feet, Graeme pulled her close and dragged his tongue up the side of her face.

Then, spinning her around, he booted her, hard, in the ass.

Suddenly, she was flying.

Emily reached out blindly, trying to stop her momentum. As she fell, her head bounced painfully off a wooden beam that crossed the upper part of the staircase. Tumbling into the darkness, she covered her head with her hands, allowing her back and shoulders to take the brunt of the impact with the steps.

As she flipped end over end, Emily listened for the crisp snap of her neck she was sure would come.

When she finally reached the bottom of the cellar steps without hearing the pop of a vertebra, she curled into a ball, doing her best to remain motionless, praying that he would think her unconscious.

Or, if the heavens smiled upon her, that he would think she was dead.

But the heavens wore a frown that day.

Emily felt Graeme studying her crumpled form from the top of the steps, knew his blistering gaze was upon her. It was an act that took moments but seemed like an eternity. Trying to quiet her racing mind, terrified her husband would descend those stairs and finish the job, she mentally took inventory of her injuries. Her whole torso vibrated with her pounding heart as it pulsed against the cool cement floor, echoing in her ears.

She rolled to her left side, the movement sending spasms of pain down her spine. Her chest ached, a knife-like sensation ripping through her with every breath, forcing her to take in only shallow gulps of air.

At the very least, she'd cracked a rib on the way down. Emily was sure of it.

Her muscles tensed, the ominous thump of Graeme's shoes as he descended the steps shooting a fresh wave of fear through her body. When he reached the bottom, he squatted beside her, gently pushed back a strand of her hair, and slammed his fist once more into her face. Snickering, he stood, turned to walk back up the stairs, then stopped.

Exhaling loudly, he whispered, "Just one more," before swinging his leg back and driving his boot into her stomach.

Emily gasped in pain, air whooshing from her lungs and bile rising in her throat. Groaning, she wrapped one arm protectively around her middle, the other around her head.

After another moment or two, Graeme turned and, wordlessly, headed back up the steps.

She could swear he was whistling.

Later that night, in a hall bathroom that smelled of bleach and soap and lavender, Emily Duncan bent in half on the toilet seat, her heart breaking as the tiny life that had been growing inside her—the life she'd prayed for since Tyler was two—slipped out from between her legs.

CHAPTER FOURTEEN

June 13

"Gabriel? Are you here?"

Tucker Simon stood outside the barn doors, hands in his pockets, heart racing. He'd come to make amends, to atone for ignoring the Apostle's phone calls earlier. But he'd had no choice. He'd been called in for mandatory overtime to assist in the postmortem examination of a young woman—a woman found bent over a trough at an abandoned farm in Buffalo, slaughtered like a swine.

He'd been summoned for the autopsy of Rebecca Sue Caraway.

Because although Tucker worked as a forensic examiner for the Wyoming Division of Criminal Investigation, he wanted more—more money, more prestige, more experience to pad his resume. Two months ago, he'd got a part-time gig with the Sheridan County Medical Examiner's office. His job in the autopsy suite entailed transporting bodies, dissecting and weighing internal organs, and transcribing the medical examiner's notes.

None of it—the broken necks or near decapitations seen in many drunk-driving accidents, the suicide victims sliced in half after jumping in front of a speeding locomotive, the snapped femurs and skin avulsions that often accompanied motorcycle crashes—none of it bothered him. In fact, he'd never been disturbed in the presence of the dead. Traumatic death was just a part of life to him.

Sure, it was gruesome, and, at times, the stench of bodily fluids and decay was so horrific, it seemed to seep straight into his soul. After one of those cases, the only way to breathe again, according to Tucker, was to "puke out the nasty."

But even that never cost him a night of sleep or dimmed his enthusiasm.

Because the more people who died an 'unattended' or 'suspicious' death, the more people required a coroner's investigation into what had killed them.

And the more investigations he did, the quicker his bills got paid

His outlook, his philosophy of 'what will be, will be,' went unchallenged—until Rebecca Sue Caraway landed on his autopsy table.

He shivered as he stood there, recalling the moment that crisp, white sheet was pulled back and the victim's face uncovered. He'd tried desperately to hide his shock and guilt from his new boss, a no-nonsense woman on loan to Sheridan from the Montana medical examiner's office.

He cursed himself now for his greed. His greed had led him to spend more time with TJ Palmer, which had led him to a bar, a back alley, and Gabriel Devine. And no amount of money was worth the shitstorm he found himself fighting through now.

He started to push open the barn door when he felt the swift breeze of an object moving next to him. A muscled arm whizzed by his head, followed by the palm of a hand slamming the wooden door closed.

"Well, well, well," Gabriel said, arm still extended and hand flat against the weathered barn door. "Look who we have here. If it isn't Simon of Cyrene—or should I call you Judas of Iscariot? Like him, you're a step below a belly-crawling, lowlife traitor, aren't you?"

Tucker's lungs grew tight, and he gulped for air. Belly cramping and bowels rumbling, he clenched his ass cheeks together to avoid an accident. He almost laughed, recalling a show he'd seen in New York where the comedian joked about going on the Cyclone ride at Coney Island and, literally, having the shit scared out of him.

So, yeah. Being scared shitless was actually a thing.

Somewhere in the recesses of his mind, despite his abject terror, he marveled at the mind–body connection. His fear, his dread in the presence of Gabriel, was causing his body to respond in the most primitive way possible. As a scientist, he found it fascinating.

As the object of Gabriel's wrath, he found it terrifying.

"Uh, no, Gabriel, sir. You have it all wrong. I-I'm not a traitor. I just had to work some mandatory overtime. It—it was for an autopsy. They found that girl from Buffalo, the heavy one. The one we put by the pig trough."

Gabriel's eyes lit up. "Rebecca? They found her already?" Clapping, he added, "Brilliant! I was afraid we would have to wait for it. Did they see the message? Understand the meaning?"

Tucker shifted his weight, uncomfortable. "I'm not sure. Maybe?" Then, suddenly curious as to why Gabriel seemed so guarded about the barn's contents, he nodded toward the door. "Perhaps we should go inside, put our heads together. You know, determine our next move?"

Gabriel eyed him suspiciously. "The barn is off limits to you, Simon. You are not to enter it. Think of it as my 'safe space.' Do I make myself clear?"

"Oh, sure, sure. I-I meant nothing by it."

What does he have in there? Tucker thought. *Another body?*

"Come with me to the house," Gabriel said, dropping his arm to his side. "I have disposed of the last sacrifice. Harry Tinning's greed has placed him where he needed to be."

Tucker swallowed. "If you don't mind my asking, where did you put him?"

Gabriel sneered. "Where he belonged—surrounded by the only thing he valued more than life itself. Money." His demeanor changed suddenly from anger to mirth. "I wish I could see the reactions of customers as they file into the bank Monday morning. Faces buried in their cell phones, ignorant of their surroundings. That is, until they push through the outer door and walk by the corpse near the ATM."

In good humor, Gabriel slapped Tucker on the back and guided him away from the barn. "Picture it, Simon. Harry's body propped against the wall, two days dead by the time the bank opens its doors. Of course, I suppose he could be found sooner by a weekend ATM user or building custodian. But it's fun to dream, right? Oh, to be a fly on the wall when they notice his bloated face and the coins stuffed into his mouth!"

Tucker remained silent, his feet scuffing the dirt as if the lower half of his body was at war with the upper half, refusing to leave the safety of the outdoors.

But even his feet knew the futility of delay. As Gabriel led him toward the house, Tucker had only one thought.

What is he hiding in that barn? And, more importantly, do I dare find out?

～

The drive to Reagan International was, to put it mildly, tense.

Once Jake learned that Gabriel had been spying on Jed's house, once he understood that the psycho bastard knew where Callie was, he insisted she go home to Virginia. He suggested Gram's house, even wondered if she should stay with her oldest brother, Finn.

Jake knew Finn Callahan was a sour guy and could be a melodramatic pain in the ass. But he also had no doubt Finn loved his sister and would guard her with his life.

But Callie would hear none of it.

"You want me to leave? Leave Tyler and Darby and Jed to fend for themselves? Leave you? Not on your life, bud."

"So, you'd rather risk getting killed? Blaze, this fucker wants you dead. Do you understand that? He has wanted you dead for months. And now, he knows where you are."

"Jesus, Jake. Try to forget about our relationship for a minute. Don't you think that, given his passion, his drive to see me gone, he would look in the only state I've ever lived in? He knows I have family in Virginia, and Gram's house would be the first place he looked. Next, he would look to Finn."

"So, we put you somewhere else, then." He thought for a moment. "We put you with Sully."

Callie shook her head, frustrated. "Even a blind squirrel eventually finds a nut, bubba. Sully was your partner for years, not to mention a close friend. If Gabriel failed to find me with my people, he would start looking at yours. Don't you see? The safest place for me to be is here, with you."

Jake gripped the steering wheel tighter, trying in vain to ignore the pit in his stomach. "I don't like it, woman."

Callie covered her mouth, hiding a smirk, knowing she was winning the argument. "It will be fine. Besides, here I have you and Jed and the entire Scooby Gang to watch my back."

Jake exhaled in defeat. "Fine. But you can't stay at Jed's right now."

She started to object, and he put up a hand.

"I'm not kidding, Blaze. I will not budge on this, even if you end up pissed as shit at me." He gripped her hand, squeezing her slender fingers. "This isn't a punishment, Callie; it's real life. You, Amara, Darby, and Tyler can stay in my parents' cabin in Pitikin Falls. It's not far from town, and we will make sure one of us will always be with you." He raised her hand to his lips and kissed her knuckles. "One of us who carries a firearm."

"Which means that Tyler will have to move away from Jed's to a new place just when he is starting to get comfortable with us. How can we do that to him?"

"How can we not?" Jake murmured into her fingers, eyes still on the road. "His physical safety should be our first concern. We can work on the other stuff later. Besides, he's a smart kid. He'll adjust." After a pause, he added, "You know, I think I screwed up with your sister. I should have been more careful, more forceful in explaining the dangers of going off half-cocked. Maybe if I had...." He hesitated. "Never mind. Just know that I'll not make the same mistake with you."

Callie's stomach did an odd flip. "Katie was her own woman, Jake. It was neither your responsibility nor your station in life to protect her."

And just like that, Callie felt herself disappearing—ripped from the sunshine that finally warmed her face, back into hiding beneath the cool shadows of Katherine Callahan.

Will I ever escape this? This feeling of invisibility, of being compared to Kates, even as she lies in her grave? Could I truly be jealous of my dead sister's relationship with Jake? Am I that awful?

A tiny sound escaped her lips, a cross between a gasp and a moan of disgust.

"Blaze, wait. Don't...." Jake started, still holding her fingers to his mouth. "Don't make this into something it isn't. I only bring up your sister to point out my mistakes."

When Callie remained mute, he shook his head, muttering, "Christ, woman. Don't you know by now how much I love you? All I want is to keep you safe."

Callie pulled her hand away from his mouth, folded her arms, and pouted like a child. She knew she was being ridiculous, petulant, about so many things.

But she couldn't help it. Her 'adulting' for the time being had gone into hiding, replaced by the reckless rebellion of a juvenile.

He wants to keep me safe? Well, who asked him? I can take care of myself!

Just as she had the thought, a wisp of air touched her ear. "He's not wrong, Shadow. Listen to him."

Kates. Perfect.

Callie rolled her eyes. "Oh, hush up!"

"Huh?" Jake asked, pulling into the airport parking lot. "Are you talking to me or a—or someone else? 'Cause I haven't said anything for the last five minutes."

She glared at him before turning toward the back seat. She saw nothing. In no mood to explain it to Jake, she answered her sister telepathically.

Don't you have a harp to play or a cloud to jump through or something, Kates?

As they exited the car, Katie Callahan's sweet laughter echoed in Callie's mind.

"Amara!" Callie called out, waving a hand. "Over here!"

Amused, Jake said, "Pretty sure she can't hear you, Blaze."

"Oh, crapbags, I keep forgetting."

Callie, noticing her sister was headed in the opposite direction, walked quickly to catch up. Stepping behind Amara, she tapped her shoulder

"Hello!" she said as Amara turned to her, then enveloped her in a hug. "So glad you got here safely!"

Amara hugged her back. "Yes, the flight was easy. Navigating the terminal, though, not so much. I'm glad you found me."

"No worries, kiddo," Callie said, squeezing Amara's shoulder. "Now, let's go collect your bags. If you're anything like me, you have more than one!"

"Oh, heck, my art supplies are in a suitcase all by themselves! I will have to pick up some stuff soon, though. Couldn't really fit my easels or a blank canvas in my carry-on." She nodded to Jake as he caught up with them.

"Hello again, Jake. Good to see you."

"You as well," Jake said, smiling. "What's this about luggage?"

"Oh, I was telling Callie I'll need to get some art supplies. I was limited to what I could bring on the plane."

"We got you," Callie said enthusiastically. "There's a very cool art store near Sheridan. We could take a ride there tomorrow if you want."

"Sounds perfect!"

They moved quickly to gather her bags and made it back to the parking lot in record time. Callie settled into the back seat of the car next to Amara.

She clapped Jake's headrest and joked, "Home, James!"

Jake smiled. "Yes, ma'am."

~

Tucker Simon sat at the kitchen table in Gabriel's farmhouse, a glass of water between his hands, and looked around. The furnishings were sparse, with just this table and two chairs, and the walls were bare.

"What news do you have for me, Simon of Cyrene? Besides the discovery of Rebecca, I mean."

Tucker took a large gulp of his water. It was warm, with a distinct metallic taste. "Um, well, about the autopsy, you mean?"

Busily scrubbing the already spotless counter, Gabriel turned to face his assistant. "I mean anything of import," he said, frowning. "Try to keep up, man!"

"Sure, sure," Tucker said, droplets of sweat forming on his lower back. "The medical examiner is still doing her exam, you understand. She found the cut on Rebecca's neck, obviously. And the 'No Temperance' message on her abdomen." He took another swig of the nasty-tasting water because his throat was raw, his tongue coated with a thick layer of white goo, and his lips were dry as dust.

He knew, just knew, that if he didn't soothe his mouth with something, anything, he would never speak again.

"The marks on her—on her breasts, though, have the examiner stumped," Tucker said, rolling the glass in his hand. "She will eventually get it, solve the riddle, and recognize the injuries are electrical. That woman doc is as sharp as a tack."

Gabriel nodded. "I hope she does figure it out. The world must know the punishment for capital sin." Watching his assistant with suspicion, he asked, "Anything else to tell me?"

Sometime in the last few days, through the miracle of faith and omnipotence, Gabriel had received a sign from above that Tucker would forsake him—that the man was planning some sort of trickery, some kind of treason.

Perhaps the imbecile had decided to go to the authorities after all or take his chances on the run. Maybe he believed Gabriel would turn a blind eye to his deception and deceit and let him go.

Fat chance.

"There—there is one thing I found out this morning at Rebecca's autopsy. The doc and I were chatting it up, talking about all kinds of things. I mentioned how her taking the reins, standing in for TJ Palmer, was a nice thing to do." He stood and brought his glass to the sink. "Then I said how sad it was to learn about the horrible death he had endured. You know, to throw off any suspicions about us."

"And?" Gabriel said, growing impatient. "What's your point?"

"Uh, well," he stuttered, turning from the sink to face Gabriel, "she told me not to say anything, but she'd heard from a doc who heard from a nurse that TJ Palmer is not...uh, he's not dead, boss. He's alive."

Gabriel's spine stiffened, and his hand stilled on the counter. Rage bubbled from the tips of his toes to the top of his head. "Alive? The Disciple still lives? Are you certain of this?"

Tucker licked his lips and nodded, slinking back to his seat at the kitchen table. Fear coiled in his belly as he watched Gabriel's eyes, trying to sense his reaction, but the man was impossible to read.

Tense seconds ticked by until Gabriel let loose his wrath. Screaming, he reached into the sink, lifted Tucker's water glass, and heaved it across the room. The glass exploded on impact with the wall, its crystal shards raining over the floor, the table, and finally, the man quaking in his seat.

But Tucker Simon was so frightened he never felt the glass splinters pierce his face.

"How is that possible?" Gabriel screeched, hands clenched and face red. Cursing, he pounded a fist against the countertop, spittle flying from his mouth with each word. "Fuck, fuck, fuck! It simply cannot be!"

Tucker sat still, too terrified to move, too afraid to raise a hand and release the broken pieces of glass that he could now feel jutting from his forehead and beneath his right eye. Blood trickled down the bridge of his nose and over his cheekbones, the sting of tears blurring his vision, just as the dozens of mini-lacerations burned his skin.

I can't stay here! This dude is gonna kill me!

A tornado of thoughts whirled inside Tucker's head as he swallowed the bile in his throat and weighed his options to get out. He needed a plan of escape, a way to get away without further injury.

He could think of nothing.

Across the room, Gabriel took several deep breaths and counted the tiles on the kitchen floor—because math had always had a cathartic effect on his anger.

Eleven across, fifteen down.

Calmer now, he faced the man with the wide eyes and trembling mouth who was bleeding in his kitchen.

Man up, asshole! I should have killed you in that fucking alley, a mistake I will soon rectify!

Wrinkling his nose in disgust, Gabriel said, "Well, I'd say our work is cut out for us, then, isn't it? This mistake cannot stand. I will go to Sheridan Memorial on the pretense of ministering to the sick. Once there, I will finish what I started."

The sky darkened, and thunder rumbled in the distance. A storm was brewing in the west.

Perhaps more than one.

Hesitant, fearing he was opening a can of worms, Tucker asked, "What do you want me to do?"

"I have several errands for you to run. But first, I need you to transcribe some notes of mine. There is a typewriter in my office."

"A... a typewriter?" Tucker sputtered. "Like, from the seventies or something?"

"You have a problem with simplicity, son? I happen to prefer my work not be hijacked by cyber thieves or stored in 'the cloud.'" He snorted. "What a ridiculous name—the cloud. As if the world's most precious documents could be safeguarded in a puff of smoke, a vault that isn't tangible. No, I'd much rather my doctrines be on paper, secured in my safe, not in the sky." He stood to leave. "Besides, all my words are to be compiled into a book, a new Bible of sorts. And, once I've located my seven sinners...." He stopped, cocked his head as if recalling a memory, then grinned. "I found it!"

Confused, Tucker asked, "You found what?"

Gabriel's eyes brightened. "I found my next sinner—a man of jealousy who strives to be like others and covets what they have." Grinning wider, he whispered, "Don't you get it, Simon? I found Envy. And its name is TJ Palmer."

Once Gabriel finished setting up Tucker, he moved quickly. His office, a second bedroom he'd converted, was in the back of the house. Secluded and virtually soundproof, the room's sole window faced the side pasture.

Which worked out well. Gabriel's plan entailed working in the back of the house, away from the office window.

Simon of Cyrene, it seemed, was a fraud: a traitor. A manipulator and a weakling who must be stopped.

Crouched down, more out of habit than necessity, Gabriel slid to the small garage next to the barn. The building had seen better days, but the structure—although much too small for his pickup truck—remained sound.

The garage now served as his workshop of sorts. Within its walls were his tools, his collection of knives and rosary beads, his secrets. He grabbed his toolbox and, whistling softly—because whistling brought him serenity—he followed the driveway as it curved around to the back of the house where Tucker Simon had parked his car.

Parked out of sight. As if ashamed, as if hiding his presence here from the world.

And yet another indication that the Apostle was doing the right thing.

Sliding on his back beneath the old Honda, tools in hand, Gabriel went to work.

CHAPTER FIFTEEN

Sheridan Memorial Hospital, West Wing
Rehabilitation and Infusion Center
Room 306

When Jake and Callie reached TJ Palmer's room, they found the door slightly ajar. JP Burke, looking sharp in his new sheriff's department uniform, stood from his metal chair to greet them.

"Agent Devereaux, Ms. Callahan. Good to see you again. I take it you are here to speak to the miracle patient." He grinned shyly. "Sure was something, huh? You two leave, and within a blink, Palmer suddenly 'wakes' up. What are the odds?"

Jake shook his head. "I wouldn't hazard a guess. Infinitesimal comes to mind. Did he get any visitors?"

"None, except you two." JP squinted at Jake. "Out of curiosity, why do you ask? Something I should be concerned about?"

"Nah, just thinking out loud. I always wondered if, aside from Gabriel, this dude had any extra help. Let's face it. He isn't exactly a powerhouse physically."

"From what I gather, he took his victims by surprise," Callie chimed in. "Some of them, like Maddie Gibbs, were drugged and then killed. His methods of luring his victims were particularly depraved. When he used the

LiveFeed site and the 'Confessions room,' it was to get inside their heads, pretend to sympathize."

"And those poor people thought they'd found a friend, right?" Jake asked.

"Yes," Callie said softly. "Instead, they found a monster. So sad."

"Well, if it's any comfort," JP said, hooking his thumb toward the room behind him, "this dickwad isn't going to hurt anyone else. We'll make sure of it."

"Thanks, JP," Callie said with a smile.

"You ready, Blaze?"

She nodded, and Jake pushed the door open.

"Honey, we're home!" he quipped. He clasped Callie's hand, and they walked to the bed and the frail-looking man with a pale face and dry lips.

Thomas Palmer appeared to have aged ten years since they saw him last—less than twenty-four hours ago.

Jake palmed two chairs from a side wall and positioned them next to the bed. After they were seated, he leaned forward.

"Hello, asshole," he whispered. "Miss us?"

Callie could swear she saw TJ's mouth twitch as if ready to spread into a grin. "Come on, TJ," she said. "We know you are no longer 'comatose.' So, let's get to it, shall we?"

Palmer remained still.

"Olly, Olly, oxen free," she said in a sing-song voice. "Come out, come out wherever you are."

Jake, elbows on his thighs, cracked his knuckles. It was a nervous habit he'd developed in high school, his go-to move whenever he was anxious about girls or acne or the exam he'd forgotten to study for.

But now, his habit had nothing to do with teenage angst and everything to do with keeping his hands busy. If he didn't, he feared they would find their way around Palmer's neck.

"We're waiting, dickhead," he said. "This is your final opportunity to help yourself."

Callie winked at Jake, placed her forearms on the bed, and leaned closer. "TJ, we aren't going to hang here forever. Start talking, or we walk, and you roll the dice regarding your fate. Do you realize that both Wyoming and Montana still have the death penalty? Help us, and the District Attorney might take capital punishment off the table."

The man known as the Disciple slowly opened his eyes and turned his head to face his visitors. "Well, well, if it isn't the dynamic duo. You caught me. I give up; I surrender to your genius." His gaze narrowed, and his lips pulled back into a sneer. "I bet you're proud of yourselves, aren't you? Catching little ol' me? Well, don't get too comfortable at the top, kids. You know what they say about standing on the shoulders of giants."

Callie giggled. "Giant? You?"

"Sure, he is," Jake said. "He's a giant douchebag, a giant pain in my ass, a giant, weeping pus pocket on the armpit of society. So, yeah, he is a giant."

TJ's face flushed, and he scooted higher in the bed. "If you're finished with the juvenile fun and games, Agent Devereaux, let's get to it." He pinned his gaze on Callie. "You're looking much better than last I saw you, Miss Callahan. You remember, don't you? Let me think. Oh, yes—it was somewhere at the bottom of that well, wasn't it?"

Jake swore and started to rise, but Callie grabbed his arm. Tugging him back to his seat, she said, "No, don't. He's just baiting you."

"Yeah, *Jake*," TJ needled, his voice an octave higher. "Listen to the woman." He ran his hands over the sheets, smoothing the wrinkles, and yawned. "Well, as lovely as this trip down memory lane has been, you both bore me to tears. So, what is it you want to know?"

Callie sat straighter and scrubbed at the vile tattoo on her thigh. "Gabriel Devine. We need to know everything about him—where he lives now, what he does for a living, and how you vile cretins found each other. Everything."

Palmer sighed. "Ho hum. You're like a record playing the same tired song—a tune with dull lyrics and a forgettable melody. I thought you would ask me something juicy, relevant. You're better than this drivel, Callie." He scowled at Jake. "Not you, though. This boring 'interrogation' has your name all over it, Devereaux." He sighed again, more dramatically this time.

It was all Jake could do to keep from slamming his fist into Palmer's windpipe.

After a tense moment, TJ brightened. "I have a grand idea! Let's play a game! Like truth or dare, except when you ask me a question, it's my choice to answer it correctly or respond with a question back. If I do answer with a question and you respond truthfully, you will, in turn, win big. You will leave here with all the answers you seek."

Jake growled and jumped up, sending his chair hurling to the floor. "Go to hell, Palmer! We have no intention of playing a game of quid pro quo with you."

The crash of wood slamming into the tile brought JP rushing into the room. Cupping the grip of his gun with his hand, he asked, "You guys okay in here?"

"Peachy," Jake said tightly. "We're just finishing up. Apparently, Hannibal Lecter over here likes the idea of dying in prison, whether on the executioner's table or as an old man."

"Got it. Explains why he don't look too bright," JP said, playing along. Then, eyeing the man in the bed, he added, "Don't hesitate to call out if you need me, Agent. I'm right outside the door, and I'm not going anywhere."

Jake picked up his chair and sat again. "Thanks, Burke."

"Oh, come now, Jacob," Palmer said after JP closed the door. "I'm just having a little fun, is all. Think of it as my last hurrah before saying goodbye to my former life."

Callie looked at Jake and shrugged. "It's not like we have to answer him, right?" Turning to TJ, she said. "Ask stupid questions, win stupid prizes. You understand that, right? If we tire of your ridiculous questions, we book it, and you gain nothing. No shortened sentence, no prison perks, no early parole. Nothing."

"That's right," Jake ground out. "Face it, asshole; you need us more than we need you. We'll get Gabriel Devine before he inflicts any more damage, but you? If I were you, I wouldn't count on sitting comfortably for the rest of your life. There is a code in prison, Palmer. Convicts aren't too happy with sleazeballs who commit crimes against children, and they aren't shy to show it."

Palmer clenched his fists. "Madison Gibbs was no child! She may have technically been a teenager, yes, but she was every bit the adult woman Callie is!"

Jake bent over the bed and, through a clenched jaw, rasped, "You keep her name out of your filthy mouth, Palmer. I mean it. You don't ever get to say her name again."

"Say whose name? Callie?" TJ goaded.

"You son of a ..." Jake started, rising once again.

"Enough!" Callie shouted, frustrated. "Don't let him rattle you, Jake. I'm fine. Let's just get this over with. The longer we're here, the dirtier I feel." She rubbed her forehead, trying to ward off an impending headache. "I'll go first, Thomas. We need to know how you and Gabriel linked up. Was it in a chatroom on LiveFeed?"

Palmer smiled. "No, not LiveFeed. But it was in what one could consider a 'chatroom.' My turn now. Tell me, Clarice," he winked, "what did Gabriel do to you? I know it was something deliciously dreadful. Something so powerful I can feel the effects from here. The anger, the hatred, ripples off you in waves when you hear his name."

Callie crossed her arms, feigning nonchalance. In truth, her hands were damp, and her heart banged against her chest wall. She feared he could see the truth in her eyes, so she stared at the floor. "He killed my best friend, Stacy Egan, and many others close to me."

She kept Katie's name from him intentionally—he didn't deserve a front-row seat to her greatest pain of all.

But TJ was astute as well as psychotic and saw right through her. "No, it's more than that. We cannot play the game properly, Callie, if you fail to follow the rules. What else?"

"That's it!" Jake shouted, furious. "This isn't a game, Palmer! We aren't here for your entertainment." He gently pulled Callie to her feet. "Come on, Blaze. We've wasted too much time on this asshole."

"Wait!" Palmer whined, desperate to keep the game going. "Don't you want to know the solution to the biggest riddle of all? The answer to where Gabriel is now and what his next move will be?"

Callie gave Jake a reassuring pat on the arm and sat back down. "Okay, Palmer, you win. Gabriel took more than my best friend. He also killed my mother many years ago. Now, answer the question that you posed. Where is Gabriel now?"

"Are you two a couple?" TJ asked, as though the thought had just occurred to him. "You are, aren't you? How perfectly boring." He wiggled his brows at Jake. "And how's the sex? I'm betting little Miss Goody-two-shoes over there is quite the hellcat under the sheets, am I right? In fact, I'm betting that pretty mouth could suck the—"

Lightning quick, Jake's arm shot out, his fingers wrapping around Palmer's throat. Pushing against the carotid arteries on either side of TJ's neck, he said, "Go ahead. Give me a reason, you piece of shit." Squeezing harder, he whispered. "Please. Give me a fucking reason."

Callie stood quickly, a flush spreading over her cheeks.

Palmer, gasping for air, pinned his panicked eyes on Callie, telegraphing a plea for her to intercede.

Instead, she cheered Jake on.

"If you're looking for a savior, Thomas, you're looking at the wrong girl. After what you did to me, to Tyler, I don't give a rat's ass if Jake chokes the shit out of you, here and now. Besides, it's not like you've decided to cooperate with our investigation. We really don't need you." She placed a hand on Jake's bicep and said, "I'll watch the door. Just get it done."

Then, back stiff, she walked toward the exit.

Jake nearly ruined the ruse, swallowing the laughter in his throat. He knew what Callie was doing, understood the psychology of her plan.

And loved her even more for it.

Letting up slightly, pretending to get a better grip around Palmer's throat, he readjusted his hold and waited for TJ to speak.

The man did not disappoint.

"Okay, okay," TJ rasped. "Don't kill me! I'll tell you what I know!"

Jake released the pressure but kept his hand where it was.

"Okay, then," Callie said, stopping mid-step but not turning around. "Where is he?"

Palmer coughed violently.

"Quit stalling, scumbag," Jake grunted.

Panting, Palmer swallowed painfully. "Okay, okay! Give me a minute to catch my damned breath, will you? In case you forgot, you were strangling me a second ago!"

The door opened, and Jake quickly moved his hand to his side. A man in scrubs, humming softly and rolling a wheelchair, entered the room.

"Sorry to interrupt, folks," the man said, "but I need to take Mr. Palmer here down to radiology. He has a bunch of scans scheduled."

"What? Why?" Jake barked, frustrated. They were so close to getting answers.

The technician, whose nametag read "R. Ramos, Radiology," eyed him suspiciously. "No idea, pal. The doc ordered them, and I'm just following those orders." He moved the wheelchair to the bedside. "You might want to come back later," he said to Callie. "These things sometimes take hours. Of course, you're welcome to stay here. Just wanted to give you the heads up that it could be a while."

Disappointed, Callie glanced at Jake. "No, it's fine. We have a few things to take care of anyway." Pouting, she walked to the bed and tapped TJ's leg. "We will be back soon, Uncle Thomas," she said, voice saccharine sweet. "Don't you go giving Mr. Ramos a hard time, you hear? Otherwise, no ice cream tomorrow."

Ramos forced a smile. The exchange between the patient and the woman, apparently his niece, was strained, stilted, bizarre.

And, he decided suddenly, none of his damned business.

When Jake and Callie stepped back into the hallway, Officer JP Burke had been replaced by a different officer standing guard.

Jake nodded to the young man, then said, "I'm sure your supervisor told you, but watch this guy closely. He's slick."

The cop stood, his acne and high-pitched voice telegraphing his youth. He couldn't have been more than twenty-one or twenty-two. "Yessir, that's what I hear. Don't worry none. I won't let him out of my sight."

Jake clapped his shoulder. "Good man."

"Great. Now what?" Callie said as they left TJ's hospital room.

"Now, we head to Jed's and see if he's heard anything from Curt or Sawyer about that body they found. Then we need to get you, Amara, Darby, and Tyler set up in my parents' place."

Callie stewed but remained silent.

"Come on, Blaze," he said as they walked across the hospital parking lot. "You know it's for the best. And just think—you and Amara can learn a lot about each other without the fear of attack looming over your heads."

Thunder rumbled, and lightning flashed in the distance. Thick, dark clouds hung overhead, stubbornly staying in place despite the steady wind gusts, but no rain fell.

"What is it with this state?" Callie said, her mood dark. "It's been threatening to rain for two days now. What the hell is it waiting for? An engraved invitation?"

Jake raised a brow. "I sense you are troubled, Grasshopper."

"Not troubled," she snapped. "I just think it's ridiculous. So freakin' dry, the trees are whistling for the dogs!" She angrily pushed a strand of hair from her eyes. "And getting back to the issue at hand, what makes you think Gabriel doesn't know about the cabin? How do we know he hasn't been watching us for months? Maybe we go out there, in the middle of nowhere, USA, with nothing for miles, and he strikes? We'd be vulnerable and alone."

When they reached their car, Jake said. "Vulnerability is a fancy word for being caught off guard. I was an Eagle Scout, woman. You'll find my handsome face plastered next to the word 'prepared' in every dictionary in the world."

Callie rolled her eyes. "Yeah, you're a regular MacGyver."

He winked and opened her car door. As she ducked inside, fat droplets of rain plopped on her back and legs. The sporadic drip became a torrential downpour within seconds, drenching Jake before he made it to the other side of the car.

He jumped in, his black hair dripping, a goofy smile on his face. Callie couldn't help but laugh.

"There's your rain, Blaze. Hope you're happy."

She laughed harder. "Delirious!"

When Jake and Callie pulled up Jed's driveway, the rain had stopped and Darby and Amara were sitting in lawn chairs on the grass, laughing and watching Tyler play a game of 'keep away' with Blue and Lucky.

Jed, hearing them drive up, met them out front. "Tell me you got something," he said.

Jake held his thumb and forefinger together. "This close. Unfortunately, just as he was about to spill his guts, a tech came in and wheeled him away for more tests. We'll go back in the morning, but I'm worried the bastard will change his mind by then and decide not to talk."

"Tyler?" Darby called over her shoulder. "Come on, bud. Bring Blue and Lucky and your sweet little face inside, okay? You can help me start dinner. It's taco night!"

Jed held the front door open. "I can't believe how close we were to a lead. When are the good guys gonna catch a break?"

"Exactly my thoughts, Jed," Callie said, entering the foyer. "I swear, it's as if Gabriel has some special power, like a force field or shield protecting him."

Jed cocked his head. "Nah. It's all just dumb luck."

"You'll have to excuse her," Jake said, a gleam in his eye. "You remember? She's all about space. Captain Kirk, Star Fleet Command, Klingons."

Amara, lip-reading Jake's words, said, "Callie, you're a Trekkie? I love Star Trek!"

Darby smirked. "Of course you do."

Callie ignored them. "Have you heard anything back from Curt or Sawyer?" Then, eyeing Darby and Amara, she asked, "Do you both know what's going on? About the connection between the paintings Amara drew and the murder victim?"

Darby nodded. "Yes, Jed told us about it. What kind of sick mind does that? A pig trough? That poor girl. So sad."

"It is," Callie agreed, turning back to Jed. "Have the police figured anything out? Anything to tie this girl in with Gabriel?"

"Hey, Ty," Amara interrupted, sensing the conversation was not one Tyler should hear, "let's go check out the ice cream selection in the freezer!"

"Great idea!" Callie said with a forced smile.

Once Amara and Tyler had left the foyer, Jed continued. "So far, I haven't heard anything new. But, considering recent events, I expect to hear from them shortly."

"Recent events?" Jake asked.

"Another victim. Do you remember Sawyer handing me an envelope yesterday when he stopped by?"

"Maybe. A lot has happened the last few days."

"Yeah, no kidding." He squinted at Jake. "Sawyer found a manila envelope propped up against the front door. I blamed the postal service."

"And I'm guessing you owe the mail carrier an apology?" Jake prodded.

"Looks like. I opened the envelope today and what I found inside leads me to believe it was hand-delivered, specifically to us. Whoever sent it wanted to make sure it reached our eyes."

Callie, intrigued, leaned forward. "What was in it?" she whispered, unsure if she wanted an answer.

"Photographs. One was a picture of a young woman chained to a pole in what looked like a barn. I think it's the same girl in the photos Sawyer sent us—the one with the symbol on her head and her throat cut."

"Jeez, Louise," Darby said, wide-eyed. "Who would send that to you?" Jed frowned. "The same man who would send these."

He walked to the high table against the foyer wall, picked up an envelope, and brought it back to her. He pulled out a small stack of photos and showed the first one to her. "This first shot was taken in a pasture or field. I can't make out the woman's features, but it looks like someone has covered her in heavy stones."

"Jesus Christ," Jake murmured. "She was pressed to death?"

Callie felt her stomach flip, sure she would puke all over Jed's fine flooring.

"I think so," Jed said, somber. "The second picture," he held it up, "is a close-up of the body afterward. Notice the symbol on her forehead and inscription on her abdomen."

"No Chastity," Jake read aloud.

Looking more closely at the photograph, Callie slapped a hand over her mouth and looked at Jake. "Oh, God. Look at her palm. She's holding a nail."

Jake put a steadying arm around her. "I see it, Blaze. No doubt this is Gabriel's work. And whatever game he is playing, whatever delusions he's operating under, one thing is certain. He means this to be a message."

"A message that he's back?" Darby asked.

"No," Callie said softly. "Not a message—a warning."

"Huh?" Darby asked.

"Callie blinded the bastard with a ten-penny nail," Jake explained. "He wants us to know he hasn't forgotten what she did."

"Not only that," Callie said. "He wants me to know he's coming."

CHAPTER SIXTEEN

Sheridan Memorial Hospital
Fourth floor

The Apostle adjusted his clerical collar, entered the elevator, and pushed the button for the fourth floor. He planned to hit the pediatric wing, make a grand show of ministering to the sick children, then use the stairs and backtrack to the third floor.

To the Disciple.

As the elevator ascended, Gabriel recalled his shock when he'd learned Thomas Palmer was still alive. Not trusting the word of Simon of Cyrene, he'd called the hospital's information desk, identified himself as Palmer's brother, Tucker Simon, and asked the receptionist about his sibling's condition. At first, the woman had played dumb, claiming to have no record of a Thomas John Palmer ever being admitted to Sheridan Memorial.

Which was either an attempt to protect Palmer from thrill seekers or a ruse created by the Feds, or the locals, to keep Gabriel from discovering Palmer was still alive.

No matter. Eventually, using his charisma and a tinge of 'Devine' intervention (he chuckled inwardly at his cleverness), Gabriel was able to charm the young receptionist with the nasally voice and shy laugh to give it up.

"Okay," the receptionist, whose name was Dawn, whispered into the phone. "I will tell you, but you never heard it from me, okay? I could lose my job."

And you think I give a shit, you twat?

"Don't worry, Dawn," he had said sweetly. "You are too kind and, if I had to guess, much too pretty to lose your job over me."

Dawn giggled. In truth, she was oceans away from pretty, making Gabriel's words strike her that much harder.

"Your brother is here," she had told him. "He was in a coma, but it looks like he woke up. He's in room 306. But, again, you didn't hear that from me."

Bored, Gabriel picked at the scabs on the palm of his hand, opening the false stigmata he'd created days ago. "I swear on the life of my brother. Your secret is safe with me."

Of course, my 'brother' will be dead soon, Dawnie, making my vow null and void.

~

Gabriel stepped off the elevator and found himself in front of a vacant nursing station. Looking right, he gazed down the hospital corridor and spotted a woman in scrubs halfway down the hall. She was standing behind a medication cart, rummaging through a top drawer. After cackling at something a colleague said, she pulled out several cards of bubble-enclosed medication and ducked inside room 418.

Familiar with the pediatric floor and well known by its staff, Gabriel headed toward the lounge nicknamed 'Fairy Tale Forest.' It was an area dedicated to recreation and downtime for the occupants of the sixty-bed wing, most of them cancer patients. The room was divided into sections, each decorated with a storybook theme. Murals of castles, enchanted forests, and mythical animals brightened all four walls. There were video and board games, puzzles, and several televisions scattered around the room. The designer had thought of everything, adding a Lego board, a coloring station, and a snack bar.

"Father Gabriel!" a woman shouted from behind him, a little too loudly.

Gabriel turned to see a heavy-set woman with rosy cheeks and curly hair bouncing toward him. He sighed in annoyance.

"Carmella," he said tightly. "So good to see you again."

Fucking cow.

"I'm so glad you're here, Father!" she gushed. "We could really use your services! We have several little Catholics on the floor this week, and I'm sure many of them would love to receive communion. I have a list here, if you wouldn't mind?"

"That's what I'm here for," he said, inwardly sighing wearily. "Lead the way."

Tucker stood and stretched his cramping fingers. Gabriel's typewriter was old, its keys stiff, and the endless hunting and pecking on the keyboard was wreaking havoc on Tucker's carpal tunnel.

He had finished transcribing most of Gabriel's notes. Tucker buried his face in his hands, feeling defeated. The man who held the strings above his head, controlling him like a puppeteer, was a certifiable maniac. The jumbled writing and cryptic messages spoke of a fractured mind, one that could no longer distinguish between reality and fantasy.

A delusional psychopath who thinks he's Jesus fucking Christ himself!

He walked to the lone window in the room and gazed outside. Several acres of greenery stretched as far as the eye could see, but he saw none of it.

His mind was too busy crunching facts, devising strategies, and playing the 'what if' game.

What if I just leave this state? Go somewhere far away? Would he look for me?

Or...

What if I went to the cops? I still know a few pretty well. Not Devereaux, obviously, but maybe that Curtis Valdez guy? He seems less dickish than most. Would he understand? Help me?

Fuck, no.

He was in too deep. It didn't matter that he hadn't killed anyone—he was an accessory now. The only person who could get him out of this mess was himself.

If he could find the stones to do it.

He needed ammunition, a bargaining chip—something to turn the tables, to hold over Gabriel's head.

And he believed that something could be found in the barn.

He walked quickly to the front door, fearing if he dawdled, he would lose his nerve. Gabriel could be back any minute now, and to be caught in the very place he was told never to enter would not end well for him.

After opening the front door, he spent several moments looking toward the road and listening for the sound of tires crunching in the gravel.

He heard nothing.

Slipping outside, he jogged on tiptoes to the barn, a steady stream of sweat running down his back, settling in the crack of his ass. He paused at the barn door, pushed a strand of greasy hair from his damp forehead, and held his breath. Legs shaking, heart pounding, he put an ear to the wooden door and listened.

At first, all was silent. He adjusted his ear, pushing it flat against the door, and listened again. This time, he heard a moan.

Or, perhaps, in his heightened state, he'd only imagined it.

He listened again, but the moaning seemed to have stopped.

Determined to get to the truth, to find the 'golden egg' to lord over Gabriel, he slowly opened the barn door and stepped inside.

≈

Gabriel felt like screaming.

He'd visited twelve hospital rooms, administered communion to fifteen bald-headed children and their anxious parents. and inflated dozens of surgical gloves as if they were balloons—to the delighted squeals of the children in the lounge.

Pretending to enjoy the company of whining, snot-nosed kids was exhausting. He faked amusement as they tugged on his vestments, their high-pitched screams of 'Father, watch how fast I can run!' or 'Father, look what I drew!' turning his stomach.

Being around the little hellions gave him hives. Just because he'd vowed never to kill a child didn't mean he had to like them.

Tiny fuckers.

Still, he'd kept up the façade, patting little cheeks and making the sign of the cross to nearly every patient on the ward, despite their religious denomination, until his communion chalice was empty and he could escape.

...to his main mission, just one flight down on the third floor.

Waving goodbye to the smiling faces—*insufferable little pukes*—Gabriel stepped in front of the bank of elevators, pressed the button, and looked at his bare wrist, checking an imaginary watch while waiting for the next lift.

Just a regular guy, mindful of the time, administering to his flock.

The elevator on the right dinged, and the door slid open. Gabriel looked around but saw no one. He made a show of moving to the open door and, at the last minute, veered right around the side of the elevator's outer wall.

To the door marked "Stairs."

Moving as quickly as he dared, he removed his vestments and collar as he plowed down the steps to the third floor. At the third-floor landing, he spotted the small duffel bag he'd hidden in a corner.

He pulled a surgical mask, white lab coat, and laminated nametag from the bag, pulling them on over the civilian clothes he'd worn under his clerical garb. Holding up the ID he'd created that read *'D. Cyple, Physician,'* he chuckled before pinning it to his lab coat pocket. He was still unclear how he would end Thomas, but he wasn't worried.

He was the impending 'King of kings,' the Messiah to the world. He had no doubt he would find a way.

Opening the door to the third floor, he tried to ignore a scene he'd just witnessed on the pediatric floor above: a toddler girl in a baby carriage, sibling to a dying child, peacefully sleeping while clutching a doll.

A doll that bore an uncanny resemblance to the one he'd found in his mother's trunk.

What was it about that doll, that scene, that seemed to trigger a memory?

A toddler with a fucking doll? What does that have to do with anything?

Troubled and confused, he swept the image away to concentrate on the task at hand—killing his Disciple.

Tucker Simon squinted into the bowels of the barn, attempting to get his bearings. The powerful aromas of molding hay and decades-old manure assailed his nostrils. He sneezed once, twice, and moved forward. A rustling to his right caught his attention, and he walked toward it, his knees trembling.

"Hel-hello? Is anyone there?"

No response.

"I-I know you're in here. Call out, or you're on your own."

A murmur, a soft groan, echoed in his ears.

"Where—where are you? Hello?"

There was a stifled cry before he heard a woman's voice rasp, "Are you real? Oh, God, I'm here! Help me!"

Tucker's respirations increased, and his bladder cramped. Scooting to the far corner, desperate to pee, he pulled open his fly and relieved himself, hoping his bowels didn't follow suit.

Zipping up, he turned slowly, debating his next move. His instinct to flee was overridden by a desire to prove to himself he was not a coward. He continued forward.

"Help me," a soft voice wheezed again.

It was coming from a back stall, somewhere to the right.

Afraid he would chicken out, he sprinted awkwardly to the corner of the barn where the sound seemed to be coming from. On the ground, in the last stall, a woman lay curled on her side. She was bound in chains, a dirty rag resting against her chin. Tucker's first thought was that she must have loosened the gag across her mouth somehow.

His next thought—*caramel-colored hair, round ass, tits for days*—was less charitable.

He bent down and examined her restraints. The chains that held her looked ancient and could probably be broken by a simple bolt cutter. He stood again and surveyed his surroundings. On the far wall stood a bench with various tools.

He immediately spotted what he needed.

After collecting the tool, he walked back to the woman and squatted again.

"What's your name, gorgeous?"

The woman gave him a sour look. "In the grand scheme of things," she mumbled, "does that matter? We can get to know each other later when we're far from here. So, please! Get me out of here!"

Tucker rubbed his chin. "I suppose you'd be mighty grateful to anyone who helped you out of this mess, huh? Like, really, really thankful."

He leered at her, and the woman choked back the bile that had reached her throat.

"Are you—are you asking me to have sex with you?" she asked, incredulous. "In exchange for your being a decent human being?"

Tucker sat back a bit. "Hold on, now. I never said that. I'm not a scumbag, miss. I've never had to beg for sex before. I'm considered quite the catch among my peers."

The woman was having trouble keeping up. "Can you just get me out? Please?"

Tucker surveyed the chains, decided where the weakest link lay, and went to work. Within minutes, metal clinked beneath the bolt cutters, and the woman was free.

"Oh, thank you!" she cried, rubbing her wrists. "I've been here forever! Come on, let's hurry! He could be back any minute!"

Tucker thought he detected an accent in her words but could not place it. "Hang on, hang on. We have plenty of time." He looked her up and down. Dried blood dotted the corners of her mouth where she'd bitten her cheeks. She had an odd emblem on her forehead, some sort of symbol, though in the dim lighting of the barn, he couldn't tell if it was permanent or a temporary henna-type tattoo.

Her large green eyes sparkled. She had scraped, dirty knees and disheveled hair. Her plaid skirt was hiked to the top of her shapely thighs.

Tucker felt his erection building. *God damn! So fuckin' hot!*

Hiding the bulge in his jeans, he helped her to stand. She swayed a bit in his arms, exhausted and dehydrated.

Tucker mistook her weakness for flirtation. Attraction.

He wrapped an arm around her and brought her closer. It took a minute for the woman to understand his intent.

She pushed against his chest, but her attempt at creating distance was laughable. The muscles of her arms were weak from lack of use.

"I got you, baby," Tucker whispered, his putrid breath hot against her cheek. "Just let it happen. I can send you to the moon and back, and you won't even need a spaceship."

Forgetting all about Gabriel for the moment, Tucker's hands roamed her body, grabbed her ass, palmed her breasts. He caressed her nipples, mistaking their erection for excitement rather than the chilly air in the barn.

"Let go of me!" the woman screeched, trying to pull herself free from his arms.

Tucker chuckled lightly. "Your mouth says 'stop,' but your body says 'go.' Did you ever hear that expression before, doll?" He ducked his head near her neck and murmured, "You smell like sweat and dirt and sunshine, baby. I'm about to blow my load just holding you."

The woman twisted and pulled, a feral sound coming from her lips. She head-butted him, making his neck snap back just enough to expose his cheek.

Opening her mouth wide, she chomped down, biting him as hard as she could and drawing blood.

"Fuck!" he screamed, backing up, slapping his hand against his face. "Are you crazy, bitch?"

The woman screamed in response, bringing up a knee and connecting with Tucker's groin.

He howled, doubling over in pain. Melting to the floor, holding his balls with both hands, he curled into a fetal position and waited to die.

The woman wasted no time. She bent down, went through his pants pockets, and found his car keys. Giving him one last kick—this one in the temple—she sprinted toward the barn door and freedom.

Tucker Simon, unable to move, could do nothing to stop her. Instead, sobbing and rocking back and forth, he watched her reach the door.

Hands shaking, she pushed the barn door open and ran to the Honda parked outside.

And Fiona Clark, aka Faith McTavish, never looked back.

∽

Sheridan Memorial Hospital
Third floor

The cop in the metal chair by the door of room 306 had his head back, leaning against the wall. His mouth was open, his breathing steady.

Fucker is sleeping on the job. How perfect.

Gabriel smoothed down the lapel of his jacket, adjusted his mask, and started down the hall, peeking into patient rooms as he went by. On the opposite side of 306, two rooms down, a woman lay still, a machine softly whirring as it kept her alive.

She was unconscious. And alone.

Gabriel ducked inside room 303 and stood at the end of the bed. The patient was older, probably in her late seventies, a breathing tube down her throat.

Life support. What a joke. Kindest thing I can do is slit her throat and end her.

But, of course, he would not. Time would not allow it.

He reached for the clipboard at the foot of the bed and read her name. *Agnes Whitmore.*

"Hello, Agnes," he said softly. "I need to borrow your clipboard for a moment. Just a prop to lend an air of respectability, you see." Walking to the side of her bed, he bent close to her ear. "I could turn this machine off, Agnes. Kink the hose, turn off the alarms, yank the tube out. I could easily stuff one of those washcloths in your mouth and hold your nose." He patted her cheek. "Unfortunately, I am pressed for time. Which means you, my dear, will remain in this living hell, trapped in a body that has forsaken you."

He tapped the clipboard against the side rail. "See ya, Agnes."

Returning to the hallway, he padded softly to room 306. The cop was still in the same position, head back and snoring, a line of drool hanging from the corner of his mouth.

Disgusted, Gabriel cleared his throat, and the young cop jumped. "Oh, sorry," Gabriel said. "I guess you dozed off there, huh?"

The officer sat up straighter, his cheeks red. "Uh, no, Doc. Just, just resting my eyes. These fluorescent lights are killers."

Interesting choice of words...

Gabriel smiled sympathetically. "Oh, I know. This assignment has so many drawbacks, I'm sure. Anyway, my name is Doctor Cyple," he said, pointing to his ID. "I need to do a neurological evaluation on this patient. It will only take a minute."

The cop eyed him suspiciously. "Can't say I've seen you before, Doc. You new here?"

Irritation building, Gabriel chewed his inner cheek until he tasted blood. "Nah, just new to this patient. His regular neurologist had an emergency and asked for my help." Pausing, he cocked his head. "You know, this exam is critical to Mr. Palmer's well-being. You could even say it's a matter of life and death. But if you're uncomfortable...."

He let the words hang, enjoying the cop's discomfort.

"Well, no, sir. I wouldn't want to put the prisoner, er, I mean the patient, in harm's way. Carry on."

Gabriel winked, clasping the cop on the shoulder. "I won't be long."

CHAPTER SEVENTEEN

"ENVY"

"A heart at peace gives life to the body, but envy rots the bones."

Proverbs 14:30

The Apostle tucked his fingers under the edge of his mask, popped a mint in his mouth, quietly entered room 306, and, one hand still on the doorhandle, eyed the motionless figure in the hospital bed. Palmer's face was ashen, his balding scalp rife with dried blood and scabs where he'd obsessively pulled his hair out.

Eyes closed, he appeared to be sleeping.

Gabriel held up the push/pull handle and gently closed the door, waiting to hear the soft clack of the latch as it slid home. In the stillness of the room, the audible click seemed more like a sonic boom than a muted tap.

Still, the Disciple slept on—oblivious, undisturbed, vulnerable.

Gabriel dropped his head against the door, his respirations easy. He narrowed his gaze on the sleeping man, contempt humming through his veins. His hostility toward TJ Palmer, his so-called 'Disciple,' was currently at war with another feeling—an unfamiliar, overwhelming sense of self-loathing for failing to kill Palmer the first time.

Padding on tiptoes toward the bed—his compulsion demanding he count the steps he took—Gabriel examined his surroundings as he moved. He needed a tool to complete his mission.

Something simple, something clean, something silent.

Fucking Judas! I could snap your neck like a fucking twig and never break a sweat.

Or he could use a pillow and snuff out the Disciple without leaving a mark. He'd done that before.

Held the bitch down, watched her puny, wrinkled hands scrape at mine as she fought for her life.

Admittedly, his mother hadn't put up much of a fight.

Gabriel harbored nothing but hatred for Meredith Sterling. He believed she was responsible for a litany of abuses, a slate of imaginary horrors, committed against him. But the accusations he leveled were meritless—false memories conjured within his mind and without a grain of truth. Regardless, to him, she was the woman who had never cared for him, never nurtured him as God expected all mothers to nurture their sons.

The warped voices in Gabriel's tattered mind spoke to him unceasingly even now, told him Meredith had looked at her only child as inhuman, a hideous creature who tested the boundaries of even a mother's love.

All because he'd killed Eileen Callahan—his father's wife—at age ten.

That he'd done it for Meredith had meant nothing to her; that he'd done it to make her happy was ignored. She had continued to look at him as if he were a monster.

Reality, however, begged to differ. Meredith had, indeed, shielded and protected her morally depraved, psychologically damaged son for as long as possible. In the end, though, she was far too broken, and he far too deranged, to be saved.

Meredith had been unable to save herself or her son.

And even if she could, by his fifteenth year, Jeremy was so far gone not even a hundred Merediths could have saved him.

He closed his eyes, recalling the day he'd brazenly walked into his mother's room at the Sunrise Horizons Nursing Facility, strangled her with rosary beads, then placed a pillow over her head to finish her off.

Karma. Poetic justice. The grand plan.

Words that meant nothing to some, and everything to others. To Gabriel, aware that the last day of his mother's life was also the first time she'd laid eyes on him in decades, those words meant more.

They meant providence.

He'd found the visit cathartic. Soon after, he'd changed his name to Gabriel Devine and taken on his greatest role of all.

The Apostle.

Along his journey, he had claimed many lives using various lethal means. But nothing compared to the near-orgasmic satisfaction of snapping a neck using the simplest tool of all—his bare hands.

More than once, he'd heard the grinding pop of vertebrae, felt it vibrate through his fingers, before his victim's head twisted unnaturally to one side or the other.

The sense of completeness, of power, was intoxicating.

Decision made, he moved closer to the man in the bed. The call bell to the nurse's station was wrapped loosely around the side rail, close to the patient, as all nursing assistants were trained to do. Gabriel removed it and placed it higher on the bed, beyond Palmer's reach, then glanced back over his shoulder.

No movement outside the door. The asshole cop probably went back to sleep.

Gabriel smiled in anticipation, lowered his mask, and bent closer to the Disciple's face.

The scent of mint and aftershave tickled Palmer's nose, and his lashes fluttered. Eyes widening in recognition, fear slammed into his gut. A scream began to build deep within TJ's chest, and Gabriel shushed him, clamping a hand tightly over his face.

Gasping for air, terrified, TJ scratched and tugged at the large hand that covered his mouth.

"Hello, shithead," Gabriel whispered. "Remember me? I'm the one who killed you the first time. Guess I didn't do too good a job, though, huh?"

TJ's nostrils flared, and he blinked rapidly, eyes darting around the room. Frantic, he swatted at the bed rail, searching for the call bell that was no longer there.

"The bell? Yeah, sorry. I had to move it," Gabriel said. "Can't have you calling for help now, can I?"

Hyperventilating, TJ's breaths came in huffs while a mixture of snot and saliva made a wet, whistling sound against Gabriel's fingers. Shaking his head violently, he continued to claw and grab at the hand that silenced him.

"I want you to know a few things before I end you," Gabriel continued in a hushed tone. "You will not be given the seal of God to protect you. You've forfeited any right to be counted among the saved."

Tears pooled in TJ's eyes.

"This is what happens when someone crosses me. You disobeyed me. I specifically forbade harming children, yet you killed Madison Gibbs and kidnapped that young boy." He pushed his hand down harder over TJ's mouth. "You took my sister, even after I expressly prohibited you from doing so! Look into my eyes, cretin!" he rasped, spittle flying. "Know my wrath! I am the Apostle, the Chosen One, the Messiah! My face is the last you will see!"

TJ bucked in the bed, trying to alert the guard outside his door. Heart hammering beneath his breastbone, mind whirling, he searched for a plan, a solution—a way to live.

But everything happened too fast.

The last thing former medical examiner Thomas John Palmer saw were the cold eyes of the mentor he'd followed; the last thing he felt, the firm grip of a madman's hands, one behind his head, the other beneath his chin.

And the last thing he heard was the resounding crack that accompanied the swift upward twist of his neck, severing his cervical spine and ending his life.

The pop as vertebral bones splintered, ripping through TJ's spinal cord just below his head, was louder than Gabriel had anticipated.

He shivered, eyes glued to his victim, waiting for the Splendor.

Five minutes later, the room remained quiet, the patient still. There was no brilliant light emitting from the Disciple, no visible rising of his soul to the heavens.

Where the fuck is it?

He continued to wait, reluctant to concede defeat, unwilling to admit that witnessing a soul's journey had, once again, eluded him.

Or had it?

As if a different kind of light shone down, Gabriel had a sudden burst of understanding—a flash of knowing that was brilliant in its simplicity yet had evaded him for years.

From the beginning, he'd been eliminating sinners—human beings who had stained the world and did not deserve to be here.

Why did I not see this before? Sinners do not ascend into the heavenly kingdom! All this time, I have been searching for something that will never be!

Nearly weeping with joy, the Apostle held onto the side of the bed and dropped to his knees in thanks.

He'd had it all wrong.

He would not, could not, witness the Splendor upon the death of a sinner. Those guilty of grievous sin were destined for hell, not for heaven.

No, a sinner would not do. He needed someone pure.

He needed an innocent.

Rising, he examined his work before adjusting the dead man's head to a more natural angle. Next, he dug into a jacket pocket and removed a marker, a roll of gauze, and a pocketknife. Lifting TJ's hospital gown, he began writing his message.

No Patience.

When Gabriel finished writing, he placed TJ's left arm on a bedside towel. Using the pocketknife, he hastily carved seven cuts into the man's forearm before wrapping the arm in the roll of gauze.

Since TJ's heart had stopped beating, bleeding was minimal.

Next, he took TJ's water beaker from the bedside table. He reached inside the dead man's mouth, pulled on his tongue until it protruded from his lips, and dribbled water over the lower part of his face and hospital gown. Medical personnel would, at first glance, surmise that Palmer had suffered a fatal seizure. The actual cause of death would likely not be known until he was moved.

Oh sure, suspicion would arise with the flop of his head, the message on his belly, the cuts on his arm. But no one would know for sure until the inevitable autopsy was performed. By then, Gabriel hoped to have all his loose ends tied up in a bright, red bow.

He straightened his white coat, positioned the mask back over his mouth, and walked confidently to the door. He didn't believe the young cop standing guard would give him a second glance. Even if he did, Gabriel was unconcerned.

He'd just killed someone using nothing but his bare hands.

And he could do it again.

≈

Tucker Simon felt like he was dying.

Curled up on the barn floor, dirt clinging to the side of his face, he touched a hand to his forehead, his fingers dancing over the knot forming there. His cheek ached where she'd bitten him, his ball sack was on fire, and vomit sat in the back of his throat, waiting to make an entrance.

Or, more appropriately, an exit.

He groaned, trying to sit up. He had to get moving, get out of here. The Apostle would be back any minute, and once he saw his captive had escaped, it would be all over for Tucker.

Rolling to his back, he sat up and looked around. The barn appeared empty. He wondered how long he'd been out of it.

Wondered how long the bitch had been gone.

"Hello?" he called out, knowing he needed to check but fearing a response. "Is anyone here?"

The only answer was the tinny groan of corrugated metal flapping on the barn roof. He swayed to his feet, patting his pockets for the car keys. As he searched, an elusive memory skated through his mind, one he knew was important to remember. The memory floated, just out of reach, until, suddenly, it was there.

His car keys, however, were not.

Shit, shit, shit! That hoofwanking bunglecunt has my car!

He half-walked, half-stumbled to the barn door. He had to get out and find help, consequences be damned. He'd rather take his chances in court and live than face Gabriel's wrath and certain death.

He found the heavy door ajar and, grunting, pushed it open. Sunlight flooded the interior of the barn, and he shielded his eyes against the burning glare. Stepping outside, he made it only a few feet before something heavy slammed into the back of his head, sending searing pain exploding through his skull.

And, for the second time that day, Tucker Simon crumpled to the ground.

❧

Faith McTavish gripped the steering wheel of the unfamiliar Honda, eyes blurry from tears, trying to get her bearings.

She knew very little about this area of Sheridan. In the months she and Caleb had stayed with Jed, she'd traveled only a few times to Wyoming.

Tyler, she admonished herself. *His name is Tyler, not Caleb.*

But forgetting their true names—Fiona Clark and Tyler Duncan— was the least of her problems. Right now, she needed to focus on getting away from not one psycho but two.

The man called the Apostle, who had kidnapped her, and the skeevy man with bad breath and even worse B.O. who had just tried to rape her.

Or had he?

Still blurry from the effects of the drug she'd been given, her mind was a murky pool of incoherent thoughts and vague memories. She assumed the drug's effects—*Valium? Rohypnol? GHB?*—were compounded by her empty stomach.

As if on cue, her stomach rumbled, reminding her she hadn't eaten in at least twenty-four hours. Adding insult to injury, she had no cell phone, and the car had no GPS. Even worse, the gas gauge was nearing the 'danger' line.

Meaning she didn't have much time to fuck around or wander aimlessly.

She knew she'd be safe if she could just get to a service station or supermarket. She could ask someone to call Jed's business line, and he would help her.

Despite everything she'd done, he would help her. She knew this deep in her bones. Jed liked her; Jed was good people.

But Jed has no idea what you've done, what you've kept from him!

As she drove, she recalled her last days in Philadelphia before she'd gone on the run. Fed up with feeling like a common whore or second-class citizen in her lover's eyes, she'd finally decided to do something about it.

As Tyler's nanny, she had access to everything in the Duncan home: money, credit cards, and routing numbers. Angry at Graeme for ignoring her and refusing to leave his wife Emily, Faith had begun a campaign to secure her future.

Because hell hath no fury.

Every day, she'd check Graeme's activity on his phone and laptop, fearing he'd found another lover. She copied his credit card numbers, stole money from his wallet, and spied on Emily, hoping to discover the 'perfect' wife was not so perfect after all.

But she found nothing to suggest Emily was anything other than what she portrayed to the world—a graceful, kind, beautiful wife and mother.

Desperate, Fiona eventually broke into the family safe, searching for money to leave Philadelphia and start over. Instead, she found dozens of newspaper articles, several polaroid pictures from years ago, and a stack of legal papers drawn up by the Weston family attorney, Gideon Sherman.

She had no idea why Graeme had papers that rightfully belonged to Randall Weston, documents that hinted at criminal activity. But before she could question Graeme about it, he was dead.

Shot point blank, in the back, three times. It was a murder that both she and Tyler witnessed.

After the killing, fearing for their safety, Fiona Clark had photographed the contents of the safe and fled with Tyler.

And had run straight to where those papers and news clippings led her.

To Montana and Jed Devereaux

≈

"Wake up, Simon of Cyrene. Your time has come!"

Tucker lay on his back, a sharp stone poking painfully against his spine, a foot resting on his chest. He opened his eyes for a second, then squeezed them shut again; the bright light only intensified the terrible pain in his head. His thoughts were muddled, chaotic.

"Where...where am I?" he mumbled, eyes still closed. "What is... what's going on?"

Gabriel stared down at the man beneath his boot. "Tell me what happened here, Simon. Tell me about the woman." He pressed his foot down harder, delighting in watching Tucker's breath hitch, and added, "Tell me what you did to my prisoner."

"Nothing," Tucker grunted. "I-I didn't touch her. I swear!"

Gabriel placed even more of his weight on Tucker's chest. "Do you expect me to believe that? The truth, now! I grow weary of your lies!"

Tucker sobbed. His hands held Gabriel's boot at the toe and heel, instinct telling him to rise, to remove the foot currently compressing his lungs.

Survival told him to stay the fuck down if he wanted to live.

"I'm waiting," Gabriel said through clenched teeth. "What happened here, Simon?"

Tucker winced. "Hard. To. Talk," he said, breathless. "Can. You. Let. Up?"

Gabriel removed his foot and casually stuffed his hands in his pockets as if they were just a few friends hanging out, deciding where to go for a beer. It was a bizarre move, one that contradicted the genuine threat that Tucker faced.

Dying via positional asphyxia.

"There," Gabriel said. "Happy now?"

Tucker was happy—indescribably so.

"Thank—thank you," he said, standing.

"Tell me," Gabriel growled.

"Yes, yes. The woman. Well, I found her, right?" he said, stalling, trying to devise an excuse Gabriel might buy. Hesitantly, he pointed. "Over there, in the corner?"

"No shit. Get to the good part."

"Um, well, I...uh, I found her, see? And I went to talk to her, just talk. But she tricked me! She was like a sorcerer or Eve in the Garden of

Eden!" Tucker watched Gabriel's face closely, hoping to see evidence of understanding, belief, or even mercy.

"So," he continued, "she like, I don't know, mesmerized me or something. She threw her body at me, talked dirty, showed me her privates!"

Gabriel raised his eyebrows in disbelief.

"No, honest!" Tucker whined. "She showed me her titties, forced me to release her using her feminine wiles. And then, when I did—on account of I had no choice—she attacked me."

Gabriel flinched. '*On account of I had no choice?*' *Who the fuck are you? Hoss Cartwright?*

Gabriel released his hands from the prison of his pockets and folded his arms. "Really? She attacked you?"

Tucker swallowed. "Um, yep, that's what she did. Attacked me, kicked me, bit my face. See?" He turned his cheek to Gabriel, theatrically pointing out the bloodied bite mark.

Gabriel sighed. "Yeah, I see. What else did she do?"

"Uh, um…" Tucker stuttered again. "She… she kneed me square in the nuts! I swear, it will be a miracle if I can still piss!"

Gabriel moved his hands to his hips and tipped his face to the sun as if mulling over the story Tucker had given.

But it was all a pretense. Gabriel knew Tucker was full of shit. His captive was not a slut or a whore, and she would never throw her body at such a disgusting creature.

No woman would.

Gabriel looked around the immediate vicinity and said, "If what you say is true, we will deal with her. She cannot have gotten far on foot."

Tucker wiped sweat from his brow and gulped. Under any other circumstances, it would have been comical—the gawky, geeky nerd with greasy hair and bad acne gulping like a cartoon character.

"I, uh…"

"What?" Gabriel snapped. "What is it?"

Tucker swallowed hard again, this time so quietly that Gabriel missed it. "She isn't on foot. At least—at least I don't think so. My car keys are...." Afraid to finish the sentence, Tucker mouthed 'poof' and patted his empty pockets.

His only hope was to convince Gabriel he was the victim of unseen forces plotting against him and was not responsible for his vile behavior.

The blood drained from Gabriel's face. "Your car? She took your car?" Arms pumping, he walked swiftly to the other side of the barn, where Tucker's Honda had last been parked. The car was gone.

"Fuuccck!" Gabriel bellowed.

Tucker ran up from behind and said, "That's what I was trying to tell you, boss. She must have taken my keys while I was out of it."

Walking in circles, boots kicking up dust, Gabriel wove his fingers through his hair and pulled, hard. "No way. No fucking way!"

"Maybe we can, uh, track her down? You know, stop her before she...." Tucker stopped, chilled by what he was thinking. "Well, we can talk to her, right? Threaten her if she goes to the cops or something."

"You really are a dumb son of a bitch, aren't you?" Gabriel screeched, punching his good thigh with a fist. "Don't you see what you've done?" He jabbed a finger toward Tucker. "You did this! You've killed her!"

Dumbfounded, Tucker sputtered. "Wha... What?"

"She has no brakes, you fucking idiot!"

Tucker looked at him stupidly for a moment. "No brakes? Why would my car have no brakes? I just had them install new pads. The garage also checked the rotors, the brake fluid, the works. There's no way they'd fail unless..." He glanced suspiciously at Gabriel. "...unless someone messed with them."

Gabriel spat and a glob of mucus landed on Tucker's shoe. Starting a slow clap, he said, "Bravo, genius! It took you long enough, though, didn't it? Yeah, asshole. I messed with your brakes."

Tucker looked genuinely wounded. "Why?" he whispered. "Why

would you do that?"

Enraged, Gabriel reached Tucker in two quick strides. He grabbed him by the neck and forced him to his knees. "Because you disgust me, pig," he growled. "You are a liability, a threat. Not to mention a pain in my ass. And I no longer need your services."

Terrified, Tucker Simon stared into the darkest, blackest eyes he'd ever seen and did something he'd never done before.

He prayed.

And he was still calling out to God as Gabriel Devine choked, kicked, bit, and pummeled him to death in a fury compared to none.

An Apostle's fury.

Later that day, after the sun went down, Gabriel loaded the broken, battered corpse of Tucker Simon into the bed of his pickup truck and drove to the back pasture, his rich baritone filling the truck cab—

So, I'll cherish the old rugged cross,
Till my trophies at last I lay down.
I will cling to the old rugged cross,
And exchange it someday for a crown.

Gabriel's plan was simple. He would bury Tucker Simon in the same grave as Bob Dietrich.

Just open the hole again and toss the bastard in. Work smarter, not harder, I always say!

But, as he drew nearer to the grave of St. Michael's former groundskeeper, something in the background caught his eye. He stopped the truck, rubbed his chin, and waited for his thought to take shape.

And it did.

A fresh inspiration, a brilliant scheme. A new and improved way to dispose of Tucker Simon.

Inching closer, Gabriel pulled next to the object that had caught his eye and hopped out of the truck. Examining his find, he walked around to the side of the machine, turned a rusted key, and smiled as the engine coughed and wheezed and finally caught.

He hadn't thought it would run; he'd lost faith for a moment.

Turning the old key back to the 'off' position, he jumped into his pickup and headed for the shed and his supply of gasoline. In his rearview mirror, like a sentry standing guard, sat the muse of his latest brainchild.

A thirty-year-old woodchipper—ready to serve.

CHAPTER EIGHTEEN

"Hey, Darbs? How's the packing coming?"
Callie stood at the doorway to Darby's room in the main house, leaning against the doorjamb.

"Almost done," Darby said. "Tell me again how putting us all together in a cabin in the woods is safer than staying in Jed's house? This place is a virtual fortress, Cal. I mean, his locks have locks. And the place is covered in high-tech cameras and surveillance stuff. What do we have in the middle of nowhere?"

Callie shrugged. "Anonymity? Invisibility? Hell, I don't know the right answer, Darby. All I know is that men with much more experience than either of us think going to the Devereaux cabin is safer than staying here. Kind of ignorant of us to double-guess the experts."

Darby dropped her head. "Of course. I didn't mean to imply I was smarter than anyone," she said softly. "I was just...curious."

Good going, Callahan! Where the hell were you when they doled out brains?

Callie walked into the room and put an arm around Darby. "Oh, I'm sorry, Darbs. I didn't mean to make you feel...." She shook her head. "Lately, I can't seem to say anything right. Forgive me?"

Darby smiled widely, hugging her friend back. "There's nothing to forgive, girlfriend. I get it. Gabriel's been stuck in all our craws like a hair in a biscuit. Be glad when that spawn of the devil gets his comeuppance."

Callie laughed. "Me too. But for now, we need to stay safe. Gabriel knows where we are and has been spying on this place for God knows how long. At least at Jake's parents' place, we can monitor the grounds better. I mean, the cabin is smaller. So is the property."

"So, fewer places to plan an ambush?" Darby said with a frown.

Callie nodded, somber. "You know, there is another option here for you, Darbs."

Darby cocked her head to the side, confused. When comprehension dawned, she shook her head violently. "Oh, hell no! You think I'm going to hightail it back to Virginia just when things heat up? No, ma'am. I don't play like that. When I make a commitment to see something through, I see it through."

Callie smirked. "In it to win it?"

"Correctamundo, my friend. Besides," she wiggled a brow, "what if Jed needs me?"

Callie laughed. "If you're sure? Anyway, it might be fun! Cozy, anyhow. According to Jed, he and Jake and the rest of the Scooby Gang will take turns staying with us at the house. We figure to leave late at night—either today or tomorrow—under cover of darkness.

"Okay, I'll be ready. After I finish up here, I'll pack up for Tyler." She bit the corner of her lip. "Never trust a six-year-old boy to remember his toothbrush and underwear."

Smiling, Callie said, "Truer words!"

Jake sat at the kitchen island, staring at Jed's cell phone and twirling a beer bottle. Next to him, Jed nursed a Jack and Coke. After a few moments of silence, Jake spoke.

"What the holy hell are we supposed to do with this?" he asked, frustrated. "Where did they find her? When did Sawyer send this?"

"Just now," Jed said glumly. "This lady," he nodded toward the image on his phone's screen, "was, for lack of a better word, 'posed' in front of a strip club in Ranchester."

"A strip club?"

"Yeah. A dive called Bushes and Boobie Traps."

"Ain't that original," Jake snarled. "We got an ID on her?"

"Not yet. But it looks like the woman we saw in the photo that was sent here, the one with the stones on her chest and the writing on her belly."

"And holding a nail in her palm," Jake added sourly.

"Right. Those pictures were sent to us by the killer shortly after he stoned her to death, right? At least, that's our working theory. But in these official police photos, the victim is posed where her body was discovered, and there was no nail, ten-penny or otherwise, found in her hand."

"So he kills her in one location, then transports her to another. And, for reasons we may never understand, he poses her twice—once at the death scene, which is strictly for our benefit, and then again at the dumping ground to toy with investigators. I think he's sending us another message."

"That says?"

Jake frowned. "That says he's in charge and not afraid to take chances."

Jed nodded. "Because he doesn't think we have a snowball's chance in hell of catching him."

"Exactly," Jake said. "What else you got?"

Jed pointed to the dead woman on the screen. "If you look more closely at Sawyer's crime scene photos, you'll see something hanging out of the pocket of her skirt."

Jake studied the picture. "All I see is red, brother. This son of a bitch left her in the most vulnerable and disgusting way possible. Her skirt is pulled way up, her legs spread... There's a freaking brand on her crushed head." He pressed his lips together. "What am I looking for here?"

"See that, hanging from her left pocket?"

Jake stared at the phone. In truth, he was so angry he was having trouble focusing.

"Here, I'll enlarge it," Jed said, touching the screen and widening his fingers.

"Shit. Rosary beads," Jake said. "Gabriel's calling card."

"Yeah. Which, for those doubting Thomases in the back, leaves little question that Callie's brother is responsible."

Jake stood. "Oh, it's him, Jedidiah. The pictures delivered here, the biblical references, the ten-penny nail, the rosary. You know, we never released that connection to the public."

"The one between the Apostle killings and the rosary beads?"

Jake nodded. "Yep. Only those close to the investigation and Gabriel know that tidbit of truth." He opened the pantry closet and stared at its contents, not really seeing anything. Turning, he said, "We need to get the women and Tyler out of this house. Gabriel is spiraling, and there's no telling what he'll do next."

"Agreed," Jed said. "I can't help but wonder where his head is, though. Why wouldn't he have killed them where they were found? Like, outside of this Bushes and Boobie Traps dive? The place is fairly remote and closes at two in the morning. I don't know, man. It's like he's acting in two different performances or playing two different roles—one for us, one for the cops."

"Gabriel is fifty shades of crazy," Jake said. "It's damn near impossible to know where his head is at. The good news? All killers—no matter how clever they pretend to be—will fuck up, eventually. They'll leave behind a partial print, cigarette butt, or shoe impression. They'll brag to the wrong person, forget to pick up a shell casing, drop their wallet while moving a corpse."

"Your lips to God's ears, Jake. I have a feeling the only way we'll catch this son of a bitch is if he fucks up."

"Oh, he will. He's too narcissistic not to."

"So, what now? We have to wait until he kills someone else?"

"Let's hope it doesn't come to that. This asshole is an organized killer with a history that, I'm sure, goes back farther than we can imagine. He follows certain behaviors we've come to expect from these types of killers, habits that help us narrow down who we are dealing with."

"Such as?"

"Such as having three points of contact with a victim—where predator and prey first encounter each other, the location of the actual killing, and the area where the corpse is found. Gabriel differs from other cases I've worked on because he takes the time to reposition his victims."

"But why?" Jed asked. "Why not just take a picture at the dump site? Why go to the trouble of posing them a second time? Just to show us he can? That he's committed to his freaking cause?"

"He wants the intimate connection with Callie, I think. The 'Only you will know what this means' kind of link between them. Posing this lady with the same type of nail Callie used to blind him creates that connection."

"Like a 'See what I did for you?' kind of thing? Showing her something that has meaning only to her?"

"If I had to guess? Yeah, that's what I'd say."

"Makes sense in a fucked-up, Gabriel kind of way. So, what's next? I was thinking with the religious slant of these killings, we may want to enlist some help. I mean, neither of us is what you'd call a 'devout' Christian. Maybe we need a fresh pair of eyes to look at this, someone who understands the symbolism. Maybe we need...."

Jake jumped on his train of thought before Jed could finish his sentence. "A priest. We need a priest."

∽

Callie climbed the outer stairs to the garage apartment and knocked on the door. When there was no answer, she knocked harder.

Then, realizing her knocking was literally falling on deaf ears, she chuckled.

Dumbass...

Twisting the knob, she let herself into the apartment. Amara was sitting on the couch, doodling on a sketch pad.

Walking up beside her, Callie tapped a shoulder. "Hey, you," she signed. "Everything okay? You seem a million miles away."

Amara blinked rapidly as if just realizing she had company. Frowning, she closed the sketch pad. "It just happened again. Twice, actually. The fugue state or whatever you call it, where I have no concept of time or place or self."

Callie sat beside her. "Okay, well, whatever is calling to you, compelling you to draw these things, we'll deal with it together. Show me what you got, kiddo."

Amara flipped the pad open to her first drawing. In it, a woman and small child, dirty and bleeding, seemed to be trapped in a deep ditch or dark hole.

Callie drew in a breath. "I'll be damned."

"What? You know this place?"

Callie nodded. "I do. It's the well Tyler and I were thrown into by that son of a bitch Palmer. That's us in the drawing."

Amara bounced her right leg up and down, a nervous habit Callie recognized immediately. It was a coping mechanism she'd used herself on many occasions.

The first time was when she'd learned about the death of her mother.

"Okay," Callie said, "what else you got there? Tell me it's just a photo of Katie and me, Halloween in 1995, dressed up and looking ridiculous as Garth and Wayne."

Amara frowned. "Garth and who?"

Callie rolled her eyes. "Never mind. Just show me what you got."

Amara flipped to the next page and handed the pad to Callie.

The drawing was a dual illustration, one portrait in the forefront and a larger image toward the top, seemingly behind the first one. In the closer of the two, a woman was slumped in front of a dumpster, skirt hiked to her thighs. The left side of her forehead was crushed, while the right side had an unknown emblem emblazoned into the flesh. A set of pink rosary beads peeked out from the pocket of her raised skirt, a bizarre juxtaposition of good and evil.

In the background image, a man's head dipped to his chest as he lay propped against an ATM, dozens of coins scattered around him. He, too, had rosary beads in a pocket.

"Oh my God," Callie gasped. "This must be so hard for you."

"Yeah," Amara said glumly. "I've been trying to figure out if there is a pattern to my drawings. Like, do I get flashes of the past and present? Or the past and the future? It would be nice to know if these folks are already gone or if we can still save them."

Callie wrapped an arm around Amara's shoulder. "I can say for certain that this woman," she touched the picture, "died recently. Gabriel was kind enough to send photographs, the asshole, so she is already gone. And the woman in the first painting you showed me, the one in chains with the slit throat, was found recently."

Amara swallowed. "Dead?"

"Unfortunately, yes."

"Then why the hell did I get this so-called gift? What good does it do if I can't save someone?"

Callie frowned. "Not sure, exactly. Maybe your ability is more for providing a chronological timeline of Gabriel's murders. Or, perhaps, it's a still-developing gift? Could be that, as time goes on and you gain more experience, it will become more of a predictive thing than a historical timeline."

Amara rolled her eyes, and Callie couldn't help but grin.

Another Callahan trait in the books!

"Well, whatever it means," Callie said, snapping some pictures with her phone, "we need to show it to Sawyer and Curt. As far as I know, they haven't found either of these people yet. Perhaps the drawing can give them a clue where to look."

When Callie and Amara opened the door to the upstairs apartment, they found Jake standing on the other side of it.

Callie jumped. "Jesus, Devereaux! Are you trying to kill me?"

Jake smirked. "Nah. I just like to watch you bounce."

Amara giggled.

Callie narrowed her eyes. "When you're done with the jokes, maybe you can enlighten us on the plan?"

"Sure, I can do that," he said with a wink. "We are heading over to the cabin in a few. Once there, Jed and I will set up some simple security measures, like cameras and motion lights. I will take most of the night shifts since I have to start my new job on Monday. He and the others will split the day shifts. We'll take turns on the weekends."

"Hopefully, there won't be a ton of weekends to cover," Callie said softly. "I'd like to get my life back soon."

Jake gave her a reassuring hug. "That's the plan, Stan. Now, let's get packed up and on the road. We're taking Jed's Suburban. He rarely uses it, so even if Gabriel has been watching the house, he probably wouldn't recognize it. Just to be safe, Jed, Darby, and the pups will follow in a rental."

Callie shuddered. "Safe? Not to be that guy, but I won't feel safe until Gabriel is behind bars."

"You and me both, Blaze. You and me both."

Fiona gripped the leather wheel tighter, her tears falling freely now. The road she'd found herself on was desolate, unpaved, and spooky as hell.

"Think!" she commanded herself.

Studying the dash of the unfamiliar vehicle, she searched again for a navigational system, knowing it was futile. The Honda had to be twenty years old. The steering wheel felt tight, the brakes sluggish, and a strange whistling sound came from the defroster.

Piece of shit car!

She studied the sky as if the answer to her location lay in a cloud. North? South? She legitimately had no idea where she had been or the direction she was traveling.

Trying to calm her racing heart, she thought of Jed and what she would say to him when she saw him again. In her fantasy mind, she would confess her sins, and he would swoop her up in his arms, kiss her madly, tell her all was forgiven.

Of course, she knew that scenario would not happen. Jed was a principled man, a man who stood on the shoulders of truth. Her betrayal, her deceit, would only cement his disgust.

But she had to try.

For it was being alone, without him, that had released the blindfold over her eyes and brought forth the truth.

She was in love with him. Probably had been for months.

A new sense of urgency filled her soul as she digested her admission.

I am in love with him. I need to fix this!

Raking a hand through her tangled, dirty hair, she focused on the winding road ahead, then tensed as she came to a particularly sharp curve.

Her foot tapped the brake pedal. Nothing happened.

She pushed down harder, panicked, steering into the curve. The pedal reached the floor, unresponsive.

No brakes? Why aren't they working? Oh God, what do I do?

She lifted the emergency brake handle, hearing only a series of hollow clicks. The car hesitated briefly but continued to careen forward.

Oh, God! I can't stop!

Rounding the bend, she tugged the wheel hard to the left, then overcorrected to the right. The car fishtailed momentarily before falling into a full-blown spin. Screaming, wrestling desperately with the wheel to no avail, Fiona fought for control as the car made its final revolution before leaping through a rusted guardrail and tumbling down a thirty-foot embankment.

Halfway down the hill, the driver's door popped open, and Fiona was catapulted the remaining fifteen feet, landing with a thud seconds before the back tires of the Honda rolled over her chest.

$\sim$

"Are we almost there yet?" Tyler said from the back seat. "My legs hurt from sitting."

"Can you wait another ten minutes, bud?"

Tyler nodded.

"Hey, do you like to fish, little man?" Jake asked. "We have a pond out back my dad keeps stocked, mostly bass and catfish. Then we have Bighorn Lake and Goose Creek nearby, just bursting with fish waiting to be caught. And Sibley Lake is a great place to sink a line and come up with a massive rainbow trout."

Tyler shook his head. "I never, ever went fishing."

"Never? Well, you're in luck! My brother Jed is the best fisherman I know." He looked in the rearview mirror and winked. "But don't tell him I said that."

"My dad was gonna take me," Tyler said quietly, "but he never got the chance."

Amara, in the seat next to Tyler, squeezed his hand. She hadn't caught most of the conversation, but you didn't need to hear it all to understand the child's torment.

His body language spoke volumes.

"Well, I, for one, look forward to learning," Callie said. Giving Jake a wink of her own, she added, "But you or Jake will have to bait the hook. I don't do worms."

Tyler snickered. "Deal!"

Jake checked his side mirrors for the thousandth time, eyes squinting in concentration, before turning to Callie. "Can you get Jed on the horn and put him on speaker?"

Callie turned in her seat and glanced out the rear window. She saw nothing.

"Why? Do you think we're being followed? Did you see something?"

"No, but I want to make sure Jed hasn't either. I haven't seen anything suspicious, but it's hard to see behind his vehicle. Just covering our bases."

"Wow. Anyone watching would think you know what you're doing," Callie said, giggling at the glare Jake gave her. Taking Jake's phone, she scrolled through the contacts and called Jed.

"Hey, Jed," Callie said, "we have you on speaker. Anything weird or suspicious jump out at you on the drive?"

"No, I think we're good. My co-pilot," he waggled his brows at Darby in the passenger seat, "has been keeping an eye out. So far, so good."

Jake gave a small whoop. "Hallelujah! Is it possible that we're catching a break on something here?"

Tyler clapped his teddy bear's paws together, and Amara grinned.

The only one not jubilant, the only one not celebrating, was Callie. She was too busy trying to ignore the black shadow that suddenly appeared, casting an aura of doom, in the seat between her and Jake.

∾

The old van idled on the side of Route 14A in the Bighorn mountains. Its passenger door opened. Kendra Douglas slipped a slim foot into her right sneaker and reached for the other shoe.

"Isaiah, are you coming? There is something on fire down this hill. What if someone is trapped or something?"

A scruffy-looking white Bichon Frise began barking in the back of the van, its deep voice a contrast to its miniature size.

"Hush, Buster!" Isaiah admonished, glaring at the dog. Focusing back on his wife, he said, "And what in tarnation do you think you'll do about it if someone *is* trapped, Kendra? That's one helluva drop. Probably need ropes and pulleys to get down there."

"But Isaiah..."

"But nothing, Missy. We are going to call the authorities and sit tight. No sense getting ourselves killed." He took her hand in his. "Honey pie, we ain't the law, and we sure as hell don't have climbing equipment in this van. Make the call. I will take a look, just a look. Maybe I can see something."

Kendra grabbed her phone from the console. "How long do you think it will take the police to get here?"

"In this area? A good while, I expect. Look around, darlin'. Ain't much here but rock and two knuckleheads in a van with their yappy dog. This is what I get for suggesting we go camping in Shell for a few days. At this rate, we'll be lucky to make it by nightfall."

Opening his door, Isaiah exited and walked around the front of the van. Inching as close to the edge as he dared, keeping the portion of guardrail that was still intact in front of him, he peered over the side of the embankment.

"Jesus, Mary, and..." he muttered, suddenly forgetting the name 'Joseph' in his prayer. Blessing himself—despite not having seen the inside of a church in a decade—he tiptoed backward before finally turning and hurrying to the van.

"What?" Kendra asked. "What did you see?"

Face pale, hands trembling, Isaiah said simply, "Death. I saw death."

CHAPTER NINETEEN

Callie stared out the window of the Suburban, enchanted by the tiny town of Pitikin Falls.

"What a lovely place!" she said, head twisting to see the shops lining Main Street. "Is that an ice cream parlor? Oh, look at that barber pole!"

Jake chuckled. "Yes, it's very quaint. They have a tiny post office, an ancient brothel that was converted to—if you can believe it—a library, and a bar dressed up like an old-time saloon. Jed and I used to love coming to this town as kids. There are several more shops and offices now, but even back then, it was like stepping through a time warp."

She rolled down her window and inhaled. "It smells like tobacco and sunshine." Checking behind her, she added, "This is Darby's dream town. She must be going nuts back there! Can we come down here tomorrow? Check out the shops?"

Keeping his eyes ahead, Jake nodded. "Don't see why not. Tell Amara they have an art supply store here as well, next to the bakery. Not sure if they have everything she would need, but it's a start."

Callie turned and signed the information to Amara, who gave out a hearty "Whoop-whoop!" at the news.

Tyler, clutching Porter the bear, had stopped listening after hearing the words 'ice cream parlor.' "Hey, Callie, do you think we can get ice cream tomorrow, too?"

Callie turned to respond just as Jake's cell phone rang. "It's JP," she said. "Shall I answer it?"

"Yeah, go ahead. Just put him on speaker."

Muttering, Callie said, "You know, Devereaux, it would have taken me a minute to set up the Bluetooth options in the car rather than this neanderthal method of holding the phone while it's on speaker."

"It works, though, doesn't it?" Jake teased. "And no setup involved."

Callie's eyes did their familiar roll, and she answered the call. "Howdy ho, JP. We're on the road now but have you on speaker. How is our former medical examiner/psycho doing this evening?"

JP cleared his throat. "Uh, that's why I'm calling. I got pulled off shift tonight on my way to guard duty. It seems Thomas John Palmer is no longer with us. He was found dead this evening, the victim of an apparent seizure."

Callie gasped. "Dead? You're sure?"

"Yes, ma'am. I haven't seen the body, but my supervisor did. He said the guy had drool on his chin, and his tongue was hanging out of his mouth. The doc on call did a cursory exam at the bedside and is calling COD as a grand mal seizure for now. 'Course, there will be an autopsy, I'm sure."

Jake made a left off Main Street, pulling onto the gravel driveway that led to the Devereaux cabin. "Who had the watch when he was found? When we left, it was a young kid. Couldn't have been more than twenty-one years old."

"Yeah, that's the guy," JP answered. "Name is Riley, though I'm not sure if that's his first or last name. I can't blame him even if it turns out to be a suspicious death. Poor kid is green, just two weeks out of the academy. Times are tough. Budget cuts, and all the calls to 'defund' us, combined with some dirtbags who don't deserve to wear the badge, have left us short-staffed. Crime is climbing, victims are plentiful, but we lack the manpower to do our jobs effectively."

"You're preaching to the choir, JP. The people who complain about long response times are the same ones who demand a reduction of officers.

Some days, I toss my hands in the air and yell, 'Jesus, fix this!' So far, though, He has ignored me."

JP laughed. "I learned a long time ago, during my years as an altar boy, that God has an incredible sense of humor."

At that, Callie's drawn brows were soon replaced by a wide grin as an idea took shape. "Hey, Jake?" she said, facing him. "You told me you and Jed spoke about needing a holy man. JP was an altar boy. As in Christian." She smiled wider. "As in church."

Jake pulled in front of the cabin and, grinning himself, killed the engine. "Excellent idea, Blaze. We don't need a priest when an altar boy should do just fine."

"Say what?" JP asked, confused.

"You busy today, buddy?" Jake asked. "How would you like to take a drive to Pitikin Falls? We could sure use a Bible lesson."

While Jake and Jed moved around inside the cabin, clearing rooms and opening windows to get some fresh air, Callie and Darby sat on the porch watching Amara and Tyler toss a frisbee to Blue and Lucky.

"How many bedrooms are there, anyway?" Darby asked. "Looks kinda small for all of us."

"It does look small, but it's deceiving. The cabin is on the narrow side widthwise, but it's quite long. I'm not sure, but I think I saw at least three bedrooms when I was here before, plus an office with a twin and trundle combo we can use as a bedroom. Not to mention this porch and a screened one out back. Plenty of room to spread out, I think."

Darby held her fingers up, counting. "Okay, three or four bedrooms. Maybe I can share a room with Tyler, and you can share one with Amara? That would leave one bedroom and the office beds open for whoever will be manning the lifeboats, so to speak."

"Sounds like a plan. And we can take turns with cooking."

Darby chuckled. "Uh, yeah. I've had your cooking, remember? I can cook. You know, do my part to keep us all alive."

"Oh, you are a funny girl, Darbs. Come on," Callie said, standing and holding out both her hands. "I'm starving. Let's grab a snack, find our rooms, and see what our men are up to."

"Oh, you had me at snack, girl! Right behind ya!"

∼

Gabriel stood in the back of the property, naked, body glistening in the waning light. He lifted his face to the sky, the scent of gasoline, blood, and victory teasing his nostrils.

He'd done it. Admittedly, it had been a stomach-churning, foul mission, but he'd withstood the challenge. Tucker Simon, or what was left of him, was either scattered among the field or stuck to the chipper blades.

The remaining bloody scraps—pieces of what was once a man— had been flung back toward the machine's controls and were clinging to Gabriel's sweat-soaked body.

Nonchalantly, he flicked a piece of flesh from his cheek and looked around. He needed to wash both his body and his machine.

Wouldn't do to discover pieces of Simon in my hair or on the chipper's blades, would it?

Oh, he cared little whether Tucker's fate was discovered after his mission had been completed. By then, the end of days would be upon the earth. The world would be too busy trying to save itself to worry about the fate of one man. But, if found out too soon, Tucker Simon's demise and disposal could jeopardize his work.

He trotted to his truck, parked half a mile away, wiping off both real and imagined bits of his former assistant from his torso. Attending to the job nude made for easier cleanup. He could shower away any trace of the man he'd just killed.

But the biggest reason Gabriel was naked while disposing of Tucker's remains was self-protection. Just one slip using the machine—a loose shirt tail or bulky glove caught in the feed rollers—could mean joining his bumbling assistant in the chipper blades.

After hopping onto a sheet spread out on the truck seat, Gabriel drove to the house. He would shower, put on an old pair of coveralls, then haul the property's water tank and hose out to the woodchipper. After cleaning it, he would burn his clothes and shower again.

Because he always thought of everything.

Impressed with how things were going so far, with a gleam in his eye Gabriel entered the house and walked down the narrow hall to the bathroom. Turning on the shower, he inspected his body—ignoring the bloody flecks of human remains that littered his torso—and instead focused on the growing erection that throbbed beneath the fluorescent lights.

Everything was coming together: Tucker's fate, the subsequent disposal of his body, his plans for Callie and Jake.

All of it. And it excited Gabriel more than he thought possible.

Stepping into the shower, he soaped his body and threw his head back, stroking himself while enjoying the scalding water and steady pulse of the showerhead. Eyes closed, panting, he embraced the image that formed in his mind.

His strong hands, veins popping with effort, encircling his sister's neck.

He saw her eyes bulge, saw her desperately tugging at his fingers as he slowly squeezed the life out of her.

Panting as the lather continued to build, he worked his hand faster beneath the pounding stream of water.

When he felt his release, when he crested that enormous wave, it was to his screams of "fucking bitch!"

And, when he finally opened his eyes, the image of Callista Callahan, naked and bloated, her swollen tongue lolling from between her dead lips, lingered in his mind.

He smiled.

~

"Tyler!" Callie called from the cabin door. "Do me a favor and grab Amara and the dogs, okay? It's getting too dark to be out there now."

Callie heard a small groan. "Aw, just a few more minutes? Please? Me and Amara are tracking lightning bugs!"

Callie folded her arms and tilted her head, resting it on the door frame. Tyler was having fun, giggling as a six-year-old boy should. She loved hearing him laugh. It broke her heart to take that joy away from him. Still, they were here for a reason.

To hide from Gabriel, to protect the family from his demented mind.

"I'm sorry, bubba," Callie called back. "If it makes you feel any better, Darby is planning popcorn and a movie tonight!"

A quick 'Yahoo!' followed by the sound of running feet made her smile. Apparently, popcorn was almost as welcome to a six-year-old as ice cream.

Callie watched as Tyler raced around to the front of the house, then took the porch steps two at a time. "Slow down there, Speedy. Geesh, for a minute, I thought that blast of air was a tornado. You're pretty quick."

Tyler grinned. "That's what Jake says!"

She ruffled his hair. "Did you leave Amara in the dust?"

Looking over his shoulder, Tyler frowned. "Um, no. She was right behind me, I swear!"

Callie's stomach plunged. "Okay, I'm sure she'll be along shortly. How about you fetch Jake so he and I can round up Amara?"

Tyler disappeared inside. Before Callie could descend the porch steps, Jake was out of the house and at her side, his Glock at the ready.

"Amara's in trouble?" he asked.

"Not sure," Callie said as they descended the steps. "She didn't come back with Tyler, and I can't call for her. Obviously."

"Don't worry, Blaze. She probably got taken by the beauty of the footbridge over the stream. The solar lights reflect off the water, creating a kaleidoscope of colors. Mesmerizing, really. Either way, she couldn't have gotten far."

"Not far? Jake, you have acres here! What if she got lost? Oh, God, what if she fell in the stream and hit her head? She can't hear the water!" She grabbed his arm in desperation. "The pond! What if she fell in the pond?"

Fell in, panicked, and went under! What if she drowned just like Kates did?

As a psychologist, Callie understood what she was doing—projecting her fears onto the current situation with Amara.

Her fear of the water; her fear of losing Katie, not once but twice.

Jake turned Callie to face him. "Panic is not allowed, okay? Amara is deaf, not blind. She would see the water long before it became a danger."

"But..."

"No 'buts,' Blaze." Grinning, he said, "Unless it's yours, walking in front of me, perky and perfect."

Callie gave a strained laugh and picked up the pace. When they reached the footbridge, her heart sank.

Amara wasn't there.

Just as Callie was fighting the urge to move from a lively trot to a full-blown sprint through the yard, she heard it.

A sniffle coming from the backyard. Someone was crying.

Hearing it, too, Jake stepped in front of Callie, and they walked cautiously behind the house. Amara, her back facing them, was sitting on a bench in front of a wall of wildflowers, her shoulders shaking with sobs.

Callie ran to her, Jake at her heels, and crouched in front of her. "Amara?" she signed. "Honey, are you okay? Are you hurt?"

Amara shook her head. "No. It just suddenly hit me that, within a short time, my life has become so dramatically different. I've lost my parents, discovered I have siblings, and found out one of those siblings is a horrible man. I've left my home, my friends, my roots. It's just...." She stopped.

"Overwhelming?" Callie asked. "Mind-blowing? Shitty as hell?"

"No, not shitty." Amara grinned. "Just odd. I think between all I've learned, the flight from Denver, and the drive here, I'm wiped. And when I'm tired, I get emotional."

Jake took in the purple smudges beneath her eyes and the paleness of her face. "Me, too," he joked. "Bawl like a baby when I don't get a solid night's sleep. But not to worry, kid." He held out a hand and helped Amara to her feet. "You still look good."

"She sure does." Callie beamed. "Come on. Let's get inside and pick a room. You and I will be bunkies! Don't worry—I don't snore. Much."

"Not that it matters, though, right?" Amara joked. "It's not like I can hear it."

Two hours later, with Tyler tucked safely in bed, the adults sat in the living room and waited for JP Burke to arrive.

Jed poured several glasses of Chardonnay and Darby handed them out. "The last message from JP said he was just a few minutes out. I've made up the third bedroom for him in case he wants to stay over. Jake and I can take the office tonight."

"Well, great," Jake teased. "Surrounded by beautiful women in a romantic cabin in the woods, and I get stuck sleeping with the Jolly Green Giant."

The knock at the front door forced Jed to swallow his reply. "Saved by the bell."

"Knock, technically," Jake teased, "but your timing is getting better."

Jed shook his head and went to answer the door.

"Look who I found," Jed said as he and JP entered the living room.

Jake stood and stretched out a hand. "Hey, JP, thanks for coming. We could sure use your help on something."

After shaking hands, Callie introduced JP to the others in the room. "JP, I'd like you to meet my best friend and calming influence, Darby

Harrison."

Darby got to her feet, and she and JP shook hands. "Pleased to meet you, Miss," JP said.

"And this gorgeous girl," Callie said, beckoning Amara to her feet and pulling to her side, "is my baby sister, Amara Grace Davies. Along with being a beauty and a very talented artist, Amara is also deaf, but she can read lips."

JP blinked stupidly but didn't move. Luckily for him, Amara did.

"How's it going, JP?" Amara said, extending her hand. "I've heard a lot about you. It's nice to put a face to the name."

JP stared, unmoving.

"Uh," Jake said, slapping him on the back, "you can shake her hand anytime, buddy."

Jake's words kicked the young cop's brain into gear. "Oh, right. Sorry. Yes, yes," he stuttered, grabbing her outstretched hand. "Nice to meet you, Amara. Sorry—I checked out for a minute, but it's not my fault." Red-faced, he bit back a smile. "Callie wasn't kidding. You really are gorgeous."

It was Amara's turn to blush.

"All righty, then," Jed said, coming to JP's rescue. "How about a drink? Beer, soda, a glass of wine? We have an extra bedroom, so feel free to imbibe. We can make ourselves comfortable while we pick your brain."

"A beer would be great, thanks."

Once the drinks had been served and they were all settled, Jake started the conversation. "JP, Jed tells me he has filled you in on all things Gabriel Devine, correct?"

Taking a sip of beer, JP nodded. "He did." To Callie, he said, "I'm sorry for everything he's done to you, everything he's taken. I believe a special place in hell exists for people like him."

"God, I hope so," Callie said.

"Speaking of God and hell," Jake said, "I'll give you the abbreviated version of what's going on with the team. Since December of last year, we've scoured the area, looking inside every crevice and lifting every rock, in search of Gabriel. But he's a slippery son of a bitch. We figured he went into hiding to lick his wounds before striking again. However, some recent homicides have given us reason to believe he is fully operational again."

"Operational as a serial killer, you mean?"

"Unfortunately, yes. A few homicide victims have turned up, each bearing rosary beads on or near the body. In the past, rosary beads have been the Apostle's distinct signature. Recently, though, his behaviors have changed, escalated. Agenda-wise, it's like he's moved the goalpost or something."

"So the 'why' of all this is clear as mud?"

"Exactly. Gabriel is building a ladder to a destination we can't see. Lucky for us, he is a narcissist on top of everything else. He's been leaving other clues, religious clues, that we hope you can help us with."

JP smirked. "Because I was an altar boy? Man, I'll do what I can, but I was just a kid. Not sure how much I remember and how much I blocked out." He chuckled. "The priest at my parish was, for lack of a better term, intense. Fire and brimstone type of stuff. And don't get me started on the nuns."

"Well, anything you can tell us would be more than we know right now," Jed said. "I'm going to print out the photos Curt sent us. Callie, maybe you can send me the pictures you took of Amara's paintings?"

"Sure thing."

"While ya'll are checking the pictures, I'm gonna peek in on Tyler," Darby said, standing. "All this talk about Gabriel gives me the shakes. I just want to make sure he's good."

Amara stood as well. "I think I'll turn in if you don't mind. I'm beat."

"Of course, sweetheart," Callie said. "I'll try not to wake you when I come in."

JP jumped to his feet. "It was nice to meet you, Amara. See you in the morning?"

She smiled. "Yes. See you in the morning."

"Can I get you another beer, JP?" Jake asked as they pored over crime scene photos.

"No, I'm good, thanks," JP said absently, squinting at one of the pictures. "Say, do you know if Gabriel is into the Old Testament?"

Jake shrugged and looked at Callie. "Blaze?"

"I honestly have no idea. He's obsessed with all things biblical, that much I know. Why do you ask?"

JP scratched his temple. "Well, I'm looking at the mark on the forehead of each victim. I can't be sure, but it looks like a Sigillum."

"A what?" Darby asked, returning from Tyler's room.

"Its technical name is Sigillum Dei, or seal of God. It's a series of geometric figures like pentagrams, circles, heptagrams, etcetera, said to contain the true name of God and all his angels."

"Okay, so what does it mean?" Callie asked.

"I have no idea. If he weren't killing his victims, I would say he is marking them as 'safe' from the wrath of God. During the end of days, the Tribulations, only a certain number of humans—those who carry the seal of God—will be taken up to heaven before the Apocalypse begins. It's called the Rapture."

"I've heard of it," Jake said. "So, this seal marks those people?"

"Yes. In Revelation, the final book of the Bible, people who wear the seal are protected from the horrors of the end time. But they are all alive. You don't need to be protected from God's wrath if you're already dead, right?" He scratched his temple again. "Another weird thing is that Revelation is found in the New Testament of the Bible. But some of this other stuff I'm seeing," he nodded to the photos, "seems more Old Testament to me."

"Such as?" Jake asked.

"Such as how she was killed," JP said, pointing to the second photo.

"Stoned to death, right? Well, see, that really wasn't a thing in the Bible. In Islam, the Quran, then sure, stoning for committing adultery is mentioned. In Christianity, however, there's a common misconception that stoning was a form of punishment mentioned in the Bible, specifically the Old Testament."

"But it wasn't?" Jake asked.

"Nope. Most likely, people who think it's found in the Bible as a form of discipline or a consequence of grave sin are probably suffering from the Mandela effect."

"That sounds ominous," Jed said.

"Not really. The Mandela effect is described as false memories shared by many people. A paranormal researcher coined the term after discovering that many people remembered anti-Apartheid leader Nelson Mandela dying in a South African prison in the 1980s. In reality, he died years later, in 2013."

"So, this Mandela effect is like a collective group-think thing?" Jed asked.

"Sort of. It's a phenomenon where people recall seeing or hearing something that never was. It is about memories and how a person's mind sometimes skews them. Take the Monopoly Man, for instance. People will swear the little guy wears a monocle, but he doesn't. Another example is Ed McMahon. People recall him traveling with a group of people, handing out checks to smiling winners of the Publishers Clearing House sweepstakes. Never happened."

"Of course it did!" Darby said, frowning. "Didn't it? I swear I can see him handing out checks in my mind."

"Yeah, that's the Mandela effect. See, Ed was on the envelope that came to your house, but not for Publishers Clearing House. He worked for another company, American Family Publishers, who gave out their own sweepstake checks."

"Mind. Blown," Darby whispered.

"Indeed," JP laughed. "Anyway, no one ever got stoned in the Holy Bible." Blushing, he added, "I mean, stoned with rocks."

"Hah!" Darby crowed, smiling. "So, you're saying those holy dudes might have taken a toke now and then?"

JP smirked. "Maybe. But stoning someone to death tells me something else about our guy."

Engrossed, Callie asked, "Like what?"

JP raised his brows and cocked his head to one side. "Like no matter what Gabriel says, no matter how much he fancies himself an 'expert' in all things biblical, he actually knows dick about it." Blushing again, he added, "Apologies to the ladies for my profanity."

Darby winked. "No worries—we aren't Quakers."

"What about the messages left on their bodies?" Callie asked. "That seems biblical, too."

"Those messages refer to sins, I believe. There are seven deadly sins and seven virtues. For example—" JP stopped speaking as Jed's phone rang.

"I'll be quick," Jed said. "This is fascinating to me."

He connected the call. "Hey, Curt. I have the gang all here, and you are on speaker. Any news?"

"Nothing good," Curtis said. "You want the bad news or the even worse news first?"

Jed glanced at Jake. "Give us the bad news first," he said dryly. "It will give us something to look forward to."

"You got it. We have an ID for both women. Their names are Rebecca Sue Caraway and Annie McCormack. Rebecca was a nurse, well-liked by her peers, reported missing by her mom when she didn't come home from work."

"Which victim was that again?" Darby asked, biting a nail.

"Rebecca was the girl at that abandoned pig farm. She had her throat slit and, from what the medical examiner tells me, burns on her body from some type of electric prod. The poor girl was tortured before she was killed."

"God," Callie whispered.

"As for Annie McCormack," Curt continued, "she was a self-employed photographer reported missing by her husband, Trevor. He admitted they were having marital problems but nothing too heavy. She was found at that strip joint with her head caved in. We checked their social media accounts, gym memberships, work history, etcetera. They lived in different areas, traveled in different circles, and were polar opposites physically. As of now, we can't find a link between the two victims."

"Even the manner of death is different," Jake said. "Rebecca was slashed, Annie killed by stoning. What else you got?"

"Unfortunately, another victim. This one is male, found next to an ATM over in Big Horn, killed in yet another way. Driver's license tells us he's Harry Tinning, a middle-aged financial adviser."

"How?" Callie asked.

"Preliminary ME report says suffocation. Basically, someone stuffed an immense number of coins into his throat until he choked to death. Oh, and guess what? He had writing on his belly, too. 'No Charity.'"

"Unbelievable," Callie whispered. "The description of how he was found is exactly how Amara drew it!"

"Christ, Curt," Jed muttered. "If that is the bad news, I don't know if I want to hear the worse news."

"Oh, trust me, you'll want to hear it. Especially you, Jed."

"That sounds ominous," Jake said.

Curtis coughed softly. "We, uh, we are investigating an accident that occurred several hours ago. I am at the scene as we speak. A woman went off a cliff on a winding back road in Sheridan. Looks like she was killed instantly."

"Okay, tragic, but...." Jake said.

"Sawyer is on his way here because the name on the car's registration is someone we all know. Right now, I have uniforms checking the area to make sure he isn't a victim as well."

Jed rubbed his neck. "What aren't you saying, Curt? Who do the tags come back to?"

Curt sighed. "An old friend of Jake's. None other than Tucker Simon."

"Okay, I'm confused," Jed said. "You mentioned I would be interested in this. But I barely know Tucker Simon, Curt."

"I know, buddy. But you are very familiar with the woman who was driving his car. When Sawyer gets here, I'm hoping he will confirm my identification, but I'm fairly confident I know this lady who was killed."

"Who?" Callie asked, almost afraid to hear the answer.

"Jed's former assistant. I'm pretty sure it was Fiona Clark driving that car."

CHAPTER TWENTY

"WRATH"

"Do not be quickly provoked in your spirit, for anger resides in the lap of fools."

Ecclesiastes 7:9

Gabriel sat at his kitchen table, coffee in hand, laptop opened in front of him. Craning his neck, he yawned as he scrolled the website of one of Sheridan's nondenominational churches, the Rock of Faith.

He was searching for something in particular; he ended up finding so much more.

In between scrolling, he gazed out the kitchen window, recalling yesterday's work. Between dealing with Tucker Simon and disposing of his body, it had been, physically speaking, a taxing day.

By the time he'd completed the cleanup, close to midnight, he was exhausted in both mind and body.

Compounding his mental fatigue was knowing that his captive, the woman he'd taken from under Jed Devereaux's nose, was still missing. He'd searched the major highways for hours, listened to the local police scanner, but there was no sign of her. He was left wondering if she really had taken Tucker's car. Could he have lied? Killed her and driven her somewhere out of town, ditching the car afterward? After all, it wasn't like Tucker Simon had been trustworthy, an honest man.

No, I can't trust a word he said. Oh, well. Not like I can ask him now, can I?

Gabriel sighed and focused on more pressing issues. It had been darker than sin on Sunday when he'd taken care of Tucker last night. As he worked, he'd been uneasily aware that he'd have to revisit the woodchipper, make sure he hadn't missed anything. In the inky black of night, it would be easy to overlook a scrap of skin or chunk of brain matter.

Gabriel knew anyone else in his position would not be so careful; anyone else would take a chance that they were in the clear.

Thankfully, he was not anyone else.

Preparing for any hiccup in his plans, double- and triple-checking his work, was the way he'd always operated. And it was why, in Gabriel's estimation, he would never get caught.

Turning back to the computer screen, he moved to the site's menu, clicked on the tab marked "Past Sermons," and searched the topics provided. The Rock of Faith was a church with only a handful of parishioners and no real following. The Sheridan area had a solid Protestant presence, and the idea of 'nondenominational' had not yet caught on.

As a result, Gabriel came to this site often, looking to steal a sermon or two. With so few members at St. Michael's, it seemed unlikely anyone would recognize the speeches he gave there as plagiarized.

Even if they did, so be it. He had more important things to do than spend hours composing a sermon no one would listen to.

Gabriel knew enough about Christians to know that false piety and devotion were commonplace. Rather than absorbing the word of God during mass, people mentally composed grocery lists or rearranged sock drawers. So, why waste time creating lessons that would go unheard?

Instead, he fished around the internet for someone else's words to take.

He thumbed through half a dozen topics, fingers drumming on the table, and played a snippet of each recorded sermon to see if anything struck a chord. At the third one in, he froze, staring at the unfamiliar speaker in the blue silk suit.

This man was new; Gabriel hadn't seen him on the site before.

Mesmerized, he watched as the red-faced man, fists clenched, screamed at his flock about retribution and consequences, preaching that only those who dug deep into their pockets and gave with a generous hand would escape the end of days.

It was nothing short of blasphemy. It was a false prophet in sheep's clothing.

Gabriel's body began to tingle, and his mind raced. As he studied the congregants' faces, he noted the fear in their eyes as they stood, mesmerized by the speaker's words.

Pastor Leland Penne. That was what the speaker called himself.

But Gabriel recognized him by his true name.

Wrath.

~

Callie stirred in bed, the enticing aroma of bacon tickling her nostrils. Keeping the lights off to avoid disturbing Amara, she wiped the sleep from her eyes, climbed out from under the covers, and stumbled to the bathroom. After washing her face, she pulled her wavy hair into a loose bun and stared at her image in the mirror. Her blue eyes looked gray today, the whites glassy and bloodshot.

Frowning, she stuck her tongue out. "What the hell you lookin' at, chump?"

To her left, a high-pitched giggle caught her attention.

"You know, sometimes you worry me, Cal-Pal," Katie said. "You are a silly goose, you know that?"

Callie cast a worried look toward Amara. "Shhh," she said, finger to her lips, once again forgetting Amara was deaf. "Hiya, Kates," she whispered. "I've been expecting you, hoping you could give us some profound insights about what we learned last night. My head is still spinning."

Katie moved to the center of the bedroom, her beautiful shimmer illuminating the darkened room. "I'm impressed, Shadow. It's barely the sunny side of dawn, and here you are, speaking in full sentences and everything! Good for you!"

Callie rolled her eyes. "Yeah, that's me. Sally Sunshine. Now, can we skip to the part where you pass over some information, please?"

Katie shook her head. "Wish I could tell you something. Part of the..." She hesitated, searching for the right words. "Part of being on this side of the veil is that there are certain rules we must obey. Rule number one, 'Thou shalt not meddle in the affairs of the living,' is the most crucial. We violate that, it's bad."

"Bad how?"

"As bad as it gets. If we violate rule number one, we go straight to H-E-double hockey sticks."

Incredulous, Callie moved closer to Katie's glowing figure, ignoring the static electricity that pulled at the hairs on her neck and arms. "Seriously? You're telling me you'll get sent to hell if you divulge anything?" Raising her voice, anger building, she hissed, "You must be joking!" Whispering, she added, "Please tell me you're messing with me!"

Katie chuckled. "Amara hasn't moved, Shadow. She can't hear us, remember?" Winking, she said, "Of course, I'm messing with you, Cal. Geesh, you need to take up yoga or something. Stressed much?"

"You started it, sister. I'd be much more chill if you hadn't up and died on me."

"Mm-hmm," Katie murmured, ignoring Callie's last remark, knowing there wasn't a proper response for it anyway. "So, as I was saying, I made up the fire and brimstone stuff, but we really can't give up any information that could change the course of history. In fact, because we are human and, right out of the gate, have proven how we handle temptation—thanks a million, Adam and Eve—we're given only crumbs of crucial information."

Callie twisted her mouth in disappointment. "So, you have nothing for me, then. Do you know what's going on, though?"

"I know most of it. And, after finding myself at Jed's, watching Gabriel spy on you, I think I understand my role a bit better."

Callie gave a half-bow. "Please, O wise one! Enlighten me, but talk quickly. You're starting to blink like Christmas tree lights with a burned-out bulb."

"Right. Okay, here's the shortened version. I'm only allowed to intercede or be aware of things Gabriel does specifically against you. I believe the cloak-and-dagger shadows we both see are like a beacon or notification system flagging me down. Every time he has you in his sights, every time something he is planning affects you, I see the blackness; I get a nudge. So, think of me as your guardian angel. But as far as the rest? These latest victims?" She began to fade. "I know as much about these killings as you do. Tread carefully, Shadow."

"Good morning, beautiful!" Jake smiled, turning from the stove as he scrambled some eggs.

He was freshly showered, his hair still damp and blue jeans clinging in all the right places. Callie felt the need to check herself before she started to swoon.

"Are you always like this in the morning?" she asked.

"Like what? Dashing, dreamy, gorgeous?"

"Chipper, happy. A ray of freaking sunshine?"

His deep laughter filled the room. "Boy, you and Kate really were twins! It makes me wonder about Finn and Ryan."

Callie snorted. "Ryan has always been a happy little morning person like some kind of freak of nature. And Finn? Let's just say Finnigan Callahan never met a morning he liked. Or an afternoon. Or a—"

Jake's laughter stopped her. "Okay, okay. Noted. Ryan is like me, you and Katie are cut from the same cloth, and Finn marches to his own beat."

"Finn never marches; he stomps," Callie said dryly.

"Gotcha." Wiping his hands on a towel, he asked, "So, did you sleep all right? Bed big enough for you and Amara?"

"Plenty big enough. She's still fast asleep, poor lamb. I think between all that has happened and her newfound 'gift,' she's wiped. So, about last night and the call from Curtis. I've been thinking—"

The back door opened, and JP walked into the small kitchen. "Oh, hey, Callie. Good morning!"

Callie grunted. "Oh, great. Another morning person."

JP smiled. "Always have been. I love mornings! Today, since I was up early, I figured I'd give myself the nickel tour of the grounds. Place is beautiful."

Jake smirked. "Up early? Is that what you call it?" Turning to Callie, he said, "He was up early because he never went to sleep."

"You didn't?" Callie asked. "Why? Was something wrong with the room?"

Jake winked at JP. "You wanna tell her, Romeo, or should I?"

JP shuffled back and forth on his feet. "Um, well, I can tell her," he said, raking a hand nervously through his hair.

Jake smirked again.

"Okay, so, ah, the room is perfect, so no worries there. I tried to sleep, but my brain had other ideas. It kept circling to Amara and how useless I felt earlier when trying to talk with her. So, I, uh, I did some research."

Jake laughed. "Research? Dude, you tried to cram in an entire semester of American Sign Language in under five hours!"

JP blushed.

"Well, I, for one, find it lovely that you think enough of my sister to make her feel comfortable," Callie said.

"Yeah," Jake said. "Sure, that's it. He went all night, balls to the wall,

228

vision blurred and body aching with fatigue because he wanted Amara to feel 'comfortable.'"

"Oh, stop teasing him, Jake!" Callie said with a smile. "No matter the reason, it was a very sweet gesture." Anxious to change the subject, she said, "Where are the others? We have a lot to discuss."

"Jed went into town for some coffee creamer. I think Darby is in the shower, and Ty is still racked out."

"Good morning!" Amara said brightly, walking into the kitchen. "It looks like a glorious day! What is that divine smell?"

Callie exhaled forcefully, a puff of air blowing a strand of hair from her face. "What's wrong with you people?" she grumbled. "It's like the Stepford Wives in here."

Jake bit back a laugh.

JP rushed up to Amara and smiled. "Good morning," he signed awkwardly. "I hope you slept well."

Jake looked on, amused.

Aware that Jake was close to spoiling JP's moment, Callie elbowed him in the ribs.

And Amara, surprised, moved her hands in a flurry of activity. "I didn't know you could sign! That's so cool! I slept like a baby, actually. How about you?"

JP felt the rush of heat move up his face and turned to Callie for help.

"Um," Callie said, "JP is just learning sign language. It might be easier to speak as you sign."

"No problem," Amara said. "I appreciate your efforts, JP."

"Okay, now that we have determined JP is a stand-up guy and Callie hates mornings," Jake said, "who wants some breakfast?"

∽

Gabriel stood in the foyer of the Rock of Faith Church, waiting for Pastor Leland Penne to emerge from the back. He'd reached out earlier as 'Tucker Simon,' asking Leland for a private audience, promising it was necessary.

He'd convinced the pastor that he was in deep trouble, trouble even his 'vast wealth' could not help.

Because nothing roped in a charlatan, a con man, like the mention of money.

After twenty minutes, Leland Penne emerged from the front of the church, the Bible nestled in his arms contrasting sharply with his swagger and smug smile.

Gabriel's first impression told him everything he needed to know.

Leland Penne was a fraud, a scoundrel who preached God's Word not for His glory but for his own.

"Hello, son," Leland said as he drew near. "My name is Leland Penne—pronounced like the writing implement, not the pasta." He chuckled at his humor. "I assume you are Tucker Simon?"

Gabriel nearly groaned in disgust, convinced Leland Penne used the pasta joke ad nauseum. "I am. Thank you for agreeing to see me, sir. I am truly at my wits' end."

Penne nodded. "I understand. Come, let us sit outside on the bench by the big tree. We can enjoy God's gift of a beautiful day while we figure out a solution to your troubles."

Fuck you, asshole. The only solution you'll be part of is the one that sees your demise.

They walked to the back of the building, along the side of the deserted parking lot, until they reached the gardens. Taking a seat on a bench beneath an ancient oak tree, Gabriel began to weave his web.

"So, this is hard to talk about, Pastor, but I need help. I have a terrible temper, sir. I've had some frightening, disturbing outbursts of anger. Some days, those outbursts are so violent, I can hardly recognize myself in them."

Leland nodded and took a seat beside him. "I see. Have you spoken to a professional about these outbursts?"

Gabriel shook his head. "I haven't. In truth, I cannot." He looked around as if expecting someone, or something, to jump out from behind a tree. Whispering now, he said, "If certain family members knew of my... my issues, I could be banished, cut off from my inheritance. Granted, I've received a monthly sum over the years and am, by most people's standards, quite wealthy. But what of my future children? Shouldn't I be worried about their financial security?"

"Oh, of course, of course. And, as you say, it's your family's money. Those funds should be earmarked for you, regardless of your issues, to do with as you wish."

"Exactly!" Gabriel said, clapping a hand on Leland's shoulder. "If you can help me redirect my anger, counsel me to control my impulses, I can also help you. I saw on your website that the Rock of Faith Church needs a roof and new windows. Is that right?"

Leland nodded.

"Well, help me and consider it done! And because I am a man of faith, I will give you a deposit right now! I am that sure you will come through for me." He nudged Leland's thigh with his own. "You know, they say the eyes are the window to the soul. When I look into your eyes, I see your intentions. I see the truth."

Leland Penne, a man whose ego was overshadowed only by his thirst for wealth, smiled. "Well, that's mighty kind of you to say. And yes, I do believe I will take you up on your offer, Mr. Simon."

"Excellent! My truck is parked over there," Gabriel said, pointing a finger. "Let's drive over to my place. I will give you a generous down payment, and we can begin our first session. It will bring you a sense of accomplishment, and me, a sense of peace."

And it will bring me one more cardinal sinner and one step closer to magnificence.

~

After the breakfast dishes were done, Amara and Tyler, fishing poles in hand, left to check out the pond with Blue and Lucky. Callie and Amara both agreed she could do more good keeping Tyler occupied than trying to sit in a meeting and play 'catch-up' with all that had happened.

Meanwhile, the remaining occupants of the Devereaux cabin sat in the living room, discussing recent events.

Jed started things off. "We still haven't heard anything from Curt about the accident or whether it was Faith driving Tucker's vehicle."

"I'm sorry, brother," Jake said. "This has to be rough for you."

Jed's shoulders slumped almost imperceptibly. Darby noticed.

"Hey," she said, reaching out a hand. "You okay?"

Jed took her hand and squeezed it. "I'm okay, Darbs. If it does turn out to be Faith, which we don't know yet, I will be sad. But I can't mourn the woman she was because she was never who she pretended to be. In truth, I have no idea who the real Faith McTavish, or Fiona Clark, truly was."

"Well, whoever she was," Jake said, "if the driver of Simon's car was indeed Faith, we have more questions than answers."

Callie nodded. "Yeah. Like, what the hell was she doing with that sleazeball? And why was she driving his car?"

JP cleared his throat. "I know I'm low man on the totem pole here, but is it possible this car accident wasn't an accident at all?"

"How do you mean?" Jake asked.

"Think about it. From what Curt and all of you have said, Tucker Simon is scum. Now, we have him possibly involved with a woman who kidnapped Tyler from Philly and altered their identities. As if they were hiding from something. Or someone."

"Okay," Jed said. "I'm with you. Keep going."

JP sat up straighter. "Okay, so we know Tucker worked with TJ Palmer in the ME's office. They worked side by side, did forensic investigations together, maybe even became friendly, right?"

Jake nodded, impressed. He knew where this was going, and it was an angle he hadn't seen, couldn't see, given his closeness to the parties involved.

JP continued. "We also know that somewhere along the way, Gabriel Devine connected with TJ Palmer, his 'Disciple.' Which, indirectly and by association, puts Tucker in the same circle of people as Gabriel. Possibly, anyway."

Darby jumped up. "Yes! It's like six degrees of Kevin Bacon!"

JP chuckled. "Kind of. So, if Tucker knows Gabriel, and Faith was driving Tucker's car, is it possible she, too, knew Gabriel? Could she have been a part of any of this? Or, if not, could she have information that Gabriel didn't want released?"

"Man, that's a lot of 'ifs,' kid," Jed said. "But, if it is Faith, we can surmise she at least encountered Tucker Simon at some point." Looking at Jake, he asked, "Can we call him? I know Curt said they were looking for his body at the accident scene, but you should have his number, right?"

Jake nodded. "I do. I'll give him a call in a few, see if he picks up."

Darby raised her hand. "JP, before Curt called last night, you were telling us about the seven deadly sins."

"Right. Capital sins are the worst of the worst. So, although the Bible doesn't mention them specifically as 'seven deadly sins,' they are referred to in one way or another. Some theologians even go as far as to say there is no way to redeem yourself if you've committed a capital, or cardinal, sin. The Bible contradicts these self-proclaimed 'men of God,' however, and tells us there is no sin that is unforgivable, as long as one repents."

Callie walked to the window, pulled aside the curtain, and watched Amara and Tyler as they cast their lines from the footbridge. "Okay, so, what are these sins? And what have they to do with the messages left on the bodies?"

"Let me think a sec," JP said. "It's been a minute or two since my

Sunday school lessons. I remember the sin of pride was considered the most severe of all the deadly sins. It has long been associated with Lucifer and how he was so impressed with himself that he forsook God."

"So, anyone vain, basically?" Callie asked.

"That'd be half the guys I've dated," Darby muttered.

JP chuckled. "Yes, anyone who puts so much faith in themselves they forget who got them there. Or, at least, anyone who fits the bill in Gabriel's eyes. Pride contrasts with the capital virtue of humility."

"Okay, so, what else?" Jake asked.

"Let's see. There's also gluttony, envy, lust, greed, and sloth."

"That's six," Jed said. "Counting pride. We're missing one."

"I'm sorry," JP said. "I'm drawing a blank here. I can tell you that the messages left on the victims correspond to the opposite traits, the virtues directly opposing the sins. For example, the capital virtue of gluttony is temperance; of lust, it's chastity. And the message left on the victim at the bank, 'No Charity,' opposes the capital virtue of greed."

Jed snapped his fingers. "So, in his demented mind, Rebecca Sue Caraway committed the sin of gluttony, Annie McCormack the sin of lust, and this Harry guy's sin was greed? What is Gabriel trying to accomplish here? Ridding the world of sinners? Passing judgment on those who commit the vilest of sins?"

JP shrugged. "Damned if I know. As I said, marking them with the seal of God tells me the killer is performing a ritual to ensure they escape the natural disasters described in Revelation—the fires, the plagues, the pestilence, and the pain. But he's killing them, the opposite of trying to save them, right? So, yeah. No clue."

"Unless he's killing them for his benefit, not theirs," Callie said quietly. "What if the murders have nothing to do with 'saving' the victims and everything to do with a perverse, hidden agenda? I mean, this is Gabriel, after all. What if he's killing them for a real or imagined gain?"

"Like?" Jake asked.

Callie looked to JP for help.

"Maybe to prove his worth?" JP said. "It could be Gabriel believes his victims are offerings, sacrifices to present to God to demonstrate how deep his faith runs. Like Abraham offering his only son, Isaac, and nearly killing him before God interceded. All to prove he believed."

Darby slapped her thigh. "Dang! Just when you think this looney bastard has used up his crazy quota, he proves us wrong!"

Callie nodded in agreement but said nothing. She was too busy following the movements of the dark entity that had entered the room, knowing that, if Katie was right, it meant trouble.

And it meant that Callie was once again in Gabriel's sights.

CHAPTER TWENTY-ONE

After showering, Callie dressed and stepped outside, following the sound of some kind of power tool. She walked to the corner of the house, her gaze traveling up a ladder propped against the siding. Jake was standing on the top rung, a cordless drill in one hand, a camera in the other.

"Need a hand?" she asked.

"Can you hold the ladder for me? Jed and JP went to Tucker's apartment and left me hanging."

Callie grabbed the sides of the ladder and joked, "Scared, are ya?"

"Let's put it this way," Jake grunted, trying to get in a better position to mount the outdoor camera. "There are two things I am not a fan of—heights and snakes. Yet here I am, in the middle of rattlesnake country, twelve feet in the air on a rusty ladder that's probably twenty years old. So yeah, Blaze, it's a little scary."

"Make you a deal, G-man," she said with a smile. "If you protect me from deep water and enclosed spaces, I'll cover your ass vis-à-vis the heights and pit vipers."

He chuckled. "Deal." Turning slightly toward her, he reached into his pocket and handed her his phone. "Okay, I think I got it. We just need to check the position. If you click the security icon, you can check the camera angle and let me know if we need to adjust it."

Callie opened the app. "Looks fine to me. It gives a pretty wide view of the entire front yard." Tilting her head back, she asked, "So, how come Jed went to Tucker's instead of you?"

Jake leaned a hip against the top rung, a shadow falling over his face. "Simon and I have a history, which is why Jed thought he should talk to him instead of me. For some reason, Jed was afraid I'd get too worked up, too pissed, and Simon would shut down."

"I can't imagine why he'd think that," Callie teased.

"Yeah, go figure."

"But, joking aside, no one could blame you if you did lose it. That man is a sneaky bastard. Did you try to call him?"

Jake nodded. "Only five times. The son of a bitch didn't pick up. So either he chose not to answer when he saw the caller ID or...."

"Or he couldn't answer?"

"Right. Either way, we figured it would be in our best interest not to introduce a spark—that would be me—to a powder keg. So, the family diplomat went instead."

"If it gets us answers, who cares?"

"Especially since we still haven't heard from Curt or Sawyer whether it was Faith who was involved in that fatal," Jake said, beginning his descent.

Callie gripped the ladder tighter, wincing as it groaned beneath Jake's weight.

"Okay," Jake said, reaching the ground. "Just four more to go. I figure another on the other corner of the house and one by the front porch. Then, two to cover the backyard. With the motion lights in place, we should have no trouble tracking any trespassers."

"Oh, goody. Nothing says 'fun' like having to track a trespasser." Callie rubbed her arms, a chill moving through her despite the warm temperature. "I can't wait for this to be over, Jake—catching Gabriel, finding Tyler's mother, discovering what Faith has to do with all this."

"Me, too, Blaze."

"And we need to find closure for you and your family, bubba. You need to find Lacy and put her to rest."

Jake squinted under the sun's rays. "If she's even dead. We still don't know what happened to her, Blaze. Jed and I continue to hope that she is out there, somewhere. Alive." His throat tightened. "Unless you've, uh, seen her as a...."

"Oh, no, sweetheart," Callie said quickly. "I haven't. No inside information, either. It was just a stupid assumption, a slip of the tongue, on my part. Forgive me?"

Jake gave her a devilish grin and waggled his brows up and down suggestively. "A slip of the tongue? Want to see my 'slip of the tongue'?"

She pushed a shoulder into him and smiled. "Come on, tough guy. We have four more of these cameras to place."

≈

Jed pounded on the front door of Tucker Simon's apartment, calling out his name.

"Simon! Come on, man! We just want to talk."

JP shifted from one foot to the other. "Maybe he's not home."

Jed knocked harder. "Tucker, you're only making things worse for yourself! You could be in some serious trouble here. Open up, and we'll try to help you."

"Want me to get management? It *is* sort of an emergency since Tucker's car was in that ravine. Maybe they'll open the door for us."

"Excuse me?" a clipped voice called from down the hall. "What are you doing there?"

They turned to find an older woman, somewhere in her eighties, eyeing them suspiciously while clutching a beaded necklace.

"Hello, ma'am," JP said. "My name is Deputy John Paul Burke. I'm with the sheriff's department." He nodded toward Jed. "And this is my associate, Jedidiah Devereaux. We have reason to believe the occupant of this apartment, Tucker Simon, may be in danger."

The woman moved closer but kept several feet between them. "Tucker? Let me tell you something, gentlemen. Tucker Simon is too selfish and too mean to get himself in the kind of trouble you are talking about."

Jed cleared his throat. "Have you seen him in the last twenty-four hours, ma'am?"

"I have not," she said, indignant. "I steer clear of the bastard, and you'd do well to do the same. And if something bad has happened to him, well, I expect it was of his own doing."

"If you don't mind my asking, ma'am, when was the last time you saw him?" JP asked.

"Day before yesterday, I think," the woman responded. "He came in at the most ungodly hour, pounding his feet and jingling his keys. I peeked down the hall, just to check, mind you, and saw him struggling to unlock the door. A few hours later, he flies out of here. I saw him jump in that piece of crap he owns and take off."

"All right. Thank you, ma'am. You've been very helpful," JP said.

When she returned to her apartment, JP said, "Well, someone isn't very popular around here. What's next?"

"Next is I get inside one way or another. And my way may not be exactly legal," Jed said. "Although I think the door may be unlocked. And I'm pretty sure I heard a moan coming from inside." He winked. "How about you go back to the car, give Jake a call, and see if they've heard anything more on their end. I'll be along shortly."

"Hey," JP said, pretending not to have heard Jed. "I'm gonna go down to the car and give Jake a call. Maybe they've got an update for us."

Jed smiled and slapped JP on the back. "Excellent idea, Junior. Be down in a flash."

Jed waited until JP was out of sight, then knocked on Tucker Simon's door one more time.

"Tucker," he said, more quietly this time. He didn't want the neighbor to come back out again. "I'm coming in now. We have reason to believe you are in trouble."

Greeted once again by silence, Jed checked the hall again. All was quiet. Taking a small tin container from his pocket, he selected a tool and began working on the lock. Inside two minutes, the tumbler released and the door unlocked.

"Shitty security, Simon. You might want to give PIPPS a call and upgrade."

He turned the knob, stepped inside, and softly closed the door.

≈

Twenty minutes after he'd finished installing the security cameras, Jake's phone rang.

"Hey, JP," he said. "Any luck at Simon's place?"

"Negative, sir. We banged on that door for ten minutes. A neighbor came out, said she hadn't seen him in at least two days. Jed's still at Tucker's door, um, waiting. He thinks maybe the door was unlocked; he might even have heard a moan or something."

"Riiiiiiight," Jake said, drawing out the word. "And he sent you back to the car to, what, make some calls?"

JP smiled. "Something like that. So, while I have you on the phone, any news?"

"Afraid not, although I expect to hear from Curt or Sawyer within the hour. As I understand it, Sawyer left the accident scene and went to speak to the ME about the bodies that have been found. Curt was going to run to the hospital morgue to see TJ Palmer's body for himself."

"Okay. I have to work in a few hours. You have tonight covered, security-wise?"

"Yeah, we're good," Jake answered. "I'll call when I hear something. Oh, and JP?"

"Sir?"

"In law enforcement, sometimes those 'unlocked' doors or 'calls for help' can bite you in the ass. Stay in the car until Jed gets back, okay?"

"Not a problem, sir. Not a problem."

"Callie! Jake!" Tyler called from the front porch. "Mr. Curtis is here!"

"Be right there!" Callie called from her bedroom. Smiling, she hung her favorite sweatshirt in the closet and headed to the kitchen. It didn't matter to her how loud Tyler yelled or that he could talk the ear off anyone who'd listen.

The fact he was talking was music to her ears.

"Hello, Mr. Curtis," she said playfully, coming into the kitchen. "Can I get you something? Coffee, water, juice?"

Curt smiled. "I wouldn't turn down a cup of coffee. You know, you're going to make someone a great wife someday. Or is that too sexist?"

Callie laughed. "Not to me. I take it as it's intended—a compliment." She started filling the coffee maker with water. "Jake's out back, playing with camera angles. We can wait until he gets inside to chat about the case."

"No problem. Jed and JP still at the Simon place?"

"I think so. JP called from the complex's parking lot. He was in the car, waiting for Jed to, um, check the apartment." She raised a brow. "Seems as though Jed heard a cry for help inside. But you didn't hear that from me."

Curt put his hands over his ears. "I hear nothing."

The back door creaked open and Jake entered, wiping his feet on the welcome mat. "Hey, Curt. I saw you pull up on my new cameras." He winked at Callie. "Good to know they work, Blaze."

"You want a coffee, Mr. Cameraman?" she teased.

"Sure." Turning to Curt, he said, "Have a seat. Jed won't be back for a while, so you might as well tell us what you've got. I can pass it on when he gets home."

"Should I get Darbs?" Callie asked.

"Nah. I saw her heading to the pond to find Amara and Ty. They've gone fishing. We can fill everyone in later."

"Okay, great," Curt said. "So, to start with, Thomas John Palmer. The autopsy results are still pending toxicology, but the ME is ruling it a suspicious death for several reasons. For starters, his neck was broken. A high fracture around the second vertebrae meant almost instant death. As far as death due to seizure activity, the doctors find it strange that he would not only have a seizure this far into recovery but also one that proved lethal."

"And one that produced such a high fracture," Jake said. "I call bullshit."

"Agreed," Callie said. "Odds would have to be astronomical."

Curtis nodded. "Indeed. And then there's the writing on his abdomen, just like the others. Palmer's message said 'No Gratitude.' In addition, his forearm had been sliced seven times, again, like the other victims. The lacerations were not deep enough to cause any real harm—just deep enough to cause intense pain."

"Which means," Jake interjected, "we don't need to wait on the official coroner's report to know they were all victims of the same killer."

"Yeah," Callie said. "Gabriel."

"Exactly. And as far as the probable attack on Palmer, I interviewed the young cop on duty when he died. The kid is scared stupid of losing his job, but he did offer up something. He told me the last visitor to Palmer's room was a neurologist named, get this... D. Cyple."

"Oh, you gotta be shitting me," Jake said.

"Nope. Ballsy, huh?"

Callie grabbed the coffee pot from the counter. After filling three cups and setting them on the table, she said, "Not ballsy so much as psychotic, delusional. This asshole is toying with us. Using that name tells me he believes himself untouchable."

"Like a cat, playing with a mouse before he devours it," Curt said.

"Yep. I seriously hate this guy."

"We all do, Blaze," Jake said. "So, what about the others? Cause of death, I mean."

Curt took a notebook out of his shirt pocket. "Sorry. I have a terrible habit of burying the lead sometimes and forgetting key points in a case. Somehow, my brain thinks if it's in my vault," he tapped his temple, "it's in everyone's vault. So, I got myself a little black book."

Callie smiled slyly. "Good for solving crimes as well as jotting down phone numbers for pretty ladies, right?"

Curt laughed. "Gentlemen, actually."

At Callie's confused look, Curt winked, "My book would be full of men's phone numbers, not ladies'. Although I do hold women in the highest regard."

Callie chuckled. "And we thank you for that."

After taking a sip of coffee, Curt studied his book. "Where were we? Oh, yeah—cause of death. As I said, all the victims had seven non-lethal cuts on their arms. We still have no idea what that means."

"Seven deadly sins?" Callie said to Jake. "Like JP was saying?"

Jake nodded but stayed silent.

"The other similarity is the mark on each victim's forehead. Other than that, Rebecca died from exsanguination. She bled to death after having her carotid arteries severed. Annie died from blunt force trauma to the head. The coroner said the impact of whatever crushed her skull sent slivers of bone into her brain, killing her almost instantly."

"Lovely," Jake said sarcastically.

"As for Harry Tinning, he died via suffocation. Several of the coins stuffed into his mouth ended up in his trachea, obstructing his breathing."

"That's horrible," Callie said, clutching her throat. After Katie's drowning as a child, dying via suffocation was one of Callie's worst fears.

Jake raked a hand through his hair. "And what about the elephant in the room? Was that accident victim Faith? I mean, Fiona Clark?"

"And did you find Tucker Simon at the accident scene?" Callie added.

"To Callie's question, no," Curt said. "The only body found anywhere near that accident scene was female." He looked down, clearing his throat. "We've made a positive ID, visually anyway. Both Sawyer and I are confident that the woman found dead at the scene is Fiona Clark."

Jake and Callie digested that information for a moment. "Damn. As much as she pissed me off lately, I was hoping it wasn't her," Jake said.

Callie grasped Jake's hand. "Me, too. I hope she didn't suffer."

"Not because of the crash," Curt said. "But to be honest, she had injuries that cannot be attributed to the accident."

Jake's face reddened, and his hands clenched. "Such as?"

"Such as circular bruising on her wrists, as if she'd been restrained by ties or handcuffs. That, along with bloodied knees and the Sigillum on her forehead, point to her being held somewhere. Probably by Gabriel."

"Jesus Christ!" Jake yelled, pounding a fist on the table. "Is there anything this fucker won't do? Any person he won't touch?"

"Easy, love," Callie said soothingly. "Curt, are you saying Faith had the same Sigillum found on the other victims?"

"Yeah, looked identical to me. But no cuts on her arms and no message on her belly."

"So, she was different to Gabriel, somehow. Or to Simon. But why did she have Tucker's car? And what caused the crash?"

Curtis shrugged. "I'd bet my next paycheck the car was sabotaged somehow. Either that or Fiona Clark, aka Faith McTavish, escaped captivity, only to kill herself by driving off a cliff."

Callie was stunned. "Suicide? Faith? I have to say there were no overt signs Faith was ever suicidal. What did you find that made you think that was a possibility?"

Curt drained his coffee cup. "It was more like what I didn't find. Specifically, skid marks. There were no skid marks on the pavement, nothing to indicate she attempted to stop or tried to avoid going off the road."

"And you think that could mean she intentionally killed herself?"

Jake brought his cup to the sink. "Maybe not. Déjà vu to our conversation with JP. He theorized early on that maybe this accident wasn't an accident at all. We might want to step away from the suicide theory and enter door number two."

"And what's behind door number two?" Callie asked.

"The possibility Faith didn't go over that cliff without help."

Callie's eyes widened. "You don't think...."

"Yeah, I do, Blaze."

Jake and Curt looked at each other before saying in unison, "I think someone fucked with Tucker Simon's car."

No one said a word for a few moments; all three sat lost in thought. Finally, Callie broke the silence.

"Okay, for argument's sake, let's assume you're both right and someone—probably Gabriel—tampered with Simon's car. Who was he trying to kill? Tucker or Faith?"

Jake shrugged. "With Gabriel, who knows? Could be he wanted them both dead."

～

"Jed is going to be crushed. He pretends like it doesn't matter to him, but believe me, it does."

Darby and Callie held hands at the kitchen table, trying to absorb the information gathered in the last twenty-four hours.

"I don't know, Darbs. Jed explained that Faith wasn't the person he thought she was. Of course, he'll be sad to know she's the one who died in that accident. But crushed? Something tells me it would take an enormous amount of weight to crush a Devereaux."

"I hope you're right. Are you going to tell Amara?"

"Eventually."

Darby raised a brow and tilted her head. "Eventually?"

"Okay, look, I know I should. But Amara has been through an awful lot. Between discovering her new ability and a bunch of siblings and then moving several states away, I want her to have a few days before we throw her into this new dumpster fire."

Darby nodded. "Makes sense. So, about Jed. How should I handle Faith's death with him? I mean, it's not like we're canoodling or anything. We're still in the 'dance' phase of this relationship, stepping on each other's feet and trying not to flinch."

"Canoodling?" Callie laughed.

"Yes, canoodling. I'll tell you, if it weren't for that man's gorgeous face and smokin' hot bod, I wouldn't give him a second glance. Oh, and that scar," Darby said dreamily. "Don't get me started on that scar above his eye. Sexy as hell."

Callie laughed. "So, you're not interested at all in Jed, then? Except to, you know, get naked with him?"

"Yes. No! Oh, I don't know! Maybe in my mind, it's like spring break at college. You know the frat party floor will be littered with beer cans and bad decisions, but you just gotta experience it once."

"Like the proverbial itch that needs to be scratched?"

Darby grinned. "Yes! Exactly like that."

Callie rested her chin on her hands. "Okay, but devil's advocate here. What if scratching that itch just one time doesn't tame it? What if it just leads to more irritation and itching?"

"Then I invest in a tub of calamine lotion. Or I—"

"Sorry, didn't mean to interrupt," Jake said, entering the room. "Calamine, Darby? I hope you didn't run into a batch of poison ivy. We try to keep it at bay, since Jed is highly allergic." He walked to the refrigerator and grabbed a bottle of water. "Man, one time, my brother had a case so bad, he stayed in bed, scratching for days. Talk about an intense itch."

Darby and Callie looked at each other before dissolving into a fit of laughter.

Jake and Callie stepped outside, each taking a rocker on the front porch. Darby and Amara were chopping vegetables in the kitchen while Tyler watched cartoons in the family room. Jed had yet to return from Tucker's apartment.

"So, about Philadelphia," Jake said, his heels moving the rocker in a steady rhythm. "I've been tossing Tyler's situation over and over in my mind, and I can't say I'm not concerned. We know his father, Graeme, is dead, murdered by an unknown individual. And his mother, Emily, has been missing for eight months or so and is, most likely, dead as well. Now, we have the person tasked with caring for Tyler since he was a baby, Fiona Clark, dead under suspicious circumstances."

"Go on," Callie said. "Although you're starting to scare me."

He took her hand and kissed her knuckles. "Don't mean to frighten you, babe. I just think it's madly coincidental."

"And there are no coincidences, only design," Callie finished for him.

"Precisely. Which leaves us with a few other options. Maybe the death of Graeme Duncan was like a catalyst, creating a chain reaction of events. Maybe whoever killed him is nervous, tidying up potential witnesses to the murder."

"Makes sense."

"The other option is more disturbing. What if the Duncan or Weston family are being targeted?"

"Which would put Tyler in even more danger," Callie said, understanding Jake's point.

"Right." He stopped rocking for a moment. "I think it's more important than ever to plan a visit to Pennsylvania. I need to talk to this Randall Weston and figure out if Tyler is in any danger."

"Agreed. Just say when and I'm there."

"Uh, actually, I figured to go solo on this one."

Annoyed, Callie asked, "Because?"

"Because if there is something hinky about Tyler's family, I don't want you in the crosshairs of it."

"Oh, for fuck's sake!" Spine stiff, Callie stood and headed to the front door. "Lovely thought, Mr. Agent Man. But meanwhile, here in the real world, I'll work on getting us a flight for tomorrow morning."

Defeated, Jake mumbled, "Great, Blaze. You do that."

CHAPTER TWENTY-TWO

Philadelphia, Pennsylvania
Eight months earlier

"Come on, Ty," Emily said. "Grandpa Weston and Auntie Elizabeth will be here in a few minutes."

"Momma," Tyler said, sitting on his bedroom floor while Emily made the bed, "your face is purple and blue. Did Daddy hit you again? Why does he hate you?"

Smoothing a hand over the bruises on her face as if it could erase the evidence and spare her child more pain, she said, "Your dad has worries, bud. That's all. Sometimes, those worries cloud his judgment, and he lashes out. It doesn't mean he hates me, though."

Liar! she thought. *He could not hate me more!*

Graeme's hatred of his wife was vicious and deep. Emily had no idea when it had started or why. There was no dividing line, no specific date, between loving whispers and sweet kisses and cruel words, hard fists, and belt lashes. Hell, she could barely remember the first time he'd hit her, much less the reason for it.

And she had no idea why she continued to make excuses for a man whose actions were inexcusable.

"Come on, kiddo," she said finally. "Let's get you some breakfast before they get here."

"Okay," Tyler said glumly. "But Daddy will be mad that Auntie Libby and Grandpa are coming over. I don't think he likes them."

She grabbed his waist and tickled his ribs. "Then it's a good thing we aren't telling him, isn't it? Daddy will be leaving for work soon, anyway."

When they reached the kitchen, Graeme was filling a thermos with coffee. "Good morning," he said as if nothing had happened the night before. "How are my favorite people this fine day? Sleep well?"

Unwilling to set Graeme off with a smart-ass response, especially with Tyler in the room, she swallowed her furious comeback and said simply, "Fine, thank you."

She found speaking difficult. Every breath reminded her of her injuries—injuries inflicted by the man who had vowed to love and honor her all the days of his life. She was bruised and bloodied, with a split lip, pounding head, and, probably, cracked ribs.

Not to mention the emotional pain of having suffered a miscarriage.

Graeme walked up behind her and put his arms around her waist. Snuggling into her neck, he whispered, "I was a jerk, love. I'm sorry I had to hurt you. But dammit, Emily, you've got to stop provoking me. We could have prevented this if you'd just remembered your place."

Bristling, Emily bit the inside of her cheek until she drew blood to stop herself from lashing out. 'Her place' would, if all went according to plan, be far away from Graeme Duncan in the coming weeks.

The loss of her unborn child proved to have a silver lining, supplying the proverbial nail in the coffin for Emily and Graeme's relationship. She was leaving, taking Tyler away from this house. If Graeme decided to fight her on it, she would report his abuse to the police. A domestic violence accusation could ruin his career as an attorney.

"Anyone seen Fiona this morning?" Graeme asked brightly.

"In the shower, Dad," Tyler said.

Graeme stared down at Tyler, frowning. "What's the use in having a live-in if she's never around when I need her? This is important. I guess I'll wait until she comes down. She'd better not make me late for work."

"She—she may be a while, Graeme. Why don't you go on ahead so you won't be late? You can always talk to her tonight."

Graeme's frown deepened. "I said I'll wait."

Several minutes ticked by; the silence in the kitchen was deafening. Emily glanced at the clock, and her stomach turned. She'd asked her family over to tell them she was leaving Graeme. They were due any minute, and putting all three in the same room was a horrible idea.

They hated each other.

She wasn't sure what had caused the bad blood between her father and Graeme, but just before Tyler's third birthday, their relationship had changed from ball games and fishing trips to snide comments and threatening messages.

As for Emily's sister, Elizabeth, she was a 'daddy's girl' and, in truth, an insufferable suck-up. She had quickly taken her father's side in the feud.

Randall and Graeme had continued to tiptoe around each other until late last year, when, after a blow-up following a family picnic, Graeme forbade Randall and Elizabeth from ever setting foot in his house again. Her father and sister hadn't been invited back since then.

Until today.

Now, with mere minutes until her family arrived, Emily started to panic. She knew if Graeme was still here when her father saw her battered body, it would mean bloodshed.

"Tyler, honey?" Emily said. "Can you run upstairs and ask Fiona to come down? Your dad needs a word with her."

Tyler cast a worried glance at his mother before running out of the kitchen and up the stairs.

"What's going on?" Graeme asked, suspicious. "You trying to get rid of me?"

"No, not... not at all," she stuttered. "Just trying to help."

"Help, huh?" Graeme said, moving closer. "You know I hate lying, right, Emily?"

"I'm not—"

His hand flew to her cheek so fast she never saw it coming.

"Shut up! Every time you open your fuckin' mouth, lies fall out!" Shouting now, Graeme slammed her against the refrigerator. The coin jar resting on top of it crashed to the floor. Moving within inches of her face, his breath hot against her skin, he snarled, "Looks like you need another lesson, doesn't it? Well, not to worry. Apparently, we have the time."

With a grunt, he pulled back his arm and buried his fist into her rib cage.

Emily gasped, white-hot pain screaming down her side as his knuckles connected with her injured ribs. Vision swirling, she lifted her head and found his eyes. They were cold, dark, blank.

Merciless.

Palming her face with one hand, he bashed her head again and again into the refrigerator. Room spinning, stomach churning, she fought an overwhelming urge to give in to the darkness. Just as she felt herself losing that fight, just when she prepared to embrace unconsciousness, she registered Graeme's confusion as he was lifted off his feet by some unknown force.

She watched, fascinated, unsure if what she saw was real or the result of a concussed brain.

Graeme was levitating. He hung frozen in midair for a few seconds before an arm flew forward and his body went flying, hurtling across the room at lightning speed.

The last thing Emily heard as she collapsed was the shattering of a window and Graeme's terrified screams.

Ten minutes later, Emily regained consciousness. Groaning, she sat up, leaned against a lower cabinet, and looked around.

It took a minute to focus, but she slowly became aware of her surroundings. The dark silhouette of one man stood to her left while the form of another man lay on the floor. Working to slow her pounding heart, burying the pain of countless injuries beneath the adrenaline coursing through her veins, she stood.

Blinking furiously, she rubbed her eyes; her addled brain tried to make sense of what she was seeing.

Graeme lay face down on the floor, unmoving, an ocean of blood surrounding him.

Emily stared at his lifeless body and felt nothing. He had been a man without scruples, without pity, without a soul.

And now, he was a man without a pulse.

As he lay there on the kitchen floor, reeking of sweat and hate and privilege, the stench of stale booze from the night before heavy in the air, Emily wondered how she'd ever loved him. He was a monster, a vicious bully whose only pleasure came from the physical pain he inflicted on her and the emotional damage he could visit upon his son.

"Emily?"

She got clumsily to her feet and, swaying, grabbed the edge of the counter for balance. Squinting, she concentrated on the man standing at Graeme's feet, pistol in hand.

"Dad?"

∼

"Tyler?" Fiona whispered, arm around his shoulder. "Ty, don't look."

Crouched against a wall recess in the foyer, Fiona Clark and Tyler Duncan remained hidden as events unfolded in the Duncan household. They'd been on their way to the kitchen, each lost in their own thoughts, when they heard Graeme's screams. Fiona pulled Tyler back to the security of the hallway, but not before they both witnessed three bullets slamming into Graeme Duncan's back.

Oh, God! Fiona thought, panicked. *What do I do?*

Tyler, wide-eyed, continued to stare at the corpse on the floor.

"Shhh," Fiona whispered, holding back tears. The man she loved was face down on the floor, deathly still, a pool of blood spreading beneath him. "It's okay, baby." She pulled him closer and, soundlessly, they stood. "We need to get somewhere safe, Tyler."

Tyler's little body shook as he peered around the corner.

"Come, Tyler," Fiona said, more sternly this time. "I have a bad feeling about this. We need to get away from here. From him."

Tyler finally pulled his gaze away from the corpse on the floor and turned to Fiona.

"Yes, baby," Fiona said soothingly. "We aren't safe here. We need to go away, make sure you are safe from...."

Tyler remained silent, only giving her a questioning look. This day would prove to be the last day Tyler spoke for a very long time.

"Safe from him, Ty. Safe from the boogeyman." She ushered him quickly back up the stairs to pack. "Safe from your grandfather, Randall Weston."

≈

Sheridan, Wyoming
The 'J. Gabriel' Farmhouse

"Oh, Pastor Penne," Gabriel whispered in a sing-song voice. "Time to rise and shine, my sinning friend."

Leland Penne opened his eyes half-mast and squinted. The glare from the bulb above his head was blinding. "Wha—wha's goin' on?" he slurred.

"Big day, Leland, my man! Today is the first day of your soul's redemption!"

Leland shook his head as if doing so could nudge his brain neurons into firing again. The chains that bound his wrists to a center column clanged with every movement he made.

"Redemption? Redemption for what, exactly?" Then, as if remembering it himself for the first time, he added, "You do know who I am, right, son? I am the pastor of the Rock of Faith Church! I am Leland Penne!"

"Penne? Oh, yes. Like the writing instrument, not the pasta, right?"

Leland's face reddened at the taunt. "I am an important man, sir! I am a man of God! Souls depend on me to save them!"

Gabriel tipped his head back and laughed. "Souls depend on you? A man of God? I've heard your sermons, Leland. The people do not depend on you. Rather, they fear you. You and your gloomy prophesies and your threats of eternal damnation unless they fill the collection basket! Those are not the actions of a man of God. There is no 'buying' your way into heaven, just as preaching with anger and hate have no place in my new kingdom."

Leland struggled to stand. His limbs felt heavy, like they were moving through mud.

"It's useless, my friend," Gabriel said. "I gave you a powerful sedative." He paused, rubbing his chin. "Do you know of the seven cardinal virtues and seven cardinal sins, Pastor Penne? Oh, of course you do. Each has its own special punishment, meant to be carried out in hell upon the sinner's death. My job is to get you into position to receive that punishment."

Leland tried to lift his head, but it proved impossible. It was as if a thousand bricks were perched upon his neck. "I don't understand," he said thickly.

"Oh, Leland. Soon everything will be clear. Your sin is wrath. In days gone by, the punishment deemed appropriate for such a sin was dismemberment. Although how they come up with these penalties is a mystery to me." He chuckled. "It's like one torment is worse than the next... Dismemberment, being boiled in hot oil, being stoned to death.

How is a body supposed to keep up? And you know what? I'm not even sure I buy it all. I swear, any Tom, Dick, or Harry can write whatever the fuck they want about religion and call it truth."

Leland's chest tightened, and he began to hyperventilate. Shaking the sweat from his forehead before it reached his eyes, he pleaded with his captor. "Please! I'm sorry, okay? I just...I just like the power preaching gives me, that's all. And I like the money it brings into the church. But, honest, I have only the best intentions!"

Gabriel ignored him, continuing with his previous train of thought. "In my work, I insist on precision and accuracy. I've slain Gluttony just as a pig would be slaughtered, and stoned Lust as the Bible has taught us. Greed choked to death on what he coveted most, and Envy died as he lived—craning his neck, coveting the gains of others while cursing their success."

Leland sobbed loudly, tears and snot gathering above his upper lip. "Please, Mr. Simon, I won't tell! Just let me go!"

Gabriel exited the barn and walked to the fire pit. After lighting a fire, he hopped into the bed of his pickup and gathered a long, thick rope into his arms. Jumping back to the ground, he tied one end of the rope to his tow hook before heading back to the fire.

Pulling on his gloves, Gabriel lifted the metal Sigillum he kept near the pit and held it in the flames. Studying the glowing embers and planning his next move, he was jerked from his scheming by what sounded like giggling. Spinning quickly, wielding the Sigillum like a sword, he pivoted in each direction, searching for the source of the voices he'd heard—laughing, whispering, mocking him.

But there was nothing to see.

Angry at the interruption, impatient to begin, he propped the iron rod in the fire pit and, tingling with anticipation, jogged back to his captive.

Oh, yes, Pastor Penne 'like the writing implement, not the pasta.' I do believe this will prove to be my masterpiece thus far.

~

Philadelphia, Pennsylvania
Eight months earlier

Emily's gaze flicked back between the corpse on the floor and Randall Weston.

"Dad? What happened?"

"Your psycho husband happened!" a female voice shouted from behind her.

"Elizabeth?" Emily said, turning. "I don't understand." Rubbing her temples, she murmured, "God, my head is killing me."

"Not surprising, since your husband was beating your head against an appliance," Randall said. "We walked into Graeme attacking you, honey. This makes how many times this year that he's raised a hand to you? So, I pulled him off you and tossed him across the room. But he just lay there, wiping the blood off his lip and laughing at me. He said you were his wife and would deal with your behavior as he sees fit."

"So, you what? Shot him?" Emily said in disbelief. "Why wouldn't you call the police, Daddy? Now we have to explain to them..."

Elizabeth moved closer. "We aren't explaining anything, little sister." She gave a furtive glance to Randall before turning her gaze back to Emily. "You are going to take Tyler to the park. We," she nodded at Randall, "are going to deal with Graeme's body. We'll get rid of him where no one will ever find him."

"Are you insane?" Emily asked, horrified. "You can't just toss him away like an old shoe, Libby. Granted, he was a jerkoff, but he was also a human being. He should have a decent burial. His extended family would want to say goodbye." She stepped to the dinette table and pulled out the chair furthest from Graeme Duncan's body. "No, we will call the cops; explain the situation. We can even contact your attorney right after we call the

257

police."

"Jesus, Emily, grow up!" Elizabeth snapped.

"Stay out of this, Libby!" Shaking now, the full implication of what had occurred finally hitting her, Emily closed her eyes. "Dad, Gideon Sherman is a great lawyer. He's been by your side since I was a kid. Call him. You were only defending me, saving me from serious injury or worse. If there was ever a case for justifiable homicide...."

Randall plopped wearily into the chair next to Emily. Taking her hands in his, he said softly, "Pumpkin, I can't do that. Do you have any idea what a scandal like this will cost the company? The stockholders will go ballistic. We stand to lose millions."

"I'm sorry, Dad, but my mind is made up. We need to call the authorities. Afterward, we will sit down with Tyler and explain what happened here. He knows what kind of man Graeme was. He'll understand."

Randall shook his head. "Can't do it, Em. I'm sorry."

Emily stood, her face pinched with regret. "I wasn't asking, Daddy," she said softly. "I'm calling the police. I could never live with myself otherwise."

"You couldn't live with it?" Elizabeth screeched. "Then, how about you die with it, you ungrateful bitch!"

Emily heard her father yell, "Elizabeth, wait!" before she felt the butt of Randall's gun, the same one used to shoot Graeme Duncan to death, smash into the back of her head.

≈

Sheridan, Wyoming
Present day

Gabriel silently gave thanks for his physical condition. Dragging a kicking, screaming, two-hundred-pound man across a gravel and dirt driveway was not for the weak of body.

Or of mind.

"Stop!" Leland yelled, reaching with bound wrists for the hands that encircled his ankles. "Let me walk! The stones! The driveway stones are ripping the skin off my back!"

Gabriel ignored him and continued to pull, sweat dripping from his brow. His biceps cramped and his thighs burned, but still, he persevered.

He always persevered.

"We're here, Leland Penne!" Gabriel huffed, dropping the man's ankles with a flourish. They were within a few feet of the pickup bed.

Leland closed his eyes, trying to catch his breath. "What are you going to do with me?" he asked, not yet panicking. *Surely, this is just a play for power or money*, he thought. *Getting killed by psychos happens to other people, not to me!*

Gabriel, his back to his captive, lifted the rope attached to the tow hitch and wrapped it around Leland's ankles several times.

"What are you doing?" Leland asked, the first tingle of real fear crawling up his spine.

Grunting, Gabriel tightened the knot at Leland's ankles and yanked on the ropes that restrained his wrists. Satisfied his captive was secure, he leaned in closer and said, "Drawn and quartered, pasta man. Have you heard of it?"

Leland, eyes wide in fright, started to hyperventilate again.

"Well, let me explain it to you," Gabriel said, his tone condescending. "It's particularly gruesome and not for the faint of heart. History tells us the punishment begins when the condemned have their intestines 'drawn,' or pulled, out of their body. The executioner gets in there and just rips 'em out. After that, the prisoner's limbs are tied to several horses. Once the animals are made to run, the 'quartering' happens—four limbs torn off, dragged in different directions, behind terrified horses. Must have been quite the event to witness."

Leland stared at him in horror.

"Now, now. Don't worry, Leland Penne! I have no intention of ripping your guts out." Chuckling, he added, "Besides, can you imagine? That would create quite the mess! And the stench? Pee-yew! Besides, I have no horses available, so I can't very well 'quarter' you, can I?"

"Please!" Leland begged, his vision blurred with tears.

"But," Gabriel continued, unfazed by the pleas for mercy, "I do have a truck. And plenty of land. If I were to drive, I don't know, thirty-five or forty miles per hour while dragging you behind it? It probably wouldn't take long for something to bend, break, or even fly off. I heard tell of a man whose head popped clean off while he was being dragged by an automobile. Heartbreaking stuff, really."

Gabriel snickered.

Leland, frantic, tried desperately to stand but only made it to his knees. A gentle nudge to the chest by Gabriel's foot was all it took to knock Leland back to the ground.

"Because I'm feeling exceptionally charitable today, pasta man," he said, moving to the glowing iron in the fire pit, "I will work quickly."

He lifted the rod, walked back to the sobbing figure on the ground and, once again, planted his foot on Leland's chest.

Bending forward, he whispered, "I find it easier if you don't move."

Leland screamed as the flaming hot iron scorched the Sigillum into his skin. He lost consciousness for a moment, and his head lolled to the side; the glowing embers stuck to his forehead, still smoking. His eyes were glazed, and his chest heaved. Little tufts of dirt lifted from the ground with each panting breath.

Gabriel patted Leland's cheek. "Good job, Penne. Very admirable."

Leland, shivering, was oddly quiet. No screaming, no cursing, no vows of revenge. Not even a moan.

"Silent treatment, eh, champ?" Gabriel said with a wink. "No matter. See you on the other side, Leland *'like the writing implement, not the pasta'* Penne."

Whistling *Spem in Alium* by composer Thomas Tallis, Gabriel hopped in the truck, tuned to his favorite radio station, and laid his head on the headrest. Classical music, especially pieces from the Renaissance era, soothed him as nothing could. After a few moments, he twisted in his seat, opened the sliding window above the truck bed, and yelled, "Here we go, pasta man! Do try to keep up!"

As he put the truck in gear and started to move, Leland began to howl. It was a scream of shock, disbelief, and unbridled terror.

It was the panicked scream of a man who knew he was about to die.

CHAPTER TWENTY-THREE

Just before dinner, Jake's phone pinged with a notification from one of the cameras at the front of the house. Smiling, he handed the phone to Callie.

"See? These cameras work beautifully, even with this steady rain. Here comes Jed."

Callie grinned. His boyish enthusiasm for the little things was part of why she adored him. Whatever he was doing, whether installing cameras, frying eggs, or nibbling on her neck, he did it with a flourish. His zest to enjoy everything life had to offer—along with his devotion to his family and friends—made it easy to fall in love with him.

Being tall, dark, and handsome didn't hurt his chances, either.

"I see, I see," Callie said. "Let's hope he found Tucker. Or, at least, found something useful in his apartment."

Darby stood at the stove, mashing potatoes in a pot. "I wonder if Curt called him. You know, about the positive ID on Faith?"

Callie opened the silverware drawer and began counting out utensils for dinner. "I don't think so."

Before Darby could respond, the front door creaked open. Jed reached an arm inside, dropped a few grocery bags on the kitchen floor, then turned and shook his umbrella and leaned it against the porch railing.

"Evening, folks," he said, stomping his feet on the 'Welcome' mat. He looked around the room before he pinned his gaze on Darby. Offering her a sweet smile, he asked, "Is that meatloaf I'm smelling?"

"It is," Darby said brightly. "Mamaw Harrison's recipe. It's got bacon and onion and a brown sugar glaze!"

"Sounds delicious. I'm starved."

Jake reached to a top cabinet and pulled out the dinner plates. "Anything at Simon's apartment? Did you find the little weasel?"

"Negative. It looked like he hadn't been home in a few days. I found a half-eaten frozen dinner next to a warm beer. And, weirdly, all the lights were on. Every damned one."

Callie felt chilled. "Like he was afraid of the dark."

"Like that, yeah," Jed said. "I also found a tiny notebook. It was in his bedroom, stuffed under a mattress, along with about a dozen dog-eared Playboy magazines."

"Tell me you didn't touch those," Jake joked.

"Not on your life, brother. But the notebook is interesting. It was almost as if Simon created it to be used as evidence in a court of law. Dates, names, places—all entries cloaked within a code, assumingly to record what was happening to him. Luckily for us, JP and I cracked that code before we even left Tucker's parking lot."

"Brilliant!" Darby shouted. "What did the freakazoid have to say?"

"Not a lot. Most of it was random dates and times, plus phone calls he had with Gabriel. JP took the notebook to work with him. He's going to dig further into it on his break."

"So, it's confirmed, then?" Callie asked. "No ambiguity? Tucker Simon was working with, or for, Gabriel?"

"It would seem that way," Jed responded. "We found Rebecca Caraway's name in there, as well as a name we haven't heard yet...Bob Dietrich."

"Who's that?" Darby asked, scooping the potatoes into a bowl.

"I have no idea. Whoever he is, I assume he's dead. There was a crude drawing of a skull and crossbones next to his name. On the way back here, I reached out to Abby and asked her to search his name in the usual databases." Jed opened the fridge and grabbed a beer. "How about you guys? Anything new pop up since this morning?"

Jake reached in and grabbed his own beer, then clapped Jed on the shoulder. "A few things that aren't pleasant, especially information relating to that accident involving Tucker's car."

Jed frowned. "It's Faith, isn't it? The woman who was killed?"

"Afraid so, brother," Jake said softly.

There was a moment of uncomfortable silence. Everyone wanted to say something, anything, to ease Jed's aching heart.

At the same time, they recognized there were no words.

Darby, being Darby, broke the silence. "Well, that's so not what we all wanted to hear. I'm so sorry, Jed,"

He reached out and squeezed her hand. "Thank you, Darby. Since we've confirmed her identity, we need to contact her family. Her parents are deceased, and the grandparents who raised her were, according to Faith, abusive assholes. But she does have a brother she was close to years ago. Last I heard, he was serving time for aggravated assault and armed robbery in Pelican Bay, a maximum-security prison in California. Still, he should have the opportunity to participate in her services and burial plans."

Jake clucked his tongue. "Uh, you do realize that an inmate doing hard time normally doesn't have a pot to piss in, right, my brother?"

Jed waved away Jake's concern. "Then I'll pay for it. As angry as I am at Faith for lying and taking part in kidnapping Tyler, she did a lot for me. She was there when I needed a friend. That has to mean something, right?"

Darby walked over to him and put her arms around his neck. "It means a lot, Jed. Sometimes, it can mean the world." She gently kissed his cheek and said, "I have some money socked away. Let me help you help her. We can pool our money and give her a decent send-off."

Jed brushed back a strand of hair from her face. "You are amazing, you know that?"

Darby smiled softly.

Callie groaned. "Oh, please! Get a room!"

"Yeah, I think I just threw up in my mouth a little," Jake countered with a grin.

Darby threw her head back and laughed. "Don't make me get my flying monkeys, people!"

After dinner and a fabulous dessert of coconut custard pie, Amara tucked Tyler into bed and joined the group in the living room, where Jed handed out notepads and brandy glasses.

"Tyler give you any trouble?" Callie asked.

"Nope," Amara responded. "He was asleep as soon as his head hit the pillow."

"Thanks for tucking him in, Amara. He's grown very fond of you."

Amara smiled. "Ditto."

"Okay, so what's next?" Jed asked, making eye contact with Jake. "You guys are heading to Philly in the morning?"

"That's the plan," Jake said. "Blaze got us a nine o'clock flight. We should get in by late afternoon. I figure we drive right to the Weston home from the airport."

Darby frowned. "You sure you don't want to wait? Why not get a hotel and hit the Westons' in the morning when you're fresh and focused from a good night's sleep?"

Jed nodded. "I second that. It's a five-hour flight, give or take. Take a minute to breathe, go out for a nice dinner, hit the hay early. We have things under control here, so there's no need to do a turn-and-burn. And Tyler's grandfather isn't going anywhere."

"We hope," Callie said, holding up crossed fingers.

"Nah, I'd bet on it. Randall Weston strikes me as the type of man who loves to be center stage and lives for the sound of his own voice. Trust me— if he knows you guys are coming to pick his brain, he'll be there."

"Maybe we could take an extra few hours to explore, Jake," Callie said with a wink. "Weston knows we are coming to talk. We can tell him to make it Thursday morning rather than Wednesday evening, right? Personally, I've never been to Philadelphia. It wouldn't break my heart to spend an evening looking around."

"Then that's what we'll do," Jake said. "And you guys have no reservations about carrying on here without us for a few days? You're good?"

Jed rolled his eyes. "Puh-lease, Jake. We were born good, right Darby?"

"Speak for yourself, bubba."

Amara, sitting quietly in the corner, cleared her throat. "Is, um, is JP coming back tonight?" she signed while speaking. "I drew something for him. It's not a big deal, just a charcoal sketch to thank him for learning to sign."

"What did you draw?" Callie asked.

"His hand, holding up his badge, complete with his badge number. I studied his hands while he was here, then had him show me his badge and committed it to memory." Amara tapped her temple. "God made up for my weak heart and crappy hearing by giving me a photographic memory. One of the best assets an artist can have."

"And to think," Jed joked, "some days I can barely recall why I entered a room."

Darby clapped her hands. "Well, I am over-the-moon impressed with you, Amara Grace Davies! Can we see it?"

Amara bobbed her head enthusiastically. "Of course! I still have a few touch-ups to complete, but once it's done, I'll be happy to hear everyone's take on it."

Callie beamed. "Can't wait to see it! JP is going to love it!"

"Speak of the devil," Jed said as his phone rang. "Hey, JP. We were just talking about you."

"No wonder my ears were ringing. I'm still at work, but I just remembered the sin I'd forgotten. It's wrath. Wrath, or anger, is the sixth deadly sin. Its opposite trait, or cardinal virtue, is patience."

"And pride is considered the first sin, right? Do you think the order means anything here?"

"Nah. Knowing the order just helps when memorizing your catechism as an altar boy. As far as this case goes, unless we are missing some bodies somewhere, this asshole doesn't appear to be killing in any order."

Jed agreed. "My thoughts, too. So, we have four victims whose supposed transgressions correspond to four of the seven deadly sins—gluttony, lust, greed, and envy. Those are the 'sinners' we know about. We need to find this prick before he puts any more notches in his belt."

"I hear that," JP said. "All right, I need to get back on the road. Text me with any developments or anything you need on my end."

"I will. And JP? Thanks, man. For everything."

Callie dried the last dessert dish and hung up the kitchen towel.

"I could have done that, Blaze," Jake said, entering the room.

"Well, my hands aren't broken either, FBI guy. Darby makes the dinner, and I do the cleanup. Only fair, right?"

"*We* do the cleanup. But thanks."

Callie wiped down the counter for the fourth time, her mind elsewhere.

"What's going on, sugar?" Jake asked. "You're a million miles away."

She threw the sponge into the basin before resting her hip against the counter. "The lady in white. She's here, Jake. At the cabin."

"So, she's following us. Or you, anyway. Has she given you anything more?"

"Not really. This time, instead of '*You must find her*,' she simply said, '*Hurry.*' I could feel the urgency, the near hopelessness, in her plea. At least, that's what my mind was telling me. Who knows? Maybe I know less than

267

I think."

"You know ghosts, Blaze. You know their habits, their messages, their hearts. You start ignoring your gut, and we're in deep doo-doo."

Callie chuckled. "Yeah, for all the good my gut does. Honestly, why can't this woman elaborate on who we are supposed to save?"

"Maybe that's a question to ask Kate." He let Blue and Lucky out to run and turned to her. "Anyway, how about some good news for a change? Abby called while you were doing the dishes. She got a hit on the man mentioned in Tucker's notebook. It seems Robert Dietrich spent his life as a caretaker. For the last thirty years, he worked as an overseer for a specific property, doing minor repairs, cutting the grass, etcetera."

"Okay, so what made him a Gabriel target?" she said, taking a seat at the table. "What was his sin in the twisted bastard's mind?"

"Not sure. The best part, though? Along with tracking down Robert Dietrich, Abby was running the search we asked her to do, looking for any property acquired under the name of Gabriel Devine or something close to it. She didn't find his exact name, but she did uncover a transfer of property—a farmhouse, old barn, and twenty or so acres—from St. Michael the Archangel Church to one 'J. Gabriel.' But what makes this even more interesting? Guess what property Bob Dietrich took care of."

"You're joking. St Michael's? I won't lie. I didn't see that one coming," Callie said.

Jake pulled out the chair opposite her and flipped it around to sit backward. Resting his forearms on the chair's back, he said, "Yeah, I hear you. Another coincidence that is too coincidental to be real."

"A secluded home with all that land. Can you imagine what Gabriel could do with twenty acres of privacy?" Callie asked.

"Trying not to think about it, actually."

"What did Abby think about the property deed? Legitimate, or no?"

Jake shrugged. "Abby thinks if someone is good enough with computers and knows how to hack into a system, it would be one of the easier records to alter. Now, I'm not saying your demented brother knows how to do it, but he did discover your cell number and your email address and sent you the videotape of...of you and Kate in that basement. Not only that, he also managed to stay under the radar when purchasing rosary beads from that military store last year, remember? So he has to have some kind of skill set."

Callie scrubbed her hands over her face. "Jesus, I'm tired, Jake. When is this nightmare going to end?"

"It's going to end with us catching this bastard soon. Jed and Curtis will check out the farmhouse tomorrow after we leave for the airport. If this 'J. Gabriel' is your brother, we will know. And Sawyer is planning to pay a visit to Robert Dietrich. Hopefully, he can shed some light on all of this.'"

"Yeah," Callie said glumly. "If Gabriel hasn't killed him already. Maybe we should postpone our Philly trip. This is the biggest break we've had in the case in, like, forever. If we can follow the trail from that property transfer, it may not matter how, or even if, Faith became tangled up with Gabriel."

"But it kind of does, doesn't it?" Jake said. "We decided to take this trip long before Faith died. We need to know more about Tyler's family before we hand him back to them. Graeme Duncan was murdered, and as time goes on, it's looking like Faith was as well. Emily Duncan is missing and presumed dead. All these tragedies in one family, and all inside of a year's time. Something is off."

"No, you're right, of course," Callie said. "I don't want to miss out when we finally bring Gabriel down, but if Tyler is in danger, his safety takes precedence. I suppose that's why we have the Scooby Gang, right? Divide and conquer?"

"Right. It reminds me of an old Sioux saying that goes something like, 'I have seen that, in any great undertaking, it is not enough for man to depend simply on himself.' So, yeah. If it takes a village to knock down Gabriel, so be it."

"Quoting Sioux?" Callie grinned. "Are you Sioux, then?"

Jake chuckled, a deep, genuine belly laugh. "Apache, actually."

Callie leaned over the table and whispered, "Well, let's get your Apache ass riled up and track us down a white man, huh?"

Jake winked. "Yes, ma'am. The sooner we catch this creep, the sooner I can show you my teepee."

It was Callie's turn to belly laugh.

~

"Let's go over some of the basics, JP," Jake said, hoisting a bag into the back of Jed's Suburban. "Jed and Curtis will be checking out that farmhouse property sometime after they drop us at the airport. Sawyer will be following up on the things in Tucker's notebook and trying to locate Robert Dietrich."

"Which leaves me, Amara, Darby, and Tyler here at the cabin."

"Exactly. So, want to know the first rule of thumb on a security detail? Trust no one. Every person you encounter outside of our circle is suspect; every event, every phone call, every passing car, is suspicious. You think about it like that, and no one can get the drop on you."

"Got it," Burke said, lifting Callie's suitcase into the car. "Don't worry, Agent. I won't let you down."

"Don't think I don't recognize that, Burke. No way in hell would I leave you to protect my most cherished people if I thought you were a fuckup." Jake winked and continued. "Jed picked up a week's worth of food on the way back from Tucker Simon's apartment yesterday, so you should be good there. No DoorDash or Amazon deliveries until we get back, all right? The less vulnerable we are to an outside party, the less risk of a target on our backs. Questions?"

"Just one. In the event the shithead does show up here, how married are you to a 'detain, not demolish' way of thinking when dealing with him?"

Jake squinted, the tiny lines around his eyes spreading out like fans. In a dark voice that brooked no question, he said, "Detain? Son, if you see that motherfucker anywhere near my people, you put a bullet in his brain. *Comprende*?"

"Copy that, sir. Happy to oblige."

Callie was sitting on the bed, tying her sneakers, when Tyler entered the bedroom.

"Cal?" he said. "Can we talk?"

Callie smiled. After months of selective mutism, Tyler wanting to 'talk' warmed her heart.

"Of course!" she said, patting the bed. "Have a seat."

Tyler plopped heavily on the mattress as if carrying the weight of the world. "It's just that I... um, I'm scared."

"Scared? Of what, bubba?"

"Of you and Jake going to Pilladelphia." He turned and glanced over his shoulder toward the bedroom door. Whispering, he said, "What if the boogeyman gets you? Fiona told me he's always watching. She said we had to run and hide from him because, you know, he sees everything."

Callie ruffled his hair. "Philadelphia," she corrected him. "And there is no boogeyman, Ty. There are just cruel individuals with mental issues, trying to scare people." She nudged his shoulder and winked. "Besides, do I look like someone who scares easily? I mean, if there *were* a boogeyman, like for real, I'd eat him for breakfast!" She tickled Tyler's ribs. "With some blueberries and cream! Those ol' boogeymen should be afraid of *me!*"

Tyler squealed and bent forward, giggling harder when Callie tickled his thigh.

"Get it, girl!" Darby yelled from the doorway. "Get down to the bone!" She entered the bedroom and sat on the other side of Tyler. "You gotta get all the way down to the thighbone. It's where all the tickle pickles live!"

Callie laughed, gave Tyler one more tickle for good measure, and then

271

turned his face to hers. "Listen here, little man. Jake and I are going to Philadelphia to see if we can figure out what happened to your family. But I don't want you to worry. We'll be extra careful."

They looked up at the sound of footsteps. Amara stood just inside the door, leaning against the doorjamb.

Tyler gave her a shy wave before turning back to Callie. "So, that's it, Cal? You're just gonna go?"

Callie looked at Amara and winked. "Yeah, I am, peanut. But not before I show Amara and Darby where I keep my secret stash of KitKat bars!"

She tickled him once more, then looked up at her sister.

Amara cleared her throat. "Um, I'm sorry to interrupt, Callie," she said. "But can I talk to you for a sec?"

There was something uneasy in her demeanor, but thankfully Tyler didn't seem to pick up on it. "Sure thing, sis." She patted Tyler's leg and turned to Darby. "Can you keep looking for those tickle pickles until I get back?"

Darby grinned. "Oh, with pleasure. I love a good pickle." She wiggled her fingers and went after Tyler's ribs again as Callie got to her feet and went out into the hallway. When she was out of Tyler's earshot, she turned to Amara. "What's up?"

Amara looked at her glumly. "I have something to show you that may change your travel plans."

Amara and Callie walked through the kitchen and out the door to the loft above the detached garage. Jake and Jed had set up some of Amara's painting supplies and an easel in the fifteen-by-fifteen space, giving her ample room to work.

"So," Amara signed, "I've been puttering around, barely picking up a brush. Just enjoying the solitude and serenity. This window," she pointed to her right, "has a fabulous view to that little bridge out back."

Callie walked to the window. "It does." She waited a moment before the eerie silence urged her to speak. "Amara? You okay, sweetie?"

Amara looked down, trying to quell her fidgeting hands. "Nope. Not even a little bit. Early this morning...."

Callie stopped her. "Earlier than now? Geesh, it's barely seven, and here you are, making sense and speaking in full sentences. Couldn't sleep?"

"I wish it were that simple. No, my being up early had nothing to do with insomnia and everything to do with this newfound 'gift.' Last night, after finishing that picture for JP, I went to bed early. exhausted. I'd only been asleep for a few hours when I was startled awake by an overwhelming urgency to paint. I got out of bed and came out here to the loft." She closed her eyes. "It was the same as before, Callie. I went into a trance of some kind and started to paint. A few hours later, I found myself standing in front of a picture that was, well... Disturbing is probably the best way to describe it."

"Disturbing?" Callie asked.

"Maybe terrifying is a better word. Or ominous. Take your pick."

"Yikes."

Amara walked to the easel in the center of the room. "Don't take my word for it," she said, pulling off the drop cloth. "See for yourself."

For a moment, Callie's mind refused to truly 'see' the picture. Instead, she found herself lost in the curve of his face, the faint lines across his brow, the vivid colors and patterns that seemed to make the painting come alive.

Amara's talent was, in a word, breathtaking.

Callie blinked as she scanned the canvas, her brain attempting to assemble the puzzle her heart was afraid to see. Eventually, the pieces snapped into place, and she bent forward, hands on her thighs, gulping in pockets of precious air.

Slowly, she lowered herself to the floor. She wasn't sure her legs would support her.

Tilting her head back, she stared once again at the canvas propped on the easel. In the painting, three people—two women and a child—were seen running away from the Devereaux cabin, heading into the woods.

Callie recognized the figures to be Amara, Darby, and Tyler. Amara and Tyler held hands while Darby hurried behind them, her head turned back toward the cabin.

As if terrified of what she'd see. As if she were tracking someone chasing them.

Inside the open cabin door, sprawled face down on the foyer floor, was Jake. His face was an alarming shade of gray, like storm clouds gathering above the sea. Beneath him, the pine floor was thick with blood.

And near the side door, arms intertwined in what could only be described as a death grip, were Callie and Gabriel, fighting for control of a very sharp, very large, Bowie knife.

Callie turned from the painting to her sister. "Are you kidding me? This is what will happen soon? This is what you saw?"

Amara shook her head. "No, I don't see these things, Callie. I just draw them."

"Without any awareness of what you're painting until you're done?"

Amara nodded.

Callie groaned before standing. "And I thought seeing dead people was freaky. On a positive note, if Jake and I are in Philly, this can't happen, right? At least, not until we return."

"And hopefully," Amara said, crossing her fingers, "by the time you get back, Jed and Curtis will have found Gabriel and put a stop to all of this."

Callie nodded. "Your lips to God's ears, little sister. Your lips to God's ears."

CHAPTER TWENTY-FOUR

"Gather together in purity and virtue and know thy place amongst the chosen. For it is those counted among the innocent who shed the sweetest blood."

—*The Apostolic Word of Gabriel Jesus Devine*
Doctrine 1:2

Leland Penne died a coward.

Not that being pulled apart limb by limb while being dragged by a pickup truck was a noble death. Indeed, it was not.

But finding grace in adversity was the hallmark of a penitent man. A humble man. Leland Penne was neither. His last moments on earth should not have been spent screaming and begging for mercy.

Rather, he should have spent that time reflecting, preparing, and pleading for forgiveness.

Gabriel stood at the kitchen sink, scrubbing at the blood beneath his fingernails. He'd been at it for nearly twenty minutes, counting slowly, his hands red from the scalding water. Somewhere in his quest to rid himself of the stain of Pastor Penne's blood, he'd ripped open his knuckles and torn a few cuticles.

He rubbed harder, staring down at the basin as swirls of pink and red circled the drain. *Where do I begin, and where does Leland end? I can't tell if the blood on my hands is mine... or his.*

It was a poetic, almost sacred, thought—more symbolic than tangible—with a certain 'blood of my blood' flavor to it.

At last, satisfied he was clean, Gabriel dried his hands and walked back outside. Leland was still secured to the back of the truck.

What was left of him, anyway.

The pastor's limbs were torn and bloody. His left arm, nearly amputated above the elbow, was held together by a few tendons and a sliver of skin. Both legs, though still attached to his battered body, were bent, lying at impossible angles.

Leland's right side seemed to have taken the brunt of the trauma. His right hip bone protruded through his skin, looking eerily like the ham bones his mother had once used to make lentil soup.

Gabriel's stomach growled.

On the right side of Leland's face, his cheek had been avulsed, the skin torn away from chin to temple. Bits of dirt, grass, and dry twigs peeked out from inside the folds of flesh—flesh that had rolled upon itself like a Roman shade before stopping at his hairline. His nose was obviously broken, and his right eye had popped free and dangled from its socket.

As for Leland's right arm, Gabriel still hadn't found it.

Unable to focus with his stomach growling, Gabriel went back to the house and prepared a quick snack of cheese and crackers before dealing with Leland's remains.

Once his belly was sated, he left the kitchen and returned to the body slumped just beyond his truck. Squatting in front of the brutalized corpse, Gabriel lifted Leland's tattered shirt and scribbled, 'No Patience' on his abdomen.

Then he half-carried, half-dragged the dead man by the rope around his ankles until Leland was just under the truck's tailgate. Working quickly, he released his victim from the tow rope, lifted the man's body, and, with a grunt, tossed it inside the truck bed.

He would take Pastor Leland Penne to the Rock of Faith Church and pose him in front of the communion table.

Satisfied, Gabriel brushed his hands against his jeans and looked around. The only loose end left was Leland's missing arm.

"Where the fuck could an arm go?" he mumbled. Then, with a hardy laugh, he said, "Leland, did you stick out your thumb and hitch a ride?"

Behind him, he heard a high-pitched giggle. It sounded like the tittering he'd heard earlier as he heated the Sigillum. It sounded familiar, like a laugh he should be able to place.

It sounded suspiciously like his mother, Meredith.

When he was a child, she had often read to him from a book of jokes. Despite how corny or lame the joke was, Meredith would often spoil the punchline with her laughter. Since his mother was dead, though, rotting in hell among countless other sinners, the laughter could not be hers.

He spun, eyes carefully scanning the landscape around him. It was the second time he'd heard a female mocking him, and the second time he'd found nothing there.

Calming his racing heart, he convinced himself the laughing he'd heard was a ruse, a trick from Satan to stop his mission. That had to be it. Any other explanation involved either a ghostly encounter or hallucinations manifesting in a delusional mind.

He believed in neither.

Confident he was more powerful than anything the devil could throw his way, he walked a small perimeter, trying to retrace the route he'd driven while Leland trailed behind.

Gabriel had dragged the pastor over several acres of land and listened to his pathetic screams before the man finally perished.

Unfortunately, Gabriel had been so intent on where he was going—to the back ten acres and its abundant privacy—he'd spent little time taking note of where he'd been.

Giving up for now, he vowed that, once time afforded him an opportunity, he would locate the missing arm and dispose of it through the woodchipper.

In the interim, he had more pressing matters to attend to. He'd received communication from a reliable source that his sister, or someone from the Devereaux camp, at least, was on the move.

And even though it was a notification based solely on technology, he'd perked up.

Admittedly, Gabriel was not a fan of cyberspace, computing, or cell phones. Oh, he could use high tech to his advantage and understood more than most when it came right down to it. But he suspected the increase in technological advances was contributing to the moral decay of the world.

Case in point—his cell phone. He rarely carried it and checked it for messages only sporadically. He saw little point, since no one in his life would send a message anyway. Today, however, when he finally checked his phone, he discovered the notification that Callie, or at least the GPS device he had planted, was on the move.

And he'd come across this intel thanks to his ingenuity and a cute little teddy bear named Porter.

Days ago, after sitting on the hill watching Jed Devereaux's home, Gabriel had decided he needed help keeping tabs on Callie and Jake. After all, he was just one man and could not be expected to sit on that hill and watch the Devereaux residence twenty-four hours a day.

Besides, he had not had a pleasant experience on his last visit. Even now, he recalled the chill that had traveled over his body, the paranoia he'd felt as, panicked, he'd raced back to his car, convinced he was being chased.

And, although he had seen no one, he had felt watched, judged, trapped.

So, he'd bought the bear, purchased the best tracker on the market, and sewn it into Porter's left ass cheek, right beneath the heart-shaped patch that said 'Share-A-Bear.' The Share-A-Bear company believed sharing was, indeed, caring, and suggested children pass the bears around to their friends for 'play dates.'

"Exchange a bear for birthday parties, sleepovers, or backyard barbecues!" the ads said. Gabriel thought it was a stupid idea, but he needed a bear and didn't have time to shop around.

He'd ordered the little-boy version of the stuffed toy on the company's website and used the overnight shipping option. Once the 'Share-A-Bear' had arrived, he'd set the virtual parameters on the GPS tracking device, planted it in the bear's ass, and sent it to Tyler Duncan at the Devereaux address.

The device was a top-rated tracker, about the size of a deck of cards, whose only drawback, according to customer reviews, was its short battery life. It came with a programmable geofencing option, designed to notify him whenever the bear moved away from the Devereaux home in Billings.

And right now, that bear was in a tiny town called Pitikin Falls.

In hindsight, Gabriel was surprised they'd let the kid keep the toy. If roles were reversed, he'd never have chanced allowing a potential Trojan horse to breach his home security.

And that, ladies and gentlemen, is what separates me from the masses.

He covered Leland Penne's remains with a tarp from beside the woodpile and wiped his hands on his thighs once again. After dousing the fire in the fire pit, he jogged back to the barn and his tool kit. He'd removed it from his truck the day he'd tampered with Tucker Simon's brakes but forgotten to return it.

The thought of Tucker's car returned his mind to the woman he'd held in the barn. He'd had high hopes for that one, fantasies about joining forces with her, ruling the world by day and making love all night. He had been able to envision a future with her, with this woman named Faith.

Faith—a name that had felt almost prophetic, divine, to him.

Of course, daydreaming of a life together with the woman now was moot. Gabriel knew the hilly terrain in the area. She had been driving an unfamiliar car, under the influence of several tranquilizers. Not to mention the vehicle had no brakes.

Yes, he thought sadly. *My woman, my future, is most likely dead.*

Still, suspecting the truth was different from knowing it. So, he'd begun his research. He'd scoured the local papers for news of an accident, finally finding one that had taken place in the mountains just off Route 14A. It had involved a woman, a cliff, and an ancient Honda.

According to reports, the woman had died on impact. Authorities had yet to release her name. They didn't need to—he'd felt it in his bones.

She was gone. And it was Tucker Simon's incompetence that had cost Gabriel a once-in-a-lifetime opportunity.

Of course, if Faith had not perished in that wreck, Gabriel knew he was just as likely to choke the living shit out of her as he was to fuck her if they had ended up together. But Simon had taken that choice out of the equation, snatching the future from Gabriel's hands.

A dream is a wish the heart makes.

He'd seen that on a T-shirt once.

And in his dreams, Faith was a loyal and loving servant, making a wonderful home for him. And Tucker Simon was still alive.

So the Apostle could have the pleasure of killing him all over again.

Gabriel glanced in the rearview mirror before leaving the Rock of Faith Church parking lot, marveling at his good fortune.

Both the church and the parking area were empty.

He could not have planned the drop-off better. Yes, the church doors were locked, leaving it impossible for Gabriel to run with his original idea—posing Leland on the communion table. Still, the grounds held many possibilities.

The gazebo, for instance. Yes.

Decision made, Gabriel carried Leland to the hexagon-shaped shelter at the side of the building. After removing the tarp from the body, he posed the dead pastor as if he were sitting at the picnic table inside the structure, enjoying the solitude, enjoying the outdoors.

And enjoying a Red Bull.

Because nothing says "Wake me up" like a potent energy drink. Gabriel had found the empty blue and white can in the back of his truck and thought it was the perfect prop. After trying out several poses with the can, he chose the one where Leland, aided by a stick wedged in the table, held the drink to his lips.

It was surprisingly life-like—if you didn't get close enough to see the bruises, the broken bones, the blood.

Satisfied with his handiwork, he climbed back into his truck, and, after one last look behind him, pulled onto the roadway and checked his phone for the latest location of Porter the bear.

Porter.

Gabriel had come up with the perfect name for the bear after he'd cut himself shaving one day. The scars that lined both sides of his face, courtesy of Deacon Billy Ray Porter and his quest to 'cut the demons' out of a young Jeremy Sterling, made it difficult to navigate with his razor while his cheeks were covered in shaving cream.

Every time he looked in the mirror, he was reminded of what his foster father had done to him as a teenager. And with that memory came another—the deaths of Billy Ray and his wife, Jolene.

Beaten and strangled, their bloodied bodies posed at a makeshift altar.

Police had questioned their foster son, Jeremy, but eliminated him as a suspect after his birth mother, Meredith Sterling, had provided him with a phony alibi.

And just like that, he was free.

Following the deaths of Billy Ray and Jolene, a new life had emerged for young Jeremy Sterling. Like a sinister butterfly emerging from a chrysalis, a bitter psychopath had materialized from the shadows and reinvented itself as Gabriel Devine, the one who was destined to become the Apostle.

And who was now on his way to being crowned King.

~

Gabriel pulled the truck to the side of the road and studied the tracker app on his phone. According to the map, Porter the bear was about a mile down the gravel driveway on his left.

He opened Google Earth and punched in the address the tracker had indicated. The house was at the end of the road and appeared to be the only one for miles. Given that information, Gabriel decided to go the rest of the way on foot.

He reached into the glove box and removed his Bowie knife. Although he was not planning on making any moves on the cabin's occupants today, he knew he needed to be prepared for any eventuality. If he was spotted, confronted, he needed a way to protect himself.

He climbed out of the truck, opened the rear door, and grabbed the fully stocked backpack he always kept with him. After double-checking his supplies—because ill-equipped is ill-prepared—he placed the knife in a side pocket and slung the bag over his shoulders.

He was ready.

As Gabriel crept closer to the Devereaux cabin, he veered from the gravel road, instead taking the wooded area to the left of the house. The right side of the house was all open land, with green grass, a park bench, and a lovely little footbridge that spanned a creek.

Gabriel clenched his jaw. The scene spoke of narcissism, snobbery, and pretense. And it cemented his opinion that Jake Devereaux was guilty of the sin of pride.

He surveyed the cabin's exterior, noting that only one car, a Chevy Blazer, appeared to be in the driveway. Gabriel acknowledged the possibility that a detached garage several feet from the cabin held Jake Devereaux's SUV.

Not that he would be able to check. Too risky.

Once he found a secluded spot that gave him a good view of the front, he took a towel from the backpack and set it on the ground. Taking a seat, he felt around the bottom of the pack for a bottle of water and a protein bar.

As he ate, he fantasized about the day he would come back, with his night vision goggles and foolproof plan, and annihilate the people who lived here.

Everyone but the kid. Unless those fuckers jump in and give me no choice.

He pulled his binoculars from the front pouch of his bag and studied the cabin. He had detected movement inside but was too far away to make out any features.

Come on, man! Someone step outside, so I know I'm at the right place!

And then, like a gift handed to him directly by God, the front door banged open and the little boy came bounding down the porch steps, a black Lab and golden retriever at his heels.

Shit, shit, shit! I forgot she had dogs!

Gabriel held his breath and waited, devising an excuse he could use if the dogs led the boy straight to him.

"Oh, hello there. I'm a Forest Ranger out here looking for a lost pup."

Or...

"You found me! I'm playing hide and seek with my kid, and he still hasn't found me! You're really good at this game!"

Or even...

"Thank goodness! I've been wandering these woods for hours. I'm lost!"

But Gabriel needn't have worried. God, it seemed, was smiling down on him once again.

He was too far away for even a canine nose to detect.

The dogs stayed with the boy, who was now running and jumping, occasionally tossing a ball in their direction. Every few minutes, the child would fall to the ground, pretending to be hurt, then giggle when the dogs nudged his neck.

It was a sweet scene, one that could melt even the hardest of hearts.

Not mine, though, Gabriel thought, smirking. *Does that make me the Grinch?*

He watched for a while before closing his eyes and leaning against a tree. He had no intention of falling asleep. He just wanted to rest his eyes.

He awoke to the squealing laugh of a child.

At first, he feared it was the demons again, laughing and giggling at him as they had near the barn. But this sound was different. The laughter sounded light, young, human.

It also sounded somehow...off. As if the producer of the sound had a speech impediment or something.

He sat up straighter and lifted the binoculars again. This time, in addition to the boy, there was a young girl he knew was not Callie's friend, Darby.

That one, Darby, had tits for days. This girl, probably in her early twenties, had a modest-sized bosom.

"Nothin' wrong with that, sweetie," Gabriel mumbled.

He watched the two of them laughing and running in the yard. There was something vaguely familiar about the girl, but he was too far away to see her face. He felt the urge to get closer.

Just a bit—just to satisfy his curiosity about who this woman could be.

Taking only the binoculars, he moved carefully toward a break in the trees about thirty feet ahead with a grouping of rocks behind it. There, he crouched behind the rocks, steadied his arms on the top of the pile, and peered through his binoculars again.

He had a perfectly clear picture of her now. Strawberry blonde hair, pert nose, a sprinkling of freckles. While her likeness to Callie was startling, her resemblance to Katie was uncanny.

Gabriel frowned in confusion. *Did my father have yet another daughter with that slut, Eileen Callahan?*

After considering that possibility a moment, he tossed it aside.

This woman was in her early twenties; Gabriel had been ten years old when he stabbed Eileen Callahan to death. He was sure that, besides the youngest child, Ryan, no other children had been in the Callahan home that day.

Certainly not an infant.

He was equally certain that the woman he'd killed that warm day in 1997 was not pregnant.

Which left one possibility.

This girl, this spitting image of his sister, Katherine, was the daughter of Rowan Callahan and someone other than Eileen.

Someone like Meredith Sterling, he thought, intrigued. *Someone like my mother.*

As he crouched behind the rocks in the woods, watching the woman who might or might not be another sister, a memory from childhood slammed into his brain, fierce and unrelenting.

In a chair much too big for him, his eleven-year-old legs swinging back and forth, Jeremy watched the hustle and bustle of the hospital corridor. Across from him, his mother lay propped up in a hospital bed, whispering sweetly to a tiny form in her arms.

"Hello, little girl," Meredith gushed, stroking the baby's cheek. "Welcome to the world."

After a few minutes, his mother called him to the bedside. "Do you want to touch your new baby sister, Jeremy? Want to give her a kiss?" she asked.

Jeremy remained silent; his hands curled into fists. He did not want to touch, let alone kiss, the child in his mother's arms. He didn't even want to look at it.

He wanted to smash it in the face.

He remembered it all now. Several months after he'd killed Eileen Callahan with a knife to the back, Meredith had given birth to a baby girl. It was in the spring, March to be exact, seven months after Rowan Callahan's death. The child was born with a congenital heart defect and was severely deaf.

A poor specimen, the weakest of the weak. But still, I had a sister back then? How does one block the memory of a sister for all these years?

Meredith, he recalled now, had named the baby Jemma after her maternal grandmother. Gabriel assumed she must have been pregnant when they'd visited the Callahan home. At the time, perhaps because she knew she would have another mouth to feed, Meredith was looking for her fair share of Rowan Callahan's life insurance; her ten-year-old son was looking for revenge.

Only one of them had left the Callahan residence with what they sought.

Baby Jemma had lived in the Sterling household for eight months, until the day Meredith walked into the nursery to find Jeremy, pillow in hand, attempting to smother the child. That afternoon, Meredith called social services and relinquished her parental rights.

It wasn't the first time she'd suspected her son of trying to kill Jemma. She feared it would not be the last. So, despite her heartbreak, she did what was necessary to protect her baby.

When the caseworker came, Jeremy had winked at the woman while handing her a baby doll Meredith had purchased for little Jemma.

"Here, lady," he had said, voice emotionless. "We have no need for this now."

The woman had stared into his young, empty eyes, and her smile had fallen away. With a fright she'd never experienced before, she shied away from both the doll and the boy with the black eyes, clutching the baby tighter to her bosom.

As the social worker was leaving, his baby sister in tow, Jeremy said, "Goodbye, Jemma. I hope I never see you again."

After they'd left, he closed the door and glanced at the living room sofa. Meredith sat there, sobbing, clutching the baby doll he'd tried to hand to the caseworker.

Returning to the present, Gabriel raised his binoculars once again. *Hello, Jemma. I remember you now. So sweet, so innocent, so pure.*

He shot to his feet, stunned by the revelation churning through his brain. *Sweet. Innocent. Pure.*

Jemma!

He'd done it. He'd found a way to witness the Splendor, found a way to see the soul's transition at death.

And all it would take was his sister, Jemma.

He'd found his innocent.

CHAPTER TWENTY-FIVE

Philadelphia, Pennsylvania
Three p.m.

Callie and Jake sat in the SUV they'd rented after landing in Philadelphia, trying to plug in directions to the Ramada Inn.

Callie glanced at her cell phone. "Google Maps says the hotel is about fifty minutes from here. And the Weston home in the Chestnut Hill development is twenty minutes from the hotel."

Jake nodded. "Okay. But before we do anything else, we need to go over the ground rules, right?"

Callie rolled her eyes. With an exaggerated sigh, she said, "When we get to the Weston house, I will not enter a room without having an exit to my back. I will not engage with any Weston family members I believe to be hostile or sketchy. If you say, 'Please check the car for my notebook,' it means leave immediately and do not return until you give me the 'all clear.' Once outside, I will wait for your signal—O mighty one—before I re-enter the premises or blow my nose. Happy?"

"You are a stubborn woman, Blaze, do you know that? Don't you understand I'm just trying to keep you safe? If anything were to happen...."

Callie pursed her lips. "Right. If anything were to happen—including natural disasters, getting hit by the Pony Express on a mail run, typhoid fever, or African sleeping sickness—it would be totally on you. Got it."

Jake smirked and started the car. "Well, that's just silly. There are no tsetse flies around here."

Eager to change the subject to a less 'Me Tarzan, you Jane' kind of vibe, Callie said, "Did I tell you what Tyler said just before we left for the airport?"

"No, you didn't."

"He begged us not to go, warned us that the 'boogeyman' would be waiting for us. He was really upset."

Jake drummed his fingers on the steering wheel, trying to come up with an explanation for that. "Maybe it had nothing to do with where we are going and more to do with leaving him again. Not to sound like a psychologist," he smirked, waggling his brows, "but could it be that he fears abandonment? His parents are gone, and he has become very attached to us."

"I'm sure he has some abandonment issues, but, honestly, this feels like more."

Jake put the car in drive and headed for the airport exit. "We're human, Cal. We can only deal with one problem at a time. Let's just get to the hotel. Tomorrow, we will go directly to the source and see what we find. Faith knew Tucker Simon in some capacity, voluntarily or not. We need to figure out if her contact with him was incidental."

"And if it wasn't?" Callie asked.

"Then Faith McTavish, aka Fiona Clark, was up to her neck in something. She was having an affair with Graeme Duncan, so maybe she had something to do with his death. It's also possible she's responsible for Emily's disappearance. And, if she knew Tucker Simon that well, as a friend or something more, maybe that's how she ended up in Montana."

"And if she met Gabriel through Tucker, that could be exactly how he traced us to Jed's."

Jake nodded. "On the other hand," he said, as if considering it for the first time, "Faith could be innocent in all of this. What if she witnessed Graeme's or Emily's death and took Tyler on the run to protect him?"

"Okay. But then, how did she meet Tucker Simon? How did she know him well enough to borrow his car?"

Jake shook his head. "Damned if I know. None of this makes sense. It's like we're going round and round and can't see where we start and where we end. If we could just—"

He stopped speaking, slapped his forehead, then let out a whoop. "Son of a bitch! We're like a dog chasing the wrong tail, Blaze!"

"And here I thought you enjoyed chasing my tail," Callie joked.

"When this case is over, I plan on doing more than just chasing that tail." Jake smirked, wiggling his brows. "But what I'm going after now is trying to understand your psycho brother. Thanks to Kate, we know Gabriel knows where we live. He's been watching the house, taking notes or some shit, probably for weeks, right?"

"True."

"And what if, while he was casing the house, he saw Faith? She is—was—a pretty lady. When she was found after crashing Tucker's car, she had no cuts on her arms and no message on her abdomen. It's like you said. She was different, somehow, to Gabriel."

"So, he spots her, and what? Kidnaps her?"

"Maybe. What if Gabriel saw her and 'fell in love'? What if he gave her the Sigillum because he wanted her to be among the counted in the Rapture? Whatever the reason, he wanted her *alive*. Perhaps he saw her as a romantic partner, not a sinner, and came back at some point to take her?"

"Scary thought, but totally up my brother's alley. But how does Tucker fit in?"

"Well, it's like JP said. Tucker worked with TJ Palmer at the ME's office. Palmer, sick bastard that he was, linked up somehow with Gabriel and became his 'disciple.' A friend of a friend, right? Tucker could have met Gabriel through Palmer and, even if he recognized what a lunatic your brother is, helped him with his twisted agenda."

"You think Tucker is that messed up that he'd say 'yes' to murder?"

"No," Jake said. "I think Tucker is a spineless wimp who would have been scared shitless to say no."

∾

Just as Jed and Curtis pulled into the farmhouse driveway, Jed's phone rang.

"Hey, Jake," Jed said. "You guys land in Philly already?"

"About thirty minutes ago. How about you? Did you get to that farm property yet?"

"Just pulled in. Curt and I wanted to make sure everything was secure at the cabin first." Jed paused. "You know, I completely trust JP. I do. It's just that the girls, Tyler... I don't know, man. They've become so damned important to me."

Jake casually glanced over at Callie in the passenger seat. "Oh, believe me, I get that. I went over several different scenarios with Burke. I think he's prepared for anything."

Jed chuckled. "Funny. I went back to the house after dropping you off at the airport to do the same thing. He's probably cursing us out right now."

"Probably. Anyway, we're heading to the hotel. I want to take Callie around town, see some sights, maybe take her to a great restaurant. Tomorrow morning, we head to the Weston home."

"Okay. I'll call you when I know anything about this farm property. In the meantime, here's something to chew on. Sawyer reached out to Curt earlier today and confirmed what we all suspected: the brakes to Tucker's Honda were cut. Whether it was done to kill him or Faith...."

"Well," Jake responded, "since Faith had evidence on her body that she was being held against her will somewhere, my money is on Gabriel trying to eliminate Tucker. Maybe he threatened to go to the cops or something."

"Maybe. I'd feel better if we could find that weasel Tucker and ask him ourselves."

"Something tells me my old pal Tucker Simon is no longer among the living." Jake turned into the hotel parking lot. "Look, we need to check in. Call me the minute you find anything out at that farm. And Jed," he added, voice grave, "watch your back, man. Gabriel has gotten awfully comfortable in this area. If this is where he's been hiding out, trust me, he isn't going to give it up so easily."

"Got it. You both be careful, too. The more I learn about Randall Weston and his empire, the shadier he seems. As my favorite brother always says, 'Trust no one.'"

Jake smiled. "I'm your only brother, chucklehead. But yeah, we'll tread lightly."

Jed and Curt cautiously exited the Suburban and looked around. The old farmhouse was to their right, a weathered barn to their left.

"As the sworn officer here, Curt, how do you wanna play this?" Jed asked.

"I've always believed the direct approach to be best, especially since we aren't sure if Gabriel Devine is J. Gabriel." Curt walked toward the front door of the house. "Let's see if anyone is home."

They ascended the porch steps, and Curt knocked on the door. "Hello?" he called out. "Officer Curtis Valdez, Wyoming DCI. Anyone home?"

They waited a moment, and when no one came to the door, Jed peered through the glass of a side window. "I see the kitchen. Looks clean. Nothing to suggest someone got up and ran when they heard us approach."

Curt banged harder. "Hello, the house! Is anyone in there? We only want to talk with you."

Silence.

"Okay, how about we check the barn?" Jed said.

They walked from the house to the barn. Curt pulled the door open a crack and called out, "Anyone home?"

Silence.

"Call me crazy, but I'd say no one was here," Jed said.

"Agreed." Curt paused a moment, then turned and faced Jed. "Wait, do you hear that?"

"Hear what? I don't hear anything."

Curt winked. "Really? Because I could swear I heard someone yell for help."

Jed grinned. "Ohhh, *that* sound. Like what I heard at Tucker Simon's apartment. Yes, I believe I did hear a scream, Curtis. Maybe we should check, just to be sure. Can't call it trespassing if someone is in danger."

Curt nodded and pulled the door wide open. The barn was pitch black, but they could make out center columns and a hay loft at the rear. Entering the building, Curtis swept his hand along the wall, checking for the light switch.

"It's here," Jed said, hand on the opposite wall. He flicked the switch, and the space was bathed in a low, gritty light. "Hello?"

"I'll take the left side; you take the right?" Curt asked.

They moved slowly, guns within easy reach but not drawn. Jed hugged the right wall, inching his way forward. He came across the first stall, and his eyes swept the space. Other than some old tack hanging on a hook, the stall was empty.

He repeated the search at each subsequent stall, finding nothing, until he got to stall six. There, pounded into a square of cement on the floor, was an iron ring. And attached to that ring, two chains spread across the dirt floor.

"Hey, Curt? Think I found something," Jed called out.

"Me, too," Curt replied from the back left of the barn.

Jed jogged to where Curt crouched over a dark stain near the corner of the wall. "Don't tell me; let me guess. Blood."

"Sure looks like. It's dried, but yeah, I'd say this is blood. Of course, that doesn't mean it's human. There have probably been plenty of animals in this barn."

Jed tipped his head. "True. Let's look around outside. I expect we need more than our gut instincts to get a forensic team in here."

Curt stood. "Right. A warrant for starters, but to get that, we need something solid to present to a judge." He nodded his head to the right. "Whatcha find over there?"

"Iron chains. They were in the last stall, secured to a piece of cement on the floor."

"Huh," Curt said. "Not something you see every day. Let's check the grounds. Maybe this J. Gabriel is mowing or something."

They left the barn and started walking, stopping when they reached the simple fire pit out front. Jed squatted, poking through the ashes with a nearby stick. "Nothing is standing out here. Definitely been used in the past few days, though. These ashes are fresh, dry."

Curt nodded. Hands on his hips, he scanned the ground. "Hey, what's this?" he asked, leaning forward and pointing to something in the dirt beside the fire pit. "Looks like a cattle prod or something." He bent lower and cocked his head, trying to see the intricate design at the tip.

"Holy shit," he whispered.

Jed moved closer to where Curt stood. Staring down at the object, he raked a hand through his dark hair. "Holy shit is right. Is that what I think it is?"

"Yeah, it is. This should be enough to give us probable cause for a search warrant." He pulled out his phone and walked toward the car. "I'm gonna go make a few calls. Sit tight."

"Got it," Jed said. Taking out his own phone, he called Jake, leaving a message when his brother failed to pick up.

"Hey, guys, Jed here. It looks like we are on the right track at this farm property. I think we just found Gabriel's Sigillum. Give me a call when you get this."

～

"I appreciate your seeing me on such short notice, Mrs. Dietrich."

Sawyer sat in an overstuffed chair in the Dietrich living room, a cup of coffee warming his hands. "I have a few questions for you. I promise I will try to be brief." He gave her a boyish, dazzling smile and added, "Although my mother tells me I'm fascinating to listen to, I think she may be a bit biased."

June giggled. "Oh, all mothers think their sons are rock stars, Agent Mills. You're lucky to have such a supportive mom."

"I definitely won the lottery on parents, that's for sure." He took out his notebook and leafed to a fresh page. "So, Mrs. Dietrich, as I said on the phone earlier, we are investigating a series of homicides in the area."

"Please," she said with a shy smile. "Call me June. Mrs. Dietrich sounds so old!"

"June it is. So, June, we have a person of interest in this homicide case who happens to be missing. This individual left a notebook mentioning your husband and one of the killer's female victims." He took a sip of coffee. "June, have you ever heard the name Rebecca Sue Caraway?"

June Dietrich clutched her throat. "No, never. Oh, my goodness! Why would a horrible person like that have my Bobby's name in his book? Do you think something untoward has happened to my husband?" Her face pinched in pain. "You know, he hasn't been home for over a week."

Sawyer sat up a bit straighter. "You're saying your husband is missing?"

She sat heavily on the sofa and nodded.

Sawyer cleared his throat. "Um, did you call the police and report him missing, ma'am?"

Uncomfortable, June bent forward and began rearranging items on the coffee table. "Well, no. Of course, I was going to. It was so unlike Bob to just— to not call or come home."

"So, why didn't you report it?"

June sighed. "Because I received information from a reliable source that my husband was having an affair, Agent Mills. A woman he met in a bar recently. Apparently, Bob had been a regular customer of several bars in the area, although I still can't believe it. How could I not know he had an alcohol problem? Or that he had a girlfriend? Makes no sense."

Sawyer was surprised. He'd been expecting June Dietrich to provide him with information proving her husband was another one of Gabriel's victims, not a womanizing drunkard. He scribbled a note in his notebook. "But your husband had a job, right? Working for St. Michael's? I'm asking because I wonder how he had time to not only hit the bars but also carry on an affair, all without your knowledge."

June, tears in her eyes, agreed. "Yes! Exactly right, Agent! That was what I thought, but then I learned the truth. Bob would rather be with his bar buddies, cavorting with a hussy named Annie or something, than be with his loyal and loving wife!"

Sawyer reached forward and handed her a box of Kleenex that sat on the end table. "I apologize, June. The last thing I want to do here is upset you."

She dabbed her eyes. "It's hardly your fault, Agent. Anyway, I was waiting for Bobby to come to his senses." She tucked the tissue inside her sleeve. "It's what Father Gabriel told me to do—be patient and wait."

Sawyer stopped writing and stared at her. "Father Gabriel?"

"Why, yes," June said. "The priest at St. Michael's. He was the one who told me about Bob's drinking and the woman."

"A priest told you this?"

"Well, yes." Then, becoming defensive, she added, "You know, Agent Mills, he could get in trouble with the church for telling me. He was worried about violating the sanctity of the confessional, but he was just as concerned about me." She frowned. "You aren't going to use this to get Father in trouble, are you? I couldn't stand it if Father Gabriel had to face the consequences of trying to help me. He hasn't been our priest for very long, what with his terrible accident and the loss of his eye. Tragic thing. But he always stays upbeat, always sees the sun in every storm cloud."

Sawyer gently took her hand. "Ma'am, I'm afraid Father Gabriel is not who he appears to be. In fact, I believe he may have had something to do with your husband's disappearance."

June covered her cheeks with her hands. "Oh, my Lord! What have I done?" Legs quaking, she slowly stood. "Agent Mills, if you'll excuse me. I need a moment."

When she'd left the room, Sawyer phoned his office to request several patrol cars meet him at St. Michael's before dialing Jed and Curtis to fill them in. If Gabriel was at the church, he wanted plenty of backup.

Meanwhile, June Dietrich, wife of Robert 'Bob' Dietrich for almost fifty years, clutched the porcelain sink in the hall bathroom and wept.

≈

When Sawyer Mills called, Curtis was securing a length of crime scene tape across the barn door. Jed, holding the other end of the yellow tape, listened in.

"Hey, Mills," Curt said. "Jed is here with me."

"Hi, Sawyer," Jed said. "You find anything at the church?"

"I did, and it's a whammy. I had an interesting conversation with June

Dietrich. It seems she was 'counseled,' and I use the term loosely, by a priest who claimed that Bob was a drunk and a hound. He convinced her Dietrich left of his own volition, free to drink himself into oblivion while fornicating with a woman named Annie."

"But you don't believe that, right?" Jed asked.

"No, I do not. It turns out this priest from St. Michael's walks with a limp, only has the use of one eye, and goes by the name of Father Gabriel. That sound familiar?"

Curt whistled. "Damn! Gabriel posing as a priest explains a lot. You call it in?"

"Yeah, right before I phoned you. I've got some marked cars meeting me at the church. How about you two? Anything at that farmhouse?"

"Plenty," Jed said. "We're waiting on a search warrant as we speak. We found a massive amount of blood and some restraints in the barn, and we're pretty sure we found the branding iron, the Sigillum, Gabriel used to mark his victims' foreheads."

"Gentlemen, it sounds like we have our man. Let's pool our resources, shall we? You stay put and wait for that warrant while I check out St. Michael's. If we don't find Gabriel, I'll send the patrol cars to you at the farm. That way, all we're waiting on is the warrant and a forensic team. Sound good?"

"Sounds better than good. I'll fill in Jake and Callie. Great work, Sawyer," Jed said happily. "I'm gonna owe you a beer or two after this."

Sawyer smiled. "And dinner. And tickets to a Seahawks game. Oh, and a jelly-of-the-month membership."

Jed laughed. "Yeah, yeah. I got you, Mills. Now, let's get him!"

CHAPTER TWENTY-SIX

"I still think we should have taken our cell phones with us," Callie said, sipping a glass of Chardonnay.

Jake shrugged. They were sitting in a quiet booth at Bellini's Taste of Italy, an Italian restaurant on McKean Street, just a few blocks from their hotel. "Probably. But Blaze, we haven't had a minute to ourselves since we returned from Falls Church. I just thought it would be nice to unwind a bit before we tear into the case again tomorrow."

Callie nodded. "You're right, of course. I'm just worried, as usual." Grinning, she added, "You know, borrowing trouble to bake a pie no one wants to eat?"

Jake chuckled. "Good to see you've taken a shine to Grandma Devereaux and her pearls of wisdom." He nodded at her plate. "How's the linguini?"

"Delish. How about your eggplant?"

"Same." He poured the remaining beer from his bottle into his glass. A steady rain tapped on the glass skylight above them. "Is it me," he said, reaching for her hand, "or are we stumbling to find common ground here? Other than the case, I mean."

"It's not you. I've been sitting here myself, listening to the soothing sound of the rain, wondering how we start a conversation like a 'normal' couple. Maybe we should pretend we just met? I'll tell you something you may not know, something from my past, like a fear or a goal or whatever, and then you tell me something."

Wary, Jake raised a brow. "Um, are you sure that's not dangerous, Blaze? Everyone has skeletons, and frankly, there's usually an excellent reason they're kept in the closet."

"Oh, poppycock!"

Jake smirked. "Poppycock?"

"Yes, poppycock! Introducing a skeleton doesn't hurt you, G-Man. It's the ones that pop out unexpectedly that wreak havoc on the unaware. And, just because I release a skeleton or two doesn't mean I expect you to dance with it, Jake. I—I want us to be close. Unafraid to share the bad as well as the good. I'm not suggesting you disclose everything because, frankly, I'm sure some stories would keep me up at night. I'm just looking for a way to open the lines of communication."

Jake winked at her. "Okay, slugger. But just so you know, my safe word is 'potato chips.'"

Callie giggled. "Original. Anyway, I'll start." She pushed her plate away and, elbows on the table, rested her chin in her hands. "When I think of us as a couple, I find myself curious about something, so curious that it's stopping me from moving forward in our relationship." Her cheeks flushed. "You know, sexually."

Jake smirked. "Now you're talkin'! This was a great idea, Blaze!"

She laughed. "No surprise there. But tell me the truth. How does this thing between us, which seems so real and powerful, compare to what you had with my sister? Obviously, I'm not talking about sex since we haven't gone there yet. I just mean the power of the attraction, I suppose."

Jake groaned. "Aw, Blaze, please... Don't go there. Isn't it enough when I tell you I love you? That you are the one I choose to spend this life, and the next, with?"

She gave him a steely look. "No, I guess it isn't. Look, you must know how strange this is for me. Do I love you? Absolutely, totally, unconditionally. And I believe that you truly love me. But, in the back of my head, there is this voice screaming at me, telling me I don't measure up. And I want to shut that negativity off. Otherwise, I fear it will seep into every aspect of our lives, our future." Softly, she added, "Our bedroom."

He waved the server over and asked for the check. After she left, he continued. "Okay. Even though I think it's a bad idea, even though I've vowed to love you forever, I will try and explain it." He rubbed the back of his neck, frustrated and a bit embarrassed. He'd had this conversation with Jed but never intended on speaking about it with Callie. "When Kate and I met, sparks flew almost immediately. I admired her confidence, her intelligence, her humor. As you know, she was funny as hell."

"Still is," Callie agreed. "But, yeah. She could leave me in stitches, doubled over and gasping to breathe, and never break a sweat."

"Me, too. Not to mention she was breathtakingly gorgeous." He cocked his head and smiled. "Not unlike yourself."

Callie blushed again.

"Anyway, with Kate and me, it was fast and furious. We only knew each other for a month, and it was like... Shit, how do I describe it? It was as if we skipped the romantic walks on the beach and the cozy drinks before dinner, instead diving head-first into the dessert tray. We were like vultures—ravenous, needy, each trying to fill an empty space inside. Kate was still hurting from her failed relationship with Kyle, and I was too busy licking my wounds after a bad shoot to notice. We both needed a physical connection, a soul to commiserate with, someone to understand our pain."

Callie dropped her head, suddenly regretting she'd ever suggested this stupid idea. The last thing she needed to hear was how intimate Kate and Jake's relationship had been, how 'ravenous' they were for each other.

Noting Callie's mood change, Jake stretched forward and lifted her chin. "But," he said sternly, "relationships that burn that hot, like the flame of a torch, inevitably run out of fuel. I believe Kate and I would have eventually crashed and burned. Our—for lack of another word—'passion' was too much, too fast. And it was for all the wrong reasons. But you and me?" He took both her hands in his. "Cal, before it was 'us,' it was just you, and it was me. Friends to the end, but just friends."

"Buddies through and through," she agreed.

"Right. But now, after spending all these months getting to know each other, falling in love the 'right' way? Man, we are on target to hit all the firsts—date nights, drive-in movies with milkshakes and popcorn, Christmas dinners with the family."

Eyes teary, she joked, "The family? You've met them, right?"

"And I adore them. Even Finn. Bottom line? I look forward to the slow burn. In truth, I crave it. I want someone who can teach me something every day, someone I can build a history with." He kissed her knuckles. "Someone to create new memories with while laughing at the old ones."

The server approached and placed the bill folder on the table.

"Anyway, does that answer your question?"

Callie sniffed. "It does. Now, I have just one more. It's about the hotel rooms...."

Jake looked at her, puzzled. "What about them? Do you want a bigger room? A suite with a king bed rather than a queen?"

Callie licked her upper lip suggestively. "Not at all. I was just wondering if we were going to spend the night in your room or mine."

Jake rubbed his chin as if deep in thought, his bristly stubble rasping beneath his fingers. Shrugging, he grinned. "Lady's choice."

Callie stood. "I say we start in my room and see where it takes us. Pay the lady, G-Man. Let's get out of here."

Smile dazzling, he winked. "Yes, ma'am."

An hour later, Callie held Jake's body close to hers. A single tear slid down her cheek.

"Oh, shit, am I hurting you?" Jake asked, pulling back some. "Sweetheart?"

Callie held him tighter, angling herself to take all of him in. "No. Oh, God no."

He brushed the tear from her face. "Then why are you crying?"

Callie kissed him lightly and wiggled her hips. She was sending him a signal not to stop. "Tears of joy, G-man, not regret. They are tears of relief, of belonging." She kissed him softly and reversed their positions so she lay on top. "We've been on a roller coaster for months. Each wanting the other, each afraid to violate that unspoken loyalty to Katie. And even though she assured me that you weren't her destiny, that Michael was her soulmate, it still felt like a betrayal to want you."

"I know," Jake murmured into her breast. "I felt it, too."

"My point is that our needs and wants have taken a back seat to our guilt all these months. But I think it's finally sinking into this stubborn Irish head. Katie wants us to live, to explore all that life has to offer… together."

She kissed him again, more passionately this time. It was a kiss that was both pure and carnal and left no doubt she was his, body and soul. "I love you, Jacob Devereaux," she said softly.

"And I love you, Callista Callahan," Jake whispered back.

He took control once again and did not stop until they climbed that mountain together, free and as one.

$\approx$

"Any word from Jake?" Curt asked. They were sitting in Jed's car, waiting for the cavalry to arrive with a search warrant for Gabriel's farmhouse.

"Nothing from Jake or Callie," Jed responded. "Either they silenced their phones, lost them, or are in an area with no service."

"In Philly? Not likely. Maybe they went out and forgot them at the hotel? They're what? Two hours ahead of us? It's dinnertime there."

Jed chewed the inside of his cheek. "Maybe," he said, unconvinced. "Did they give you an idea of when we could expect the warrant to be issued?"

Curt shook his head. "The Sheridan County judge is on vacation, so we're waiting for the judge in Johnson County to issue. Could be a while."

Anxious, Jed shifted his weight from one foot to the other. "Do you mind if I head back to the cabin and check in? I don't want to leave you stranded here without wheels, but I need to lay eyes on Dar—on the girls and Tyler. Especially since Gabriel isn't here."

Curt nodded. "Yeah, I'm fine. If they don't locate Gabriel at St. Michael's, Sawyer will leave two units and come here to the farm. Take your time checking on, uh," he smirked, "on whoever it is you're really worried about."

"Guilty," Jed chuckled. "See you in a bit."

∽

"Well, shit!" Jake said, hopping out of bed. "I forgot to check my phone when we got back from the restaurant."

Callie sat up, the sheet pulled over her chest, and swore. "Damn! I didn't check mine either. Unbelievable! A maniac is on the loose, undoubtedly planning our demise, stalking us. Yet here we are, footloose and fancy-free, turning off cell phones and shit. What the hell is the matter with us, anyway?"

Jake, sans underwear, pulled a pair of jeans over his bare ass. Callie found that sexy as hell.

"Let's not beat ourselves up, Blaze," he said, zipping his fly. "After all, we were a bit preoccupied." He gave her a beautiful smile, and she momentarily forgot what they were talking about.

"Just put a shirt on, G-man. You're distracting me."

Jake laughed and grabbed a black T-shirt from his duffel bag. "There. Happy now?"

"Ecstatic."

"Good. I'll be right back. I need to go to my room and get my phone."

Once he was gone, Callie dressed quietly. She quickly made the bed, out of habit more than obligation, and grabbed her phone from the zippered pocket of her overnight bag. She turned it on, noting the four missed calls from Jed.

"Shit, shit, shit!"

Before she could check her voicemail, Jake was back, banging on the door. "Blaze, it's me."

She opened the door wide and held up her phone. "Four missed calls. You?"

"Six. Let's call Jed and see what's so urgent."

~

Five minutes later, Jed was filling them in on the latest developments.

"So, that's where we stand now," Jed said. "We're waiting on a search warrant. Sawyer's interview with Bob Dietrich's wife pulled it all together. Gabriel has been posing as a priest for months. We think he found the deed to the farmhouse property and amended it to look like he'd bought it years ago. We found chains, leg irons, and, most telling, the Sigillum branding iron he used on the victim's foreheads."

"Damn," Jake said softly. "So, he's been close for months, keeping tabs on us, no doubt. And as a Catholic priest? Great way to find sinners, isn't it? Masses, confessions, counseling sessions. Hate to give the fucker credit, but it's genius." He rubbed the back of his neck, frustrated. "I have so many questions. When did he get here? How did he find us? Did Tucker have anything to do with it?"

"No clue," Jed said. "Although, if I were looking for you two, I'd start looking at people close to you."

"Like my brother," Jake mumbled.

"Or our parents. He must have known you both left Falls Church after

Palmer tried to kill Callie and Tyler. And he didn't need to search for Callie's family since he knew they were in Virginia. I would bet he researched you and somehow found out you had family in Billings."

"Wouldn't be too hard. I grew up here. An internet search would find my high school track records, football stats, anything in the news with my name on it, even as a kid. Once Gabriel had that, it's a hop, skip, and a jump to Asa and Jane Devereaux and their son, Jedidiah."

"More than likely," Jed said.

Callie leaned in toward the speaker. "And Tucker Simon? How does he fit into all of this?"

"Not sure, but I'm thinking Jake's theory is spot-on—Tucker encountered Gabriel through his association with Thomas Palmer and, somehow, threatened him if he didn't cooperate."

Jake sighed. "Guess we'll learn the whole story once we catch the fucker...if I don't kill him first. No sign of him at the property or the church, I suppose?"

"Nothing. I left Curtis there and came back to the cabin. I was uneasy leaving the girls and Tyler for too long, especially with this new information. JP just left to go home and get some sleep. He'll be back in the morning."

"Okay, good. We're heading to the Westons' early tomorrow morning. I figure we can have a look around, question him about Faith, show a photo of Tucker Simon."

"And get a feel for Randall Weston's relationship with Tyler," Callie said. "Isn't it odd that he's let his grandson stay with us all this time? Wouldn't you think he'd be insisting the child belongs with family? That Tyler has been with us long enough?"

"You would think so," Jed answered. "If it were me, I'd be your worst nightmare, banging on your door every damned day. Hopefully, you can get a feel for the guy when you visit tomorrow."

"Yes, hopefully. I also want to see if I can sense Emily," Callie said. "Who knows? If she's dead, maybe she's hanging around the house. But make no mistake, guys. I will not hand Tyler over to his grandfather until I'm sure he had nothing to do with Emily's disappearance or Graeme's death."

"Don't worry, Callie," Jed said. "I will protect him with my life. No one is taking that kid anywhere until we're sure it's safe."

∾

Sawyer squatted closer to the fire pit, his hands on his thighs. "So this is where you found that contraption? The Sigillum?" he asked Curtis.

"Yep. It was lying right beside the pit. Neither Jed nor I touched it."

"Excellent." Sawyer stood and waved his cell phone. "I got the notification on my way over from the church. We're good to go on the warrant. My guys are bringing it, along with some crime scene techs from your department. They should be here within the hour."

Curt huffed. "Long as it isn't that screw-up Tucker Simon, I'm good with using DCI people. Of course, after checking with the human resources department, I'm told Simon hasn't been to work in a while. Chances are Gabriel killed him as well as the others." He tilted his head and eyed the horizon. "Let's hope the warrant comes sooner rather than later. We're losing daylight."

Sawyer nodded glumly. "We are. Worst-case scenario is we keep some uniforms here and at St. Michael's and return at first light." He started walking back toward his car. "Come on, Valdez. I have a piping-hot coffee in the cup holder with your name on it."

∾

After Gabriel left the woods near the Devereaux cabin, he headed to a small hardware store close to his parish. He needed supplies and equipment to prepare for his next mission.

A sister! And, from the looks of it, a young and pure sister! Ripe for the Splendor!

His plan was simple. He would return to the cabin, neutralize the occupants, and take the young woman. While conducting his reconnaissance, he had noted not only the two females and the little boy, but some young stud he'd never seen before.

Boyfriend of busty Darby Harrison? Or Jemma?

No matter. Whoever he was, he was as good as dead. Gabriel had the upper hand. The dumbass was being watched, yet he had no clue. It would be like stealing candy from a baby.

And that baby is my baby sister!

It still fascinated him how he'd wiped that entire memory from his mind. After all, it wasn't as though he'd been a toddler then. He'd been ten years old, nearly eleven, when Jemma was born. How could he not recall it?

And she wasn't even a healthy baby. A weak baby girl with a fucked-up heart and ears for shit? Wouldn't that stand out in my mind?

Guess not.

By the time he arrived at VJ's Hardware Haven, he had composed a mental list of items he would need: ropes, duct tape, zip ties, flashlight. He already had a Bowie knife but wanted to grab a few bandannas to use as a blindfold and gag.

The store was nearly empty, with just a few patrons milling about. Gabriel grabbed a small red basket and began to make his way up and down the aisles. A yell from behind caught his attention.

"Father! Father Gabriel!"

Charles Ryan, a seventeen-year-old parishioner, jogged down the aisle, trying to catch up to the priest. Gabriel hadn't seen Charlie for months, not even at Sunday services.

In fact, Gabriel realized he hadn't seen Charlie since the day he'd arrived in Sheridan to take over as parish priest.

"Young Charles," Gabriel said, tone stern. "I'm glad to see you in town.

I thought for sure you had moved and not let the church know." He put his hand on the boy's shoulder. "I can only do so much for your soul, Charlie. You need to do the rest. Regularly attending mass is a good start."

Charlie's face flushed. "Yes, you're right, of course. It's just between school and studying..." He shrugged. "Oh, and I got a job at that new garden center in town, so I work all weekend. I'm not even home to get to mass."

Gabriel nodded. "I see. Then I suppose you must ask yourself, 'Am I worth more? Is my soul something I can buy with a job that pays me minimum wage?'"

The boy stared at the floor, his blush deepening. There was no answer to that question. Charlie needed to help his family pay the bills and was confident God understood. "I will try, Father. Honest. Anyway, I'm glad I ran into you. I was wondering what was going on at the church today. Do you know?"

Gabriel stared blankly.

"I—I mean with the police. There are several cop cars parked in front of it."

Gabriel struggled to maintain a neutral expression. "In front of the church?"

"Well, not exactly in front. Kind of kitty-corner, I suppose. It's like they're watching but don't want people to know they're watching. But if that's the case, they're doing a piss-poor job of it, dude." His face reddened once more when he realized what he'd just said. "No offense meant, Padre."

Gabriel ground his back molars. "None taken, son. So, do you know how long ago that was?"

Charlie's Adam's apple bobbed up and down as he nodded. "Just now! I passed there about five minutes ago. Looks like a big operation, too. What could the police want with a small-town church like ours, Father?"

"No idea, son. Go on, run along with your chores. And Charles? Thank you for letting me know. I will get right on it."

Anxious to finish up, Gabriel moved quickly. He would do a drive-by of the church in his 'All Bark, No Bite' pickup truck and check things out for himself. Afterward, he would park a mile or so away from the farm and walk in, just to ensure the cops weren't also camped out there.

Because, if they were, things were going to get very ugly, very fast.

CHAPTER TWENTY-SEVEN

"I am the way, the truth, and the life. No one comes to the Father except through me."

John 14:6

Gabriel hunkered down a safe distance away and studied the farmhouse with his binoculars. A dozen or more investigators, some in Tyvek suits, were setting up perimeters and yellow tape and taking notes on clipboards. Earlier, he had passed by the church, seen the miles of police tape in front of the building, and kept driving.

Now, thirty minutes later, it was nearly sundown, a cool blanket of darkness settling over the property.

How the fuck did they find me?

Enraged, Gabriel lowered his binoculars and began counting the fence posts surrounding the house. Counting calmed him, brought him to center. He needed that balance before he lost his shit and started screaming, giving away his location.

He searched his mind, trying to find where he'd slipped up. It came to him almost immediately, and he cursed his stupidity.

Bob!

His downfall had to be in eliminating Bob Dietrich. He was the only one of his sacrifices who attended St. Michael's. Somehow, the police had linked Bob to St. Michael's and, eventually, to the farmhouse property.

It was possible June had reported Bob missing after all. More likely, the information had come from that slimeball, Tucker Simon.

He probably couldn't keep his mouth shut and started flapping his gums to someone. Pity I could only kill the son of a bitch once!

Once police found out where Bob worked, all they needed was one well-placed inquiry, one crackerjack interview with a churchgoer, to discover the parish priest went by the name Gabriel Devine. He could hear it in his head now.

"So, ma'am," a random cop would say, "can you tell me who assigns Mr. Dietrich his work here? Who signs his paychecks?"

"Oh, that would be Father Gabriel."

"Father Gabriel..."

"Yes. Father Gabriel Devine," this traitorous person would tell them. "He's the new pastor. Nice man, but, my goodness, he's been through the wringer, physically speaking. He walks with a limp, poor dear. Oh, and he wears a patch over his left eye."

It was over.

He had always known this day would come—that one day, his ruse here would come to an end. He'd just hoped it would have been later, after his work was completed. Now, he must tread carefully. He was so close to completing his mission.

So close to emerging as the savior of the world, the gatekeeper for the Father.

No mortal shall know the Father without worshipping the son!

He sat down on a damp rock about two miles from the house, pulled out his notebook, and composed a list of things yet to be done.

1) Claim Jemma—my innocent—from the cabin, mark her forehead with the seal of God, and free her from the shackles of earth. (Note: Make sure to record the Splendor in real time with the cell phone.)

2) Eliminate Agent Jake Devereaux, guilty of the sin of pride, preferably using the Hell Wheel I've developed.

3) Stop the Antichrist, Callie Callahan, from fulfilling her destiny as a catalyst to the Apocalypse.

He put his pen down, raised his binoculars, and took one last look. There was nothing left for him here. No reason to—

Fuck! The Sigillum!

He had left it by the fire pit. Now, with the place crawling with cops, there was no way he could sneak in and grab it.

What will happen to Jemma if she dies without the seal? Will she suffer eternal damnation?

She was an innocent. He could tell that, feel that, right away. Chewing on a nail, a habit he hadn't indulged in since he was a boy, he engaged in a mental sparring contest with himself.

—What if I don't kill her? What if I wait it out instead? I can find the Splendor elsewhere.

—No, you can't, fool! You've been looking for the Splendor for years. It's now or never!

—But what if I can't do it?

"Can't do it?" he mumbled, disappointed in himself for even thinking something was out of his grasp.

He wondered if it was mercy or anger that seemed to be choking his breath.

There is no 'can't'! he thought. *I will be king and, as such, can make an exception. I will tell the Father that Miss Jemma needs to be protected!*

With one last glance at the farmhouse, Gabriel stood. Crouching low, he tiptoed away from the hedgerow and back to his truck. He would drive to Dayton tonight, get a hotel room, perfect his plan. He had Pride in his sights but still needed to find Sloth to complete the first steps of his journey.

Once his seven sinners were taken care of, he would focus on the beast who bore the number 666.

His sister, Callista Callahan.

It would be a victory that secured his crown and ushered him into eternal life.

Driving away from the place he'd called home for months, he headed to Dayton and the cheapest hotel he could find. It was there, his inner voice whispered, that he would find his final sinner.

∼

The 'J. Gabriel' Farmhouse
8:45 p.m.

Sawyer Mills and Curtis Valdez stood side by side and addressed the uniformed officers and crime scene technicians standing before them.

"As you can see," Sawyer started, "night has beat us to the punch. We've obtained the search warrant for the house, barn, and twenty acres of land. Obviously, beginning a massive search in the dark is not ideal."

He nodded at Curtis, a sign to chime in.

Curt cleared his throat. "Right. And if we miss something, it could be gone forever. We suspect the owner of this property is a serial killer named Gabriel Devine, who goes by the name of the Apostle. He's killed at least eighteen people over the years. Keep in mind, those are only the ones we know of."

Sawyer's phone vibrated, and he blinked at the screen, trying to make sense of the message it held. "Uh, make that nineteen, Curt. I just received a text notification that another body was found."

"Shit. Where?" Curt asked.

"A nondenominational church in Sheridan called the Rock of Faith. The dead man, or what's left of him, has been identified as Pastor Leland Penne. According to the text message, Pastor Penne was beaten, mutilated, and posed in a gazebo outside the church. My partner says they have been scouring the grounds, looking for the guy's missing arm."

"Good Christ," Curt muttered.

"They're sure this guy is another of this Apostle's victims?" one of the uniformed officers asked.

"Seems likely," Sawyer responded. "The cop who caught the call spotted rosary beads, his calling card, dangling from the gazebo ceiling and found the words 'No Patience' written on the dead man's belly."

Curt nodded. "Right. The presence of rosary beads left on or near his victims was never released to the press or the public, so it's highly doubtful this is a copycat killer." Curtis took out his notebook. "Another fun fact to know here, people, is that this killer leaves a burn mark on the forehead of the deceased. The design is circular, a religious symbol called a Sigillum. Etched within the pattern of the Sigillum are said to be the names of God's angels."

"I knew I should have paid more attention in Sunday school," a voice from the back said.

Curt smiled. "You and me both, man. Anyway, as Agent Mills mentioned, this suspect also writes the cryptic messages on the abdomens of those he's killed. There are many levels of crazy here, ladies and gents. Gabriel Devine is a dangerous man. The good news is we're confident that Gabriel has been living on this property for months."

Sawyer looked over the group. "As far as tonight goes, Curt and I agree that it's best to lock down the scene and start our search first thing in the morning. The sheriff's department and Sheridan PD have agreed to give us units to sit on this site overnight. We also have two units monitoring St. Michael's Church, where we believe the suspect is posing as clergy." With a toothy grin, he added, "And because Curt and I are both single men with no lives, we'll be hanging here overnight as well."

Curt chuckled. "Single, but not for lack of trying, my man."

"You and me both, partner." Sawyer winked, then turned back to the officers. "Thank you all for coming out. The crime scene teams are dismissed for tonight. Please meet us back here tomorrow morning at six. As for the rest of you, we need two radio cars to stay. Headquarters has agreed one of those units should be a K-9 unit, just in case this guy shows up and tries to jackrabbit us."

Two hands shot up from the group. One of them, attached to a copper-headed cop who looked barely old enough to shave, spoke up. "Officer Bryan Jensen here, sir. It will be K-9 officer Nick Petrowski and myself taking watch tonight. Where would you like us stationed?"

After the units staying behind were given their assignments, the remaining officers dispersed in a sea of blue. Curt dug into a pocket for his cell, planning to call Jed and fill him in. "You know what this is, right?" he asked Sawyer, thumbing through his contacts. "This latest victim? According to JP, patience is the direct opposite of anger."

Sawyer rubbed his chin. "And the sin of anger is better known by another name, right?"

Curt nodded, sullen. "Yep. It looks like Gabriel found his Wrath."

∾

Dayton, Wyoming
'Sleep with Us' Travel Lodge
11 p.m.

In the words of Woody Allen, 'If you want to make God laugh, tell Him your plans.'

Life can really fuck with you sometimes. Gabriel was at the end of his mission, forging a path to glory and omnipotence. He had it all figured out, had dotted his I's and crossed his T's, and still, it happened.

Despite his care and planning, his next target—slow and lazy and known as the least offensive of all deadly sins—got away.

The irony was not lost on Gabriel.

Fuckin' Sloth.

Hours ago, after arriving at the motel, cheekily named Sleep with Us, Gabriel had gone in search of his next sacrifice. The majority of motel 'residents' were jobless drunkards or drug-addled twenty-somethings with a chip on their shoulder and a desire to piss off their parents.

No, no one here held down two jobs while taking night classes and volunteering in a soup kitchen.

Instead, the patrons of Sleep with Us Travel Lodge were a bunch of angry, privileged assholes who tore through their trust funds by age twenty-two, then stuck out their hands for more.

They were complainers of the 'injustices' of life, allergic to work yet insistent that their right to be 'taken care of,' financially and emotionally, be recognized.

Which, to Gabriel, meant Sloth lived here.

Plan in place, Gabriel stepped outside the motel and moved into position. From his vantage point—tucked near a dark alcove—the doors to each room of the L-shaped motel were visible.

He stood with his head down to obscure his face, his mind bouncing from thought to thought as, giddy, he reined in the urge to scream out his accomplishments.

I'm almost there! I'm so close to omnipotence!

Of course, he still had Callie and Devereaux to dispatch. But he knew where to find them and had a detailed plan.

Standing in the shadows, he paid particular attention to a room two doors down from his own. Earlier in the evening, a strung-out, emaciated female with rotting teeth and scarred skin had kicked the bottom of the door to Room 10, cursing and slapping the weathered wood in frustration.

A female? Was Sloth a woman? Gabriel didn't think so.

After she'd fumbled with the lock for a few moments, Gabriel stepped in.

"Can I help?" he asked, walking toward her.

"Can't harly open the fucker," she slurred, her fetid breath assailing his nostrils.

"Here, let me help," he said, taking the key from her hand. After unlocking the door, he winked. "Don't worry; it's not your fault. The locks in this place are ancient. Hell, I haven't seen these old-fashioned keys used in years."

He turned the knob and pushed the door open. "There you are."

"Mush obliged," she mumbled.

"I'm Gabriel, by the way," he said, trying not to cringe as he held out his hand. He wondered what kind of rank diseases she was carrying.

"Hattie Mae," she said, ignoring his hand and clumsily entering the room. Inexplicably, a flash of discomfort moved through her, and she rushed to add, "My old man, Ari, is on his way. Sum bitch is always late."

So, Ari is Sloth then. Perfect.

Gabriel smiled. "Well, it's nice to meet you, Hattie Mae. Ya'll have a good evening now."

After bumming a cigarette from her, he returned to his alcove and pretended to smoke.

Gabriel hated tobacco—hated the taste and the smell and the choking haze it left in its wake. But he was nothing if not resourceful. Since smoking was not allowed in the rooms, it was a good cover.

Just another guy out for a smoke. Nothing to see here.

Five minutes later, Ari came back to the motel. Gabriel, still outside feigning a smoke, nodded in greeting when the young man turned toward him. Although it was too dark for Gabriel to see his facial features, he could make out that Hattie Mae's boyfriend wore cut-off shorts, a tattered shirt, and canvas sneakers without the laces, as a younger person would do.

Gabriel estimated him to be about twenty-five.

Ten minutes after Ari entered the room, Gabriel heard what sounded like a knock-down, drag-out, free-for-all before the door to Room 10 opened with a bang.

317

"An' don't forget my chips!" Hattie yelled from somewhere inside the room.

"Yeah, yeah. I'll get your damned chips," Ari yelled back before slamming the door closed. Unlit cigarette dangling from his lips, he muttered, "Long as you're happy, motherfucker."

Pulling his ball cap lower, he lit his cigarette and, still mumbling, ducked into the night. Gabriel followed, hugging the shadows, slinking behind him on the dimly lit road.

It was eerily quiet, with only Ari's occasional sniffle breaking the silence. Head down, hands in his pockets and strides long, he moved with purpose.

When Gabriel realized his destination, he smiled. *Good ol' Ari. This is almost too easy!*

The man from Room 10 was heading southeast, directly toward a liquor store, precisely as Gabriel knew he would.

Because the best way to catch a sinner is to travel their path!

As Gabriel followed from a safe distance, he contemplated the best way to end the man when he caught up with him. In the literature he'd studied, the punishment for Sloth was to be dropped into a pit of snakes.

Not bloody likely.

So, it was on to plan B. He would use his knife. But there was another problem.

He no longer had the Sigillum, and without the seal, his victim might not reap his heavenly reward. No matter. Gabriel would do for Sloth as he would do for Jemma—ensure the angels understood his sacrifices were marked safe from Judgment Day.

When he got to the alley beside Spirit Liquors, he leaned against the side wall of the building and waited. Once his target exited, he would pull him into the alley and finish him.

But the man never came out.

Fuming about the delay, Gabriel slipped inside the store to search for him. Ari was near a rear door, speaking with another man who looked just as pathetic, just as shady.

Oh, for fuck's sake! A drug run!

Pretending to scour the shelves, Gabriel watched the men from the corner of his eye. He heard a muttered agreement, caught the exchange of money, spied the small plastic bag with white powder inside.

When the transfer was complete, Ari and his dealer turned and began moving toward the front door. The wail of police sirens stopped them in their tracks.

"Cops!" yelled Ari unnecessarily.

Pivoting on feet that never seemed to touch the ground, they pushed through the back door and disappeared into the alleyway. Gabriel followed as close as he dared but lost them after they sprinted into someone's backyard.

He wasn't about to risk it all for this tweaker. The last thing he needed was a homeowner calling the authorities to report a trespasser.

Son of a bitch! How am I supposed to finish this with all these delays?

A vein in his temple bulged as, fists clenched, he walked back to the hotel. He despised failure, not only because it weakened character and resolve but because it was beneath him.

A supreme being did not fail; a holy spirit did not stumble.

He reached his room and let himself inside, slamming the door behind him. The urge to hit something was overwhelming. "Motherfucker!" he roared, pummeling the bed with his fists. He grabbed a lamp from the end table and, eyeing the wall, prepared to throw it across the room.

A light tap at the door stopped him.

"Um, Gabriel?" a muffled voice said. "It's Hattie Mae. You know, from next door? I, uh, I was wondering if you had any chips you could share with me? I'm dying for a salty snack, and the motherfucking vending machine is busted."

Gabriel closed his eyes and set down the lamp. Smoothing his hair back, he pasted a smile on his face and opened the door.

"Hattie, come in," he said. "Let's see what I can rustle up."

Shuffling her bare feet on the filthy carpet, she staggered into the room.

Gabriel smiled and closed the door. He had a new plan, a better idea.

Because who said Sloth had to be a man?

Facing her, he reached behind his back, felt for the deadbolt, and quietly clicked it into place.

Then, he began.

CHAPTER TWENTY-EIGHT

"Holy crapbags!" Callie said from the passenger seat. "Is this really a house? It looks more like a hotel."

Jake looked through the top of the windshield, counting the levels of the Weston house. "It's big, all right. I count three stories." He pointed to the left corner of the house. "Elevator, too. How do the occupants even find each other? Be a great place for Tyler to play hide and seek."

Callie frowned. "But only if we decide Weston had nothing to do with Graeme Duncan's shooting or Emily's disappearance, right?"

He lifted her hand to his lips. "You are adorable when you play momma tigress. Don't worry, sweetheart. Tyler will not step foot in this house until we decide what kind of man Randall Weston is." Unbuckling his seatbelt, he said, "Ready? Don't forget what I said, Blaze. Keep your back to an exit, not a wall. And if things look hinky, get the hell out of there."

"Aye, aye, Captain," she said with a mock salute. "Wonder which door we use? I can see three choices in front."

"Center door, maybe. Let's go."

They walked along the brick pathway, past a center fountain, and up the brick steps to a porch that wrapped around three sides of the house. Several feet ahead, a huge mahogany door with intricate stained-glass inserts welcomed them.

Callie whistled. "Good grief, but that's a beautiful door."

Jake clucked his tongue. "That door probably cost more than your house in Falls Church." He put an arm around her and squeezed. "But I will buy you one if you'd like. Couldn't afford the house to go with it, but at least we'd have a great door."

Callie giggled. "Yeah, probably not." A golden door knocker in the shape of a lion's head hung in invitation. She lifted the handle and knocked. "Always wanted to do that," she whispered.

Jake smirked. "Now *that* I could probably afford to get you."

Callie's retort died with the sound of shuffling footsteps drawing close. They heard a latch click before an elderly woman opened the door.

"Can I help you?" she asked, wiping her hands on her apron.

"Yes, ma'am," Jake said, digging into his front pocket. Producing his badge, he said, "I'm Agent Jacob Devereaux, and this is my partner, Callista Callahan. We have an appointment to see Mr. Weston this morning."

"Of course," the woman said, opening the door in invitation. "I'm Myra, house manager for West Wind Estates. Mr. Weston is expecting you. Right this way."

They followed the woman through a spacious foyer with shining hardwood floors, an antique grandfather clock, and several elaborate chandeliers. On their right was a double grand staircase with deep red carpeting, and to their left, a sitting room or parlor.

Callie nudged Jake and whispered, "Good grief, Barney. This is amazing."

"Yeah, but those electric bills have to be brutal," he whispered back.

"Here we are," the woman said, opening the door to a beautifully appointed library. "Make yourselves at home, and I will let Mr. Weston and Mr. Sherman know you are here."

"Mr. Sherman?" Jake asked.

"Yes, Gideon Sherman, the family attorney. Mr. Weston requested he be included in the meeting."

"No problem. The more, the merrier, right?" Jake said.

When Myra left, Jake leaned closer to Callie. "Why would Weston think he needs a mouthpiece present for a few questions?"

"No clue. Maybe we should ask him," Callie said. "I wonder what kind of attorney Gideon Sherman is?"

They sat on a rich leather sofa and studied the library. It was at least forty feet long by twenty feet wide, roughly the size of a three-car garage. The walls were lined with floor-to-ceiling bookshelves that held thousands of books. A rolling library ladder stood beside one of the units, hooked to a track at its top.

"You can tell a lot about a person by the books they read," Callie said, walking to one of the shelves. She ran a finger over several hardcover classics. "Shakespeare, Twain, Steinbeck. He has some heavy hitters here. I bet many of these are first editions and worth a fortune."

Jake stood and stretched. "Yeah, but how many has Weston actually read? That's the question."

"All of them," a deep voice said from behind them.

Jake and Callie turned to find two men standing at the library entrance. One of them, a short, balding man wearing a crumpled suit and wire-rimmed glasses, said nothing. The other man, who looked to be around sixty-five years old, wore a pair of khaki pants, a polo shirt, and a sardonic grin.

Randall Weston.

Jake and Callie recognized him immediately from media photos they'd seen.

"I apologize if that sounded crass, Mr. Weston," Jake said. "In my line of work, skepticism comes with the territory. No offense intended."

"And none taken." The men entered the library and met Jake and Callie in the center of the room. "Proper introductions are needed, I think. Randall Weston," he said, offering his hand, "and this is my friend, Gideon Sherman."

Jake introduced himself and Callie and shook hands. "So, Mr. Sherman is your friend? I thought Myra said he was your lawyer."

Gideon pushed his glasses up the bridge of his nose. "Can't we have both? Randall and I go way back. If I weren't his legal counsel, I'd still be his friend."

"So, you said Devereaux, right? That name rings a bell. You'll have to forgive me. I seem to be having trouble with my memory lately, Agent."

"Not a problem. We've spoken about Tyler a few times but have never met. And it isn't like my last name is 'Smith,' right? You can call me Jake if it's easier."

Randall smiled. "That's very gracious of you. Aging is a fool's game, Jake. There's no way to win—everyone goes home a loser."

Gideon frowned. "How utterly depressing you are today, Randall."

Attempting to change the subject, Callie moved to an arrangement of framed photographs on a side table. Pointing to a picture of a beautiful, smiling young woman, she asked, "Is this Tyler's mom? Emily?"

Randall walked to the table and lifted the frame. "Yes, that's Emily. Spitting image of my Amanda, God rest." He put down Emily's picture and picked up one at the far end of the table. In it, a smiling, radiant Amanda Weston sat in a rocker with a baby in her arms.

Callie had seen her face before—had been seeing it for months.

Amanda Weston was the lady in white.

Callie itched to let Jake know but was unsure how to do it in a crowd.

"Sorry to hear about your wife," Jake said, unaware of Callie's dilemma. "How long has she been gone?"

Randall set the picture back on the table. "Coming up on ten years now. Cancer. Beast of a disease." He clapped his hands together. "Before we get started, can I offer you anything? Tea or coffee? Myra baked up a decadent pecan coffee cake this morning."

Jake looked at Callie, who shook her head. "I think we're good. Shall we sit?"

Before they could take a seat, the clack of heeled shoes against hardwood flooring drew their attention. A woman of about thirty-five, in a red skirt and cream-colored blouse, entered the library. "Don't forget about me. I want to sit in on this get-together."

"Of course, darling. Come in," Randall said. "Agent Devereaux, Ms. Callahan. This is my oldest daughter, Elizabeth."

"Nice to meet you," Callie said. She studied the woman's face before deciding Elizabeth was the sister who was Amanda's spitting image, not Emily.

"So," Elizabeth said sourly, "what is it, exactly, you are inquiring about? Because I have to be honest here. I'm not thrilled at your refusal to release my nephew into our custody. He is my sister's child, for God's sake. He belongs with us." She dropped her head as if overcome by a sudden wave of sorrow.

Callie and Jake didn't buy her act for a second.

"Now, Libby, play nice," Randall admonished. "You can't very well blame them. Good Lord, Tyler's father was murdered! And his mother is missing. I, for one, am thankful my grandson is in such capable hands. How is he, by the way?"

"Tyler misses his parents," Callie said. "Although he seems to enjoy being with us. He loves Blue and Lucky, our dogs, and takes that teddy bear you bought him everywhere."

Randall frowned. "Teddy bear? I didn't get him a teddy bear." He looked at Elizabeth. "You?"

"Nope," she said, bored. "Can we get this thing going? I have a salon appointment in an hour."

Callie chewed on her inner cheek, worried. Looking at Jake, she said, "Maybe we should call JP and let him know? If Randall didn't get that bear for him, where did it come from?"

"You're right. I'll call after this. Faith is still a possible source, though. Remember, her favorite beer is porter."

"Faith?" Randall asked. "And who would Faith be?"

They all took their seats, and Jake began. "Faith McTavish. You know her as Fiona Clark."

"Oh, her," Elizabeth sneered. "She took Tyler, kidnapped him right from his home. She should be in prison."

Jake huffed. "Yeah, well, difficult to do since she's dead."

Randall paled. "Dead? How?"

"Murdered, we believe. Faith was being held against her will. She escaped, but as she fled from her kidnappers in someone else's car, she rounded a steep bend and couldn't stop. We're still gathering information, but it appears someone tampered with the brakes on the vehicle she was driving. The car jumped a guardrail and tumbled about thirty feet down an embankment."

"Jesus," Randall whispered.

"Anyway, her connection—voluntary or not—to a serial killer is one of the things we wanted to talk with you about." Jake reached into his suit pocket and pulled out his phone. Scrolling through pictures, he stopped at Tucker Simon.

"Do any of you know this man?" he said, turning the screen toward the group. "It was his car that Fiona was driving."

Three faces peered at the phone; all of them denied knowing Tucker.

"Odd," Jake said. "You see, this Tucker guy was working with a man known as 'the Apostle,' a serial killer we've been tracking for months. His real name is Gabriel Devine, and he is Callie's half-brother."

"And your point is?" Elizabeth asked.

"My point is we have Fiona Clark, a woman connected to your family through Emily and Graeme Duncan, driving a car belonging to the associate of a killer."

"So, why do you think she was a kidnap victim, Agent?" Gideon asked, taking off his glasses and polishing the lenses. "How do you know she wasn't an accomplice to this Apostle's crimes?"

"Because," Jake answered, "when Fiona was found dead at that accident scene, she had rope burns on her wrists and chain marks on her ankles, injuries consistent with being held against her will."

"Or maybe she was into kink," Elizabeth said, annoyed. "Look, I'm sorry she's dead, but I don't see how we can help you." She snapped her fingers. "You know what? Check that—I'm *not* sorry she's dead. At all. Fiona fled my sister's house before Graeme's body was even cold, taking my nephew with her. We had no idea where he was until recently. Frankly, I'm not so sure she wasn't the one who killed my brother-in-law. The bitch was Graeme's mistress. Hell hath no fury, right?"

Callie watched Elizabeth's posture, analyzed her body language. She was hiding something; Callie was sure of it. "Elizabeth, it's more than just information on Tyler's nanny. This man we've been looking for spent months targeting my family, killing my people. He murdered my twin sister, Katie."

Elizabeth, eyes cold, remained unmoved.

"We were trying to track his location," Callie continued, "but Gabriel found us first, in Montana, two thousand miles from Virginia."

Elizabeth continued to stare at her impassively. *What the hell was wrong with this woman?*

"Don't you see? If Faith knew Tucker, and Tucker worked for Gabriel, then isn't it possible she mentioned us to him? Mentioned the two people who came to town to investigate a killer?"

When Elizabeth continued to wear a bored expression, Callie tried a different approach. "Don't you find it odd, Elizabeth, that Emily went missing the day your brother-in-law was killed? Or that both Graeme and Fiona, two people connected to your family, were murdered within less than a year of each other?"

Gideon stood and held up his palm toward Elizabeth. "Don't answer that, Libby." Giving Callie a stern look, he asked, "Just what are you implying, Missy?"

"Missy?" Callie said, irritated.

"We aren't implying anything, pal," Jake said, getting to his feet and squaring up to Gideon. "Just asking questions."

"Sounds more like throwing out accusations to me," Gideon snarled.

"It's fine, Gideon," Randall said. "We all want to learn the truth here. As for your question, yes, I find these two murders unsettling. And I fully understand your reluctance to return Tyler to his rightful family, given the circumstances." He chuckled lightly. "In your eyes, we must look pretty suspicious. But I can assure you, the three of us? We're harmless."

"And the fourth?" Jake asked. "What about Emily? Is she harmless as well?"

Elizabeth snickered. "Harmless? Good God, she's fucking Mother Teresa." She lowered her voice. "Not that I think she couldn't have plugged Graeme, mind you. Graeme was an abusive asshole. If she did kill him, she had good reason."

"Elizabeth!" Randall shouted, standing. "Your sister did not kill that bastard! Despite how he treated her, Emily didn't have a mean or vindictive bone in her body. If she were here...." His voice cracked.

"*Didn't* have a mean bone, as in past tense?" Callie asked. "So, you think she's dead, then?"

"No, no, of course not. I would appreciate it if you didn't put words in my mouth, Ms. Callahan."

"Those were your words, Mr. Weston, not mine."

"So, if she's not dead, what do you think happened to Emily?" Jake asked Randall. "Where do you think your daughter is?"

Callie got to her feet. Discreetly, she checked her surroundings, an icy tingle rushing down her neck. Something was close by—she just couldn't see it yet.

Before anyone could answer Jake's question, Callie faced Randall. "Excuse me, Mr. Weston, but I wonder if I could use your restroom?"

"Of course. We have many renovations in progress, so you'll have to use the one on the second floor. Take the set of stairs on the right. The powder room is on the left, second door down the hallway."

"Right stairway, second door on the left. That doesn't sound too difficult. I may actually have a ghost of a chance finding it," she said, hoping Jake got the message.

"By the way," Randall said, "the west wing is closed for elevator repairs. I'm afraid our workers have building materials scattered about so, for your safety, please stay in the east wing."

"Of course," Callie said, excusing herself.

She needed to find a ghost.

Callie walked through the foyer, searching her surroundings. The parlor, entryway, and staircase to the east wing were empty.

But standing on the staircase leading to the 'forbidden' west wing was Amanda Weston, her long hair flowing in an imaginary breeze, gesturing for Callie to follow.

And so, she did.

≈

The farmhouse that had once housed Gabriel Devine was crawling with uniforms.

Sawyer and Curtis stood outside the barn, coordinating the search with members of the sheriff's department, Wyoming DCI, and local law enforcement.

"Okay, so where are we so far?" Sawyer asked one of the crime scene technicians.

"We've swept the barn," said the woman, whose nametag read K. Simmons. "We have some solid prints, a few partials, tons of pictures. Right now, our guys are swabbing the barn chains and that weird branding iron with the symbols on it."

"The Sigillum," Curtis supplied. "It was used to mark the foreheads of the victims, so you're bound to get some DNA from it."

"Let's hope," she said. "We have a few cops from the local PD searching the grounds. So far, they've found some plastic garbage, a dirty bandanna, and an old woodchipper."

Sawyer's head, buried in his phone, popped up. "Woodchipper? Where?"

She pointed beyond the house. "In the back, almost to the property line, I think. But the cop who found it dismissed it. He said, and I quote, 'That chipper is older than some of my underwear.' He doubts it has been started for years."

Sawyer rubbed his forehead. He and Curt had been there all night and were exhausted. "Be that as it may, I'd like to take a look at it."

An older deputy came jogging toward them, sweat dotting his brow, beer belly swaying over his too-tight duty belt. "Agents," he wheezed, bending forward to place his hands on his knees, "I found something."

Curtis patted his shoulder. "Take your time, man," he said, concerned. It wouldn't surprise him if the man keeled over. "We aren't going anywhere."

The cop straightened, his respirations slowing. "Thanks, but it's important. I found—uh, I found," he stuttered, "I found a...a body part. An arm, I think. It's pretty chewed up, so I couldn't swear to it in a court of law."

Sawyer looked at Curtis. "How much you want to bet it belongs to Leland Penne?"

"Negative. That's what my momma calls a sucker's bet."

Sawyer turned back to the cop. "Where did you guys find the arm? And more importantly, where is it now?"

"We found it in the back, about ten feet or so from the side of the barn. It was in some tall weeds, so we almost missed it. My partner put out a few cones and is keeping an eye on it right now. Chain of custody and all, right?"

"Okay, let's take a look," Sawyer said.

The cop began leading the way, then turned. "You know what's bizarre?"

"You mean, besides finding an amputated body part?" Curt teased.

"Yeah, that too. But the fingers on the hand are spread out, like the last thing that arm tried to do was stop momentum or something. And the watch that is still on its wrist? I think it's still ticking."

~

Jed and Darby were sitting on the front porch swing of the cabin, coffees in hand, watching Amara and Tyler play with the dogs.

"Have you heard from Callie or Jake yet?" Darby asked.

"Not yet. I'll give them a call later. I did reach out to Sawyer's contact, Kelly Deegan, at the Philadelphia PD. He'll swing that way and chill outside until Jake and Callie wrap things up at the Westons'. Just in case."

Darby paled. "In case what? Do you think they're in danger?"

Jed put his arm around her. "Probably not. But if anyone in that household had anything to do with Duncan's murder or Emily's disappearance...."

"Then there's a lot at stake," Darby finished for him. "Like freedom."

"Right. I'll call Jake as soon as I finish my coffee. He needs to know about Deegan."

"Things are such a mess, aren't they?" Darby said. "I cannot wait until this is over and we catch that knuckle-dragging bastard."

"We will. It's only a matter of—" Jed's cell phone rang, and he answered it. "Hey, JP, did you get any sleep, brother?"

"Some. I'm at headquarters now and have some news. A movie crew shooting footage about the Bighorn Mountains found Fiona Clark's car. It was backed into a semi-wooded area on a seldom-used road. Inside were her purse, luggage, passport, and cell phone."

"Well, that's great news. Maybe check her messages and calls. I know her password if you need it."

"Already got in. It's an older Android phone, so it wasn't much of a challenge."

"Good job. Did you find anything?"

JP hesitated. "Uh, yeah. No texts or calls, but some photographs you will want to see."

Jed's stomach began a freefall, though he wasn't sure why. "Copy that. Go ahead and send them. I'll take a look and call you back."

"Got it. And Jed? I plan on coming to the cabin in a few hours if you need to...to go somewhere."

"Well, that doesn't sound good," Jed said. "Just send the photos, Junior. We'll deal with the fallout later."

∾

"So, you were giving me your theory on Emily's whereabouts?" Jake said to Randall.

"Right, right. I wish I knew, Agent. When Libby and I arrived at the house, Graeme was already dead on the kitchen floor. Fiona and Tyler were missing, as was my daughter."

"And why were you going to the Duncan home? Just a visit?"

"Emily asked us over, but I never had the chance to find out why. When we got there, she was gone."

"I see. Is the Duncan house accessible? I'd like to take a look, maybe check out Fiona's room. I'm sure local investigators tossed the place, but they weren't looking for what I need."

"Which is?"

"Evidence that Fiona was involved in Graeme's death or Emily's disappearance. And any suggestion of a prior relationship with Tucker Simon."

Gideon Sherman cleared his throat. "Randall, I strongly advise against allowing that. I believe that a search of the Duncan home would be a clear violation of Emily's civil rights. Now, if Agent Devereaux cares to get a warrant, we have no choice but to comply. Until then, I suggest we move on to another topic."

Jake frowned. "I'm not sure how trying to locate a missing woman violates her rights, Counselor. Personally, if it were my family member, I wouldn't blink an eye."

"You're right, of course," Randall said. "If it can bring Emily home, you have my permission to search her house."

Gideon sighed. "As I've said, Randall, I'm against it. But if you're dead set on doing this, I insist on being present. Consent can be withdrawn, you know."

"Fine. We'll all go."

Jake glanced toward the library door, wondering what was taking Callie so long.

"All right. As soon as Callie returns, we can go." His cell phone rang, and he excused himself to the foyer.

"Hey, Jed."

Jed skipped any small talk and dove in. "Where are you?"

Jake watched Randall, Gideon, and Elizabeth, huddled together, whispering among themselves. "We're still at the Westons'. We have a flight back in a few hours. Why? Something happen?"

Jed ground his teeth. He was ready to explode, to spit out the new information JP had uncovered. Information that could change everything.

But he held back, afraid Jake would do something he shouldn't.

Instead, he said, "They found Faith's car and cell near the mountains. JP and his crew were able to get into the phone and found some pictures."

"Uh, okay. What kind of pictures are we talking about?"

"I'm just going to send them to you. I need you to keep calm, though. A Philly cop named Kelly Deegan is parked outside near the Weston's security gate. He's a friend of Sawyer's."

"A cop? Why did you send a cop here?" Jake said, alarmed. "What aren't you telling me?"

Jed rubbed the back of his neck. "Just look at the pictures, Jake. The images speak for themselves."

CHAPTER TWENTY-NINE

J ake sat, stunned, on the bottom step of the staircase, trying to process
the images Jed had just sent him.

Papers.

Photo after photo of various legal papers and newspaper clippings,
taken as they lay scattered in what appeared to be a strongbox or safe. Jake
enlarged the first picture, a birth certificate for Emily Weston. The next
images were legal documents regarding the adoption of a young female.

Why did Faith take these? Was Emily Weston adopted?

He scrolled through a few more views of the same pictures, confused.
The birth certificate listed Emily's birth parents as Randall and Amanda
Weston. Yet, the strongbox also held adoption papers.

Curious.

Hearing footsteps, he raised his head and looked to the library. Randall,
Gideon, and Libby were heading toward him.

He flipped to the following picture, again wondering what was taking
Callie so long.

"Everything okay, Agent?" Elizabeth asked.

Jake nodded absently before returning to the image on the screen. It
was a newspaper clipping dated August 14th, 1995. The article had been
published by the *Montana Record*, a now-defunct local newspaper in

Billings, and described the recent kidnapping of a five-year-old child from her front yard.

The kidnapping of Lacy Jane Devereaux.

Jake blinked twice. Questions ricocheted around his brain, nearly overwhelming him.

Where did Faith get these? How does she know my sister? And why did she take pictures of the news coverage of Lacy's kidnapping?

"Agent?" Randall asked.

Jake looked up from his phone, the pieces of the puzzle finally clicking into place. Faith had found these legal papers and recognized what they meant. Maybe she had been looking to blackmail Randall, or maybe she'd just wanted to ensure her own safety.

These photos had given her leverage: she'd had knowledge that could destroy the Weston family.

Jesus Christ! Jake thought, fists clenched. *Lacy!*

Angrier than he'd ever been, Jake leapt up and charged Randall Weston. Grabbing him by the throat, he pushed his back against the foyer wall and lifted the old man off his feet.

"Where the fuck is she?" he ground out between clenched teeth. "Where is Lacy?"

"Let go of him!" screamed Elizabeth, trying to pull Jake's hands away from Randall's neck.

"Agent Devereaux!" Gideon thundered. "Unhand my client!"

Jake turned his head to the lawyer but never loosened his grip around Randall's neck. "Your name is all over this shit, Sherman. Make no mistake—you're next."

"Please!" Randall said weakly. "You're choking me!"

"I'm gonna do more than choke you if you don't tell me where she is, motherfucker!"

"Daddy!" Elizabeth screeched. "Don't worry! I'm calling the cops!"

"Call them," Callie said from the top of the steps. "I think they'd be interested to know what this is about." She disappeared from view for a moment before returning to the steps, her arm secured around a young woman.

Emily Weston.

"Well, fuck!" Elizabeth grumbled.

Jake dropped his hands from Randall's neck, ignoring the man's grunt as he hit the floor. Eyes pinned to the top step, he whispered, "Lacy?"

Emily Weston, twenty pounds lighter than she had been on the day of her husband's death, appeared weak and pale. With Callie's assistance, she began slowly to descend the steps.

Jake took the stairs two at a time, lifted Emily in his arms, and carried her the rest of the way down the stairs and into the library. After placing her in a chair, he turned to Callie.

"Blaze?"

"I found her in a back room," Callie said, glowering at the three individuals in the foyer, disgusted. "In the wing supposedly closed for renovations. The room was set up as a tiny apartment, with all the comforts of home—including restraints on the bed and a shit-ton of pharmaceuticals on the dresser."

"I can explain...." Randall whined from the doorway.

"No, Daddy, you can't," Emily said quietly, looking up at Jake. There were purple smudges beneath her eyes.

He could see it now, see his sister beneath the gaunt face and pale lips. The urge to beat Randall Weston to death almost overtook him.

"Callie gave me the shortened version of my past while untying me from that bed," Emily said quietly. "I'm sorry I don't remember you. My life has been centered around being a Weston for twenty-seven years. And a Duncan. I have vague memories of another life, but over the years, those memories have come in quick snapshots, like flashes of pictures appearing in my mind without context."

Jake kneeled in front of her. "It's okay if you don't remember me, sweetheart. It's enough that I remember you."

Sniffing, Emily gently touched his cheek. "My father killed Graeme," she said, her eyes finding Randall's. "He walked in on Graeme beating me, choking me, and was just trying to protect me."

Callie grimaced. *Protect? God, I hope we aren't looking at Stockholm Syndrome here.*

Jake turned to Callie. "Blaze, a cop is parked outside near the gate, a guy named Kelly Deegan. Can you bring him in? We have some arrests to make."

Callie turned to leave, but Gideon grabbed her arm. "You aren't going anywhere, Missy. I don't think you realize who you are dealing with. We've done nothing wrong!"

Jake was in Gideon's face in two strides. Jaw tight, he said, "I'll give you two seconds to let her go before I break that arm."

Gideon let her go in under one.

"I'll be right back. Are you going to be okay alone?" Callie asked Jake.

He patted his sidearm and smiled. "Don't worry. I'll be just fine."

Gideon stepped closer to Randall and looked defiantly at Jake. "As I said, Agent, there's been a misunderstanding. We haven't committed any crimes here."

"But you have," Emily said weakly. "You all have." She rubbed her wrists; the faint red outlines of her restraints were evident.

"Daddy shot Graeme and wanted to cover it up," Emily said, turning back to Jake. "I insisted we contact the authorities. After all, as I said, he was only trying to save me. The police would understand it was justifiable. I truly believe that if he had lived, Graeme would have killed me one day."

Jake glared at Randall. It didn't matter that the old man had tried to protect his sister.

He still wanted to pound him into the ground.

"Both Dad and Elizabeth refused to involve the police. They feared repercussions for the family business. But I insisted. The next thing I knew, it was lights out. Someone hit me, knocked me out."

"Who?" Jake asked gently.

"Not sure." She jutted her chin at Gideon. "Maybe him."

"I will not stand here and be slandered!" Gideon yelped. "I had nothing to do with that! I told her she could have killed you!"

"Told *her*?" Jake said. "Told who? Elizabeth?"

Gideon clamped his mouth shut.

"Fuck you, Gideon!" Elizabeth screamed. "You're the one who's been drugging her! You're the one who insisted we tie her up!"

"Shut up, you stupid little cunt!" Gideon hissed.

"And," Elizabeth said, a glint in her eyes, "you were the one who kidnapped her all those years ago." She smiled coldly as the little man's eyes bulged. "Don't look so shocked, asshole. I didn't get this far in life without learning how to find out information."

"Why the hell would you do it, Sherman?" Jake said, fighting for control. He was furious. "Trying to cash in on a family's misery? A family who, maybe, couldn't have children?"

"No!" Gideon shouted. "Amanda needed...help. They suffered a tremendous loss in 1994."

"Shut up, Gideon," Elizabeth snapped. "You're a lawyer, for fuck's sake. Don't you know when to shut up?"

"I'm not going down for this alone!" he shouted back. "Look, the Westons lost a little girl, Everly, to a tragic swimming accident. She was only six years old, and her death destroyed Amanda. She couldn't have more children, and Randall... Well, Randall wanted to help.'

"So, you kidnap a fucking kid for him? Take her away from the family that adores her?" Jake said, his voice cracking.

"Why, Daddy?" Emily asked.

Randall dropped his head. "Your mother was dying, Em. Not physically, but emotionally. We talked about adopting from an agency, but I feared it would take months, maybe years, to get a child. Your mother didn't have that kind of time."

"So she knew? Mom knew I was taken from my family?"

Randall shook his head. "No. She believed it was a legitimate adoption. We told her Gideon was working on estate planning with a dying woman. We told Amanda the woman had no family and needed a home for her five-year-old daughter."

"Unbelievable," Jake snarled. "You have all the money in the world, and instead of hiring a surrogate or going to a legitimate agency or exploring a fucking orphanage in the ass-end of the world, you take the brightest light in our lives."

Emily was crying so hard she could barely see. "And then you kept me prisoner, drug-addled and tied down, for months."

Randall, in a fog, sat heavily on a leather chair. Eyes teary, he said to Emily, "I'm so sorry, pumpkin, but I couldn't bear to lose you. I thought maybe, once you had time to sort it out, you'd see things our way. But it doesn't matter now, does it? It's over. We're finished."

"No shit, Sherlock. Murder, attempted murder, kidnapping, assault. The list is endless," Jake said. "And all because you couldn't step up and do the right thing."

"You took everything from me," Emily said, showing anger for the first time. "My freedom, my dignity, my life with my real family. And my son. You took months of life away from Tyler and me."

Randall wept softly.

The front door opened, and Callie entered with a middle-aged man in a police uniform. "Jake, this is Lieutenant Kelly Deegan, Sawyer's friend. I've given him the highlights about what's going on here, and he's called it in."

Jake nodded in greeting. "Thanks for coming. We're going to owe you one."

"No problem. I have units responding momentarily. If you want to get Ms. Duncan cleared medically, I can meet you at the hospital for your statements."

"That would be great. Callie and I have a flight in a few hours. If we get permission from the doctors, I'd like to fly Lacy—I mean Emily—back to Montana with us." He took Emily's hand. "I'd like to take you to see Tyler and Jed if that's okay." His eyes welled. "And Mom and Dad. My God, they are going to flip. They never gave up hope of finding you, Emily. None of us did."

Emily smiled, her first smile since that dreadful day when everything had changed. "I'd like that. Very much."

≈

"How long has she been in there?" Jake asked Callie as he paced the waiting room.

"Five minutes longer than the last time you asked, love," Callie said, holding out her hand. "Come on, bubba. Sit next to me and hold my hand."

He sat and gave her a gentle kiss. "Can you believe this shit? We found Lacy!" He grinned. "And Tyler is my nephew!"

"Crazy, right? It's nothing short of miraculous. And you want to hear something that will blow your mind? If it wasn't for Gabriel, if it wasn't for us coming to Philly to find information on him, we might never have found your sister."

"You're right. I'm still gonna fuck up that bastard brother of yours, but yeah, you're right."

Callie chuckled. "Not if I fuck him up first! So, have you spoken to Jed? Your parents?"

"Not my parents, but I did call Jed. Obviously, he put it together when JP sent him the photos. We decided not to tell Mom and Dad yet. I want to see how Lacy wants to play it."

Callie rubbed his back. "She did tell us she wanted to hold off for a few days, get her bearings, before seeing them. Tyler, too. She just wants to get stronger, Barney."

"I know. It will work out better this way. I've asked Jed if he's willing to return to Billings, just him and Lacy. We can keep Tyler and the girls with us at the cabin for now. It will give Lacy a few days to adjust and clear the remaining drugs those fuckers used to sedate her out of her system."

"As long as the doctors give the green light, it's a good plan," Callie said, laying her head on his shoulder. "I switched us to a later flight and added a ticket for Lacy. Or Emily. Gosh, what are we going to call her?"

Jake closed his eyes and leaned his head on the wall behind them. "As long as she is home, I don't care." His eyes snapped open. "Hey, in all the excitement, I forgot to ask. How'd you know Lacy was up there, in that supposedly closed wing?"

Callie smiled. "Her mother. Amanda Weston, as it turns out, is the lady in white. I guess 'find her' meant find Emily. I felt a ghostly presence and went to investigate. She was standing on the stairs and beckoned to me."

"Huh," Jake said, brows drawn. "I thought Kate said ghosts couldn't interfere with the natural order of things."

"Yeah, she did. I'll ask her about it next time she pops in. I am hoping to introduce her to Amara. Well, sort of introduce them. I'll have to translate, obviously."

Jake smiled at her warmly. "You must be so psyched for that. All three Callahan girls in the same room." He pushed a stray lock of hair behind her ear. She was wearing a messy bun today, strands of shining auburn waving around her face.

"You have no idea how gorgeous you are," Jake said. "Last night, you and me together? Man, that was nothing short of amazing."

He tilted her chin and kissed her, his lips soft against hers.

Callie sighed in contentment. "Amazing? It was spectacular, G-man. And I can't wait to do it again."

Jake's laugh rumbled through his chest. "Yes, ma'am. I think we can arrange that."

"Are you sure you're okay to fly, sweetheart?" Jake asked Emily as they headed for the airport. "We can stay back a few days, give you time to get your bearings. You spent a long time locked up in that room."

Emily was in the front passenger seat of their rental car; Callie sat behind Jake.

"Yes, I'm fine. I just want to get to Tyler and Jed. And Mom and Dad." She paused. "Saying 'Mom and Dad' sounds so strange. I wish I had a better memory of my life before, well, before Randall Weston had Gideon kidnap me. With any luck, I haven't buried the memories too deep."

"You know, occasionally, a person's brain will tuck certain memories in a seldom-used corner," Callie said. "Sometimes, it's a type of defense mechanism; other times, it's a way to isolate random facts and figures we don't use every day. Kind of like a hall locker at school."

"Oh, that's right. While Jake and I waited for the discharge paperwork, he said you were a psychologist. So, tell me, how do I find the combination to open that locker?"

"Patience, counseling, maybe even hypnosis will help. The best advice I can give is don't force it. The recollections will surface eventually, usually when you least expect it. It could be a phrase you hear, a photo you see, even a particular aroma that can trigger your memories."

"I hope so. I only need a day or two. I look washed out, unhealthy, and that might scare Ty. The doctors said I'm malnourished and dehydrated."

"Did they abuse you? Not feed you?" Jake asked, hands squeezing the steering wheel.

"No, they brought me food. I just chose not to eat most days." She turned to Callie. "What I ate, when I ate, were the only things I could control. Refusing to eat what they put in front of me was all I could do to, I don't know, be me," she said apologetically.

"With the bonus of pissing them off, I'm guessing," Jake said, grinning.

"That, too," Emily smiled. "So, yeah. I plan to spend a few days with Jed, stuffing my face and detoxing. I do need some things, though, basic stuff. I left everything behind."

Callie leaned forward and patted her arm. "Oh, girl, we are gonna shop! Well, not right away, of course. I have plenty of clothes at Jed's that will take you through until we get you some stuff of your own."

"I appreciate that, Callie. I couldn't return to the house I shared with Graeme, and I didn't want to wear anything associated with my captivity." She looked at her brother's profile. "What do you think will happen to them, Jake? How many years in prison?"

Jake drummed his thumbs on the steering wheel. "Not enough, if you ask me. I'm sorry, kiddo. This must be incredibly hard for you." He squeezed her hand. "As for your question, I imagine Randall will face the most serious charges—murder, kidnapping, assault. He is looking at a huge chunk of prison time. Gideon and Elizabeth will also see the inside of a cell, but with less time than Randall."

Tears slid down Emily's cheeks. "He'll die in there, you know," she said quietly. "He won't be able to handle it, and he'll die long before his ticket should have been punched. And that just makes me sad. It's difficult to verbalize how hurt I am at what he did to me, but you need to know he was a very loving and attentive father when I was a child."

"And the only one you've known," Callie added.

"Yes. But I can't dwell on that now. I am starting over, creating a new beginning with my son and my new family—who used to be my old family." She chuckled lightly. "Boy, this is like a cheesy reality show or something."

Jake winked at her. "Yeah. But someone has to make the cheese."

Once they landed, it was only a half-hour's drive to Jed's place. On the way, Callie and Emily ducked into a department store to pick up some essentials for Emily.

"Thanks for stopping," Emily said to Jake when they returned to the car. "I didn't even have a toothbrush."

"Of course. While you both were gone, I phoned Jed. He is home as we speak and preparing a room for you. JP," Jake looked at Callie through the rearview mirror, "is at the cabin with Amara, Darby, and Tyler."

"And this is to hide from that horrible man you told me about on the plane?" Emily asked.

"Yes," Jake said. "Jed's house is huge, so it would be tough to cover all the exits and entrances. Not to mention being so close to a major highway. On the other hand, the cabin is off the beaten path, with only a few doors to watch. We installed cameras, and JP was going to work on a 'poor man' alarm system—string-type wires between trees, bells tied to doors, more motion sensor lighting."

"Well, I hope you get him soon. I need to see my son."

"And you will. I promise."

Emily yawned and rubbed her eyes.

"Why don't you close your eyes and take a twenty-minute catnap, Emily."

She nodded and laid her head back. "Hey, Jake?" she said, eyes closed. "If you want to call me Lacy, I won't mind."

Jake's eyes filled with tears, and he smiled.

CHAPTER THIRTY

"My God, my God, why have you forsaken me?"

Psalms: 22

Dayton, Wyoming
Sleep with Us Travel Lodge

Hattie Mae, as it turned out, was a bleeder.

After punching, kicking, and stabbing her to death, Gabriel took a moment to enjoy the intricate patterns of blood splatter against the wall.

It reminded him of an abstract painting, allowing the viewer to interpret what they saw.

Gabriel saw power, control, and brilliance within the varying shades of crimson.

Once the fight had left Hattie's cold, dead hands, Gabriel used a Sharpie pen he'd found in a motel drawer to write 'No Diligence' on her belly. Next, he attempted to hand-draw a Sigillum on her forehead but couldn't remember the order of symbols he had used before.

Tough break, Hattie, me girl. Hopefully, once the end is upon us, I can save you.

His final task was to wrap a set of rose-colored rosary beads around her hands. Satisfied, he took a shower.

And then, he took another. Because the blood stains covering his hands proved to be stubborn ones.

As he packed his small duffel, he reflected on his accomplishments thus far.

He had dispatched six of seven vile and capital sinners. He was about to claim his seventh, Pride, as well as witness the Splendor with Jemma.

My innocent.

Best of all, he would soon face down Callie Callahan—the Antichrist, the devil.

The Beast.

∼

After watching the tear-filled reunion between Jed and Emily, Jake and Callie headed back to the cabin in their rental car.

"That was beautiful to witness," Callie sniffed. "They were so happy to have found each other."

"Jed and Lacy were only four years apart, so they were pretty tight," Jake agreed. "I was twelve and she was just five when she was taken. Jed saw her as a playmate." He smiled. "But, to me, she was an annoying baby sister."

"Kates and I were annoying younger siblings to Finn, too," Callie said. She flipped down the visor and checked her image in the mirror. "Jesus, I look like I could haunt a house," she joked.

Jake waggled his brows. "Dead or alive, I'd still do ya "

"Of course, you would," she teased.

"Get real. You couldn't look bad if you tried," Jake said. "Speaking of bad, do me a favor and give Curt a call. I'm dying to know how the search is going at that farm."

Callie plugged her phone into the console and scrolled for Curt's number. He picked up on the fourth ring.

"Hey, Callie," he said. "You guys back?"

"Yes. We just dropped off Jake's sister at Jed's place and are heading to the cabin."

"That's great. Jed gave me the abbreviated version. I'm happy for you, buddy."

"Thanks, Curt," Jake said. "It's amazing, seeing her again, knowing she's alive. I don't mind telling you, I had my doubts." He swallowed back tears.

"Anyway, we need to relieve JP at the cabin, but we're calling to see if you found anything at Gabriel's place."

"We found plenty," Curtis answered. "Aside from the Sigillum and a box of rosary beads, we found a severed arm in some tall grass. It belonged to a man named Leland Penne. We believe he is Gabriel's latest victim."

"You got a body to go with that arm?" Jake asked.

"Not on the property, but yeah. The rest of him was posed in a gazebo beside the Rock of Faith Church, where Penne was pastor. There were rosary beads on scene and 'No Patience,' written on his torso."

"So, he's Wrath," Callie said simply.

"Right," Curt said. "As far as this farm, we have blood, hair fibers, and a ton of material to analyze from the Sigillum. Oh, and there is a working woodchipper out back."

"Ruh-roh," Callie said ominously.

"Yeah, what you said. Crime scene guys think Gabriel disposed of at least one person using it. And, since Tucker Simon hasn't been seen or heard from in days, my money is on him."

"Well, I won't lie—not gonna lose sleep over that one," Jake said. "Guy was a peckerhead."

Curt chuckled. "You ain't wrong. Still no sign of Gabriel, though. I wonder if he found out we were onto him and skedaddled."

"I don't think so," Callie said. "At least, I'm sure he hasn't left the area yet. He's not finished. He has to conquer 'pride' and 'sloth.'"

"I hope you're right, Blaze," Jake said. "I'm tired of chasing this fucker."

They pulled into the road leading to the cabin. "We're here now, Curt," Jake said. "I will reach out later for an update. Jed is going to stay at his place for a few days, just until my sister is a little stronger."

"Got it. Keep in touch and watch your back, kids," Curt said. "This dude is seriously messed up."

Callie shook her head. "It's worse than that. Gabriel will not stop until we're all dead."

"Or he is," Jake grunted.

~

Gabriel sat in the woods, binoculars in hand, and stared at the cabin.

He needed to get rid of the dogs.

He'd spotted them playing with that kid, Tyler, the first time he'd spied on the cabin. For some reason, the little boy seemed to enjoy their company.

Gabriel couldn't stand animals of any kind, but he especially hated drooling, hairy canines.

But the kid liked them. And, since the boy was going to be the only one left standing in that cabin, Gabriel couldn't bring himself to kill the flea-infested bastards.

But he did need to neutralize them.

Sitting on the same rock he'd occupied before, he rummaged through his oversized duffel bag. Unable to get back to his house, all he had was a few bottles of pills, the clothes on his back, and some travel-sized toiletries he'd taken from the motel.

After he was done with Hattie Mae, he'd left the Sleep with Us Travel Lodge and driven to a supermarket nearby, purchasing two sirloin steaks and a jar of peanut butter.

He pulled the steaks from his bag and cut slits in them. Next, he took out several small pills from a prescription bottle and crushed them on a rock, using the hilt of his Bowie knife.

Gabriel was guessing at the amount of Valium he needed, so he used more than he thought was necessary.

A lot more.

He sprinkled a good amount of the pulverized, yellow powder into the slits on the steaks, then covered each of them with a finger-full of peanut butter.

Eat this, you little fuckers!

The sound of tires crunching on gravel drew his attention from the steaks to the driveway. An unfamiliar car was pulling in with two occupants. Gabriel ducked lower and watched as Jake exited the driver's door, moved to the passenger side, and helped Callie out of the car.

After a short embrace, they walked, hand in hand, toward the porch steps.

Although he was nearly a half-mile from the house, the faint bang of the front door—its sound carried by the wind—reached Gabriel's ears.

Both dogs bounded outside, followed closely by the little boy.

Grinning in delight, the boy squealed and jumped into Devereaux's arms. Callie ruffled the child's hair and patted the dogs before the three entered the cabin.

The dogs, however, remained outside.

Perfect.

∾

"Good to have you home!" Darby said, hugging Callie.

"And it's great to be here. Honestly, it seems as though we've done nothing but travel the last few months," Callie said, taking a seat in the kitchen. "I, for one, will be dancing naked in the streets when this is over!"

Jake smirked. "I'd like a ticket to see that one."

"Ticket for what now?" JP asked, entering the room.

Callie blushed. "Never mind."

"Yeah," Jake said, winking at Callie. "It's an 'invitation only' kind of show. So, what's new from the world of JP Burke? Anything to report?"

"It's been quiet here. I'm glad you're back, though. I have to get going for my shift. Call you later?"

"You bet. And JP?" Jake said. "Thanks, man. We couldn't do this without you."

∾

Gabriel watched through the binoculars as the man Jemma had called 'JP' drove off.

"See ya, douchebag," he muttered.

A few seconds after JP's car went by him, Gabriel heard dogs barking. In seconds, they were almost on top of him.

The stupid fuckers are chasing JP's car!

Passing Gabriel, unaware of his presence, they flew by, jowls swinging in the breeze. Gabriel waited, knowing they would have to pass him again eventually.

He got ready.

~

Saying that Callie and Jake were having a bit of a disagreement was like saying the eruption of Vesuvius was a tiny inconvenience to the citizens of Pompeii.

"Did you hear what I said, Barney?" Callie said, face flushed. "Amara drew another picture. This one has you on the floor, bleeding out, while she, Darby, and Tyler are running toward the woods, and I...I am fighting with Gabriel!"

"Okay. So?"

"So?" she asked, incredulous. "Oh, for fuck's sake! Amara has been spot-on with every other painting, Jake. Why aren't you more concerned?"

Jake opened the fridge and grabbed a soda. "What would you have me do, Blaze? Run away, tail between my legs, and leave you and the rest to fend for themselves? Do you really think I would leave the woman I love, my nephew, to the wolves?"

"I'm not saying leave us here to die, Devereaux. I'm saying go to Jed's house, stay with Emily, and send Jed back here. Curt and Sawyer are tightening the noose around Gabriel's neck. It's only a matter of time."

He pulled a chair in front of her and sat. "Sweetheart, I don't have a death wish. Believe me, I don't. But don't you think Amara's painting gives us a leg up? We know what can happen here, so we'll be extra cautious."

Tyler came running into the room before Callie could provide her counterpoint. "Callie, have you seen Blue and Lucky? I can't find them anywhere."

"I haven't, bud. They couldn't have gone far. If you go outside and yell, "cookies!" I guarantee they will come running. If not, we will form a search party. Deal?"

Tyler nodded and took off running.

"Still can't believe that's my nephew. I wish I could tell him," Jake said.

"Soon, babe. Give Emily some time," Callie said soothingly. "But, back to the matter at hand. I was explaining to you how dangerous your staying would be and telling you, in my charming way, what a child you're being about this whole thing."

"Am not!" Jake joked. "Poopy head."

His phone rang, and he pretended to wipe sweat from his brow. "Whoever you are," he said into the phone, "I am indebted to you."

"It's JP, and I can't wait to hear why. My cell died, so I'm using my partner's phone. There's been another murder, and it has Gabriel's name written all over it. A young woman, Hattie Mae Clemson, was found in a sketchy motel in Dayton. She was beaten and stabbed, and the words 'No Diligence' were written on her belly."

"So, this is Sloth, then?"

"Yes, sir. This motel is, for lack of a better word, a tweaker's paradise. They have hourly rates, dope dealers around every bend, and three liquor stores within walking distance. I feel like I'm starting to understand this asshole. Choosing this place to find Sloth is what I would have done."

Jake scrubbed his face. "Super. Okay, keep us in the loop. I'm going to do a perimeter check. Callie," he looked at her, frowning, "seems to believe I will die today. I'll do my best to ensure that doesn't happen."

"Be careful," JP said. "Whether he is that good or really does have some kind of divine intervention, this guy always seems to have the jump on us."

~

Dogs are boringly predictable.

The golden retriever and shiny black Lab followed their noses, finding the steaks he'd left them not thirty feet from where he hid.

They were so obsessed with the thought of delicious meat that they ignored their innate instincts to protect their charges.

Stupid animals.

He waited until they both collapsed, barely conscious, before dragging them out of sight.

Bowie knife tucked in his waistband, Gabriel began the half-mile march to the Devereaux cabin.

To his destiny.

~

"Blaze, where is Tyler?"

Jake had just come in from checking the cameras, motion detectors, and outdoor lights.

"I thought he was with you," Callie said, heart kicking up a notch.

"Don't worry, sweetheart. I'm sure he's with the pups. But it's getting dark. He should be inside now." Jake checked the camera app on his phone and said, "I don't see him."

Callie's mind went first to the pond before arriving at a more terrifying prospect.

Gabriel!

"Don't," Jake warned, noting the fear in her eyes. "I'm sure he's fine. I'll take another look around."

"Let me come with you," Callie said. "Safety in numbers."

"No, I need you here, Blaze. Darby is new at this crazy stuff, and Amara can't hear danger if it approaches. I'll bring one of the radios JP left us." He handed her the other walkie-talkie and grabbed a windbreaker from a hook behind the kitchen door. "Lock up, and don't open the door to anyone but me."

"Christ, I hate this shit," she mumbled, locking the door as he walked down the porch steps. She pushed the talk button on the radio. "Watch your back, Devereaux!"

She peeked out a curtained window, terrified that the next time she saw the man she loved, it would be as he lay bleeding in her arms from a stab wound to the gut.

Just as Amara's painting depicted.

Darby and Amara sat in the kitchen with Callie, shoving cookies into their mouths.

"Want one, Cal?" Amara asked. "When I'm nervous, I eat."

"Me, too," Darby said, grabbing a third chocolate chip.

Callie sighed. "No thanks. My stomach is in knots." She picked up the walkie and spoke into it. "Jake, what's going on out there?"

Silence.

"He's probably just out of range," offered Darby.

Callie chewed a cuticle. "These suckers work up to two or three miles, I think. Unless he's left the property, he should still be in range."

"How about the cameras?" Darby suggested. "Have you checked them?"

"No. The app is on Jake's phone, not mine."

Darby raised a hand. "Um, isn't that Jake's phone on the counter?"

The three turned to where Darby was pointing. "Well, crapbags," Callie said. "Yeah, it's his. I don't like that he left without it."

"Well, let's check the app. Maybe we can see them."

Callie unlocked the phone and opened the app. Each of the cameras appeared on the screen in a grid-like pattern. She clicked on the square that said 'Camera One.'

The front yard came into view. Callie's eyes roamed over the image, checking for movement.

"Anything?" Amara asked.

Shaking her head, Callie moved to each camera in succession until she came to the fifth camera, aimed at the side yard.

There! Movement near the tree line!

Callie squinted, bringing her face closer to the screen. She gasped.

"What is it?" Darby asked.

She tossed the phone to Darby and grabbed her boots from beside the back door. "Gabriel has Tyler!"

Darby and Amara, heads together, watched as Gabriel—one arm snaked around Tyler's neck—walked the boy toward the house.

"Oh, my God!" Amara cried. "Where is Jake?"

Callie shook her head, wrestling a boot in place. "Didn't see him. Didn't see Blue or Lucky, either. I'm going out there. I'll go out the front and will double back."

"The hell you say!" Darby yelled, her tone decidedly un-Darby-like. "Are you fixin' to die today? We need to call the cops and wait for help!"

"And by the time they get here, I will have lost my family. No, I'm doing this, Darbs. Call the police, then call Jed. Make sure to lock the door after I leave. And guys," Callie said, taking a butcher knife from the drawer, "no matter what you hear, don't come outside."

∾

"Don't worry, little man," Gabriel whispered into Tyler's ear. "All I want is to talk to Callie. That's it."

Tyler, lip trembling, whispered back. "Liar."

Gabriel chuckled. "Good for you. You're a smart kid, you know that? Come on, genius. Let's go say hello to my sister."

∾

Heart racing, Callie crept around the right side of the house. Her hands shook as she held the knife straight out in front of her, as if daring someone to attack. Ears straining, she tried to pick up any kind of movement but the grounds were eerily silent.

Cursing her stupidity for taking a knife rather than the spare revolver Jake kept in the hall closet, she continued to tiptoe forward. Within a minute, she had cleared the side of the cabin and was staring into the backyard.

The yard was bathed in varying shades of black and gray. Shadows flickered across the concrete bench near the flower garden, giving the illusion it was composed of dozens of slithering snakes. Callie shuddered, momentarily frozen in place.

Just as she willed her feet to keep moving, a soft moan, originating from near the back door, stopped her in her tracks.

Shit!

Hugging the wall, heart pounding, Callie moved slowly toward the back door, sliding her feet along the grass, trying to mask the sound of her movement. Her foot hit something solid, and she nearly toppled over.

"Jake!" she cried, dropping next to him, all attempts at silence forgotten. He was lying on his left side, a dark puddle of liquid pooling around his abdomen.

"Callie," he said weakly. "What... what are you doing? Get out of here." He attempted to sit up but fell back with a thud.

"I'm not leaving you, Devereaux!" She reached up and pounded frantically on the back door, screaming for Darby. "Darbs! Open up! It's Jake!"

She heard the click of the lock, followed closely by the door creaking open. "Christ on a bike!" Darby cried. "What the fudge? Come on—get him inside!"

Callie grabbed Jake's arms while Darby took one leg and Amara the other. Together, they half-carried, half-dragged him over the threshold of the back door.

Before they could get him fully inside, Tyler came running at them from behind. "Callie! Jake! Help!"

Callie's head snapped up, and she caught Tyler in her arms before he plowed her over. "Ty! It's okay, bud. You're safe now. Go on inside, stick with the girls and Jake. I'll be back."

Tyler, eyes wide, scooted passed Amara into the house. Darby watched him go before grabbing Callie's arm. "Did you see his face? He's scared to death! Girl, you cannot go out there!"

Callie bent down and removed the Glock from Jake's duty holster. In the hallway light, she could see that his face was ashen, his eyes closed. Sometime between finding him and the three of them carrying him to the door, Jake had lost consciousness.

"I have to find Gabriel," Callie said with a calm she didn't feel. Kneeling, she pulled Jake's shirt up. "Oh, God, this is not good! He's been stabbed and he's bleeding badly. Call 911 back, tell them we need an ambulance as well as the police. Keep pressure on the wound and try not to move him around."

"I don't like this, Callie. I don't like it at all!"

"Me either. But I have a gun, a knife, and a radio. If I'm still out there when the cops come, use Jake's radio to let me know they're here. Otherwise, unless it's a dire emergency, don't." She gave her friend a sad smile. "I'd hate to have the drop on the bastard only to have my position given away by one of your famous Darbyisms."

"Darbyisms my—okay, never mind. Just please, be careful," she said, hugging Callie. "I've already lost one best friend. I don't plan on losing another."

"And I don't plan on going anywhere. Lock up. I'll be back."

Gabriel stood behind a tree, watching Callie creep further into the backyard.

That's it, bitch. Come to papa.

He studied the back side of the cabin. He could see Jemma and the boy pacing in the kitchen but couldn't see the blonde. He assumed she was attempting to save Devereaux.

Devereaux.

It was unfortunate the way it had gone down. Gabriel had hoped to prolong Jake's death, to make it unbearably painful.

But Devereaux had appeared out of nowhere, ranting about Gabriel using Tyler as a human shield.

Afraid to take the shot, Jake had instead pulled back a fist and landed a powerful right hook to Gabriel's jaw.

Gabriel had staggered, but he didn't fall. Instead, he'd pulled the knife from his waistband and buried it to the hilt in Jake's side. The agent grunted, then went down in a heap.

Gabriel had kicked him in the head several times before moving to another tree several yards away, where he waited with the boy.

Now, watching Callie getting closer, he knew his wait was nearly over.

Callie scanned the yard, seeing nothing.

"Hey, moron!" she called out. "You must be a special kind of stupid. What did you expect would happen here? Did you think I would fold?"

She moved lightly, quickly, toward the corner of the property and the last place she'd seen Gabriel with Tyler. There was a light breeze, causing the trees and bushes to sway, making it hard to distinguish human movement from nature's hand.

"You do realize the cops will be here any minute?" she shouted. "And when you go down for this, for all the people you brutally killed, your ass will never see the light of day." She was about twenty feet from the tree line. "Of course, if there was ever an argument for the death penalty—"

A twig snapped to her left, and she spun. Gabriel charged, knife at the ready.

Callie fired the Glock, hitting Gabriel in the shoulder.

"Fuck!" he screamed, stunned. He slapped a hand over the bleeding wound and continued to move toward Callie.

"Stay back!" she warned.

He thrust the knife toward her, and she raised her arms in front of her face, feeling the blade's sting as it sliced her forearm.

Her arm jerked down and away from him. She took a step back, and her finger unintentionally pulled the trigger.

The bullet nicked his leg.

"Goddammit!" he yelled.

"That's what happens when you bring a knife to a gunfight, asshole!" she screamed.

His head spun as, panicked, he tried to figure out his options. This wasn't supposed to happen; he was supposed to be invincible.

He could continue to attack and risk being shot a third time. Or he could flee, tend to his wounds, and then return sometime later to finish what he'd started.

Dragging his injured leg behind him, one hand firmly on his shoulder wound, he stumbled toward the woods again, his only intent now to get away from this cabin.

If he could circle around, using the trees for cover, he could get to the safety of his truck, and out of this fucking nightmare.

Callie watched Gabriel duck into the tree line, and paused. The landscape was unfamiliar and he was armed. Only an idiot would go chasing after an armed killer in the dead of night.

She knew this, felt it with every fiber of her being.

She ran after him anyway.

Callie lost Gabriel almost as soon as she'd entered the woods. It was impossibly dark, with an abundance of black shadows and thick brush to hide behind. Thinking quickly, she reversed direction and ran back toward the cabin and the rented SUV parked out front. Jumping into the driver's seat, she checked the ignition and flipped the visor.

Keys! Where are the keys?

She found them in the console, started the engine, and took off down the driveway.

And after the man who had taken everything.

Gabriel's arm was on fire.

He had never experienced pain like this, even when Devereaux had plugged him in the leg all those months ago.

Run faster! Live to fight another day!

He nearly had his truck in sight when he saw the headlights behind him.

Callie's heart pounded as she squeezed the steering wheel.

Where are you, asshole?

Rounding a slight bend, her headlights caught his fleeing form emerging from the woods and onto the driveway. Callie's boot pressed harder on the gas pedal, as if her foot had a mind of its own.

Or had a plan her brain was still unaware of.

As the SUV's headlights bathed him in their glow, Gabriel stopped at an immense aspen tree and turned. Grinning, eyes sparkling as if he had a secret, he waited.

Callie, lightly tapping the brakes, inched closer to the man near the tree.

"Eat me, bitch!" Gabriel cackled, slapping a hand over his crotch in an obscene gesture. He dug into his waistband as if ready to draw a gun.

Not today, pal. Not ever again.

Callie floored it, ramming the Tahoe into Gabriel's lower half, pinning him to the tree. His arms flew backward, catching on a tangle of thin branches on either side of the immense tree. He stood sprawled, unable to move, his arms splayed wide.

As though he hung on a crucifix like Jesus himself.

Callie tried to calm her pounding heart and, gun in hand, exited the Tahoe. She studied the man before her, trapped between the front fender of the vehicle and the tree, arms flung out on either side of him.

"Game over, scumbag," she said through gritted teeth.

He moved, and she raised the gun.

"Aren't you clever," Gabriel wheezed, his blood-stained teeth turning her veins to ice. His head moved slowly from side to side as he took stock of his predicament. He noted his position on the tree for the first time, and a faint smile tugged at his lips.

"My God, my God," he cried, "why have you forsaken me?"

Tipping his head back to the heavens, he muttered, "It is finished."

Callie watched his chest carefully. He didn't appear to be breathing.

Relieved, the adrenaline slowly waning, she allowed her arm to fall to her side. She was numb, dazed, unsure whether to laugh or cry.

She turned to leave but heard his voice again.

"This isn't over, little one," he hissed, spraying blood from his lips with each word. "It will never be over. There isn't a prison in the world that can hold me. I will come for you until the end of time."

Callie raised the gun again.

In an instant, a cool breeze touched her face, and Katie appeared at her side. "Shadow, don't. Don't get down in the mud with him. He's not worth it."

Gabriel caught Callie's hesitation and winked. "Second thoughts, Callista? I always knew you were the weaker sister."

Callie steadied her hands and took a calming breath. She dropped her head to one shoulder, cracking her neck and thinking how 'Hollywood' this moment felt.

Her eyes found Gabriel's once more. He winked again.

"Shadow, please," Kate said. "You're better than this."

Callie closed her eyes briefly. "Sorry, Kates," she whispered, "but I don't think I am."

Hands steady, finger on the trigger, she locked on her target and squeezed.

And blew a hole, dead center, between Gabriel's eyes.

EPILOGUE

Three weeks later
Devereaux home
Billings, Montana

"Callie!" Tyler yelled from the foyer. "Me and Mom are taking Blue and Lucky for a walk! Want to come?"

Callie stood at the kitchen counter, assembling sandwiches. "I'm making lunch, but go ahead. I'll save you guys a few tuna sammies."

She felt Jake enter the room before she saw him.

"Got one of those for me?" he asked, leaning against the kitchen door. He was still pale, still hurting, still recovering from a splenectomy following Gabriel's attack.

And still handsome as hell.

"Of course I have one for you. How are you feeling, big guy?"

"Like someone cut me open and took out an organ," he joked.

"It's only been a few weeks, Barney. You lost a ton of blood and underwent major surgery. It's going to take some time."

He walked toward her and gathered her in his arms. "And how are you, Blaze? You went through something pretty rough too." He kissed the top of her head. "You saved my bacon, darlin'. In fact, you saved us all. But to do it, you had to kill a man."

"Not a man, Jake. A maniac. And I would do it again to save my

361

family." She placed the cutting board in the sink. "Everything worked out. Blue and Lucky are fine, Tyler has his mom back, and we have our sisters. I'd say a few spirits were looking out for us."

"Like Kate?" Jake asked.

"Yes, Kate, for one. She's been with us the whole time. I spoke to her this morning, and she isn't even mad at me anymore."

"Oh?"

"Nope."

"And the dark shadows you've seen? Gone?"

"Yes. Not to sound dramatic, but Kates thinks the darkness was a manifestation of Gabriel's energy. He was pure evil, and the blackness of his soul manifested within the shadows that we saw. I think seeing evil is all part of this gift I have. Whether I want it or not."

"Well, all this stuff is way above my pay grade. You mentioned a few spirits having our backs. Who else?"

"Amanda Weston. She helped us find Lacy."

"Yeah, about that," Jake said, taking a seat at the breakfast counter. "I thought ghosts couldn't meddle in human affairs."

"I did, too. I asked Kates about it, but she was vague. Something about how if the interference produces a result that's 'ordained,' it's more like the spirit is guiding someone to a foregone conclusion. Sounds like a load of crap to me, but don't tell Kates I said that."

He laughed. "Deal."

Callie put a sandwich on a plate and pushed across the counter. "Here. Eat something."

He took the plate and thanked her. "By the way, I spoke to Curt Valdez this morning. He told me they found that caretaker, Bob Dietrich. He was buried on the farmhouse property. They also found a manifesto, a new 'Bible,' among Gabriel's effects. That guy was one twisted motherfucker."

"Do tell," Callie said dryly. "What was in there?"

"Just rambling, nonsensical plans to rule the universe or something."

He took a bite of his sandwich. "He found us through a GPS in that teddy bear, Porter. That was my bad. I should have tossed it as soon as I knew it didn't come from Randall."

"Not your fault, G-man. Gabriel was a sneaky son of a bitch."

Jake nodded. "He also wrote about Amara being his sister. He believed she was his 'innocent' and that her death would allow him to witness the soul's journey to heaven. He was going to kill her, Blaze."

"Yet another reason I'm glad I took him out." She wrapped two sandwiches in plastic wrap. "What else?"

"Curt thinks Faith was held captive by Gabriel and escaped using Tucker Simon's car." He took another bite. "By the way, Tucker's DNA was found in that woodchipper."

"Damn," she said.

"Anyway, JP and I tried to fill in the blanks when he was here yesterday. We believe Faith and Tyler witnessed Graeme Duncan's murder. I mean, Fiona and Tyler. I can't seem to wrap my head around that."

"None of us can," Callie said. "But no one will call you out for calling her by Faith McTavish, the only name we knew."

Jake nodded. "True. So we believe that Faith, about to go on the run, searched Duncan's safe and found those papers about Lacy Jane. Knowing Tyler had no other relatives, she ran with him toward the family his mother was stolen from."

"Wow. I take back everything I ever said about Faith. She really did want what was best for Tyler. Wonder how the adoption stuff got into Graeme's hands, though."

"Not sure," Jake said, "but I would bet he was blackmailing Randall Weston."

"Wow," Callie said. Quirking a brow, she added, "Speaking of...I wonder how good ol' Randall is enjoying the penal system."

Jake wiped his mouth and pushed his plate back "JP said Weston is on suicide watch. There are questions about his mental state. His attorney says Weston is in the early stages of dementia, which would explain how he didn't recognize the Devereaux name."

"Right, especially since it was in all the newspaper articles."

"Exactly. As for Elizabeth, although her hands are by no means clean in all of this, she's working on a plea deal—her testimony against Randall's and Gideon Sherman's, in return for a reduced sentence. Personally, I hope they all rot in prison."

"Me, too," Callie said, leaning across the counter. "And Emily? How is she coping with everything?"

Jake smiled. "She is amazing, Blaze. Everyone feels a sense of closure, but in a good way. Mom and Dad are over the moon, of course. And Jed feels like a missing piece of his heart has been returned."

"And Tyler is a little boy again, happy and in love with his momma," Callie said softly. "I assume they will stay here? With Jed?"

"Yeah, at least for a while," Jake said. "Everyone has a lot of catching up to do. How about Amara? Where will she end up now that the danger has passed?"

"Falls Church," Callie smiled. "She has some catching up to do as well. She plans to sell her home in Denver and move into the garage apartment to get to know the family. Darby has promised to help her put together an art show once she's settled there."

"So, it sounds like everyone is where they belong," Jake said with a smile.

Callie came around the counter and gingerly sat in his lap. "And what about us, Barney? Where do we belong?"

He smiled. "Come with me, and I'll show you."

∼

Jake pulled his car in front of the Devereaux cabin in Pitikin Falls and cut the engine.

"What's this?" Callie asked. "Why are we here?"

Jake kissed her and got out of the car. "Come on, Blaze. I'll show you."

They walked, hand in hand, beyond the cabin and over the tiny bridge, to the open fields behind the house.

"Pick a spot," he said.

"Excuse me?"

"Pick a spot for your new home." Turning to face her, he took her hands. "We need to go back to Falls Church, sweetheart. It's where we belong. My job is there, your family, our friends. And Amara will be there, too. So, I propose a compromise."

She smiled. "I'm listening."

"My parents offered us some land here. We can build a second home, a place to stay when we visit. And knowing how important family is to us both, I expect we will be back often."

They stood arm in arm, looking over the land, both envisioning what life could be. Content, Callie laid her head on his shoulder.

"You know, Barney, now that Gabriel is out of our lives, things may get a little boring."

"Yeah. I can do boring for a while." He took her left hand and caressed her fingers. "No rings, huh?"

Callie frowned. "Um, no. Why?"

Jake kissed her. "Just imagining how beautiful this land would look with a ring on your fourth finger. Come on, Blaze. Let's go plan our lives together."

As they walked away, two figures stood in the woods, watching them leave.

"I imagine they will have a wonderful life together, Kate," Michael said. "One I wish we'd had."

"But we have each other now, Michael," Katie said, smiling up at him.

"And yes, Callie and Jake will have an amazing future."

"You know, Callie is so good at this investigation business," Michael said. "Do you think she'll join the FBI? Become a profiler?"

Katie pursed her lips. "Someday, maybe. But first, she needs to play her greatest role yet."

"You mean?"

Katie's smile was radiant. "Yes. The only question is whether, in nine months, baby Katherine Eileen Devereaux will have the same fiery curls as her momma."

THE END

ACKNOWLEDGMENTS

And here we are—closing the final chapter in the Shadow Sister's Trilogy.

If you are still reading this, congrats! Most people would rather watch paint dry. ☺

How fun this journey was! How much I've learned about perseverance and strength and dangling modifiers! Still, as enjoyable as this road has been (except those dangling modifiers, obviously) these books, though written by my hand, were not written alone.

Family and friends were crucial to completing this series. First off, I'd like to thank my husband and partner in crime, Mark, who knew enough to walk away when I was close to taking a hammer to my laptop. Sometimes, your silence was all I needed to put down the weapon.

To the greatest children a mom could ever have—Jennifer, Brian, Jared, John, and Jordan—thank you so much for never wavering in your support. I am so proud of you all and love you with a ferocity that is, at times, frightening.

The only thing better than having wonderful children is having amazing grandchildren! To Declan, Ava, Raylan, David, Connor, Mila, Dean and Piper... there is no greater joy in my life than hearing your giggles and watching you grow. I love you all beyond measure.

An additional honorable mention goes to my youngest daughter, Jordan. Publishing a book is almost as tough as writing it. If not for her technical savvy, these books would still be sitting on a thumb drive, all sad and gloomy, waiting for a home.

Thank you, Jobes. I love you.

Thank you to my beautiful mom, Mary Quinn, who checked and rechecked my grammar, never once busting my chops for being a comma freak. I wish everyone in the world was blessed with such an amazing mother. Love you, momma.

To my siblings, Lori Martin and James Quinn. It's been a rough, sometimes scary, few years, but we're still standing! Together, the three of us can tackle anything. I love you both crazy mad.

In our family, there is no such thing as in-laws—only bonus sons and daughters. To those we've been fortunate enough to embrace inside our crazy circle—Lara Noll, Peter Barreira Noll, and Jessica Noll, your presence and light make our circle complete. Love you all to the moon and back.

Speaking of family... To my brilliant and gifted cousin, Brian Quinn. I gave you a monumental task when asking you to not only create the covers for this trilogy, but to put on your 'formatting' hat as well. You succeeded beyond my wildest imagination. Your talent, patience, and extraordinary artistic eye make me wonder if we are truly related. ☺

A special shout out to my dear friends Debbie and Andy O'Connor and Walter Ferenc. You guys are my constant cheerleaders and biggest fans. I thank you from the bottom of my heart.

Every author needs unshakable and loyal supporters. In my case, that award goes to Phil and Ginger Brady. You've both been to countless book signings and are always the first ones to jump in to lend a hand. I am so grateful to have you as friends, and I love and appreciate you dearly.

To Hilary Barber—book lover extraordinaire as well as pal and confidante—who knew when to push, when to pull, and when to run.

Just kidding... you never ran! Thanks a million for your support and your friendship.

To my bestie on the other side, Lisa Ferenc... I cannot see you, cannot touch you, but I can feel you. You're in the steps I take, the words I write, the air I breathe. Until we meet again, keep watching over us and know that I will love you until the end of time.

To my lifelong friend and the inspiration for the character of 'Darby Harrison'... Mary Hoffman, I would be lost without you. You are an essential piece of my life 'puzzle,' and a huge part of my favorite childhood adventures. As we continue to move through life, creating fresh memories, I am so thankful for your presence. No one can make me laugh like you can!

Love you more.

To my fabulous editor, Jennifer McIntyre. What can I say (besides bring out yer dead?) In life, if we are fortunate, we meet people we feel an instant connection with; people who pull us into their circle and make us feel as if we were always there. We share a love of writing, a love of cats (occasionally!) and a sense of humor (or humour? ☺) You took a chance on me, guided me, helped me convey what I wanted to say without changing my writing style or the tone of my voice. I cannot tell you how much you mean to me, and I look forward to many more 'jam' sessions with you.

In closing (yes, you are almost free to go!) I would like to give a special thank you to all the fine men and women in our law enforcement community. Policing society in today's climate is a difficult task. Yet, despite being vilified by the people they have sworn to protect, they continue to show up, trying to make the world a better, safer place for everyone. I tip my hat to you all, and I ask God to protect you and keep you safe.

Peace out, my friends.

—Q

WHAT'S NEXT?

I hope you enjoyed reading the last installment in the Shadow Sisters Trilogy, '*The Final Fury.*' Although I will miss the love, banter, and humor of these characters, the feelings of warmth and sense of 'family' elicited within these pages will go on for a long, long time.

So, what's next? Glad you asked! I am currently enjoying some 'me' time in between doing a great deal of research for my next book. In keeping with the 'Quinn' tradition, the next adventure will be a tale of ghosts, mystery, and suspense.

In the tentatively titled, *'Rosemear,'* we follow the story of Spencer and Isabella Boyd, a wealthy couple with two children. After a devastating loss and Isabella's struggle with mental illness, the family, in desperate need of a fresh start, move into an old mansion in Savannah.

Once a magnificent manor, *Rosemear* is now in dire need of repair. Locals warn the couple of the mansions ugly history and claim it to be haunted by the victims of an unspeakable tragedy.

Spencer Boyd has never believed in the supernatural. Instead, he is certain that the stories of a haunted Rosemear were merely created to keep children away from the abandoned building.

His wife, however, is not so sure.

Within weeks of moving in, Isabella witnesses some terrifying ghostly activity…lights flickering, disembodied voices, scratch marks on her arms and legs. Frightened and concerned for her children, determined to find the truth, she begins a quest to discover exactly what occurred in Rosemear over one hundred-sixty years ago.

And comes face-to-face with a frightening possibility...

Either Rosemear is, indeed, haunted by angry sp_rits, cr Isabella's worst fears are coming true.

And her fragile mind is, once again, threatening to return her to an endless abyss of chaos, paranoia, and madness.

ABOUT THE AUTHOR

Quinn Noll's passion has always been her five children, eight grandchildren, and her husband of 41 years, Mark. A registered nurse, she recently switched careers, happily pursuing a lifelong dream of writing. Quinn makes her home on the Eastern Shore of Virginia with her husband and a shiny black Labrador named Mr. Beauregard.

The Final Fury is the third installment in the thrilling 'Shadow Sisters' trilogy.

Want More Quinn?

For updates, bonus content, and special giveaways, be sure to visit me at Quinnnoll.com and sign up for my newsletter!
Shadow Sisters: The Beginning—a short story detailing the Callahan sister's early years—is available to download free when you sign up for my newsletter!

Happy reading!

Quinn Noll

Quinn Noll
Writer. Poet. Dreamer.

www.Quinnnoll.com
Facebook.com/Quinn.Noll
Instagram.com/@Quinnnollwrites